The Complete Stories of
MARY BUTTS

By Mary Butts

THE TAVERNER NOVELS
THE CLASSICAL NOVELS
ASHE OF RINGS AND OTHER WRITINGS

THE JOURNALS OF MARY BUTTS
Edited by Nathalie Blondel

About Mary Butts

MARY BUTTS: SCENES FROM THE LIFE
A Biography by Nathalie Blondel

A SACRED QUEST: THE LIFE AND WRITINGS OF MARY BUTTS
Edited by Christopher Wagstaff

MARY BUTTS

The Complete Stories

PREFACE BY JOHN ASHBERY

EDITED AND WITH A FOREWORD
BY BRUCE R. McPHERSON

McPherson & Company
Kingston, New York
2014

The Complete Stories of Mary Butts

Published by McPherson & Company,
Post Office Box 1126, Kingston, New York 12402
www.mcphersonco.com

1 3 5 7 9 10 8 6 4 2   2014 2015 2016 2017
MANUFACTURED IN THE U.S.A.

Library of Congress Cataloging in Publication Data

Butts, Mary, 1890-1937.
  [Short stories. Selections]
  Mary Butts : the complete stories / preface by John Ashbery;
edited and with a foreword by Bruce R. McPherson.
     pages cm
  ISBN 978-1-62054-009-1 (pbk. : alk. paper)
  I. McPherson, Bruce R. (Bruce Rice), 1951- editor. II. Title.
  PR6003.U7A6 2014
  823'.912—dc23
                                   2014036418

✤ ✤

Contents

❖ ❖

❖ ❖

Preface

JOHN ASHBERY

I FIRST HEARD OF Mary Butts in the summer of 1949 when, after graduating from Harvard, I had moved to New York and taken a summer job at the Brooklyn Public Library. It was a time when I was looking for contemporary writers, especially fiction writers, who had somehow escaped classification in what is now called "the canon." Only a couple of months earlier my friend Frank O'Hara had introduced me to the then-unknown Jean Rhys, Ronald Firbank, Flann O'Brien and Samuel Beckett (this was in the pre-*Godot* days), and I had stumbled on Ivy Compton-Burnett, Laura Riding and Henry Green. All of whom began to persuade me that there was a lot more to twentieth-century literature than Harvard was then letting on.

My immediate superior at the Brooklyn Library was a man in his forties named Richard Elliott who, rather unexpectedly, turned out to be an expert guide to the esoterica I was interested in, and was himself a talented author of strange short stories of which only a few, as far as I know, were published, in obscure little magazines. Of the many writers he suggested I look into, two in particular have remained favourites: Jane Bowles and Mary Butts.

Except for Mary Butts, all the writers I've mentioned so far will doubtless be known to most readers of twentiety-century literature; doubtless she will not be. However, that is about to change. As Patricia Beer wrote in the *London Review of Books* recently: "She is one of the current victims of the fashionable drive to exhume 'forgotten women writers.' The category is dreary. Mary Butts is not."

Originally published in *From Altar to Chimney-piece: Selected Stories* by Mary Butts, McPherson & Company, 1992. Reprinted by permission of the author.

Yet as recently as 1988, Humphrey Carpenter in *Geniuses Together*, his survey of the 1920s expatriate Montparnasse milieu in which Mary Butts moved, referred to her in passing as "a woman named Mary Butts." Still, she was admired and encouraged by Pound and Eliot; Ford Madox Ford published her in his *Transatlantic Review* (she also appeared in the American review *Hound and Horn*); she was a friend of Cocteau (who drew her portrait and illustrations for two of her books, and is the model for the character André in her story "The House Party"); had a close relationship with Virgil Thomson (who reportedly once proposed marriage to her); and she seems to have frequented Gertrude Stein's salon. Of course, these credentials wouldn't matter if she were a negligible talent—the pages of 'twenties little magazines like *transition* and *The Little Review* are crammed with forgotten names that will doubtless remain so. Butts was an extraordinary original who deserves to be remembered on the strength of her work alone—one of those *femmes maudites* like Jean Rhys or Djuna Barnes, shadowy presences on the fringes of the Lost Generation in Paris. Until recently, despite the efforts of a few stubborn fans (the American poets Robert Duncan, Robert Kelly and Ken Irby among them), none was more spectral than Mary Butts. Then in 1988 her memoir of childhood, *The Crystal Cabinet*, was reprinted in England (Carcanet Press) and America (Beacon Press).

It was not, however, an ideal vehicle to launch a Mary Butts revival, since it will interest mainly those already won over to her fiction. It rambles occasionally when she sets out her ideas on the education of children and Freudian psychology, and tells us almost nothing of her certainly tumultuous adult years in London and Paris. Fortunately, there is now this collection of stories, as well as an omnibus edition of the novels *Armed with Madness* and *Death of Felicity Taverner* with a preface by Paul West (also published by McPherson & Company). The world can decide whether it wants reprints of her first novel, *Ashe of Rings*—actually quite different from the others, in an "expressionist" style rather like that of the extraordinary novella "In Bayswater," reprinted here—and of her two historical novels, *The Macedonian* and *Scenes from the Life of Cleopatra*, as well as the still unreprinted stories and the uncollected and virtually unknown poems.

A biography of Mary Butts is said to be on the way, but until it materialises, our knowledge of the person behind the fictions will remain tantalizingly slight. The charms of *The Crystal Cabinet* lie mainly in her evocation of memories of early childhood and of the Dorset landscape which recurs constantly as a setting, a character really, in the novels and the stories. Family relationships are not dealt with in depth. Her brother Tony, obviously an important person in her life, barely appears, and though she speaks fondly of him, Virginia Woolf reported he told her that he had always hated Mary. (Tony was the companion of the writer William Plomer, and committed suicide in 1941.) Hence, it's difficult to know whether to look for traces of Tony in Felix, the heroine's sympathetic gay brother in the *Taverner* novels—he sounds more like Felicity's cruel and capricious brother Adrian in the latter one, just as Adrian's mother and several scheming dowagers in the stories resemble, given certain of her traits set down in *The Crystal Cabinet*, Mary's mother.

We know that Mary Butts was born December 13, 1890, at Salterns, the family estate near the Dorset coast. The pleasantly eccentric house was notable chiefly for its collection of William Blake paintings (the phrase, "the crystal cabinet," is taken from Blake). They were acquired by her great-grandfather Thomas Butts, Blake's enthusiastic patron. She was educated at St. Andrews school in Scotland, went to live in London before World War I, and married the poet and translator John Rodker, by whom she had her only child, Camilla, in 1920. She seems to have lived mostly in Paris in the 1920s, with occasional revivifying visits to Dorset. Divorced from Rodker, she married the painter Gabriel Aitken (who designed the jacket of her book *Several Occasions*); they too were later divorced. She spent the last years of her life in Sennen, Cornwall, where she died in 1937, aged forty-six.

Paul West mentions her disjointed, dislocated style, and indeed she can be a difficult writer to "follow." Her fondness for double and even triple negatives ("Nothing upstairs makes me believe anything but that you are all mad, but she is too young to tell nothing but lies"; "It is getting more and more inopportune to suppose women have no secrets unconnected with sex"); her occasional carelessness in indicating who is saying what, to the point where we don't always know who is still in the room; a lapidary terseness that verges on mannerism and is sometimes merely mannered: these traits abound in her stories, which nevertheless succeed oftener than the novels. Perhaps she was aware of this, since in *Death of Felicity Taverner* she tries harder than elsewhere to construct a plot (in this case one rather like that of a detective novel), but it sags under the weight of too many stylistic *trouvailles*, often beautiful in themselves.

I seem to be building a case against her; that is by no means my intention, but since I've begun I should perhaps point to her other flaws before going on to her virtues. It will be noticed that the same character-types appear throughout her fiction, sometimes with the same names: the gay brother (her brother Tony?); the taciturn painter-husband (Aitkin?); the selfish dominating mother; the Russian gigolo-in-Paris, Boris, who is sometimes *méchant* (to lapse into French, *à la* Butts), sometimes (as in *Felicity Taverner*) a perverse savior; and the central female character, sometimes called Scylla, who must confront Charybdises of her own, through whose eyes we see everything and who is Butts herself. The supporting cast includes a number of sharply etched expatriate Americans, sometimes heroic and almost as smart as the Europeans (like Carston, another savior, in *Armed with Madness*); sometimes victims of European corruption (Paul in "The House Party"), sometimes victim-tormentors (Cherry in "From Altar to Chimney Piece"). Indeed, her take on Americans is fresh and unconventional, though it is hard to believe that the Stein-Toklas salon was a coven of satanist bolsheviks, as she seems to be suggesting in "From Altar to Chimney Piece."

The problem is that it isn't always possible to sympathize with these decadent darlings, so determined to put up a brave front in their reduced though hardly indigent circumstances, who have secret access to the earth's magic, who "know," as this passage from *Felicity Taverner* puts it rather too bluntly:

> *The Taverners were the kind of people who, if they have to choose, choose a boat and a library rather than a car and a club; cherry blossom before orchids, apples before tinned peaches, wine to whiskey, one dress from Chanel to six "from a shop."* . . . *They knew what in relation to Chardin has been called "all the splendour and glory of matter." Like him, they were in love.*

This is atypical of the author. Usually she brings on her characters without explaining them, especially in the stories, where there is little room to do so. In the amazing one called "Brightness Falls," a character named Max tells the male narrator: "I feel I've got to tell someone, and it might as well be you. I won't ask you not to repeat it, because you won't be able to." This is in fact true of "Brightness Falls" and of her stories in general. They start just about anywhere. "This happened in the kind of house people live in who used not to live in that kind of house, who were taught to have distinct opinions about the kind of people who lived in them" is the first line of "The Warning." They unfold, rather than unroll, with lacunae and bits of seemingly irrelevant information interrupting the flow, and then, having brought us somewhere, they leave us. Thus, at the end of "Brightness Falls," Max has just finished describing his wife's and her girl friend's hilarity after all three had passed through an episode that seems tinged with witchcraft:

> *"Anyhow, they got livelier and livelier; out of their clothes and into them again, telephones, taxis, dancing somewhere; more mischief—"*
> *"Did you go out with them?"*
> *"No, I would not do that."*

End of story. But meanwhile we have been to some extraordinary places without leaving London: the enchantment scene takes place in Lincoln's Inn, where

> *The air was wild and mist-softened, moisture everywhere, but without shine. Like a picture that might easily become another picture, and has to be very good to stay put at all. It was all so dull, a London pool, and not deep enough.*

Before that, when Parmys, Max's wife, is starting to explain the mystery, he says:

> *"I didn't want to listen, but I found myself attending to noises. In November the third week was still, you remember. A few leaves left to fall, and each one I thought was like a little word that you just couldn't catch. Light and brown and so few of them—whispers in the air. I used to stand at the window and watch, until I thought of coral and pearl and how red and white they are."*

Where are we? Where have we come from? But the narrator has already warned us in the story's opening sentences: "There is no head or tail to this story, except that it happened. On the other hand, how does one know that anything happened? How does one know?

Paul West likens Mary Butts to a hummingbird, and he is right: we admire hummingbirds because we can't quite see them; their erratic motion prevents that and is what we like about them. After reading Butts one is left with an impression of dazzle, of magic, but what made it is hard to pin down. Rereading after forty years her marvelous story "Friendship's Garland" (all the stories set in London as well as the London parts of *Ashe of Rings* have a haze of madness in them, the author being indeed "armed with madness"—a phrase, incidentally, that I would dearly love to trace), I found that the only thing I remembered from my first reading was a single metaphor. We are in rather sinister company at a café called the Craven.

> *Through the noise and the iron streets, even through the racing wind the sun poured, roaring its heat through the wind at the huge buildings and the crowd. Those are the hours when the city pays for being a city, and is delivered over to the wind and the sun and their jackal the dust. All the earth pays, but principally the city. On the other hand, inside the Craven there is no nature at all. These things are not natural, marble like cheese, red velvet, and plaster gilt.*

"Marble like cheese" was all I had retained, except for a sense of the whole story as something evil, glittering, funny and, and the end surreally beautiful, as the narrator sees her face in a mirror looking "half old, like a child's recovering from a sickness," and later "like a child that has been dipped in dew." To remember the stories, even just after finishing them, necessitates rereading them; there is no other way to hang onto their breathless skittering as it evolves before us.

Though Mary Butts was not exactly unknown during her lifetime, she became so almost immediately afterward. Only now, after more than half a century, is the public discovering her. The very features of her writing that taxed earlier readers—her startling ellipses, especially in conversations; her drastic cutting in the cinematic sense; her technique of collaging bits of poetry and popular song lyrics ("Lady Be Good" and "What'll I Do?") into the narratives—make her seem our contemporary. So do the freewheeling and disordered lives of her characters, who can be "wired" in a very 1990s way—the homosexual ones, for instance, whom she treats with a sympathy and openness astonishing for the England of her time. One keeps getting the feeling that these stories were written yesterday.

"The old man belonged to the majority who do not approve—say of cats or earrings or 'bus tickets," she writes in "In Bayswater." Today that majority is bigger than ever, but so is the minority that opposes it—the minority who approves. We need Mary Butts now, to guide us, "armed with madness," through mazes and forests to the pure sources of storytelling.

❖ ❖

Foreword

BRUCE R. MCPHERSON

MARY BUTTS first "spoke" to me in 1988 or '89 when the poet Robert Kelly handed me a copy of *Death of Felicity Taverner*. I knew of her very slightly. I was surprised to discover an unknown and free-spirited literary adventurer possessed of an original style from an era I had studied deeply; suddenly there was an exciting distaff counterpart to D. H. Lawrence; and I was appalled that her work had been erased from the history of the 1920s and '30s.

Her disappearance added to her allure. After her death in 1937, her work fell out of print, with a few minor exceptions, for more than fifty years. She is not the only significant Modernist whose writings dropped from view between the world wars, and in the drastic reordering of the world following the second war; cycles of obscurity and rediscovery happen to writers all the time. But while the works of Virginia Woolf, Djuna Barnes and H.D., along with many lesser English and American women writers, were enjoying a renaissance during the feminist wave of the late 1960s through the '80s, Butts seems to have been cold-shouldered. Was it for being politically incorrect, or insufficiently feminist, or seeming to embrace an excessively libertine lifestyle, or perhaps for writing work too challenging?—choose whichever you like, but all would be hard to substantiate. The problem, rather, may be that Mary Butts had never quite *arrived* in the estimation of the British literary establishment. In a working lifetime of about eighteen years, she published five novels, a novella, two collections of stories, two pamphlets, various poems scattered in little magazines, and roughly a hundred reviews and essays for prominent journals and newspapers. Given her stylistic originality, one would have thought that would be enough. Her work was mostly praised and even occasionally anthologized; but sales were modest, her audience small, and her aesthetic allegiances remained with avant-garde writers and composers—French, ex-pat Americans, and British. She died young, leaving a substantial body of unpublished and unfinished work. Her departure, therefore, went unremarked, and her absence quickly forgotten except by poets and outsiders and connoisseurs.

I began to read everything of hers I could find. With *Armed with Madness* (in the form of a xerox copy) I became convinced of her lyrical genius and began to plan how she might be republished. A year or two later I learned I was not alone, that a young English scholar, Nathalie Blondel, had been working with Butts's daughter, Camilla Bagg, in the same pursuit—at first by arranging for an unexpurgated edition of *The Crystal Cabinet*, an autobiographical memoir of her childhood. The difficulty, however, was that no-one remembered her.

My approach was to create a single volume in 1992 for the novel *Armed with Madness* and its sequel *Death of Felicity Taverner*, and at the same time to publish a selection of sixteen stories, titled *From Altar to Chimney-piece*. I did not imagine that the project would grow to include another four volumes by and about her: *The Classical Novels* in 1994; Christopher Wagstaff's compilation of critical essays, *A Sacred Quest*, the year after; and in 1998 Natalie Blondel's stunning biography, *Mary Butts: Scenes from the Life*, as well as an omnibus featuring Butts's first novel, *Ashe of Rings and Other Writings*. By century's end, her work had found a small but devoted readership, and captured the attention of academic scholars. Nathalie Blondel's publication of Butts's *Journals* (Yale, 2002), a prodigious feat of scholarship and longhand decryption, fittingly capped a long decade.

Having come so far, how could I escape the rest of the journey? Even before the stock of *From Altar to Chimney-piece* was exhausted, I was investigating MB's uncollected poetry and unpublished fiction (including a first novel in typescript) among her papers at Yale's Beinecke Library. Plans for a revised volume of stories quickly enlarged into this complete edition, and when another young English scholar, Joel Hawkes, proposed an edition of her essays and reviews, a second campaign took shape. So *The Complete Stories* heralds another four- or five-volume project that will bring all but the most fugitive works into print by 2020.

·　·　·　·　·

Mary Butts is known primarily as a novelist, but she practiced the short form throughout her career, and an argument could be made that she built her novels, particularly *Armed with Madness* and the historical novels, from smaller units. All the more reason, then, for this new collection of thirty-eight stories, which adds new facets to her oeuvre, and a few surprises for its readers. When planning a "complete" edition of stories the choice is either to offer them in their original collections or to order them by date of composition, supposing the latter can been determined. Each approach has its advantage: either we gauge the development of a writer over time, or we experience the work as her audience did. Butts kept dated journals where she often mentions initiating stories or their completion; but there are ellipses and uncertainties, particularly because so few of the original manuscripts and typescripts are among her papers in the Beinecke and must be presumed lost. (Butts wrote longhand in composition books which were sent to a typist; she would hand-correct the typescripts and, one expects, the typeset proofs.) Some day scholars will have sorted out the details. Meanwhile, the original collections are presented here, but with a proviso.

Mary Butts published two story collections containing twenty-one pieces, *Speed the Plough* and *Several Occasions*. Just before her death, a third collection had been requested for consideration by T. S. Eliot at Faber & Faber (title unknown, receipt uncertain), and its acceptance might have altered significantly MB's reputation. Instead, under the title *Last Stories*, the volume appeared in 1938 from the publishing house of her great friend and benefactor, Annie Winifred Ellerman (a.k.a. Bryher). A note regarding the thirteen stories preceded the text, reading in part: "None has previously appeared in book-form. They are printed in two groups—first, those written during the author's last years at Sennen, and then those written from 1925 onwards." The demarcation (coming at "After the Funeral") suggests that the arrangement may not be Butts's. Furthermore, Bryher's Brendin Publishing ran afoul of English libel laws when one Geoffrey Dunlop threatened to sue for defamation over the story "A Lover"; Brendin was forced to destroy the remaining book stock. The book was well reviewed, but its publication was inconsequential to the larger scheme.

The last piece in *Last Stories* is an epistolary fiction from 1917 titled "Lettres Imaginaires," which is not to be confused with a novella Butts wrote in Paris in 1924 and 1926: that book, *Imaginary Letters,* was published in 1928 in a limited edition with drawings by Jean Cocteau, and the text is to be found in the omnibus *Ashe of Rings and Other Writings.* "Lettres Imaginaires" clearly heralds its epistolary twin, but the status of *Imaginary Letters* as a novella argues against its inclusion here.

After *Last Stories* comes a section of seven uncollected stories, two of which, "The Master's Last Dancing," and "Fumerie," were transcribed and edited by Camilla Bagg and Nathalie Blondel, and published in 1998 in *The New Yorker* and *Conjunctions* respectively. Both are significant works, and border on the gonzo fictional journalism of another contemporary, Henry Miller, as unlikely as that may sound. Two other pieces, "A Magical Experiment" and "Untitled," are published here for the first time; they are slighter, but exert their charms nonetheless.

· · · · ·

Butts occasionally uses Greek words to express particularly numinous ideas. *Daimon* is not a demon but generally a tutelary or presiding spirit, or perhaps a voice within; whereas *kêr* (pl. *kêrês*) is a lesser and more puckish spirit, represented in popular art, according to Butts, "as little fluttering winged bodies, and imagined as a cross between a bacillus, a boy and a ghost."

· · · · ·

Originally, three different publishers issued Mary Butts's collections, each with its own house style for spelling and punctuation. For this edition, a standard orthography has been established in general conformity with our other MB editions, referencing *The Concise Oxford Dictionary*, third edition, 1934. Occasional stylistic idiosyncrasies according to demands of individual stories, e.g., interior monologue, have been allowed. Obvious errors have been corrected.

This project has been greatly benefited by the on-going counsel of Robert Kelly and Dr. Roslyn Reso Foy; the kind cooperation of Mary Butts's grandsons and executors of the Estate, Daniel and Edward Israel; and the generosity of the artist Pat Steir in allowing the reproduction of her paintings on the covers of our editions.

The Complete Stories of

MARY BUTTS

✦ ✧ ✦ ✧ ✦ ✧ ✦ ✧ ✦ ✧ ✦ ✧ ✦ ✧ ✦ ✧ ✦ ✧ ✦ ✧ ✦ ✧ ✦ ✧ ✦ ✧ ✦ ✧ ✦ ✧ ✦ ✧

Speed the Plough

Speed the Plough
In Bayswater
The Saint
Bellerophon to Anteia
Angele au Couvent
In the Street
The Golden Bough
In the South
Madonna of the Magnificat

1923

❖ ❖

Speed the Plough

HE LAY IN BED, lax and staring, and obscure images rose and hung before him, dissolved, reshaped. His great illness passed from him. It left him too faint for any sequence of thought. He lay still, without memory, without hope. Such concrete impressions as came to him were sensuous and centred round the women of the hospital. They distressed him. They were not like the Kirchner girls in the worn *Sketch* he fingered all day. La Coquetterie d'une Ange. One need not know French to understand Coquetterie, and Ange was an easy guess. He stared at the neat counterpane. A tall freckled girl with draggled red hair banged down a cup of cocoa and strode away.

Coquetterie, mannequin, lingerie, and all one could say in English was underwear. He flicked over the pages of the battered *Sketch*, and then looked at the little nurse touching her lips with carmine.

"Georgette," he murmured sleepily, "crêpe georgette."

He would always be lame. For years his nerves would rise and quiver and knot themselves, and project loathsome images. But he had a fine body, and his soldiering had set his shoulders and hardened his hands and arms.

"Get him back onto the land," the doctors said.

The smells in the ward began to assail him, interlacing spirals of odour, subtle but distinct. Disinfectant and distemper, the homely smell of blankets, the faint tang of blood, and then a sour draught from the third bed where a man had been sick.

He crept down under the clothes. Their associations rather than their textures were abhorrent to him, they reminded him of evil noises…the crackle of starched aprons, clashing plates, unmodulated sounds. Georgette would never wear harsh things like that. She would wear…beautiful things with names…velours and organdie, and that faint windy stuff aerophane.

He drowsed back to France, and saw in the sky great aeroplanes dipping and swerving, or holding on their line of steady flight like a travelling eye of God. The wisps of cloud that trailed a moment behind them were not more delicate than her dress.…

"What he wants, doctor, to my mind, is rousing. There he lies all day in a dream. He must have been a strong man once. No, we don't know what he was. Something out of doors I should think. He lies there with that precious Kirchner album, never a word to say."

The doctor nodded.

He lay very still. The presence of the matron made him writhe like the remembered scream of metal upon metal. Her large hands concealed bones that would snap. He lay like a rabbit in its form, and fright showed his dull gums between his drawn-back lips.

Weeks passed. Then one day he got up and saw himself in a glass. He was not surprised. It was all as he had known it must be. He could not go back to the old life. It seemed to him that he would soil its loveliness. Its exotics would shrivel and tarnish as he limped by. "Light things, and winged, and holy" they fluttered past him, crêpe velours, crêpe de Chine, organdie, aerophane, georgette.… He had dropped his stick…there was no one to wash his dirty hands.… The red-haired nurse found him crying, and took him back to bed.

For two months longer he labored under their kindness and wasted under their placidity. He brooded, realizing with pitiful want of clarity that there were unstable delicate things by which he might be cured. He found a ritual and a litany. Dressed in vertical black, he bore on his outstretched arms, huge bales of wound stuffs. With a turn of the wrist he would unwrap them, and they would fall from him rayed like some terrestrial star. The Kirchner album supplied the rest. He named the girls, Suzanne and Verveine, Ambre and Desti, and ranged them about him. Then he would undress them, and dress them again in immaculate fabrics. While he did that he could not speak to them because his mouth would be barred with pins.

The doctors found him weaker.

Several of the nurses were pretty. That was not what he wanted. Their fresh skins irritated him. Somewhere there must still be women whose skins were lustrous with powder, and whose eyes were shadowed with violet from an ivory box. The brisk provincial women passed through his ward visiting from bed to bed. In their homely clothes there was an echo of the lovely fashions of *mondaines*, buttons on a skirt where a slit should have been, a shirt cut to the collar bone whose opening should have sprung from the hollow between the breasts.

Months passed. The fabric of his dream hardened into a shell for his spirit. He remained passive under the hospital care.

They sent him down to a farm on a brilliant March day.

His starved nerves devoured the air and sunlight. If the winds parched, they braced him, and when the snow fell it buried his memories clean. Because she had worn a real musquash coat, and carried a brocade satchel he had half-believed the expensive woman who had sat by his bed, and talked about the worth and the beauty of a life at the plough's tail. Of course he might not be able to plough because of his poor leg…but there was always the milking…or pigs…or he might thatch.…

Unfamiliarity gave his world a certain interest. He fluttered the farmer's wife. Nothing came to trouble the continuity of his dream. The sheen on the new grass, the expanse of sky, now heavy as marble, now luminous; the embroidery that a bare tree makes against the sky, the iridescent scum on a village pond, these were his remembrancers, the assurance of his realities. Beside them a cow was an obscene vision of the night.

Too lame to plough or to go far afield, it seemed as though his fate must overtake him among the horned beasts. So far he had ignored them. At the afternoon milking he had been an onlooker, then a tentative operator. Unfortunately the farmer recognized a born milkman. At five o'clock next morning they would go together to the byres.

At dawn the air was like a sheet of glass; behind it one great star glittered. Dimmed by a transparent shutter, the hard new light poured into the world. A stillness so keen that it seemed the crystallization of speed hung over the farm. From the kitchen chimney rose a feather of smoke, vertical, delicate, light as a plume on Gaby's head. As he stamped out into the yard in his gaiters and corduroys he thought of the similitude and his mouth twisted.

In the yard the straw rose in yellow bales out of the brown dung pools. Each straw was brocaded with frost, and the thin ice crackled under his boots. "*Diamanté*," he said at last, "that's it."

On a high shoulder of down above the house, a flock of sheep were gathered like a puffy mat of irregular design. The continual bleating, the tang of the iron bell, gave coherence to the tranquility of that Arte-misian dawn. A hound let loose from the manor by some early groom passed menacing over the soundless grass. A cock upon the pigsty wall tore the air with his screams. He stopped outside the byre now moan-ing with restless life. The cock brought memories. "Chanticleer, they called him, like that play once...."

He remembered how he had once stood outside the window of a famous shop and thrilled at a placard.... "In twenty-four hours M. Lewis arrives from Paris with the Chanticleer toque." It had been a stage hit, of course, one hadn't done business with it, but, O God! the London women whose wide skirts rose with the wind till they bore them down the street like ships. He remembered a phrase he had heard once, a "scented gale." They were like that. The open door of the cow-shed steamed with the rankness that had driven out from life.... Inside were twenty female animals waiting to be milked.

He went in to the warm reeking dark.

He squatted on the greasy milking stool, spoke softly to his beast, and tugged away. The hot milk spurted out into the pail, an amazing substance, pure, and thick with bubbles. Its contact with caked hides and steaming straw sickened him. The gentle beast rubbed her head against her back and stared. He left the stall and her warm breath. The light was gaining. He could see rows of huge buttocks shifting uneasily. From two places he heard the milk squirting in the pails. He turned to it again, and milked one beast and another, stripping each clean.

The warm milk whose beauty had pleased began to nauseate him. There was a difference in nature between that winking, pearling flow and the pale decency of a Lyons' tea jug. So this was where it all started. Dimly he realized that this was where most of life started, indifferent of any later phase. "Little bits of fluff," Rosalba and all the Kirchner tribe...was Polaire only a cow...or Delysia?... The light had now the full measure of day. A wind that tasted delicately of shingle and the turf flew to meet him. The mat on the down shoulder was now a dissolving view of ambulating mushrooms.

.   .   .   .   .

"Yes, my son," the farmer was saying, "you just stay here where you're well off, and go on milking for me. I know a born milkman when I see one, and I don't mind telling you you're it. I believe you could milk a bull if you were so inclined..."

He sat silent, overwhelmed by the disarming kindness.

"See how the beasts take to you," the voice went on. "That old cow she's a terror, and I heard you soothing her down till she was pleasant as yon cat. It's dairy work you were cut out for.... There's a bull coming round this forenoon...pedigree...cost me a bit. You come along."

As yet they did not work him very hard, he would have time to think. He dodged his obligations towards the bull, and walked over to an upland field. He swept away the snow from under a thorn bush, folded his coat beneath him, and lit a cigarette.

"And I stopped, and I looked, and I listened." Yes, that was it, and about time too. For a while he whistled slowly Robey's masterpiece.

He had to settle with his sense of decency. It was all very well. These things might have to happen. The prospect of a milkless, meatless London impressed him as inconvenient. Still most of that stuff came from abroad, by sea. That was what the blockade was for. "I've got to get away from this. I never thought of this before, and I don't like it. I've been jockeyed into it somehow and I don't like it. It's dirty, yes dirty, like a man being sick. In London we're civilized...."

A gull floated in from the sea, and up the valley where the horses steamed at the spring ploughing.

"A bit of it may be all right, it's getting near that does one in. There aren't any women here. They're animals. Even those girls they call the squire's daughters. I never saw such boots.... They'd say that things were for use, and in London they're for show... Give me the good old show...." He stopped to dream. He was in a vast circular gallery so precipitous that standing one felt impelled to reel over and sprawl down into the stalls half a mile below. Some comedian had left the stage. Two gold-laced men were changing the numbers on either side. The orchestra played again, something that had no common tune. Then there swung on to the stage a woman plumed and violent, wrapped in leopard skin and cloth-of-gold. Sometimes she stepped like a young horse, sometimes she moved with the easy trailing of a snake. She did nothing that was not trivial, yet she invested every moment with a significance whose memory was rapture.

Quintessence was the word he wanted. He said..."There's a lot of use in shows."

Then he got up stiffly, and walked down the steep track to the farm, still whistling.

When the work was over he went out again. Before the pub, at the door marked "hotel," a car was standing, a green car with glossy panels and a monogram, cushioned inside with grey and starred with silver. A chauffeur, symphonic also in green and bright buttons, was cranking her up. Perched upon the radiator was a naked silver girl. A woman came out of the inn. She wore white furs swathed over deep blue. Her feet flashed in their glossy boots. She wore a god in green jade and rose. Her gloves were rich and thick, like molded ivory.

"Joy riding," said a shepherd, and trudged on, but he stood ravished. It was not all dead then, the fine delicate life that had been the substance of his dream. Rare it might be, and decried, but it endured. The car's low humming died away, phantom-like he saw it in the darkling lane, a shell enclosing a pearl, the quintessence of cities, the perfection of the world.

He had heard her deep voice. "I think we'll be getting back now." She was going back to London. He went into the bar and asked the landlady who she was.

"Sort of actress," the landlord said. And then, "the war ought to have stoped that sort of thing."

"Why, what's the harm?"

"Spending the money that ought to go to beating those bloody Germans."

"All the same her sort brings custom," the wife had said.

He drank his beer and went out into the pure cold evening. It was six o'clock by the old time, and the radiance was unnatural.

He walked down the damp lane, pale between the hedgerows. It widened and skirted a pond covered with vivid slime.

"And that was all they had to say about her...."

He hated them. A cart came storming up the hill, a compelling noise, grinding wheels and creaking shafts and jingling harness; hard breathing, and the rough voice of the carter to his beast.

At the pond the horse pulled up to breathe, his coat steamed, the carter leaned on the shaft.

"Some pull that."

"Aye, so it be." He noticed for the first time the essential difference in their speech.

Carter and horse went up the hill. He lit another cigarette.

Something had happened to him, resolving his mind of all doubts. He saw the tail lights of a car drawing through the vast outskirts of a city. An infinite fine line went out from it and drew him also. That tail lamp was his star. Within the car a girl lay rapt, insolent, a cigarette at her lips.

He dreamed. Dark gathered. Then he noticed that something luminous was coming towards him. Down the hollow lane white patches were moving, irregular, but in sequence, patches that seemed to his dulled ears to move silently, and to eyes trained to traffic extraordinarily slow. The sun had passed. The shadow of the hill overhung the valley. The pale light above intensified its menace. The straggling patches, like the cups of snow the downs still held in every hollow, made down the lane to the pond's edge. It was very cold. From there no lighted windows showed. Only the tip of his cigarette was crimson as in Piccadilly.

With the sound of a charging beast, a song burst from him, as, soundless, each snowy patch slid from the land on to the mirrored back of the pond. He began to shout out loud.

> "Some lame, some tame, some game for anything, some like
>   stand-up fight,
> Some stay abed in the morning, and some stay out all night.
> Have you seen the ducks go by, go a-rolling home?
> Feeling very glad and spry, have you seen them roam?
> There's mamma duck, papa duck, the grand old drake,
> Leading away, what a noise they make.
> Have you heard them quack, have you heard them quack, have
>   you seen those ducks go by?
> Have you seen the ducks go by, go a-rolling home?…"

The way back to the farm his voice answered Lee White's, and the Vaudeville chorus sustained them. At the farm door they forsook him. He had to be coherent to the farmer. He sought inspiration. It came. He played with the latch, and then walked into the kitchen, lyrical.…

"And I stopped, and I looked, and I left."

A month later found him on his knees, vertical in black cloth, and grey trousers, and exquisite bow tie. A roll of Lyons brocade, silver, and peach, was pliant between his fingers as the teats of a cow. Inside it a girl stood frowning down upon him.

Despair was on her face, and on the faces of the attendant women.

"But if you can't get me the lace to go with it, what am I to wear?"

"I am sorry, madame.… Indeed we have done all that is possible. It seems that it is not to be had. I can assure madame that we have done our best." He rose and appealed to the women. His conviction touched them all.

"Madame, anything that we can do…"

The lovely girl frowned on them, and kicked at her half-pinned draperies.

"When the war starts interfering with my clothes," she said, "the war goes under...."

His eyes kindled.

In Bayswater

"Some passages in the life of an only son."

He FOUND THE ROAD behind Westbourne Grove where there was the cream and laurel-green cottage where he wanted to live. He had heard that it was to let and was persuaded that it would be cheap, because of the neighbourhood, because there was no tube, because of the Portobello Road. A woman made of dirt-stiffened rag was its caretaker. She told him a fantastic rent. He had begun to live in the cottage years before. In that last resort, he liked to wound himself observing his own piteousness.

He crossed the ivory boards in his muddy shoes. There was clear yellow paint inside and a round window over the porch, set in deep wood. He put his elbows in it and listened to the wind in the poplars and thought that he was in an old, resting ship. If four shared it, it might be possible. He had not four on whom he could rely. A clean laurel grew in the back yard. He picked a yellow leaf and wrote on it and put it inside his shirt. The great window at the back was made in small panes. He wished he had a diamond in a ring to cut his longing on it. The kitchen was flagged. The larder had a marble shelf for cooling and in summer the butter would not run or the milk sour. There was a glass and white wood cupboard, and shelves for books.

"It is nice," he said to the woman, "but there is no geyser in the bathroom." He knew that she knew that he could not pay the rent. He thought, how, if he took it and could not pay, a life of beastly evasion would begin and corrupt the still beauty. He had no nerve to dodge bills, the technique of frightening him had been too developed. He went out, the leaf pricking him, and forgot to give the woman her tip, so that the wretchedness might be completed by a bad exit, and the shilling still be there for tea.

The round window followed him that was the house's eye, a ship's window, the shape for the eye of the wind. Small, square windows are good, and wide plate sheets; well, he could not have them and must go back to the sort that rattle and stick, that look out on mean arrangements and illuminate them.

These are the fancies of a man looking for a house. His next was the Portobello Road because of its crime. It was a fair walk, as Londoners count it, into a hollow full of bright shops, a market and a crowd, a moving, merry place. There were squat glass pillars full of sweets, called cushions, of the texture of silk. There were little pieces of meat classified and no carcasses. The poor like thick gold watch-chains, and little earrings stuck on cards. He pretended to be envious, while he had no sense of it at all. He imagined a freedom, but the rich vitality, the bestiality, the arrangement of wit, innocence and corruption had no relation to his nature.

He wanted his tea.

The leaf had made a small sore. He pulled it out. On the yellow underleaf was a red line he had scrawled: *From the house with the round window we are kept out of,* and his name, *Alec.* The letter was broken by the veins of the leaf. He put it away. He did not notice the people who had noticed him unbuttoning his shirt. He walked away to the right into a district of tall houses whose doors stood high above the streets at the top of high steps. Some had pillars. The dogs ran along lifting their legs against the high, frayed area rods. The road also ran up.

Into a city of charwomen. They climbed out of deep areas. Soon he saw they were everywhere, descending, rising, in their rhythm; young in glazed cotton furs, mature and very pregnant, old with scum in their eyes. Rooms would be cheap and include the services of one of them, and that would make a gesture.

Rain began. Wetted at dusk, the streets' patina of filth gleamed like stale fish, and out of the crests of the houses came noises of weeping that never was, that never could be comforted. A stiff old gentleman with white whiskers and a red face let himself into a boarding-house with a long bright key. Alec saw him and remembered that the family of a man he knew lived in one of these streets, and that his friend used to live with them. If he called, there might be tea, and he liked the idea of contact with the man again. He filled a coloured disc in Alec's mind, violet and blue with little gold flecks. He looked up and saw the street. At the first number there was a brown visiting card with the man's

name under a bell that did not ring. With his lips against his fingers
Alec called up the tube. His breath beaded its mouth and moved a clot
of grit. A woman let him in. He went up the high stairs that smelt of
dust. At the top of the stairs he found their flat, the door flush with the
step. He was half-enchanted, saying *these are not natural,* forgetting he
had come for human contacts and tea. A little old woman opened the
door, dressed in dull silk, and a small coat of black wool over it. Her
wedding ring was of bright gold and very thin like her hands. For an
instant she peered at him and then began to smile.

"Come in; you're a friend of Charles, I expect. I'm afraid he's not
in, but he may be back." He was drawn inside, and separated from his
hat and stick. A tall, sullen, pretty girl left the room at once to make
him tea.

.   .   .   .   .

"You see," she was saying, "I am Charles's mother, and that makes
it so difficult. How can I say anything against my own son? But sometimes I must…before my daughter comes back. A girl's innocence
should be respected. Once it's gone, it's gone forever, as Landor says…
But he drinks, my dear boy,—you'll forgive a short acquaintance and
an old woman, I know. He drinks, and stays out half the night—all
night, and I don't know what his journalism brings in, but he gives me
nothing.…"

It had been going on some time, and the impact of the idea, substituted for his idea of Charles, was like the pricking of the leaf. He took
it out of his pocket and split it down the back. So a generous man like
Charles was a cad to his mother. —What was she saying?

"He says he is fond of his sister, but he does nothing for her that a
brother should do. He brings men to the house who ignore her. He
says she is not smart enough. He sneers at her. There is something in
him all the time that makes me afraid."

Rubbish. What did she mean by that? This was not interesting. It
was mean. As Rutherford he stood for charm, as Charles he was becoming wicked, just simply wicked like a man who starves his dogs,
and also obliquely, medically wicked, responsible and irresponsible, a
double treasure for the connoisseur.

"I'm so glad you came. I like to meet his friends. Charles tells them
I am a spiteful old woman. But I am all alone, and I have to keep it
from the girl."

Why? Poor old thing. I don't suppose she has to.

"We all thought him a good fellow. He is our authority on periods and décor." That ought to please her—mothers like to swank.

He wanted to hear more, and was beginning to be ashamed. He did not attend to the shame, and was arranging a fresh cast when the girl came back into the room, staring contemptuously over the tray. He took it from her. She blushed and scowled. There was bread and margarine and with them a superb cake.

The delicate voice spoke like a gramophone, round and round, to no one.

"My daughter is a good sister, she loves her brother Charles."

"Don't, Mother."

"Why not, my dear? Wasn't it only last week that you replaced the eyeglass he is always breaking? I know it cost ten shillings, and on your salary.... I tell you about this, Alec, I knew that you were the one Charles calls Alec as soon as I saw you, because of what you said about his being an authority on dress. Oh, my dear boy, if you saw his room, the filthy state in which he keeps his things, his rubbishy novels, his ukulele that makes such a wicked noise, I think; the cigarette holes in his sheets. I know I am a nervous old woman, but some day there will be a fire, and he will burn to death and we're very fond of him, all the same, aren't we, dear?"

"Mother!"

"But, Mrs. Rutherford, what does he do that you don't like?" He wanted his appetite quickly glutted.

"Charles...I can't bear to go into it..." She paused and winked: "I must leave you and see about dinner. Charwomen can't cook, and I'm determined that my children shall have one good meal a day. Charles..."

He was left alone with the girl. A more abstract part of him had already sketched a mask from her pale bold face, and hot ignorant eyes.

"Your brother Charles..."

"You must not take my mother too seriously. She does not quite understand about young people. Charles..."

He thought: You are ten years younger than he, you silly maid. You want smacking. And he said:

"Yes, I agree, but what does Charles really do?" He rearranged himself, raking back his beautiful gilt hair.

"Charles drinks—he leads a bad life, whatever that is."

"We would admit nothing, but that he is sometimes drunk."

"There was a night here once—anyhow he thinks dreadfully. He told me to read a poem once about a bad woman. Mother was frightened—I know too that he is friends with a woman who is not married and who has a child. He would not tell us that it was not his child." Alec thought: But this is ordinary rubbish. I'm wasting my time. Good advice, and I'll go. He said:

"You should try and be matey with him then. You should go out with him, make him show you people. He might not drink so much if you were sympathetic. Nothing is so beastly as when brother and sister aren't friends?"

"Mother would not hear of it. You don't understand."

"What don't I understand—" —I'm off, but I did say the only thing that's always true when I told her to be matey.

The girl went on: "Charles does not think that one can do anything wrong. I don't understand these things. I never go out except to work. It is lonely."

He forgot the stiff lines of the mask he had made of her, lost himself in psychology, and psychology in pity.

"Well, now I know that Charles has a sister, perhaps your mother will trust me." This is going it—I am off home. "Make my apologies to your mother, I have an appointment."

"What did you come here for?"

"I've been looking for a flat."

"There is one to let on the floor below. We have the keys. Mother, let us show him over the flat below."

The mother came out of the kitchen. "Do you like apple dumplings? I hope you'll stay to supper and only hope Charles will come in. I've kept my hand for pastry." She led him affectionately downstairs.

The flat was frightful, a low room with jumping panes and sprawling flowers and yellowing paint. A hot blue bedroom. From the streets he had fallen into domestic anguish, and into rooms that were the interior version of the streets' unrest; and though the retreat was open, he was not sure of it, because the old woman was a witch and would diddle him, the girl her apprentice, and Charles their conjuration. He saw Charles as a stone idol that walked. He was damned if he would take the place.

"Charles. Charles. Charles."

Someone was coming upstairs. To his active ear the slow step sounded deliberate. Here was Charles coming, who did not think anything

wrong, who was cruel to his sister. Who would not take his sister out.
Who had an old woman cooking for him upstairs. Whom Alec knew
as another person. He was out of the door and after him.

Charles marched past him, did not look at him. He followed him,
feeling kicked, up the black stairs. He saw the girl beside him suck in
her mouth, and then a frail call: "Charles, my dear boy, here's a friend
you'll be glad to see. Alec whom you've told me about so often. He is
staying to supper," and lower, "You will be nice to him, won't you?"

They crowded on each other into the little room.

"What in hell does he want?" asked Charles. "I'm going up to my
room to be sick."

"Have you no respect, Charles, for my drawing-room?"

"None."

His sister screamed. "I can't bear it. I can't bear it."

"What can't you bear?"

"We were having tea with your friend and showing him the flat, and
it was nice and amusing, and you can come in and shame us."

"And what would you do if I didn't? Exploit me till there was no
telling which was your son and which was your husband, eh, Ma?"

Drunk—dangerous. Might be sick.

"Rutherford, hadn't you better come up to bed at once?"

"In the absence of that woman's spouse, I am the head of this
house—

> *My fathers drew the righteous sword*
> *For Scotland and her claims,*
> *Among the loyal gentlemen*
> *And chief of ancient names,…*
> *Like a leal, old Scottish cavalier.*

In Bayswater we have other occupations."

He had taken the hearth-rug position, his arms open, grasping each
end, working his olive neck. They waited. "Charles, why do you mind
us knowing your friend?"

"Alec, I must apologise for these people. This is why I don't bring people home. I am as drunk as drunk, and where's some food?"

"In the kitchen. I'll bring it up to your room if you're going to be
sick."

"I'm not going to be sick. Is there anything to drink?"

"You know—"

"I know there is going to be some. Go out and get it, girl, and we'll play *pass the keystone*."

"Give her some money, Charles."

"Damn her, why should I?" The girl went out. Alec rushed after her.

"Go back, my dear. I'll see to it. You must let me. I insist. It is abominable." This is not possible. He sings: *His golden locks time has to silver turned.*

In the street Alec shouldered people left and right, ran into the wine shop and out again with the sour drink.

When he got upstairs, the women were talking low in the kitchen, and up and down the tiny sitting-room Charles was pacing, talking, striking at the air. An ugly boil showed above his collar, a patch of skin on the heel above his shoe. Alec noticed that a great ring was gone from his elegant yellow hand.

He stood in the doorway, licking his mouth. Then he said: "Here's the keystone," and then: "I say, Rutherford, wouldn't you be better in bed?"

"How long have you been here?"

"About an hour."

"What's she been telling you?"

"I never knew you drank like this."

"Turn it into a nice mime, man. That's your job, isn't it? What did she say? Tell me, or I'll wring your neck."

"She minds your drinking. What mother would not?"

"Go on."

"Oh, and the way you keep your room; you've got such a flair for beauty, you know."

"Good man, you've told me, now I'll kill her." He spun Alec out, lifted him, dropped him, hitting the ground with him, and went into the kitchen. There were screams. Alec rushed in. Mrs. Rutherford was sucking her hand. Charles was leaning against the dresser, tears falling down his face. He spoke first:

"It is finished. I am going up to bed." He went out on a light swing, and as lightly up the bare attic stairs.

"This is too awful. Mrs. Rutherford, I am going to take the flat below. I may be able to help you. I could come up at a sound. You are all alone here."

"Bless you, dear boy, bless you."

He was just conscious that this was the sort of good deed to be done quickly. He ate her dinner, he went out to telephone, he slept on the sofa. The women whispering in their bedroom were quiet. He sat over the fire. There had been no sound from Rutherford's room since his door had shut. Suddenly his mother in a red dressing-gown came into the room and sat down by Alec.

"Dear boy. What an entertainment for you. Must I tell you that it might have been worse? Poor, poor, poor son of mine. To think of his singing like that. You know we really are people of that sort. The last poor ghosts of a great family. May I have a cigarette?"

She sat slim and straight, head back, hand up, like a boy. Alec saw the boy. He saw the room and its implications. He thought he saw the possibility of romantic adventures. He saw his retreat closing. He acquiesced.

II

ONE OF THE charwomen was creeping about his bedroom. Alec stood about the living room afraid to touch anything lest the dirt-scum should rub off before the woman had given it a semblance. He could feel her revolving slowly, on an unfresh, quiet morning, when his mouth was sore and his body dazed, with only the sleep interval between him and the dreadful stories upstairs. What a family—compact of malicious and sexual crime, tragic lives and comic deaths. He remembered a great-aunt who had had twins, who had crawled to her husband's bed and left the bodies there, and had hung herself from the chandelier, and her toes tapping the foot of the bed had waked her husband in the morning.

…The girl would leave the room with her irrelevant hauteur and the mother's voice would drop to a hiss and out would drop a toad and Charles would improve on it. *Putting the jewel in the toad's head*. Phew. There could be a series: Bayswater nights.

The flat was horrible. He slept at one and two and three, and woke at nine and ten and eleven, and often went out without washing, re-hearsed, idled, ate too little, ate too much, till late night, like a black madness, drove him back. Not to study, talk and imagination, but to a dogged run up the black, smelling stairs. There he found them, not often Charles, not always the girl, but always the old woman, and a series of obscene, absorbing stories. The flowers he brought them withered in the vases, the classics they borrowed were not read, and it seemed to him that if he took them away it would make a position clear of which he was afraid. He was on a tide and felt it, with reprobation, with amazement, with anguish, curiosity and fear.

The mother fed him, and he sometimes cooked for her, but she would not learn his dishes though she praised them. There was always praise. Instead of a small clean green house and some pretty bits of furniture, praise.

Charles, since that night, had been charming. He had not come there often. He kept his disc in Alec's imagination, night-blue, spangled with gold; and another arrangement where he might murder his mother, and terrify his sister, and refuse to explain why.... He was in a circle by himself. Alec heard his soft bitter voice, whose sound was lost in the mother's reiteration of praise.

"Charm, my dear boy, of course he has charm. All my husband's people have charm. He reminds me of poor Lord Byron."

"Where has he gone, Mrs. Rutherford?"

"Oh, to his room to work, I hope."

Alec thought it must be cold up there with the stars shaking over it.

"He drove Mrs. Sumner out of it this morning. What a state it must be in. You are so particular, Alec. I like to see that in a young man. There is an uncle on his father's side—"

Alec felt for the cigarette he had long ceased to enjoy. It was the first time she had got down later than a grand-parent. It had been saga as much as scandal. She had said "uncle." That might mean that they were coming to the history of living beings, not death-gilt heroes and heroines he had dressed in their costumes as she had moved them naked in their sins.

She had a husband "away at his work and shortly to return." She was preparing him.

"His uncle Ramsay won't speak to us."

"Because of Charles?"

"Because of something that happened before Charles was born." Among the various properties of Uncle Stewart's career had been a collection of obscene books. "He was like Charles about his bedroom, and when he died they were found. I sometimes think that Charles may have something up there."

Charles knew any number of amusing things that had happened about cod-pieces and beds and medicines and make-up and songs.

"Of course you must not think that I mind the classics—I don't

think it's a book, but he locks the door, and if only he'd trust me a little— Do you know what he said to me when I asked him?"

"I heard him tell his sister she had a mind one could make toast
at—"

"He said *to the filthy all things are filthy*, staring at me with that ridiculous eyeglass. An eyeglass with the clothes he wears." She fretted on.

In the afternoon of the next day he was alone with the flesh-raw
flowers, and when he had thought of blood and flaying and Assyria,
and the uncommunicative shapes of cuneiform, he had backed to the
door, and stood rattling the handle and let himself out and then went
upstairs. There was no one in. He pretended that Rutherford might be
in, and for the first time went up his stair. His door was not locked.
Alec's conscience went on squeaking like a ghost.

The room was stirring in the thin wind.

There was a pale stone Buddha, an iron bed with a red blanket, and a
night table with a marble top, and a blue quicksilver ball. A nice set. He
saw these and began to look for something to see.

It takes time to look at books. There was a basket-handled sword.
No fireplace. The servant's room. Pink tooth brush. Did his mouth
bleed? A chest of drawers the colour of mustard to write at and dress. A
piece of silk on the wall in Charles's colours. The wine-dark. If he finds
me here, I came up to borrow a book. The devil take him. He never
told me he had these....

He squatted down on the boards.

There were all the Italian writers and portfolios of fallen columns
and standing columns and well-heads whose contemplation should
occupy a gentleman's leisure. There was Boccaccio, on parchment, the
page spaced with small witty cuts. Alec turned over on his face, and an
hour later, put them away with guilty accuracy, and went downstairs.

If there was a secret, it was hidden. He had not believed in it, only
hoped for it as he might hope for a drink. He left the women alone
that night, and the night after Charles came down to his rooms, and a
friend came and another, and they sang, but Charles would not sing,
and Alec fancied he might be going to cry, and put off telling him that
he had gone up to his room, because one confidence might force another. He knew now that everything would happen in its time, and
this was the root of his perception, the excuse for his weakness, and
made him a happy man.

The next night they were not cordial and he hardly noticed it. The night after, he was making a stage-model and there was a sharp knock and he had let in the girl, sulky and liquid-voiced and fresh from tears.

He noticed that he would like to force her into a corner of the room, twisting her arms, and supposed that one or both must be in a high state of erotic excitement.

"I'm not supposed to come," she said, and scowled, then, with a prepared vulgarity that scandalised him: "You won't let on to Ma, now, will you?"

He wanted to say: "My dear, it is quite proper for you to spend an evening with me, and I shall not make a mystery about it," and felt again that mixture of disgust and vital interest, when she fell down into his armchair and began to shiver without crying, so that he could only say: "What is it?" and at his gesture, she exclaimed: "What must you think of me?"

He looked down into the hot eyes, at acting become obscene through excess of lying, but at raw hunger. It was personal and impersonal. It was the impersonal that interested him. Her race was boiling there. She ought to be singing, not squirming there like a typist, singing another bit of that infernal saga that was coming up-to-date, that was coming up-to-date.

Poor ravenous kid. She should be given flowers and kisses and taken to bed. *Cover her with flowers.*

"I'm glad you've come—listen to this." He went to the piano and sang the pretty song, and played some Mozart to sensitize and detach himself. When he joined her she was bolt upright and sneering:

"What a good chaperone a piano makes."

"What is this fuss about propriety? It is awfully silly."

"I was only thinking that we need more than a piano upstairs. That's why I came. That's why I came." She said it the first time with sober tragedy, the second time like a caress.

"Has Charles been unkind to you again?"

"Oh, là, là. Don't let's go into that. Please, Alec. Yes. Yes. He sneers at me. Oh, God, why aren't I dead?" He thought: I'll get the truth out of that girl if I wring her beastly neck: "Now, look here, tell me the truth."

"Yes, Alec, I will. He sang a dreadful song about—I can't tell you, but you can guess, and when Mother told him to stop and he wouldn't, I ran into the kitchen, and he followed me in there still singing."

"Now, mind you tell me the real truth."

"He frightened me. I ran downstairs."

"You must explain it more. You haven't told me anything to believe."

"I can't, I can't. Oh, comfort me, comfort me."

They're all mad. I must start from that. They're all mad. His brutal temper is making the girl neurotic. Poor little beast. Is it a trick to get hold of me? No. No. Charles is off his dot—I needn't be careful—it's awful. "My dear—"

"Alec, it's silly to mind, but when I minded he snatched my little seed-pearl bird out of my frock and threw it out of the window. It was very old, and I haven't any ornaments."

Alec found he was beginning to cry, and when he checked himself, the sense of danger rose behind the pity and interrogation and balanced him. He was leaning over her staring when Charles came into the room.

"What have you been doing to the child? How dare you throw her bird out of the window?"

Charles took no notice and said to her, "I want to talk to Alec, wouldn't you be better upstairs?"

Alec, expecting heroics, saw her face swell into a puffed, white, whimpering mask.

"Rutherford, you leave that girl alone. She came down her with a horrible story I don't believe."

"Believe it, man. It will have truth enough to suit you."

"Until I know it's a lie, I must protect her. Nothing upstairs makes me believe anything but that you are all mad, but she is too young to tell nothing but lies."

Charles frowned: "Will you listen if I tell you the truth?"

"You said that her truth should satisfy me. Suppose it does?"

"So?"

The girl turned in her chair. He thought of a daschund lying on its side.

"Sit up." She sat up immediately, a young gentlewoman.

"It is good of you to take care of me."

"Look out," said Charles laughing.

"Man, how dare you laugh when you have driven the child so crazed, she doesn't know what she's doing or saying?"

"Alec," said Charles, "are your intentions honourable?"

"God, man! Are yours?"

"What are my intentions? They are to leave this place tomorrow morning, and my mother can try my father for a change."

Alec was just going to ask Charles humbly for the truth, when the girl began to wriggle and chatter, bolt upright in her chair, turning her body from one to the other.

"Charles, please, please go away. This is the only refuge I have. It hasn't been all fun being shut up with mother. Alec, you know I came down…I was afraid it was wrong, but I came because it was quiet, and you would let me cry. Oh, Charles, you might give me a chance. I will tell Alec all the truth."

The men felt that they were acting in a story from a magazine, the present race-fable. They saw each other. "You go to bed," they said.

It was not easy to get rid of her.

"I hate Mother as much as you. Let me stay with you. Show me, and I'll be the kind of girl you like. Give me a chance. I ought to have a chance. You are my brother."

"I agree there," said Alec, and immediately the image of another kind of living was clear to him and he said:

"I wanted to live in a small green and white house that was quiet with a tree, and a round window and stones on its floor. I came here instead without wanting to. That was mad. Without being mad I have lived in an asylum I am going to rationalise for myself. I give in to it. I do not understand what you are all about. But I'm going to."

Mrs. Rutherford slipped into the room.

"My dear, what are you doing here? I am very surprised. Alec, what is my daughter doing here? She's not a bohemian, to be in a young man's room."

Alec and Charles each noticed the other was feeling sick.

"I followed Charles down to get my brooch."

"What brooch?" said Charles.

"My brooch he threw out into the yard."

"It will never be found," said the old woman, "you had better go upstairs."

"It does not exist," said Charles.

"Something exists," said Alec, and then: "Charles, what have they done to you?"

"It is time," said Charles.

The old woman said: "Haven't you done enough for one night? If you will excuse me, I will take my daughter to bed."

Charles said without violence or pleasure: "Will it surprise you to hear, Alec, that I have just come in?"

"There is rain on your shoulder," said Alec. "You have just come in."

"Then I could hardly have been bullying my sister. At present I have no hat."

"Stay here with your friend, Charles. I did not know about this. I will get as nice a supper as I can, and call you both."

Charles fell into his sister's place in the chair by the fire. Alec said: "I smell burning." He did not move. They both said: "It is nothing," but Alec ran out of the room, mad with the feeling that he must be there first, and up the chocolate stair he would see history-making, saga-history, the drama and the psychology caught for a moment in the event, the *historiê*.

Upstairs in an iron tray on the kitchen floor Charles's *Decameron* was burning to death. There was the white core, curled edges that glowed and went out, brittle metallic pieces lifted in the draught to the four corners of the room. The cover his mother and sister had torn off lay on the table like a sham. Their mutilation had left a block of sheets, too well sewn to come apart, whose lit edges had gone out. Many loose sheets were burned away. The book was dead.

He did not hear them following. He stood about.

Poor Charles. His treasure. This was what they did when there was no one looking. He was convinced at once and became Charles's man. He wanted to put it all away, just to hide it, then to bury it. He burnt his fingers on the try.

"Charles," he cried over the banisters: "Charles. Come and see what they've done." Charles came.

"There they are," he said, "now do you see?"

"Yes," said Alec. "I mean I don't quite, but I want you to forgive me. Let me do something. Oh, your book, your book!"

"It is the way they relieve themselves," said Charles. "She is malignant against the pleasant things, and the kid is mad with thwarted instinct. That's what they do."

"What can I do for you?"

"Nothing."

"For God's sake don't say that."

"I didn't like the way you came in here. You told them, I don't doubt, that I was the devil of a fellow."

"You know them. It was like going on falling."

"All right."

"I'd better tell you. I sneaked up one day to your room and read there because they said—"

"That there was something obscene there."

"No. I did not tell them."

"Are you keen on my sister? Why did you stay?"

"No. I was interested. At first I was really taken in. Then—"

"When my mother overdid it—"

"I felt that I was in a current—I wanted to find out the truth. I was inside the houses of these streets. It is the opposite of my values. I wanted to get through this way into what *is*. Living with demons made me a cad. I am begging your pardon. I will pack and go."

"And leave my mother responsible for the flat and rent."

"What am I to do? I'd beat the girl and wring the old woman's neck."

"It is time to shuffle the cards. You might stay and see what we can do."

Alec felt beaten, forgiven, blessed.

"They're still here," he said.

"Coming in too," said Charles. "It is more than a stanza, it's a canto. I'm glad you see that." He guided them in and pointed to the floor.

"That is what you have done to my book."

"If I were you, I would be ashamed to have such a book for a girl to read."

"How did she come to read it? She sped up to my room at your orders."

"You must have left it about. I found her hysterical."

"So did Alec. Stop it, Mother. You have overdone yourself this time. It was also a valuable book. I had meant to sell it and have given her the money. However, she amused herself with it another way."

"Why couldn't you have laughed at it? It is a jolly book. You've got its sheets for domestic uses."

"Alec, would you allow your sister to read it?"

"I should be ashamed of her if she couldn't."

"Come," said Charles. "I am going to bed. I am going away tomorrow. Perhaps, Alec, you can give me a bed for the night."

"They have all left me but you."

"You have my sister?"

"A girl. You are the head of the house."

"While my father lives?"

The girl wailed: "Alec, persuade him sometime to forgive me." He went across to comfort her, and when he put her through the door he heard Charles saying:

"Prospero burned his book: they burned mine: my book is burned: they could not bite, they hid the tooth: they could not see, they stole the eyes. I am starving. I am blind."

Alec's heart climbed up his throat; he took Rutherford away. He remembered the streets, three weeks back, where there was weeping going on that never was, that never could be comforted. He would like to have had the girl, too, and run all night from one to the other, and patronise one while he worshipped the other. He felt sickly and refreshed himself, remembering that he was finding out a truth.

He saw Charles undress, feebly, dropping his clothes for him to pick up and fold, gaily, silently.

He said: "It's a pity we've no drink."

"Have you any tea—China tea?"

"Yes. My mother sends it to me. She is kind—"

"Tar and jasmine. Make some."

He fell into his bed and lay flat, smoking. Alec came back.

"It's been going on for two years. Since I came back sick. I thought they might give me a roof. I meant to shape the girl. I heard a bolt snick. I was curious too. There is a great smooth tide we call a rost. I was drawn on it.

"I don't know why it happens. Why the old sow eats her farrow. Why the farrows are eaten. I couldn't make the girl see, though there's not much difference between a paralysed rabbit and a paralysed fox.

"She's not omnipotent either."

"Why didn't you quit?"

"Fatigue. They are wretchedly poor."

"But, tell me. I heard you speak brutally to them."

"Oh, man, when there is nothing but untruth, one must *make* a reality, or become one of the lies. Any reality will do. It is a quality that one famishes for.

"I made myself part of what she said, to give her truth, which stops madness, which is a release for her and for the girl. I am a man of my race, I want truth. Universal truth if I can get it, anyhow particular truth. Even my décor I hitch on. More tea. But she won on me. I am brutalised, gelded, spoilt."

"Listen to me," said Alec. "I have got some cash. We are going to take that house."

"What house?"

"My house with the round window, the dear place."

"I should improve it. I tell you I'm next door to mad. I even need food."

"You'll have it. You must let me do it for my own sake."

"All right. I used to have a will. I suppose one can recover even from a mother. You know, I have a terror that one can't. I am very sick to-night. My God, what harm had the book done them that they must destroy it—the clean page. When I was a boy she gave us things to break, she was a scolding housewife that soiled things in secret with grease.

"She told me the great poems were filthy. 'I am guarding you against yourselves.' *An exile I have washed me clean.*"

"Peace," said Alec. "We'll do better by our own children."

"I've lost faith in truth. I'll leave no children. I'll do my bit to end the world."

Alec devoted his life to him.

"This persecution is over for you now. Don't you know that? Do you hear?"

Rutherford tore away the clothes and began to toss.

"They murder, they are murderers—"

"We're at an end," said Alec, "that is sure. At the end of a set of evils. Slowly, one after another, they're going to be eaten. There won't be any left."

"You mean," said Charles, settling down in the easy bed, "there is going to be destroyed *all things but beauty alone?*"

And Alec to whom beauty must be mixed with love slept beside him.

III

It had been Alec's intention to take Charles away, but next morning he found him occupied and disagreeable, inert in every part but his body. Alec was shy and took his cue, accustomed by life to these disappointments. He had an idea of paradise that was a state uninterrupted by breaks in fortunate continuity. Upstairs it would be quiet for a time. He did not know what the mother and the sister would do, but they would find a way out for themselves. Man must do that, and those people always do. The worst of men do the most impossible things, have to do the most terrible things. *God is not mocked.* He winced that he could still think like that.

He loathed his occupations till they relieved him. By the evening he was tranquil enough to say: "There will be an empty week. Perhaps a week and a week. *A time and a time and half a time.* We shall begin again. These Scots families carry Scripture with them. There is the father to come back."

He passed the girl on the stairs with her head up, slowly stepping. He wished her an illegitimate baby and went off.

Two nights later a little old man hopped upstairs in a dreadful hurry. Alec was afraid that it was not time for life to become again a condition of music, but went about his room remembering what that condition is.

And Charles was not interested.

"Pa's back," he said. He called him that always, with a spit, and "Ma" with a contempt that masked hunger.

Alec could not bear it and took him out to dinner, and with friendly cunning gave him all the drink he wanted, letting him choose and suggested "tell me about your father." Charles, glowing at a red velvet bench, refused.

In the street Alec said: "I think I shall walk home," and Charles said: "Do you mind if I come with you?" and in Holland Walk Charles sang.

First he sang:

> *My father is a clergyman, a good and honest man,*
> *My mother is a Methodist, so I do the best I ca-a-an.*

"You said he was a schoolmaster."

"No, he was a priest."

"Oh," said Alec, excited at the Roman mystery, "how did he get out of it?"

"He left a note on the vestry pin-cushion, after he had celebrated mass, that he had lost his faith. But it was because he loved my mother. He has never lost his faith."

"How has he combined the two?"

"Not at all."

"But what has he done?"

"Perhaps he maternalises her. He has been the great cuckoo squalling in our nest."

"And the cuckold?"

"I expect so. She hates him now."

Then he would talk of nothing but of some discoveries made in Etruria, but he talked so well that Alec's mind sprang wide and he gave him his attention, keeping the rich morsel of story to enjoy alone. Charles had brought a camp-bed and placed it along the opposite wall at the foot of Alec's, and slept there, neat and formal, chilling his host.

Alec saw the father next day running up the stairs with a bunch of flowers. He was like a greying dog, and by no means, in himself, a formidable man. Alec gave up the effort *de se taire* and began again observations that would end in spying on matters that spying would not illuminate. In his life he had known too much ill luck to believe in good luck, but still felt that it might be induced. When his sitting-room door did not shut easily, he left it open. When a friend came, he held him in talk on the stairs. Charles was out all day, came in late and sober, asked politely for his bed, slept in it folded like his figure on its tomb; did his share of the breakfast, ate it and left the house. But on the fourth day he asked for his father. He was restless for a little, and said, "I must see my father." He went into the bedroom and drew a comb that smelt of sweet oil through his black hair, and went over his face with a little wad filled with brown powder.

Alec, who made up well, in the theatre, never did more than wash and whip a wet comb through his magnificent hair. He feared that he would not be able to go upstairs again. A saga is not heard by inference. He was sad, and was careful not to examine the point of anguish behind the disappointment—the sense that he and Charles had nothing in common...

Before he had expected him, Charles came down.

"How did you find him?"

"Not so bad. There are times when I quite like him. My mother improves when he first comes home."

Alec was disappointed till he had tasted this.

"My mother gives him such a time. He still thinks her incomparable, like an infatuate with a mistress he condemns and can't live without. Not that he condemns her. He only wishes they were both angels before God. Oh, how he wishes this business of living over, and so do I, and so do all our house."

"I don't see that," said Alec. "I still like things, green leaves and frisking and the good hearts of friends."

"No," said Charles. "I want Venetian palaces, which, once and for all, are not to be had, and cannot be won."

"While your mother is the worst housekeeper I ever met. She can't make a pattern of plates on a dresser-shelf." This annoyed Charles and Alec was not sorry. His irresponsiveness had bruised him.

My little son, do not take sides in a family quarrel. My mother's advice. Damn the old ladies. They knew things.

When he got home that evening, he found a little blue note that Charles's mother would be so pleased if he would come up and meet her husband, he was very solitary and so liked young people. Alec's going upstairs was like the passage of a nightmare, slow, and swift in extreme opposites, and he was not himself when he pushed in the door, but a stuttering greed for sensation of which he was no longer connoisseur but glutton. He grinned at the bowed backs about the fire.

The girl would not turn round, or look up. He thought he would tell Charles that when she was old she would be a nasty woman, and remembered that no one knew that better than Charles, and that Charles must not think that he talked clichés…

Charles was shewing off a point of erudition.

The old man listened with respect. Alec listened, fidgeted, had no comment. He was crying to himself that this was a Volsung house, and they should be singing. Charles's ivory stick in the corner by the fire was the sacred tree.

But they didn't grow round Charles. Yes, in a way they did. Alec did not see exactly how. But he would have liked to hear them sing.

The old man said: "Don't you think, Charles, it would very interesting to have an article on Byzantine monasticism in the new quarterly. I'd rely on you a good deal."

The girl said: "Do you remember the wonderful dance you took me to when you wore the gold dress and the curled purple beard?" and Charles said: "Yes, and you wouldn't stay out of pure, sullen refusal to play—"

"I had warned her, Charles, that it was not a proper place for her, but I don't doubt you'd find her more broad-minded, or shall I say more corrupted, now? But here is Alec. I'm so glad to see him again. Didn't I tell you, Father, all he has done to cheer an old woman up?"

"Do you know, Alec, she has broken the most horrible silence about that dance? What truth is there in them?" Alec felt readmitted....

The old man began to fidget. He did not look directly at his wife and daughter, but obliquely at the men. Alec said: *he was once a priest.* An operation of magic was done to him: if he had eyes, he has seen something outside the course of Nature. I say that it depended on his eyes. They say that it did not depend upon his eyes. He has heard confessions. He has elevated the host and censed it and given extreme unction and called Mary an ivory tower and exorcised ghosts. Here he is with wife and children. He has done too much.

The old man belonged to the majority who do not approve—say of cats or earrings or 'bus tickets. He tried to get a denigration out of Alec, who could not think of one. He was wondering at him and trying to remember a piece of theology, when Charles began to give his father a piece of his mind.

"I tell you, people ruin their lives trying to mean both sides of a question as both sides. You can mean a question one way or another, or as many as you damn well care to invent; but you are not to mean two opposites at once. Of course you can mean them if you do not think of them as opposites. You can mean *everything*. But then you have to know what everything is, don't you know..."

So Rutherford was drunk. A good beginning for the night. Alec began to ask him to come to bed.

"I want Father to see what I mean."

"I see that you are drunk, sir, and in your mother's drawing-room. I have known since you were born that you would come to no good end. You say that you can make no money, that I never gave you a profession. Your mother needs a winter coat. Look at your collection of books—"

Charles spat into the fire and sat rigid, while Alec's heart beat.

—"I do all that my circumstances warrant. My son should supply my deficiencies. I am a much ill-used man, and Mother, Mother,—she is not kind to me."

His voice ran up. Alec stared and shrugged to himself. Rutherford flung his arms round his mother's neck. "We understand one another, the old lady and I. Don't we, Ma?"

Alec knew that the gears had been changed, and the engine that had balked would now climb. He blew his nose and looked over the crest of his handkerchief. Charles and his father might be going to cry, no common tears. The old lady had unwound a small roll of braids, tacked on blue paper, and began to knot some dirty threads. Alec cocked his head. That was a web. She was making lace. She makes lace when her men are beginning to cry. The girl looked as though froth would bubble out of her heavy mouth. He lost his sweet feeling for Charles. Charles was part of a play. Not even protagonist. He had no time to feel ashamed. Sometimes love is restored to the quiet soul that Alec wished to have and that his simplicity encouraged and prevented.

Would the song never begin? It did not begin. They bickered. Then Mrs. Rutherford said: "Why should he sell his things when you could give me a coat if you cared to? If you had kept your post in that secular school, we should have been well-off. There's a man for you, worrying about his soul and not his wife—not even about his pretty daughter."

"Don't, Mother."

"There are times when I must speak out. Do you know, Alec, that whilst she was being born, four old priests sat outside our house, in a cab, cursing her as she made her first cry, and me for bearing her to a man who had been one of their priests. Isn't it like them, the shaved men!"

This was reward. There are rewards and fairies. Was this fairy land? Certainly not. "You must not make those curses real," he cried and was not noticed.

"It is she makes them real," the old man cried.

Alec wanted to hide his face....

Mrs. Rutherford and her daughter went to bed. Alec recognized that brightness in the air which marks the appearance of a form of life to which man is not unusually sensitive. His mother would have said: *There is magic about.* The father and son discussed projects and literature. Gradually they began to move. One looked for cigarettes behind a photograph, the other for matches, for a handkerchief, for a suitable piece of coal. In the cramped rooms they swelled, and round Alec grew shadows that met on the small ceiling, drove into one another, mixed and moved out. The son said:

"I shall go and see if Mother is all right," and the father: "I want to ask the girl something." The women slept together. The men did not go. Alec saw the women laid out like saints in neat iron beds, the old woman thinking, the young woman feeling. Nasty, ill-educated girl. No. Charles's sister was capable of thought....

Charles was not drunk enough? How much would it cost to make

Charles drunk enough—drunk to ecstasy, not drunk to witless brag-
gings, drunk to possession by the dark daimon?

Outside, the miseries were streaming up through the roofs, the constant incense that did not even smell nice. It was not much of an exchange for the old man for the sweet scents of his altar. He remembered a barrow of cherries fresh with rain outside a Paris church. His
innocent cocky youth made a face at him and dropped its mask. Misery—*Miserere.*—There was no lord. We are not allowed to believe in a
lord any more. There is a great prince in our hearts. Rutherford knows
that and I, he and only I, that we are lie'd for ever: But that prince is
in prison. I take him out when I can, and Rutherford shuts him in. I
want the salvation of Rutherford's soul. Do I mean anything when I
say it like that?

The salvation of his soul means that the prince has come out for
ever. A thing that has never happened in the world.

Alec left them moving about and went downstairs to bed.

Charles came in to breakfast and said that he had spent the night
wrangling, and then gone for a walk in the pale morning rain. He
added: "Are you sure that you do not mind if I stay here, because the
old man is getting ready to turn me out of what he calls the house?"

Alec said that he could stay for ever, but that it seemed strange because his father had asked for his opinion on several important matters
and had listened with attention. "You will see," said Charles. Alec went
out to work. Observation had become a creation like a piece of needle-
work to be picked up, added to, and perhaps be finished.

A few days later Charles said: "I have made a great mistake—I
wanted a recommendation from an old friend of Pa's, and I asked him
to get it for me. He promised, but he warned the man not to give it."

"And what will that cost you?"

"A great deal, I am afraid. It was for an excavator's job in South Italy.
I shall not go now."

"Oh, Charles, it is insupportable."

"It is," said Charles. "I sink and it lies on top of me. How dirty one
feels when one says: 'I am doing my suffering.'"

Alec saw that it was a small, beastly tragedy. Charles could do that
work, it fed his imagination and would feed his body. It would lead
him back to consideration, honour, luxury. He thought that Charles
must have these in order to be himself. The old man had lain in am-
bush for this. Alec hated him and tried to be rude to him, but he

went on looking peaceful and wretched, fussing about the rooms, never leaving his wife, still asking his son questions. His son answered patiently until, two evenings later, he went up to his father and said:

"You are trying to ruin my life and you still pick my brains, you wicked old man. The sooner you die the better."

Alec had expected something more from Charles than this commonplace. It was a little better when he added: "In spite of you I will live and do the work I like. My mother and my sister can starve. They are your job"—and the old man skipped with rage and said nothing. Alec laughed, too, when Charles added: "I will not accept your responsibility," because he articulated like a good Scot.

The girl opened a rosy mouth and sang:

> *Charlie is my darling, darling, darling,*
> *Charlie is my darling*
> *The young—*

"Blackguard," shouted the old man.

"Hit someone your own size," said Charles, lifting his noble height, and above his laughter, Alec watched and could make nothing of his eyes.

"You will never come into this house again."

"Do you challenge me? I am going out now and my last state will be worse than my first."

Alec followed him out. "You've done it, this time, Charles." He made him no answer—Alec wanted to catch at his sleeve and was afraid. Only a woman could do that. He had to stop a sob of excitement, pain and humiliation. Then he thought that Charles was going out to drink and had he enough money to get as drunk as he wanted to get? He crumpled a ten-shilling note into his hand. It was taken without recognition. Alec went into his sitting-room and left the door ajar. Not for an hour. Before midnight, Charles, who had fallen in the road before a 'bus, was carried up, they presumed to die, and laid on his mother's bed. There was a dry hole where Alec's heart should have been. He helped them that night, and, when the doctor said that Charles did not seem intoxicated, went out on to the stairs and cried and thanked God. He wanted to help more and went back, and from the living room he heard the girl crying in hysteria, and her mother controlling her with great sense. The doctor was in the kitchen. He went to the bedroom door. Charles was on the bed, black and white and young, and by his side his father stood, in exaltation, his hand lifted, absolving his son; and, as Alec saw, absolving himself also, not from past malevolence, but from carnal generation and from women. Alec also saw the father exulting in the son, and afraid that he would see what was being done to him, and that Charles had seen, and was curious, angry and amused.

Just then the mother came back, past Alec, into the room and spoke cheerfully: "My son is not going to die."

IV

AFTER HIS parents thought that Charles was as good as dead, Alec did not leave the affair alone. Independent of his preferences he had an eye for truth, he was preoccupied with Charles. He knew that Charles wore masks. If Alec could not unmask him, there was trouble about that might strip him. He was not afraid that anything common would be exposed. If he had thought that, he might have been afraid and gone away because he was looking for something that was greater than life. Instead, in sensual fever, he evoked pain on this man, ready to stage him and weep over him at once.

After his accident he took Charles away into the country and talked to him about his complexes, his father's complexes, his mother's complexes. He was invaluably silly to Charles. There was an idol once taken round Scandinavia in a cart. He went about through the villages with Alec. He did not tell him anything.

Alec decided to find Charles a woman, a girl of parts to play baggage. He brought Charles back to his people's flat, his visual mask red-gold that had been yellow-gold. Alec explained that he could not find the money to take another place; probably Charles insisted. They lived again in the pagoda, Charles on top, then Alec, and a creeping woman in the basement. She cleaned for Charles's mother and the old lady sat on the dresser and they would talk. Alec's contact with the district was over. He had described it to his friends. Over the street there was a set of empty rooms. In league with Charles's mother he let them to a white girl called Billy.

The flat was damp. Her furniture came tied up with ribbons. She went about like a blooming, fresh toadstool on its stalk. From the first Alec lost interest in her, but his instinct for treachery made him bring her upstairs to see what the old woman would make of her. They made

it a favour to have her, she made it a favour to go. She asked for a foot-
stool. The easy tea-party became formal, a duologue between the old
woman and the young. The girl hated her, deep in her sullen pool. Alec
was bored. Charles had bruised him. He could take the girl or leave
her. He might take her since his people disliked her. Billy rose to go.
She engaged the party to return, dropped a little veil half-way down
her face, and went down to her flat. She put on a dirty dress. Her eyes
set into grey glass beads. She lay with her hair in a fish skeleton the cat
had left by the fire.

Alec went away for a short tour. He came back into a windy, violent
spell of spring, and found about one quarter of his flat occupied by a
young man. He said that Charles had put him there and had paid the
rent. He was called Festus.

"He wrote to you for permission, but the address was lost. I will go
at once if I'm in your way." Alec's sentimentality was not vulgar; his
weakness, by which he meant to inherit the earth, was also kind.

"Of course not, my dear boy. You must stay of course." He was not
sorry even when Charles came in looking like a tree trying not to put
out a leaf.

"Festus was homeless between the jobs."

"I gave in and did what Charles told me."

After tea Festus washed up.

"Hard, bright and sweet," said Charles at the slight, elastic back and
drew in the ashes with his stick. "I am very fond of him."

"How long have you known him?"

"A long time. He rationalises his affection for me."

"I can see he adores you." The small change chinked in Alec's pocket. He had set the stage and he was not to play. He saw a young saint
and an old saint walking in a paradise that was a cold hillside.

This was something that Charles had found for himself. Charles
was warm. There was a deadlier cold about. He felt himself run upon
icy sticks.

"Is he as mad as the rest of us?"

"Yes."

"Only adolescence I suppose?"

"He is formed for his age and very intelligent. But you must be
right. By the way, Alec, why did you bring that girl, Billy, here? Mother
is saying that she won't know your cast-off mistresses. Festus would like
to save me from her and I can't gratify him—"

"Your mother wanted the place let—" He was pierced and weary; "I can't please everybody. If you keep a tenement, you try and let it. I see what unites you and Festus. Some new humbug about sex. I'm sorry you don't like Billy. I'm off to look her up."

"I hardly know her."

At the door he turned back to see Charles lie back and smile at Festus as he brought in the dish-cloth to dry it at the fire.

Billy let him in, yawning inattention. Billy at home was new. He sniffed about. On a table representing a mushroom there was her photograph in chiffon and a rose. Stuck on the frame there was an abominable portrait of her in orange-peel and buttons. She shewed it to him. "Festus did that."

"Did he give it to you?"

"No, Charles."

Really. She did not see that it was not kindly meant. What fun. He readjusted.

"How is life getting along?"

"I'm waiting for my contract to go to Los Angeles. It is all settled. The director is taking me over with his wife—"

"Or as his wife?"

"I wouldn't think of such a thing. I'm getting my clothes—"

Swank of the métier. Why try it on me? We all starve together. Play up. "How many people are dying of love for you, Billy?"

"I'm tired of love. A little quiet spinsterhood suits me at the moment—"

Pale hands I loved. Dear—dear. He thought of a piece of white, smooth, dead wood.

"Sergius wants me to marry him and go to Russia. I might."

"But you're married already."

"Only technically, after all. The Soviet would divorce us."

Lord, the vanity of these fancy-girls.

She began to be eager.

"Do you know, Alec, if I had not been brought up a Catholic, I should like to be a Buddhist. What do you think I'd better do?"

"Be a Buddhist."

"I can't get over what I've been taught. A clairvoyant told me that I was once the wife of a Samurai. A man no one can see follows me about. What do you think of reincarnation? I haven't seen him for a long time."

"See who?"

"My spirit-husband. Some day he will materialise and give me everything I want."

"Meanwhile you might as well go to Russia with Sergius?"

"Why not? I want to get this life over, you know. It's dull."

"I'm surprised to hear you say that." This ass I tried to foist on Charles. I must tell him this.

"He comes when any danger threatens me. He tells me what I am to read. Once I was staying in a house when a murder was done and I saw him. I don't know why I am telling you this, Alec."

Nor I. "Have you seen him lately—since you came here?"

"Not at all. Your friend Charles would be sufficient to keep away any real psychic manifestation—"

"You don't like Charles?"

"He seems to be simply negligible, that's all."

"And Festus?"

"He seems a nice boy. It's a pity he's so neurotic."

"What's his trouble?"

"Oh, he imagines it is his duty to kill himself. Didn't Charles tell you? I imagine it was Charles put the idea into his head. He is just the sort of man to suggest morbidities and give them a greater value than normal facts. Festus has had a hard life. He has told me all about it. His father was a brute—"

"It sounds a plain doctor's case. But he mustn't die. Charles wants him."

"I can't see that Charles ought to be considered. His life is spoilt already. Can't you see he is rotting where he stands."

Alec wanted to bounce. Wanted to box her ears and smack her behind. Charles had not told him everything and she'd guessed. She had asked him in to say what she had said about Charles. She had poured dirty water on Charles. She had a spirit-husband. That bright, righteous lad was going to die. Charles would be upset. Oh, dear. They could not have it to themselves because Billy was here. Billy at other people's houses. Billy drunk, Billy sober, Billy broke, Billy amorous, Billy-by-the-fire. Two men called to see her. Alec was sent to fetch more cups. Two boys with a car. Festus was not that kind of boy. One of them took his chair. Billy was standing up. Beasts. He went away.

Charles was rotting. He saw Festus out of doors, giving Charles blood out of a spoon.

"She says you're no good, Charles, my Charles."

.   .   .   .

"Follow up," said Alec. "Let it be quick, let it be quick, my God." It had happened quickly. He had left Charles to his darling and gone off with Billy. She was always ready to talk about them, but he left it to her. He asked her to interfere, to consult Charles about Festus, but this she always refused. For reasons she would not give, for no reason, because Alec did not understand, because Charles was responsible, because no one could approve of Charles.

Alec said to himself, "Charles does not come to me. I am entitled to find out what Charles is like." Then he discovered that Billy saw Festus, and was doing her duty on behalf of him. "He spent yesterday evening with me, and I've found out all about it."

"No one has told me yet," said Alec, "why he should be killing himself at all."

"He thinks that he is fated to kill his father," and this from Billy seemed enough, because Billy did not understand pride, innocence and torment. He could not think of a better answer. Festus had gone to lodge in another house.

One day Alec was coming in quietly, he heard Charles talking to Billy in her room. After the first interest and inhibition of listening, he listened. A high voice and a low noise. The acute interest went out. He was irritated and knocked at the door. They did not say "Come in" at once. He went away.

Billy said: "That was Alec. We'd better ask him down."

"He will find out what he wants without our telling."

"He might think that there was something between us. Will you fetch him?" Charles looked at her and then, slowly, did what he was told. Alec would not come. "Tell me yourself."

"Festus is going to commit suicide."

"Can I help you?"

"I don't know."

"Are you trying Billy?"

"Alec, will you take Billy away?"

"No. How can I? She doesn't count. Why do you want that?"

"For the sake of the clean issue."

"I don't think, Charles, you are quite the man to manage a young suicide." Charles sighed. Alec went on: "Why don't you take him away yourself? And you mustn't be jealous of him."

Charles giggled.

—"From the look of you I should say you could do with a change. Can't you leave town?"

"I don't want to at present." Charles went away.

Alec began to shiver. It was then he prayed for it to come soon and suffered because he had deliberately offered Charles sense.

Charles had earned sense.

He went downstairs after him.

"I'm sorry you're troubled. Please let me be of use." Billy said: "Festus has gone out by himself. I think we ought to follow him."

They went out. Billy in a purple coat, Alec in grey, Charles in black. Through the dull spring streets and the grit-laced air they hurried to Festus' lodgings. He was not there. "I know where he sits." Charles walked them to Holland Avenue. It was getting dark. They walked on the right side under the trees. "There he is." Alec saw a dark boy upright, alone on a bench. He looked at Charles. Billy said: "I suppose I had better go. He ought not to be left." He wanted to push Charles on and hold him back. She left them instantly. "Not her," he said to Charles, but she was sitting on the bench, a black cap at the back of a white neck, and purple shoulders sloping.

"It is your place and all you'll do is to save it up against her that she took it."

"The pubs are open," said Charles.

．　　　．　　　．　　　．

When they got home, they called on Billy. "It's all right," she said. "I've got him to promise that if I'll help him to do it later, he'll put it off for three months. It's a bargain. But he must have company."

"We'll all keep him company. Good for you, Billy. Now I must be told why he wants to do it at all."

Charles said: "He is going to do it because he believes he can never express in himself his idea of excellence."

"But we none of us can. Why can't he see that. Why should he want to? The vanity!"

Billy said: "I said I would go round at eleven to his rooms. I'll tell you everything in the morning—"

Alec was dazed. His mind would not focus.

There was a tightness and a white blur. He felt he must strangle or be strangled.

"Is she doing her best d'you think, Charles?" he asked as they went upstairs.

"The pubs aren't shut," said Charles.

.   .   .   .   .

They sat in the saloon.

"Aren't you letting Billy have all the responsibility? Can you trust her? I wouldn't. You won't like it if anything goes wrong."

"I am enjoying myself so much up to the present."

"Why do you let Billy act for you?"

"My hands are tied," said Charles.

"They're not, they're not," Alec shrieked. "Use your great wisdom."

"I have none. Let the female do her part."

"You're afraid of the responsibility."

"I am *not* afraid of you or Billy or myself. Believe me, Alec, in the past I did everything that suggested itself to me. Now we are on an ideal plane, and I have no ideal solution."

"Ideal plane! Can't you see it's an adolescent neurosis?"

"Believe me, it is like that now, and nothing less. Let the flesh do its bit."

Alec did not think of Billy as flesh. Charles frightened him. Charles was playing up. He squirmed.

"You'll be in an awful state." And what state am I in throwing silly fits before my friend in his necessity? When it's over, I'll help.

They did not go to Festus' lodgings because Billy would be there.

Next morning Alec woke up feeling sick. Billy was about, very brilliant.

"I've sent up a note to his mother to let Charles sleep, whether the charwoman wants to do his room or not. Go round and call on Festus."

"Won't you come?" She was uncertain.

"No, I must get my place straight. I've left everything because of that boy. I should like to—"

He could not bear to stand about. He went.

He found Festus dead in his bed. He sat down beside him, feeling very cold.

Get the news to Charles. I have to do that. Thank God the girl didn't get here first. She mustn't see him. So that's what he took. I must find the landlady. *In any case you leave a body behind you. Such a want of method.* Can we persuade them it's accidental? We must try. Charles would wish that. I must see about…

But he walked out into the street, and, at the impact of the air, he swam and drank it.

Festus is dead. Charles knows it, but he has to be told. How unfair. I'll tell Billy and she can tell Charles. That's a frightful idea.

I've got to tell everybody. I found the body. Who killed cock-robin? It's quite all right. I hardly knew him.

Take Billy down a peg. Petty cat. Suppose Charles says nothing. If Charles doesn't come off it—

Come off it, you bitch. Leave us men alone. The pretty dead. People go mad and die to illustrate Charles. The illustrated life of Charles. He tore along: with a thick throat shouted up to Billy on the doorstep: "Festus is dead."

She flung out her arms, and strained her palms on the door frame and opened her mouth. She stretched back her head and then led him in.

"Had I better tell Charles?"

"No," shouted Alec, "you go and tell the landlady, tell the police, tell the postman. I am going to Charles."

On the stairs he met the charwoman.

"There's a glove, sir, from one of the gentlemen who was here last night." A huge motor-gauntlet like a dead animal.

"None of us. What gentleman?" Suppose Charles should come downstairs.

"Last night, sir, a gentleman called. Before eleven it was. I heard him with his car. One of Miss Seton's young gentlemen. He took her for a ride in his car and they didn't get home till it was nearly two, I heard them."

"Give it to her."

"Oh, oh, oh." He sat on a stair. We left him to her. He asked her to go. She said she would go. She did not go. He killed himself.

And well the car Love guideth.

Follow up.

He walked firmly upstairs, straight in and up to Charles's room. Charles was awake, propped up, his elbows tucked in to his sides.

"Charles. Festus is dead. He took poison last night. I found him. Billy did not go to him as she said she would. She went out in a car."

"Dead is he," said Charles, and threw himself out of bed, into an overcoat and went out past Alec. "You can tell my people."

Alec told them and went out after him. There was no Billy. Beside Festus' body, Charles was giving directions to the landlady and the police. He gave Alec telegrams written out to send. They worked all day without speaking to each other.

They had the inquest and buried him, received his family and sent them away. They ran it between them. After two days' absence Billy went about among them again. When they could not repeat the story, she told it. Eventually she did all the telling. She invented a mysterious silence when the men began to talk about their affairs again. Then she left the flat and went away.

Alec followed Charles about. It seemed to him that Charles carried a quiver of shafts when a shot meant salvation.

Brightness falls from the air. It had fallen when Festus died. He wanted an arrow to stick. He followed Charles up to his room. Charles had offered a contact like brushed velvet. Alec wanted a kick or a blow. Charles sat up against the wall. Alec, sitting, reached across the table to him.

"Do for God's sake tell me, Charles. Do you understand about Billy?" he cried at him. "Did she know what she was doing when she left him that night? Did she want it to happen? Yes, want it to happen? I can say it now. It's a good thing she's gone. What does your mother say? You must admit, Charles, I've been reasonable and asked no questions?

"*Approfondir* the business for me, for pity's sake.

"Aren't we friends enough for that?

"Stop playing the velvet cat. You've played it since that morning. Can't you see you're being too proud to shew your broken heart? But I know it's broken. You might occasionally come off it with me. I'm not in training for a hero. I've been helping you bury your friend, and a ghastly week it's been. I'm going off for the week-end. I wish we could go together."

Charles listened to this. Alec became ashamed and stopped. He had exposed himself to Charles. Perhaps all this had happened that he might be lured on. Like a split plum he was lying in Charles's mouth to be spat out. Excess of shame squared him against Charles. Charles said:

"Let us take Billy first. There is a common girl, detached from the pre-occupation of her class-type, and who dares not be bored. Her ennui was like a vacuum, into which everything was sucked.

"You brought her here. You have an uncritical reliance on the female principle. After the example underneath us. You have not got the key of the mothers.

"I suppose you thought that Billy would satisfy your curiosity, but not as a rival. She cancelled out with my mother, but that was no gain for she was unready for fresh action.

"I was asleep with Festus. You got tired of Billy. I'm not her size. There was Festus like a thin rod incapable of evasion or compromise or the least adaptation, stripping a male reality, and you two around clapping your female disks."

We laughed.

"Then Festus' little obsession came to a crisis—"

"What was it?" Alec muttered.

"A simplicity. He had stripped certain aspects of virtue and when he found that he could not exactly reproduce them in his daily life, he decided that he was not fit to live, and must immediately die.

"There was also a boy who was better than he was at his job.

"I made the mother's circle till you came along and charged the air with that blonde bitch. A young man does not do it easily. She got going. He died as easily as falling off a log.

"They were getting on quite nicely, you remember. She was busy saving and pushing us gently away. He was full of gratitude and simplicity. He felt he would not die, and wondered how I could have been so right without knowing her. She withdrew and he instantly died. And there rushed into her vacuum intoxication, orgasm, flesh for dreams. She will feed on that for a time. She will be something for a time. And that's that.

"These were your arrangements, Alec, to enlarge your theory of me; to illustrate, explain me, punish me. The developments took their own line. When I could not act, I stood out. Now you are shocked, but you will find that you have gratified your nature. You will not describe its instinct to betray, you will only feed it.

"I betrayed you when I practised my feminine element on you. Superficially you sentimentalized yourself into pique, into indifference, but your instinct found Billy. She has done the job for you. My boy is dead. My mother will be stimulated."

"I can't stand any more," said Alec. "Kick me, kill me—"

"Or cry to you. That's your sensuality, but I'm not under the obligation. I am on exhibition here before you, but I give my own show—"

Alec took out his pocket-knife and sawed the blade into the hard bend of his wrist.

The blood and the good pain saved his reason.

"You are right, you have given your own show. I see myself. I am your slave. I will go away forever and become not your slave. Some time I shall be at peace and not your slave. I mean I understand and thank you for this explanation, for your show. I'm going off because you'd be justified in treading me in like a slug— You'll feel better if you know you'll never see me again—"

"By no means," said Charles.

❖ ❖

The Saint

WE ARE TOLD that they shall burn for ever and ever." She had listened to his preaching for twenty years. That evening his voice was unusually hard, but it did not convince her. Her mind ran on to the conclusion which would make anything else he said insignificant. "And now to God the Father, God the Son and God the Holy Ghost."

She felt the sweet evening outside the lights and smells of the church. The altar lights were lit, and a double row in the nave, yet the hard light poured in and put out the candles and the brassy gleams.

A sparrow flew in. She heard the wings drum against the dark roof. She felt as though her own breast were dashed there. She turned round. The verger was pulling the cords of the top windows. The bird flew out. Half the congregation had turned. She remembered the sermon and was sorry, and began to attend.

For a quarter of an hour the preacher described the rebellion of the angels, and the foundation of the kingdom antithetic to God's. The old lady listened.

For sixty years she had basked in Christ's sun, and balanced her prayers with works. She had not married, but had seen how people behave, and out of her experience her innocent mind had polished its mirror to reflect the heavenly world. She had an image of life as particles sucked into the charity of God's breath, all but certain black specks her church and the preacher called the evil spirits, the enemies of souls. He was describing the choice they had made, to be outside God, Who was sorry for them, but could not because of His justice, exercise His power. Then he hesitated.

The old lady wiped her glasses, and made a short prayer that God would help him out. He continued:

"Who among them could say what had happened to the devils now, but that they were active in the world? In the dissensions of nations, men might observe their impure actions. Might they not suppose that a child pilfering in the shop was an instance not indeed of the influence of the great angels, but of the smaller powers it might not be inaccurate to call imps of darkness."

She liked that. That was true. All her life she had felt that. Of course there would be small devils, children of the children of grace and light. Cast out from it.

"... Need man despair when he considered this? There was no need at all, did he realise that there lay within a power that lies in all that is of God, a power to make them suffer. Now, by his good actions, had he the power daily to put back the devils sevenfold deeper into hell. Let him realise that. His triumph was their despair...."

But that was terrible. She remembered a cousin of her youth whose body had been found shriveled on an island off Cape Horn. The ships had passed him, and their fortunate passage had marked off his torments till he died.

"... Until eternity begins with their annihilation they must remain outside the kingdom of eternal love....

"And now to God the Father, God the Son and God the Holy Ghost...."

The people stood as though sucked on to their feet.

On her way home, on a grass strip of garden, three children were playing cockshies at a battered wooden face.

"Who gave you that Aunt Sally, children?"

"That's not Aunt Sally."

"Who is it then?"

"That's the devil."

It hurt her. She walked away through the delicate light, under squeaking flocks of sparrows to her house, and sent her maid out for a walk. Images rose out of the fire. She watched the angels falling out of heaven in a glittering rain. One by one she saw them go out like a rocket's flare, and stand on the earth weeping, leaning on swords still fiery at the point. And after them their children, smaller and darker, who had not the comfort of remembering heaven. She saw her cousin so withered and enfeebled, but death had come to him with the passing ships.

Lastly she saw Lucifer fall out of the sky, a most beautiful young man with wings. She wept, and went into the garden to line the bird-box with wool.

It did not end there; the sermon had only strung together the thoughts in the old saint's breast. For weeks she was comforted with a picture of the devils' return into the kingdom and charity of God, but she found that there was no authority for this, and it tormented her.

Then the summer came, with a heat no one could remember. The dust choked the leaves, and when no rain came to quench it, moved continually, filling up lungs and pores. In the evening the water in the bedroom jugs was warm, at six the pipes were cut off and the tap that was left all day to trickle in the sink.

Outside the town the woods were worn and littered with bodies looking for rest. The trains could be heard crawling, bringing more bodies from the great towns, and carrying out people she knew to coolness far away.

She did not go, but sent a girl and her baby instead, and went out at evening into the wide Georgian streets where the grass grew, and the paper whirled in white dust spirals.

Then, in the night, she would see her cousin, with his body nearly as thin and light, among the stones.

There was a moment in each day when the heat rose like a flood tide of water and broke. For an hour the ears would throb, and there bubbled in her mind what seemed like black tadpoles, some legged, some winged, red with interior heat that blew most dreadfully white in contact with her.

At evensong when she was restless in church, she would look up to the steps and then the altar, and see behind its glitter there were spaces, dark walls upheld by stones.

There was the lamp that never went out, and the Cross tilted forward, and under these the quiet confusion of lights.

She had read once that the candles had been used in the service of an Egyptian goddess. She was sorry for the goddess whose light had been taken away.

These fancies, which might have spoilt another's faith, brought her in the end to a crisis of pity and love.

The love of Christ she knew, and since Christ is God, and God is Love, that one might love God's enemies, as well as God. She went into the state of rapture, until the idea of the soul in pure union passed out and became a need for action.

Some would have been contented with transcendental benevolence, some would have written a book, she could only add new works to a life of works. She prayed: "O, God, if Thy angels suffer in exile from Thee, remember also my cousin who was a sinful man and suffered in loneliness, for a time, what they must suffer through eternity. Grant that in praying for him, I may pray for them also; in pitying him, pity them also. For the sake…"

With the autumn the heat passed, but no rain came. The leaves fell in a night, clashed and whirled; the old dust flew among the streets. People had ulcerated throats. It was cold. There were fires on the moor, but no rain. Everywhere in nature there was pain, the cold of hell when its heat went. Her prayers were no more than thunder drops. She understood that her love must make her one with the beings for whom she suffered; that, to do that, she must sin.

One large sin would be enough. The universal God would understand her mortal weakness and let it be enough, and the devils would be comforted.

She wrote out the seven deadly sins to find that for those of the flesh she was too old, and for those of cruelty incapable. She thought that she might send her nephew back to the light women he followed, but he had gone already and it seemed at least a kind of offence by proxy.

But the next time she knelt to receive the communion, she saw what she must do, hanging like a picture in the air. She had the care of the altar vessels. Among them there was a pre-reformation communion cup of silver-gilt, used only when a Bishop celebrated.

When she touched it, it had been a cold treasure of the Saints. Now she saw it red as if there were a coal inside. She would steal and sell it.

Two days later, but not at a time when she was accustomed to arrange the altar flowers, she took the cup out of its case, and put a piece of cement there instead. The use of a weight made her unhappy, but so it seemed to her that a devil would have acted, or one of their agents here. Next day she went to London to see her sister, and in her bedroom in Camden Town took out the cup.

She wondered if she should shew it contempt, use it, perhaps, to clean her teeth. Then she saw its beauty, not as a sacred vessel, but as a piece of jewellery, and the memory of holy cups in stories made her raise it to her mouth. A bitter wash seemed to rise out of its dry pale gold. She understood that it had become, for the time, the devil's cup. She was afraid, until she saw a picture of a woman with the body of a suffering man laid across her knees.

Next day she put it inside her muff and went out. At Mornington Crescent she asked a policeman where she could sell a valuable piece of family jewellery. He told her to go to Attenborough's in Shaftesbury Avenue. She got into the 'bus, but at Tottenham Court Road she got off and walked through some streets on the right till she saw a small dealer in jewellery and antiques. There she sold the cup for fifty pounds, or about one-fifth of its value.

She came home in a storm. The west wind emptied out sheets of rain; the gutters brimmed on the house edges, and her cat was mewing, drenched against the garden door. Her life began again exactly as it had always been. Only, by what she had done, she knew she had related herself to everything that there is in the world. She said, "I feel myself less lonely now," and once, "I have seen the Son of Man!"

She knew too that when the time came for the loss of the cup to be discovered, she might be afraid and forget for whom she had done it, and against this she prepared herself.

A week later, sooner than she had expected, the Vicar found out. He told her about it, beating with his stick on the flat stone of a grave, and anger and anxiety made him look unshaved. It occurred to her to say the cup, though lost, was not destroyed, and was still carrying its holiness about the world, and also that a man might have taken it to sell and give money to the poor. She did not say it out of delicacy, and then, later, forgot, and said it to try and comfort him. But he was shaken out of his priest's attitude, and as an angry man turned on her with his version of the wisdom of the world. She listened and, although it made her unhappy, it calmed and strengthened her.

She had known him a long time; now it seemed that she saw truth. She was exceedingly sorry and tender for his distress.

A week later it was Hallowe'en. She was used to keep it as a feast of holy souls, but that night she kept it as a feast of dismissal for those by whom they had become holy. When her maid was in bed she laid the plates on the table, one of bread, one of marzipan cake, one of apples, and with them a decanter of wine. She said grace over them in the name of her now universal God. Then she said, "Come and eat. Come and enjoy yourselves. Forget the brimstone and the ashes."

She saw that if they came they would eat too much, and that she must do that as well. It did not make her laugh as she listened at midnight to the rocking, roaring wind. The casement strained. "Let them in." She shut it again, and poured herself out a glass of wine, and ate a cake quickly. The disciplined stomach stopped her half-way through.

For a moment she thought that there was more that she might do, a deeper summons she might make, but the idea only began and went away. She took the food off the dishes and put them away, and threw the food on to the fire, and stood at the empty table.

"*And now to God the Father, God the Son and God the Holy Ghost.*"

Next day she had forgiven the Vicar his cynicism, that had, without her knowing it, made her angry. She stopped him, in the churchyard, without speaking. He was wretched. There was no news of the cup. It would be, without doubt, sold in America, and the people there would hardly know for what it had been used. It was wrong to despond. The loss had brought him much sympathy. They must turn their thoughts to the active duties of life. He walked along beside her.

"You do not think that they will melt it down?"

He did not.

"Its value, if one does not consider its sacred use, is not so much in its material."

The tide of her tranquility rose. Then she remembered that she had done nothing with the money she had received for the cup, and she laughed.

"What has been done about the School for Mothers we are all anxious to have?"

"There is nothing to prevent it, but the want of money."

"I have been thinking of that. You know I have a small sum put by, and it seems that so much of the happiness of our town might depend on it."

✢ ✢

Bellerophon to Anteia

"...and when he became hated of all the Gods,
he went away...eating his heart."

WHEN ALL IS SAID and done, I should prefer that you should
know, Anteia, how I came to be here. It seems that you have a
right to know, since you liked me so much. I thought that I knew what
our preference for each other would mean, but here I am in this place
where the grasses are grey and the sand white and the dull sea is never
quiet or coloured and the wind does not stop.

I cannot stop, but I am going nowhere, and there is nothing but
the memory of it to remind me that I hunted the chimæra in mid-air.
I knew that, after what happened that day in the corridor at Scyros, I
should come to an end of the sun and colours, on dead beaches, and
that a spin of sand racing the dunes would be the hero Bellerophon.
I do not know why it should be so, only that you took a fancy to me
that rich autumn so that I had to go away, even from myself, to dance
in the sand, a thin ghost.

In this there is nothing I would have chosen.

Already the wind is fingering me. A hero must be sorely winnowed
and withered to be turned so light. When I left you, you will remember, I had on gold armour and a purple crest. I am not wearing them
now. I should like to tell you how I got here, how I found the place.

You never know what adventures may lie in caves. I was already
half-way up a hill when I saw an entrance where I hoped to find a beast
that would engage me in fight. My armour was already a little dull,
and I wished to exchange it for a light skin to protect me until I should
have found a way out of my exile. There was nothing in the cave, but
some way back water dripping from the roof. The cave ran low, oiled
and green, but stooping I went under it and found myself in a black
hall that glittered. The sand under my feet sparkled, dry and glorious. I

70

marched, and thundered my name, *Bellerophon*. I honoured that place at least. I saw myself dipped in dry star-dust. It seemed a day's march through. At the end there was a small arch and a passage of pebbles and slow water, a stream two inches deep but not pure. There were too many green ferns, one could not see out of what soil they grew. It was certainly daylight. I hurried through.

I stood on stone at the edge of a round pool that was open to the sky. There was a belt of rocks round it. I could not see over, but I rubbed, even with my tongue, the dry bloom on the gold stone, and was reminded of a terrace at Scyros and of the painful names given to our intimacy. Then I forgot even these, I was so pleased with the double circle of sky and water, a blue lid over a blue plate—I could have broken the plate and eaten it like cracked sweet ice. I crossed in a bowl floating there, which may have been the one Herakles left.

After that there was another passage with the same quality of light as a brown blight gives over a strong sun. It came from one side, through windows, and there was sometimes a sighing sound. I went down it indefinitely, until I heard a noise of banging repeated with a roar between strokes. It was instantly dark. There was a cave and up it a sea running from some ocean, on to a black beach. There was a gleam when the wave ran up, and a horror to hear it strike, and, as it slid back the suck, suck, on the stones.

I stripped and leapt upon a breaker, and, parting it with my hand, rode up, and lay a long time on the beach of black stones while the water screamed past me. I leapt up the oiled face of the cliff, and heard the waves mount after me, climbing each other's backs. Through a hole in the face of the rock, I entered a hall of unrecognizable gods. I think you might know some of their names. They were saying, "There goes the hero Bellerophon," but not kindly.

After that I watched confusedly. I remember that I studied in great expectation some writing that formed itself on a scroll, where our affair was described in sentences that depended upon a sentence that was not written. I spent some time at this until I fell into disgust. Again, there was much that I should have wished to refer to you.

You will now want to hear the end. I can tell you that. For some time the nature of my walk had changed. There had come a tender light. I particularly remember a green and violet light that sometimes turned rosy; and the ground was spongy but not disagreeable, except through an apprehension of its wetness I could not help feeling. I had known when I entered the ocean cave that it was all up. I could not be-lieve it, of course, but I was surprised when I found at the end a small dry room with a floor of clean sand and at the further side a shelf or an altar cut out of the rock, powdered with clean sand and empty. The light sand on the floor drifted up to it. Later I found a way out on to these beaches.

That is all I have to tell you. Adieu.

✧ ✧

Angèle au Couvent

THEIR SCHOOL WAS BUILT inside the ruins of a monastery on the coast of Fife. The playing fields were enclosed with huge walls. Among them were a few garden-plots and a thin line of trees. On one side of the wall the sea went roaring night and day. At the intersection of the walls there was sometimes a tower. One was a pigeon-tower, full of holes. The trees, that were a row of whistles for the wind, grew small out of the bright grass. Outside the wall there was a ruin and a saint's tower. The school-tower, ill-proportioned and built of the same stone, overlooked the square. There was never anything but wind in the town whose pride was to grow in spite of nature and also to outdo nature and laugh at nature.

The girls went about the country in solitary couples, trudging, chatting. At night they were shut up under the towers, inside the walls. Those who loved the school rarely went outside. They were girl-athletes, running like deer inside the walls, leaping, turning, charging in a group, scattering to reassemble, passing slowly, cowled like young monks, into lit, stone houses at dusk. They were young monks, vowed to obedience, labour, chastely ignorant of chastity, rewarded by authority and power. The model was a god-centred word, and sometime the god had been lost, and his place taken by rules and ranks, and by great cold, and at night by the voices of the sea.

They were girls grown as boys and turned, occasionally, into animals who had lost their sex. There was to be found in them a cynicism and a true accidie that they sweated out running in the wind.

A girl walked on a path cut off from the wind, under young lime trees, on soaked gravel. The sun splintered on the top of the wall, bright, cold gold. It would soon rain-in the March night.

She pulled on her hood lined with bright silk and enjoyed its touch, and out of her serge tunic pocket, over one small breast, took out a rosary she had made of nutmegs and peach-stones, spaced with red beans and finished with a cross. She was taught that it was wrong to pray to the Virgin, so it might be true. "Hail, Mary," she said, also the *sursum corda* and a psalm of penitence, going from bead to bead till she had had enough of it and there were seven beads left. She tried to make up a prayer. The sun had sunk behind the wall into wet, gold air. At supper, because it was Saturday, there would be richer food. She paced back, her eyes watching inside her hood, contemplative, up-and-sideways-looking, underscored with blue on a milky skin. Her head went up, safe inside her hood she was all attention, calling to any daimon to come and play, at anything, in a darkening garden, in Scotland, at the beginning of night.

God is a spirit. The cold wind rose.

God is the helping of man by man. Who helps me with my algebra? A mouse ran across her path, a gull cried over her.

God is a gentleman. No, that's the devil. The devil's a part of God. I always thought that myself. Lord, give me something to play with. Make my Cicero translate right. Forgive the devil and comfort him. Let Doris be my friend. Make tomorrow all right. I must finish my beads. A poem will do. She went on and looking at the dark grass said, *Round the stem of the Fairy Tree.*

A house-mistress with a lantern overtook her.

"Are you out so early from the Confirmation Class?"

"I do not go, Miss Mackail; I have been confirmed."

"I see." She went on. The girl stepped out into the dark and trudged in her round snow-boots after the swinging light circle, and the powerful idol travelling on its edge. She wanted her to be a jolly old lady, who would call her and give her buttered toast and ask her what she thought about life. There was supposed to be a house-mistress who did that, who let her girls stay over when they had colds.

The night arrived. The clock-tower struck half-past six. The old tower sank into the night's iron sky. Her head was cooled and rested from the schoolroom's noise. Her colt's legs ached. Dry wires of hair rubbed her forehead under her hood.

In the schoolroom, on her desk, she found her sewing returned for the blood-stitched buttons to be taken off and put on again. The spread of calico had knocked over her flowers. "That woman's a beast," she said, and put a head of cotton through a darning-needle and tied the ends. The child's infinite capacity for leisure was being introduced to another kind of time, full of ends and beginnings and things which had to be done.

The Saturday night crowd, rested and expansive, saw her.

"Crazy Terry in from the playground so early," they sang and jerked the back of her chair.

Her only chance was to amuse them, to be a little crazy. A small, chlorotic matron interrupted them to say that her sewing was disgraceful. She sucked a finger rough with threads of skin....

"That's right," said a girl, "go on. You like being called Crazy Terry because you think you're different. But you aren't. You're just like everyone else. Ruth's going to give you a prefect's jaw about trying to be different." The tribal life whooped off.

"Silence," called a prefect.

"Why?" said a girl who knew a great many boys and wore her hair all the holidays in a white ribbon, and lived near London, in a large red house and grounds and went up to London in a car.

"Fifty lines by tomorrow morning to anyone who speaks again."

In the silence the cold could be felt passing in at every window of the long room. Terry noticed that the low sky looked as if it were dark blue and was glad to be quiet.

"It's because of the people who're going to be confirmed," whispered the girl and put out her tongue.

The new kind of time stopped. Terry had ruled off the end of her Latin dictionary into squares which were the days of the term, and she now had a square to fill in with a design for the kind of day it had been. The day before had a crescent inside a smaller square, which meant the new moon seen through glass, and accounted for the return of the buttons. A coarse darner makes a large hole in a linen button. She looked through it at a piece of the room. The gas whistled in the hazy air.

I saw a tree with gold fruit. It didn't mean anything. I was top in English, that's a Solomon's Seal. If I score off Rachel I'll draw a swastika on Monday because she's a Jewess.

She practised swastikas and counted up the days to the term's end.

There was a girl who had asked Terry to explain the Faerie Queen. She had interesting square bones and a blonde skin that tanned. Terry with dark spiral curls admired her, but she belonged to another girl, the daughter of an Indian Colonel, whose life was on a pert convention. Terry did not understand. She had thought until lately that there was a god who gave things it was good for people to have. She had asked him for Doris. There had been delicious scraps. She understood she was no match for the girl who had Doris, but did not understand why.

The Sunday was brilliantly cold. At the end of the afternoon walk their shins were sore through their wool stockings. The schoolroom fire roared. The prefects had tea in the house-mistress's warm drawing-room. Time, that all the week hummed like a taut rope, moved into a slow beat, and Terry, at her ease, made her own time.

Doris and her friend had been confirmed the night before. Unexpectedly Doris came over to her and said:

"Will you come out into the playground, Terry? I want to talk… You can't come out like that. Go and get a sweater or something."

Terry ran, and at the foot of the stairs stood still, glowing and in pain that there should be someone to tell her to put on a sweater when it was so cold.

In the Blue Dormitory Doris's friend was in her cubicle as Terry passed, putting up a sickly head of Christ, by Dolci, on the wall.

Terry knew that that sort of picture was not a good picture. It did not help her at all to think of a man like that. Old maids liked him and people called Pale Virgins in the old song. The child did not identify herself and correctly. She intended that Doris should not think like that.

The girl saw her.

"Do you like my picture, Terry Vane?"

"Well, not very much. Stiff plain Christs I like better."

She was busy giving the girl a sensibility equal to her own.

"I don't suppose you would see what's in it," said the girl, who was overwrought and whom Doris had told that Terry had a wonderful mind and whom a little daring would have sent whimpering to another friend.

Then Terry would have been protected and Doris sensitized, but Terry thinking only of the playground, ran away from her into her cubicle and snatched a sweater and with her cloak unfastened, walked her friend out and away.

Doris unhooded her bold, intelligent head. Terry seldom wore her hood because, as the house suspected, she loved her own hair. They shook off other strollers and reached a wide drive that commanded the sea.

"Well?" said the child.

"Look here, Terry, for three weeks I've been to the parson's lectures and all I remember is that there was a council at Nicaea where some-body decided that the Son was one substance with the Father. There's one thing, and what has it to do with my duty to my neighbours and what have either of them to do with eating bread and wine in church? I was so nervous this morning I might have been sick. My sister used to have tea and a biscuit before she went, but she doesn't go now. What is one to believe? Or do, once one believes?"

Terry said: "We can chuck the council of Nicaea, anyhow."

"Then the catechism?"

"That's just how people would like us to believe."

Doris grinned.

"But, Terry, who cares if we believe? That's what I want to know. Is there a God at all that we've any reliable information about? I mean is the Bible true? There's something called the higher criticism that says the Bible didn't happen."

"My bishop talked about that and told us to ignore it. So I asked. It's about the flood. All those animals couldn't have got into the ark."

The blue-pearl-coloured sea hammered on the reefs that are the coast of Fife. *Black rock and skerry* ravelling the pure water that comes from the pole into a mantling for the sea. The bitter air was cold gold, the smoke of the Scots town enchanted it. A star came out. Terry looked at it and a white ivy leaf on the wall and at the texture of old stone. The sky was green in the South. She smiled, passing into those beauties.

"What would God say, Terry, to my brother? He likes horses and he drinks, and knows about life, and when he comes into the room it goes with a swing and father's friends look small, and father gets mad and Dick just laughs. On all accounts Dick's damned. But if God isn't decent to Dick—"

"God's got to be—"

"Well, if the parson's God isn't true, is there anything? Muriel says it's Christ that matters. I can't see there's anything so wonderful there. Would you mind a few years' bad time if you knew you were going to be taken off directly it was over by millions of angels to have a good time for ever. Besides, He was never married and books are about be-ing in love."

"Her picture is awful."

"Good for you, Terry. She got mad when I didn't like it. Now you've said so."

Terry's cheek was like milk and wine.

"Doris, I know there is a God. But the point about God is that parsons and churches spoil Him. He exists only when you are by yourself and see that things are beautiful."

"Yes," said Doris, "go on."

"He writes His name everywhere for us to see. Look at those purple cabbages. Think of an ice. That's God being friendly. Like your brother's horses. They said Christ ate and drank."

"Never too much, Terry."

"Wine and things He liked, if He was God at all."

"Wasn't He God? You don't think He was God?"

More stars came out. Terry saw a feather-moon turn into a gold knife. They were out in the centre of a great playing-field. The whole sky was over them. She put up her face for it to kiss.

"No. I understand. It is not a man or a woman. It's more like the bird they call the Holy Ghost.

"It is every beautiful thing.

"It is the stars coming out and the orange square of those windows. Where we must go back.

"It is every good thing.

"It is especially love.

"It is us when we see it. We are God.

"There, that is all I know. Will that do?"

"I am going to try and believe it. Oh, Terry, you've said everything."

"Remember, if it isn't true, we've got to go to hell with the people who wanted it to be true."

"Heaven for climate, hell for company. I'm with you, Terry."

Terry thought: Will she stay with me now?

Across the brightness of her suddenly simplified conception, the question wrote itself in black. She was breathless with pleasure, but she understood that the answer was not yes.

"Still thinking, Terry?"

"Yes."

"Well?"

"Only that what I have seen is good enough. I mean that it is all that I shall have."

Doris looked aside.

"It seems to me that you have everything. Do you mind if we go back. I promised Muriel to make toast and go through tomorrow's prose."

"Yes, if there's time."

And Muriel does not mind, —Terry thought and had not the courage to say, and this understanding lay, like a bitter almond she would afterwards learn to appreciate, in the honey of the child's mind.

II

A GIRL BLEW a whistle. On a remote playing field they put on their cloaks and sorted out, two and two, to return. Terry under a tree saw them coming and turned back over squeaking wet turf. The even rollers of the sea ran up the beaches. She looked to see if the sun had coloured them. There were birds in the gold air behind the leaves whose turnings made her sick, and no colour in the grey water she could hear all day and all night, except when she was in school.

She imagined that she was ill and would not go over to school, but sit out there all night under a small tree and watch the uncoloured sea till it could only be heard. She was afraid of the people of the place. She was not ill and they would find her, they would ask her questions and punish her. It did not occur to her that they could be right in anything they did, or that she could defy them. She ignored them because she could not do anything else but—she was at their mercy and in fear. The wind was cold, the ground was wet—she went in at the tail of the cloaked girls.

"Where have you been, Terry? Mooning about the courts. We saw you."

"Who cares if you did?"

Anyone could see I care. God how I hate them.

In half-an-hour there would be the hour's preparation, food, then another hour's work, then bed in the icy whistling dormitories. She did not understand the work. She did not always listen when they explained. They said she could do it if she liked. This morning she had not listened. She had forgotten to attend to the beginning and there was no one who would tell her. There was a lesson to be done about Hebrew prophets. "One hour a week at that and five at algebra," she said, and drank a mug of weak tea. The tiny stimulus acted. In the hall she hung about and looked at the curve of the old stairs.

The house-mistress came out of her room. "Isn't it time you went over to school?"

"Not for five minutes," said Terry simply, and went away. She did not know that the sight of her, all sizes and none adjusted, exasperated the athletic woman.

"She is not wholesome," she said, and thought of the splendid machine she captained, also of the kind of girl she liked, neat, sturdy, predictable, smart. These were her pride. There was her technique.

Terry went back and drank some tea from the bottom of the pot. She began to see night coming, light ebbing and replaced by light. Between their pools she could be lost. She threw a Spenser into her satchel and ran across into school.

High up there was a varnished hall where the lower school did its preparation. From the roof, enormous lights threw a just-sufficient glow on to the desks. On the platform one of the sixth form kept the room, doing her almost grown-up work, writing with a fountain pen. From time to time a girl left her place, walked up the steps, asked permission from her and went away. That was all that would happen for two hours. Terry would not have to go away. She slid sideways into her seat, curled down and looked about her. The tea worked. She thought of the fast waters of the burn bubbling, and of a girl she admired and had seen throwing up a ball and jumping to meet it and of her beautiful legs. That she was called Clumsy Terry and that she could describe what they did and that it did not count. "Writing is my only joy," and that was like a song. Songs were literature. She could do literature better than them all. She knew things in a flash, out of nowhere. She spoke when no one else could. There was silence and she felt warm for days. But it was not possible to trade the flesh with the grown-up women for the algebra and the arithmetic. They would only be paid in their own coin and she could not earn it. Not if all day and through her sleep she tried to find their pennies. She could not pay them. She did not know what they wanted. The others all spoke together, "Yes, yes," they said and handed in clean competent pages and grumbled for swank. She never pretended not to understand a lesson when she did. Oh, yes, I do unless they call me conceited. On the days I can't stand them I pretend not to understand. The things they can do they won't help me with. No one ever told me how they began, why you have to take a and b away from each other. Mother says she had no education, and if I make such a fuss about it, I can look out for myself. Mother is not like the mothers in books.

She did her algebra wrong, and comforted herself preparing a poem, satisfied her sense of justice, quieted her fear of the next day. She got word and sense perfect, she rested, she lived, she began to be hungry.

Next day the algebra was returned to her to be done again, alone, that afternoon, when the others were out in the fields, the headmistress to be told, the house-mistress, the captain of the house. Terry could not see. Sweat broke out of the milk-bright skin, on to the rough wood. Cold followed sweat. Lead crept in her veins. Before her the heavy disgusted face of the mistress sucked the corners of its mouth. Horrible tears rushed up her and were held, bolted back by her teeth. *They shall not pass the barrier of my teeth.* She went into literature class, where now her back was broken she could still speak. She knew it all, and she could not make a mistake; she was praised. It counted for nothing. Like quiet it half restored her. Like a little cup of wine it heartened her for something that she could not bear. Her isolation among the insatiable women became a state she had entered.

She reported after school to the headmistress and was contemptuously dismissed. "You here again, Terry Vane." It banged in her head, a dance-step trodden by great beasts. She was all small in a wood. A baby terror woke.

Hark, hark.
The dogs do bark,
The beggars are coming to town.

Enemies were singing towards her. She went over to the house, too sick to eat.

After lunch she had to sit and sew. The other girls had seen her outside the headmistress's door. She wanted them to say things. A prefect whispered to another, and a girl she did not like joined them.

Her house-mistress was more explicit. "I wish you to understand, Terry, that your conduct is disgraceful. It is utterly unsatisfactory. Until I have evidence of improvement I shall recommend that you do no more literature."

At first she could have stunned herself with crying; wailing, imploring, have drooped before the woman. She had not the courage of abandon. She looked stupidly out of the window, lived a long time, forgot.

She was outside. "Devils," said the child. "Devils. No God." She thought of God as quite helpless too, and went clumsily downstairs.

"I'm sorry, Ruth, I can't play till half-time, I have to go to a detention."

"Really, Terry, I call that carrying slackness rather far. You won't work and you won't play except at things you think you are good at."

A monster that would not work and would not play formed in her mind. She remembered that at night it was dark. Then her mind ran out into a place where people were free and pranced along with grapes in their hair. It was either silly, or too good to be true. She wanted to be out and moving in the cold. In the passage they were fighting to be ready for play. She took her books and went back again into school.

Now it was empty, the great skeleton house that rushed with life and murmured with classes, quite empty. She could not hide in it. One or two others, also sent back, passed her without speaking. She could have smiled, but thought they despised her and acquiesced. She thought of an impudent game they might have played before the mistress came, and imagined it played, went into an empty classroom, opened a clean page and waited.

No one came. She was cold. She had been six terms in the place. The end would be in two years. She had been driven up north. She had only asked to be taught like a boy. She would go back south, from one failure to another, into dusty gold out of grey wind.

"I did not think I could not do anything. They are making me so that I can't do anything at all." A band outside began,

> *O ye take the high road*
> *And I'll take the low road*
> *And I'll be in Scotland afore ye.*

The tune rose in her head, it was good to be alone, high up in a room all windows, and hear music. She began to walk about, singing quietly, not in tune, swinging her curls. She warmed, tune followed tune. The mistress, coming along the passage, saw her through the glass door, saw her come back again and again to the window, and sit on it, looking down into the town and up into the sky.

"I told you to wait for me in B. This is D."

"I'm sorry, Miss Keith, I thought you said in here."

"Your work is disgraceful. I don't know what to do with you. You have ability."

The tune had drawn the child into a pattern. Terry said: "I can do one thing well. I can understand the value of words and quantities. The words in this stuff are just made up. It doesn't interest me. It might—"

The woman was astonished into attention. "It might if what—?"

The music stopped. Terry looked round the dull walls.

"I don't know. It doesn't matter." If I could tell the woman. If I could ask her to explain from the beginning. It isn't worth it. She wouldn't. They like to bully. I can't say it. I must get it over. I must get away. She saw herself running, first against the woman beating her with her hands, then past her crying till the need for steady breath stopped her, and she was out of place, out and out on the Fifeshire roads, till she met a man on a horse, who picked her up. She wondered how long she had taken thinking. She opened the textbook.

"It was seven and eight I got wrong."

"I set from six to ten."

"I got six right."

"I returned your work for gross inaccuracy in the eighth example."

The man was with Terry, waiting for her at the classroom door. She shrugged her shoulders.

"Show me what I did wrong, please."

"Terry, that is not the way to speak."

She sighed into herself. The woman looked at her. She was white and she had been red. She showed her exactly what she had done.

"Don't let it happen again. I am sure you could do better work if you liked."

Better. She could do it perfectly or not at all. She withdrew herself. The band began again. *Turn ye to me* it played, and a point was touched to bliss like sexual pleasure in a little star. Never listen to anything but that sound. "May I stay a moment?" she said cunningly. "I should like to go through it again while I remember to understand." The pretty appeal worked. Pleased, she put out her tongue as the mistress went through the door, and sat behind her desk listening.

The tune was new. She waited for the repeats and sucked them in. "Ai, ai," she sighed in exquisite desolation.

She remembered that she was not to be allowed to learn literature any more. There would not be a band every day. Bands were not verses. Her nerves, plucked by the music, resolved into active passion. She was strong and went into agony. She leapt up and ran, down the stairs, into the playground. Scotch mist was brimming the air softly. Balls were clicking through it, all the school was playing. She could not be alone. She did not want the old kind man on the horse.

"*Turn ye to me*, it's called. *Turn ye to me*," she said to the great wall. A bird flew out of it and the haar curled. "*Turn ye to me*," she said evoking the girls of the house and gave a little shriek of pain walking up and down, up and down the cinder track, drenched and wild. The rain increased. There were hooded figures coming up the path. She turned back, the rain driving through her coarse stockings. She ran up to her cubicle. In the old green passage the lights were lit. She was afraid of colds and tore off her stockings and tunic, put on a white frock and her evening shoes.

"Turn to me. Oh, something turn to me. There is nothing. If I am not to learn literature I shall die."

"Die," said the wind rising out of the inaudible sea. In the dormitories the white enamelled walls glittered like ice. The old, green passage had deep windows. She sprang on to a sill and played that she was lying in the arms of the sea.

The tune ebbed in her brain. She noticed that it was not so important now if she did not learn literature. She could teach herself. She could not help learning it. She would certainly learn nothing else. The deprivation was a mask, the house-mistress pushed up to be a pasteboard cow for the enemy that would stalk her all her life. The enemy moved in every person. It was not a person but a reaction in persons from her yet uncrystallized sensibility.

"*Look out, my lovely one.*" A charming young man was speaking to her. Nicer than the old man on the horse.

"*Good luck to you*," he said and vanished. She sighed and came to herself.

"God is a beast. Perhaps He is miserable like me."

She thought that the young man on the screen of her imagination was sad. A girl passed her, a stock-broker's daughter, with leering eyes and a rich frock.

"I suppose you're ashamed to go down."

"No."

"Well, I should have some tea if I was you and get it over."

"Thanks."

That's June. Insult one and pat. I must have something that lasts in this world.

She went downstairs and found that she could not pass the schoolroom door. She remembered scented woods by the sea. The house-mistress called down the bannisters.

"I wonder if you would go over to school and fetch me my purse? I left it on the table in the mistress's room."

Terry heard the drawing-room door shut. As if nothing had happened. It was their bluff to pretend to mind what one did. She went out by the forbidden front door, across the quadrangle, running delicately in her thin shoes. She was going somewhere interesting. In the mistress's room there might be curious things that explained what went on there and the secret ideas that govern the regiment of women. Halfway up the stairs she felt very tired. The place was enormous now it was dark. She had heard of a ghost. She hurried, sighed and cooled her forehead against the door. She knocked. There was no answer. She went in, saw a bead of gas in the dusk, pulled the little chain, saw the purse and looked round. The room was full of shabby papers, but there was a fire and a deep empty chair. She lay down on it. There was nothing interesting. Only a re-statement of some of the poorer girls grown up. The chair only was good, and the fire. She wanted to lie there for the rest of the day, in the heart of the enemies' country, be found lounging in a chair. It was like playing Indians.

She could not move. She must not. She must not rest. She thought of the school getting darker, that would not be filled for an hour.

The men were lighting up the place into a blaze. She did not remember. She lay before the rich fire. She saw the purse on the table, struggled up and fell back. Then she forgot what she was doing.

She saw a young man on the wall. He was Hermes with a child on his arm. She had gone out of life and he was taking notice of her.

She saw that it was a large print of a statue, unwound off a roller, and hung on a wall and she began to remember who Hermes was.

That's a great statue. That's beautiful. I suppose men's bodies are like that.

Oh, the old woman's purse.

She dropped off the wheel of her environment and saw the feelings of the day in a pattern unrelated to the pain of her small pains. They interested her, and there passed into her curiosity, elation, power. She saw the image of Hermes and that it was outside the time in which she was living and the people to whom she was subject, and that through her pleasure in him, she could live in his time and turn round in it and come out again. The old woman wanted her purse.

I shall see things in the world where Hermes is, and when I come out these people will leave me alone.

She chewed on the prospect of alarming the mistresses. She annihilated the years to her maturity and remembered them.

Divine Hermes, don't let me forget you. The old woman wants her purse.

Hermes, Hermes, before I saw you here, you were the boy who came and talked to me this afternoon instead of the old man.

I must take the old woman her purse.

❖ ❖

In the Street

"A *boy's best friend is his mother.* Perhaps he found you one. I am not your son. I have analysed some inversions of passion. What can I do with my passion about you? I am so weak tonight. I think I shall get no further than a rhetorical question about my passion over you. As I leave the Ballet, the rain is filling the Square with gently shaking wires. I can feel the fever coming on, and gnawing me in the back.

"It is up to me to walk a certain distance in the rain till I reach a Tube Station, and stand a certain distance in a smelling golden heat, and leave it, and go out where it may not be raining, into a high black cold. My coat and skirt is very fine, worn and thin. Underneath it is a wool sweater I am very thankful to possess. It is raining, and the rain is freezing. In the Tube the foul heat dries the iced rain.

"I did not have any dinner.

"It all works logically back to you. I have seen the best dancing in the world. I am very ill. When I get home there will be some soup in a saucepan I must heat up. And some milk. And a sweet apple. And someone who will speak sweetly to me: 'Sweetheart, will you sleep up in your room, or down here by the fire?'

"I do not always listen because I am counting out the change in my bag and arranging it, and scolding because the cigarettes have not lasted, and a great piece of bread and butter has been dropped face-downwards on the floor.

"I thought I was there. I haven't moved at all. I am where I was, out-side the theatre. I have got to get there. I have nothing to wrap round my neck. It will harden my throat. Good.

"The street is full of little houses—travelling houses—boxes of light, the great cars throbbing and filling. You have one. You are in it now,

87

asleep because it is night, running down the dark lanes after a gold path.

"I'm going to be ill. I have seen the best dancing. I shall stare at the people coming out and warm myself at their bright dresses till I remember what I have to do.

"God! that lucky brute to be so wrapped in fur. One could swoon away to sleep in those folds and tails. A spatter's caught her stocking. Hooray! I'll brush. There's a woman I used to know. Pray she doesn't see me. I can't be seen like this. I would feel her cloak between my finger and thumb. There they are. The brown fur's stupid. She wouldn't want to know me. I'd *shew*. I believe they're frightened. Click-bang. Gone—Same old address. Dive in headfirst. What legs!

"There's a rich circle of mud in the gutter with a piece of orange peel, a match in it, and what looks like a ten shilling note. Just where the cars stop. I must get it. Either before or after that orange pole of a woman.

"I haven't the nerve. I say it is because of the pain, and the pain may be because of it.

"Oh, God, it's cold. I will go home… And leave that ten shilling note? The mud's moving down. Now. Got it and it's not. If any of the servants has seen and laughs I'll beat his face.

…"We're off home, right, left, left, right, first on the right, and over and over and over and along. Suppose I went on walking, it's easy now I've begun. Spend the sixpence on greasy-sweet chocolate. The twigs would be beating on Primrose Hill, little black tea leaves and crooked pieces of wood and posts and a field with its back up. Round green hills once, like there are in the South. It does comfort me to remember them, and one must be sincere at all costs.

"I've not started, and I don't remember—oh, yes. It's all because of you that I'm out ill in the rain, or I would be laughing at it. You horrible old woman. I get that out of it, the appropriate words for you. I might have called you something else and got it wrong.

"I'm off now. The blazing crowd's gone. I've passed them.

"I should be with you now in bed by a wood-fire, in the soft air. The fever is turning my bones to iced sticks.

"There was a man outside in an eyeglass with a huge ribbon. I knew him when he was poor. As poor as my young husband. And he used to tell me you were nice. But you knew that I could be tormented through him, because he was my young love.

"He left me to bear you alone. He left me to be hated by you. They have all done that.

"The earth nurses us all alike, your opinion and mine for which I dislike myself. There is the endless wrong done to the young by the old. That is the sin against the flesh. Philoctetes' wound.

"I should not see my child again…the blazing crowd's gone. I shall be noticed if I stay longer. There was a man outside, the sort of man who would take care of me. It does not matter. When I am at home I can sit in the dark sometimes with my old friend, and we can tell each other the dreadful things our people did to us.

"You great gilt and pink idol down there in the South, my young marriage was one more raw scrap for you to eat.

"Now this is the way one goes mad. One goes mad. One goes mad. I have got to get home and attend to my life. It is not the time to go mad. I am not, and I won't be. What rubbish. I should not mind at all but that there's some chocolates at home with nuts in them, and if I were mad I should be too mad to eat them, and they crunch up well. I shall never reach the corner of the street,

"I should like to be lying down in candle light, with my baby, with nothing to do, and see you in a bright dress putting flowers beside me.

"That's what you would be doing if I were dead.

"Let us say now that I am dead, and it will be easy for my soul to slip through the street and take itself home. Now I am dead. This is good. I now see everything luminous, and the dimensions no hindrance, without my senses' criteria against me.

"Free at last. Now I am a ghost and dead, I can do what I like. Invisible too in a city of souls. It is over then.

"Now I'm well off, and the walls pass easily. I can pick the ghosts I would meet. Not you. Not you. I choose the imagination I made of him. Not his ghost, but my ghost.

"In the Charing Cross Road we shall meet, a glass ghost, but clear, clear through. Smoke in autumn in the old woods, and a grey plume. That is so. Oh, there you are. We pass sideways together, and in the million-needled branches brush off the raindrops, and in that sea's light clashing, step off into the boat called millions of years.… And you, old woman, the tides of our bay always made you sick.

"Good God, what is it? I'm inside the station, and can't find that money. It was sixpence. There, that's done. Sink down into the yellow heat. We shall shriek as we fly north.

"It is heavy work coming up the left shaft, like being born again.

"I don't remember what I thought down there in the town. I'd better not remember.

"There is the awful air. Now I'm out.

"God, how cold. Not rain but the pure wind. It is the hardest thing of all on my body full of dregs. It must walk the last five minutes with no distraction looking down the wind into the dark.

"Impudent old woman. Here am I, and I drift about in the night saying that an old pink witch is murdering me.

"I am turning you into an *immortal house, imperishable, starlike.* Who said that the old have peace? Not if I can help it."

❖ ❖

The Golden Bough

SHE STOOD BY the door at the party. The man who had brought her did not speak. He left her and crossed the room. She sat down on a plain, small chair. He came back, and sat carefully beside her. It occurred to her he might be drunk. He laid a finger on her wrist. Very unwillingly she attended to him.

Then he said: "It's a poor show. Shall we go?" Then: "What is it like outside?"

It was in London, and late in February. She felt the year-stream winding about the streets. Solid, vibrating, it ebbed at morning, but by three in the afternoon it rose, lapped up the steps of the houses till the rooms brimmed, always moving, moving its huge stream.

The man who had brought her was like a dipper filled at midnight with that black water. The room she looked into was under the sea. The people were not fish.

He had only said: *"What is it like outside?"*

She had come to London to join this life from a coast-town where there was a pier sticking out into the sea. A wounded officer had told her about the life in studios, and at the end of his conversation she had taken the paste combs out of her hair, and prepared a new attack upon the world.

The bubble of her fancies lolled out of her brain. Now the man beside her had suggested that she should see what he saw. She seized and popped him inside her bubble, a neat black mannikin, and looked out into the room.

In the centre was a girl like a rag doll who was called Lois. She gathered up her lovers like an innocent mother who has born devils and not sons. Anne had talked to the man about herself.

The man who had brought her had told her about the loss of his virginity, as though it had not been his, and something that had happened to him in the war, and then something neurotic. The pits of Lois' eyes were dark. Anne sat against the wall, a fair, gilt idol, conscious that it has not yet been worshipped and blackened, and smeared with scent and blood.

Lois was passed from hand to hand, bounced and sprawled, till a young man came and moved her away to dance. She was between his arms, a barrel of bright silk on sturdy legs—Anne saw his spine draw up, and his shoulders pass sideways with the least spring. His chin was up over Lois' head, his feet were together, he moved in a small pattern in which all variety was included. Lois followed him, and slowly abandoned herself, her legs flying, her face on his breast.

She was not asked to dance.

His hair was laid over his skull like a black wing.

Outside the brown night was waiting. It would receive her later, exhausted with envy and desire.

Her bubble contracted round her peering skull. She drew back into the wall, and pulled a slow face.

There was the man who had brought her. When the music began again, she forced him to dance. He was so drunk that he fell down immediately, and lay looking up. Two of his friends dragged him into another room. A dull, ugly boy came and sat beside her. She talked to him occasionally. An hour passed. A very young girl fetched him.

The man who was giving the party began to turn out the lights. One was left, closed up in a blue cap. The semi-mystery made it easier and duller.

A knot of men pulled Lois about. One of them burned her arm with the stump of a cigarette. "It won't do," said the man who was giving the party, and pushed him away.

Anne rubbed her back against the wall, a nerve thrilling. She noticed later that she did not understand what it was all about. Yet she remembered with contempt the past simplicity of the pier, and the cinema, and the wounded young men migrating with their secrets.

Later she got up, and went to look for the man who had brought her. He was on his host's bed among the overcoats, arguing about the nature of reality,

"There is," he said, "absolute beauty and absolute truth, which man, by reason of certain elements in his nature, is conscious of, and separate from. Both these equals are equal. So that he can live neither with, or without, absolute beauty and absolute truth."

"I have never heard of that sort of truth and beauty. Some little thing goes wrong, and you forget about it, and years after you can't face a crowd, or go into an empty room."

"And that is because you wanted your grandmother for wife."

"What is there in this that accounts for the disproportionate nature of one's pain?"

The room was nearly dark. The unshaded mantle had been broken by a passing head. Its thread tried to whiten in the whistling flame. A man got up off the floor, and sat on the bed, and turned out one of his pockets counting:

"I'll tell you a thing. One does not see half of what is happening round one. There's a trick, though, by which you can. Bang a door at midnight, You'll hear the noise break up the quiet and let something through. Pull up the bathroom plug at the same hour. Go through quick into a dark room to the window. You'll see skeleton birds crossing the white sky."

"That's funnier than absolute."

"Not more interesting than physics."

"Their observation leads you to conclude that anything may mean anything."

That was the man who had brought her. They had thrown their overcoats on him, and he spoke over a wall. Over him the gas whistled, and lit the deadly staring face. The young man she had seen dancing had come in and began to lift the coats off him as he looked for his own.

"It's a bloody world. Let's be rude to it."

She moved out a little on the floor, and he trod on her hand. She hid it in her dress and looked up at him. He did not see her, but Steevens sat up and asked her if she wanted to go home. They went out together.

"Have you enjoyed yourself?"

"I can't say that I have."

"Why not?"

"You are all such dreadful people."

"Why?"

"You drink and you pretend you are in love with those girls, and you believe in ghosts."

"You are not used to the idea of people moving about and watching themselves try new combinations."

"What is it all about?"

"I knew you would ask that. I rather agree that it's a question. As a matter of fact, I think it has got to a time when a little death would do our set good. No, I don't mean another war, rather a ceremonial blood-letting. A ritual death. Not another suicide. Besides, an old order's changing, we must inaugurate. I haven't got my eye on a victim yet.... What are you interrupting for? You can stand sexual talk, why not this?"

"How do you know I like it?"

He grinned. "You little seaside hack. If you want to learn the catchwords, you'd better talk to me."

She trotted along sullen beside him.

.   .   .   .   .

She went to Lois' flat and watched her. Lois sat on the floor and cleaned a pair of grey shoes. Their surface brushed pale and dark like the light on fields. She powdered, rubbed and blew.

"Whose are they?"

"Leo's, the boy I dance with."

"I saw him at the party."

"We were blind and they burnt my arm. They're a thick lot, but he's all right."

Lois sat back on her heels, a shoe in each hand. She clapped them and dropped them.

"Some girl has got to darn his socks. He won't be dressed when he comes in because he's resting his good clothes. I collect the pawn tickets." She took two pounds out of her stocking. "Nobody knows you have it there. Would you mind popping round the corner and getting these out?"

"Certainly."

He was drinking his tea in a girl's dressing gown and a pair of cotton pants.

She looked curiously into the milky, hollow chest.

"You are a friend of Steevens', aren't you?"

"Steevens? Oh, yes. We were in the same asylum. Our families put us in. We got ourselves out."

"It was the war, I suppose?"

"Not at all. That was the excuse."

"How did you get out?"

"Our mothers came to visit us, and when they'd seen them they took our word for it we were sane. It takes ten mad boys to make one old mother."

"Are you all right now?"

"No."

"Surely Steevens is all right—"

"That's where he gets you. Once a month we go on a blind together, and at the end of it we write a letter to God. Shut up, Lois."

"—Once you start, you don't sleep at night."

"I do with you, when it's a waste of time. But don't let Steevens take you in. He has an idea and he makes faces at it, and when you see his faces, you'll be surprised. We practise them together. Do you dance?"

"Of course."

"That's something like real life. You'd tell me to read a Russian novel, but I know what I like."

"I think everyone should read them because they're psychologically absolutely real."

"You haven't seen our letter to God. That's the stuff."

"You believe in God then?"

"God. I'd spit in His face. Do you?"

"I think he's the enlarged idea one had of one's father and mother."

"What, those people! Lois, come here, Lois. It isn't fair. She's laying a trap for me. She's doing it on purpose. She says they're doing it all over again. I really should be mad if I thought that."

"She's only being clever."

They drew away from Anne.

Steevens' advice had been very dull, and very difficult and it did not work. But she was afraid of him. At his orders she martyred herself.

"I'm sure I didn't mean to say anything against your religion."

"There, Leo, and you mustn't be rude."

"There I was ragging. Let's dance. No, my weakness is for owls, and they're impotent."

They danced. She minded her steps til she forgot, and stared up in his face, and he stared over her head.

She went back to Steevens, who said :

"I am sorry I behaved so badly that night. I should not have got drunk and left you alone. How did you get along—?"

"Perfectly. Who is the boy who can dance, Lois' friend?"

"Leo Pollard."

"Has he been mad?"

"That's what he says about himself."

"Were you in hospital together?"

"I was never really there."

"What sort of a person is he?"

"Charming, in spite of his little artistic stunts."

"I heard you talking about beauty the other night, but perhaps you don't remember."

"I have no objection to a universal arch. Boys like Leo are a decoration, a jewel, a cap-feather. One retrims you know. Life's always preening herself up with one of them."

"What is Lois?"

"The sound shoes that will see more than one of us to our journey's end." He turned her wrist between his fingers and thumb. "It is amusing to see how you get it all off by heart. Now look."

She was squatting in a mist where there were stones and white grass. It was unvaried and colourless, without the sound of water running, or settling, or wind. There were stones. She passed into a large dusty room.

He had only pinched her wrist and told her that she was inexperienced, while her experience had not been of his kind, but that suited to a lady-animal and no more.

She remembered his face under the whistling gas. He dropped her wrist. She looked round his dark, red room.

She went constantly to Lois' flat. Leo showed her his seven cigarette holders, in seven colours, for each day of the week. He also taught her to dance. Alternately she saw Steevens, and endured him for practise in what she must do in the world.

In May, Lois took her out into the country with Leo, because it was good for him to be in the air.

One day they came to a wood. Outside it there was a tree. They hurried to it through the sun. A grass road ran through the wood up to a hill with a bare cap. A red animal ran along the branch. They told Lois its name, and she did not listen. They lay down in the wood.

"Why do they paint aspidistras in a window-frame instead of a bacchante running from the hounds of spring?"

"People say the bacchante does not represent pure form."

Then Leo read them his poems, and when he had done he said:

"I shall write next a hymn on Anne's virginity. I don't doubt it's only mental, but it's good enough."

She did not hear. She had selected that he liked bacchantes, and that was plain sailing, the old formula in the new world.

She saw that they were neither in London, nor on any esplanade and that this was something like something real at last. Up or down her hair did not matter. It would take itself up and down in its time. Something like bark peeled off her, she felt herself white and cool like a peeled stick. She did not remember to remember anything. She forgot. Then a thin wire of active hate passed from her to the boy. He would have to admire her, who had so loved dark, tender girls. It was pleasant. She could now do what she liked, it did not matter. There was something exactly right for her to do. It was coming.

Lois went away to gather sticks for the fire. Anne looked at the tree.

"Lift me up on your shoulders, Leo, and I'll climb it." He lifted her up. She wound her skirts tight round her knees, and mounted one after another the huge arms. She dropped a leaf into his hair. He looked up and away, and began to throw sticks at his dog. The leaves filled in their net. She was shut up in a tree. There was a green room with holes in the floor, and a brilliance over her head. She rested a moment. A breeze, stopped in the breathless wood, broke through. The light filled the upper rooms. She went up them, and stepped out on to the tree-top. Above the forest the hill came over to the tree. She leaned back on the main shaft and opened her arms along two boughs, and began to sing in German, which she knew he did not understand. Presently he came out and glanced up. She hurried down hand over hand.

There was an empty six feet between the lowest branch and the ground. He came over, and she slid through his arms, and tore away.

"Come on. Let's run a race."

They ran again and again. He left her to match himself with his dog. She was under the tree watching him. Out in the ride, he fell and cried out. She ran to him, and from another part of the wood came Lois like a settling partridge. They turned him over, and blood was on his bare chest. A fly hurried up.

"It's his lungs," said Lois. "Oh, quick. There's a village over the hill." Anne went away. At the top of the ride she saw Lois crouching, with Leo laid across her knees.

⋅ ⋅ ⋅ ⋅ ⋅

"What did you do?"

"I wired to his people."

"Where was he then?"

"At Lois' flat. He could not stay there."

"Why not?"

"It was not suitable."

"There was Lois."

"They sent a car and took him away. Also Lois has no money, and he needs everything."

"He needs nothing.… He might have been left with the girl he liked.…

"There, be quiet. What were you doing when it happened?"

"Running races."

"And you forced him on and on till his lung burst. Active little animal, aren't you? It's funny you should have done it, you little green thing."

She suffered. She looked down with empty lungs, while an enormous pain like a steel bubble rose and burst in her throat. A stretch of vacant time went on after the bubble had broken, and she looked surprised at the unfamiliar torture.

"It was in a wood. Green to green. You were in a wood. They've taken him to another."

"Who? Where?"

"His people. Don't you know where he is now? Down where his people live, a hundred miles from here. There is a house set low in wet grasses like a slug. The river sweeps past it and the trees advance on it. Blue troops of trees with great rides cut out of them. If you follow one out and up, you will see the house in an eddy of fog. It moves because the river runs so fast, and the grasses dip and the snails are in squadrons, and in winter the wind squalls in from the woods, and sinks and breathes out there.

"The stinking, wet hole! There's a plaster nymph on the lawn that sprouts ferns, a green fringe waving all the way down her back-bone. The place where pure bone turns into bright smelling leaves."

"It is a good thing," said Anne, "he is so young, and a very unconscious person."

"You're probably right. Only I've seen a dying baby and it looked wise. Even the flowers are sallow there. We'll order him red roses, bloody warriors."

"That's a wall-flower," she whispered.

"Have it your own way. I believe you've had everything your own way. I didn't mean to train you for that, you rotten little death-priestess.... Since you are a priestess, you damned well behave like one. You come back here and tell me when he's dead."

❖   ❖   ❖   ❖   ❖

Lois was reading.

> *My little cherie, They've given me a fortnight to shuffle off in. The holders are for you to keep, and my kit for you to make what you can on. By the way, see Steevens has all the ties. He goes hopelessly wrong on ties. Dud cheques send on here—after I'm dead. In change for the ties, Steevens will get my poems printed. I've written a hymn on Anne's virginity.*
>
> *This is a horror; the feel of the wall here makes your nails throb, not really hard or nice and bristly and like your racoon muff. When I was in Canada. They've put me in the drawing-room—all the time I dance in and out and round about the fancy tables.*
>
> *See Anne sees that hymn.*
>
> *But it's all right. I'm well away now. I must tell you something. I've had an idea about God that settles it. God's always young and funny—He always has to be killed. He doesn't want anyone to believe in Him, and they hang Him up for us to have a look at death. The pretty girls cry. Lois, don't you see? This is a real idea at last. God's a young nut, and one of us, and He's killed all over again. There was Adonis.*
>
> *Oh, smile at me like that. I see the treasure that has given me eyes. Lois, you are one of the pretty girls. When it's over, get blind at parties, and sing that hymn I wrote about Anne. When we're two stars together, I suppose she'll be one, too. We'll bump into her.*

She was out that night crying:
"Stand me another drink, and I'll sing. Stand me a drink."

❖   ❖   ❖   ❖   ❖

Steevens got up and tied the sash of his dressing gown, and staggered to the door. Anne came in.

"You show up like a blue light on a red stage." He lay down again and she sat beside him.

"Do you lie here like this always with the curtains drawn?"

"And think of *fire and sleet and candlelight*? Now Leo's dead, yes."

"But it's midsummer—"

"It won't be forever. Then I shall get up. I shall be all right once this terrible sun is over. What have you been doing?"

She looked up at him like a dog.

"I've been writing a play about Leo, you said something ought to be done."

"Tell me what it is about."

"Of course it is made up. Marcus Adair, a young man about town, has lived previous to the war with a beautiful girl divorcée. When he comes back from the war his nerves are shattered. He becomes engaged to a middle-class girl, which angers his aristocratic relatives.

"Finally, on a visit to them, they induce him to neglect her for the daughter of a neighbouring squire, and she breaks it off. He returns to London, and by his dissipated life estranges himself from them completely. His fiancée meets him there in company with the divorcée. They return to the divorcée's flat, and after a long conversation with the beautiful woman about her past, the girl learns that her own outlook on life has been too narrow. Later they visit Marcus in his rooms, where he asks them both to forgive him, and shoots himself.

"Phyllis—that's the girl—induces the divorcée to return to her husband. In time Marcus' family are won over by her goodness, and together, in the old village church, they unveil a tablet to his memory."

"Well?"

"And I've sold it to a film-company!"

"What? Sold it? Is it going to be produced?"

"Yes. They've paid me."

"Thirty pieces of silver, I hope. Good for you, Anne. That's the stuff of immortality to give us. Or are you sharper than we think? Did you do it for revenge? But I think you're proud of it. Tell me."

"Steevens—you must know. I can tell you now. I was in love with Leo. I had to write about him. I couldn't bear it till I had."

He changed sides. She looked down at his back. The dark dressing gown mixed with the red sofa.

Two rings of white bones were on his ankles, and there was another round his neck. The heavy shoulders heaved up and did not sink.

"You little idiot. Green I called you. Filthy aniline dye."

She felt she was being stoned, and began to cry. She was physically afraid.

"Go away and don't come again."

When she got to the door she thought of something she could not remember and made another face. When she was gone, he began to cry.

"It's not for myself, it's for you, Leo, all the epiphany you've got for the fine clothes, and the fine movements, and the sensual elegance, and the silly imagination, and the pain."

❖ ❖

In the South

IF YOU WILL walk up. I've told the car to meet us at the top."
"I'll come, *My one and only dear*
And walk about with you anywhere."
The wind shivered her silk dress and her hoarse, small voice shivered into the song and, as she took his arm and trembling pressed his elbow against her side, she felt his bone was her bone, a piece of herself going about, to return and tell her what it had done, that, when he came to find her, he was stone returning to its rock, wood to its tree, water to its source in a place of stones and small trees. The country they were in, their own country, was made of turf hills, patched with small trees and stones and hammered by the sea.

Their bright clothes came up beautifully out of the grass together, their active feet sprang, their sticks struck and sprung. The wood they called the Sacred Wood tossed in its sorrow, not theirs. They were lords of the land, brother and sister and sister's lover who grudged them nothing and they were going to the tops of the green hills and over and down. At the end they would dine at an inn and part, but never again for long.

They opened a gate that led into a flock of brown cows. The fear of cows could be indulged in like *the blemish in the joint of a well-shaped body*, because she was with those who would never let her be hurt. A naked sun went over, a fair sea was behind them, the hill road mounted easily, a long flight up to the east, away from the sun.

She strained ahead between them and they told her stories of cows. Her lover's were real Argentine cows who charge men, making a circle round them and walk in and in.

"God help you if you're on foot. You have to go down on your knees and bark like a dog. Then they think you are a dog and respect you."

Her brother's were toy English cows, that sharpen their teeth on their sides and stare from the make-believe world that was the property of the two who had grow together, and a game that was their creation and an expression of their love. At the top of the down, where only the sheep go, there was grey, savage grass and furze bushes the wind had moulded into balls. They could see a long way, over a great part of their world and every kind of living beauty. They praised and adored it, their backs turned on the way they were going, so that their faces should be towards the sun. Inwardly they thanked him for taking care of the land, for making it grow, for adorning it and displaying it. They praised it for him to hear, till the lover, who came from the north, found a mushroom and they found more and sat them, stalks up, on a loose stone wall to find when they came back.

At a gap in the down a car was waiting. They put her in between them. The wind of their gathering pace moulded her thin dress to her shape, the ribbons of her hat tore out. She leaned forward, linked in their arms. They could see she was a woman and their love. They flew down the white road.

Half-way down the boy said : "Stop her here—you two go round. I'll walk through the wood you say is haunted and you can pick me up on the other side. I don't suppose I shall get anything," in a solemn voice, his camera unslung to photograph the ghost.

"If he's so earnest, he'll scare it," she said as the car crept round.

"God help the ghost you babies catch."

She lay back, in her peace, watching a man drive a tiny donkey round a field.

The boy came out of the wood. "I saw nothing," he said, with a slight air of offence.

She apologised for the shy ghost.

As the car started, the boy let out a deliberate note like a bird call and after a few bars gathered them with him in a song of the day, full of quick effects and comic rhymes. She saw the skin pull under the driver's ears and knew that he was laughing. The hedges tore past. The sweet wind bowed a field of wheat, whose heads rose as they rushed by. Sweet air and a sweet tune. They gathered up the chorus and poured it out again. It had the crunched pleasure of the last sweet in the box. They would never sing it again perhaps. It had the transience of a sweet. But they would always sing. They were not musicians, they would sing transient songs and repeat very classic poetry and talk baldly or else a rather elegant slang. Anyhow, today there would be nothing but triumph on triumph of recognition. The lover did not mind. They were his children. The car went painfully up the hill. They got out into the square that fell down the hillside.

"Do you want to come into the castle with us?"

"Well," he said, "I don't know. It looks like a climb, while the man in the bar knows how to mix cocktails. I think I will have a drink before dinner, if you don't mind. In fact, I'll wait for you and if you don't come back and I'm hungry, I'll eat and tell them to keep something for you. Will cold chicken do?"

"Do just what you like, my dear."

The brother and sister shot away over the square to the stone cross, an invisible transit on their way to a place where they could be together and alone.

"First of all, come into a field and I'll take your photograph."

They turned into a walled track between two cottages, between flowers rising over the tops of old walls. In the blowing field he posed her, under an apple-tree, under an oak, on a bank, in a ditch. The camera clicked, her light clothes streamed. He took her out of the field. There was a moment's hesitation.

Both looked at the small, steep hill and its ruin that was the hub of all the long hills and shallow valleys, out of which they had come, from high valleys, empty and powdered with flint, and from low, where a brook crawled, where everywhere, as the wind fell, the sea could be heard knocking.

"We might go up," he said.

"It's years since we've been and the excursion is coming down."

"It takes more than people to put this place off its stroke. Do you know, it frightens me? It has been here so long watching us come and go."

"Think of it the other way: that it only exists because we are here to look at it, and because we love it. Let us go up."

They went back through the warm stone houses that breathed quiet, where they were known and recognised, where food was waiting for them and courtesy, where they were lords. The sun dropped, streaming its light.

They walked up the turf to the towers and the castle walls. To the east, from the grass hills, there was the purple land, flat and sea-laced and not crossed like the green hills. There they did not often go and were easily lost. They were not invited and did not sing.

A purple cloud came out of the far woods and mounted over the land.

"Look at that," said he.

She thought how it would pass over to the sun behind them and put on a gold mantling, and that, when a dark coloured cloud and the sun go down together, there is a noise like a deep voice, or a bell. She thought:

"Love will reduce all things to the condition of music, but now I have observed the tunes, I must forget them. I have a living brother to enjoy, the motif of the world, not its accompaniment. They are no more than our décor.

"Have you ever seen any country you like as well as this? In Spain, I mean, or in Scotland?"

"No, but it's old, sister, so old. Sometimes it makes me afraid. Not when I'm with you, but in winter when the wind screams, and when the wind falls the owls hoot and the bats squeak and I have to say *owls are impotent, bats are bastards* before I can get up out of my chair."

"After all, where you live isn't here, it can only see here."

They sat down on a fallen stone under a wall where a courtyard had been. Two heavy youths were scrambing up and down in trousers and braces, squalling at each other. They were pleased that they recognised without philanthropy, or commiseration their contrasted pride and grace. They were back in their own country. *One that composed their beauties* and knew its own and took them back.

They settled themselves. She took a deep breath. There was something to say that would be difficult, but which must be said because there had been a hole in the temporal foundations of their life.

"Do you know, cher ami, that I think it is time that the family habit of quarrels should stop. Look at us. Why should we bang cursing out of each other's doors? And when has there been a time when we have not? Quarrels about aunts, about politics, about nothing, about cash—"

"About sisters, about brothers." He took her hand. "I agree, I agree. It comes to this. There is only you and me left. We're the last that's left of our rows and lovers. The saga ends with you and me. We're the last word of the genius of our race. They will die, and there will still be you and me—

"I don't know about myself. I'm not yet sure of myself, but I am of you. You have got yourself out of yourself. I shall do that. If I can't, I shan't play. But I've a shot to make, too."

"I knew that. I'm waiting for your shot."

"We shall never be separated again."

"We shall never be separated again. We've made peace between each other. After first loving and then misunderstanding we've made peace."

"We have made peace."

"Because we have made peace, brother, here I end my hate of them all. I stop in myself every impulse of malice, indignation, despair. I don't do it strenuously, but it is done. Help me to make my peace."

"I will. Sooner or later it will happen. By the way, I don't see what's to be done with Aunt Vera and Uncle Claude. They've gone too far."

She considered, "No, I can't. Let's forget them. It's about all we can do."

"But you and I will have pleasure in each other for ever and ever."

He put his arm round her and began to kiss her. It was cold in the shadow of the wall. Her skin was cold where she had sweated. The grass was darkening and iced to touch. The ruined tower was very tall. The boys had gone away.

She was trembling now she had said it, that because of him she could put love above pride.

It was almost night. All the warm day had gone into the orange tip of his cigarette. It was simple. The cold, powerful night had come. Warmth had gone into a little coal three inches away from his hand. They carried it, if the world didn't.

He struck a match. They rubbed cheeks in the flame. There were two coals now.

"We shall never get across each other again," he said. "You've got nothing on. Come down the hill, or the food will all be gone and the drink will all be gone, and Aubrey and my train, and we'll never face the cows and have to spend the night on the cold hillside."

❖ ❖

Madonna of the Magnificat

IN THE THIRTEENTH year of her virginity Mary, the daughter of Anne, sat in the dark storehouse, listening to feet running in the alley, flicking her tongue in and out. The dark was cool and smelt of grain. She sat on a sealed oil-jar, cooling her soles on its side. A handful of rotten dates shot in through the window slit. Then a dead puppy. She sat still, with shut hands. Then nothing happened in the gold-patched dark. "Pig," she whispered, rocking, her tongue stuck out. Later an arm passed a bunch of red lilies through the slit. She looked at them for a time, then snatched them and tried to look out of the windows without being seen. When that was over, she heard a small shout: "Hail, Mary," and turned and saw an angel that was like her idea of an angel.

Angels are usually homosexual figures, more or less draped and winged. That will do. She remembered that she had never considered the evidence of her being, or of her not being, a descendant of David, and with another part of her mind she was listening until she said without reflection: "Am I to have a husband so soon?" And then: "Need I marry Joseph?"

Meanwhile the angel took a lily from his bunch, turned it white, replaced it and vanished. She stood for a few moments glancing round the shot gloom, not reassured. She ran into a corner. The lily was visible in the dark. She tightened her little skirt round her knees.

In the next room was her mother, who was told everything, from whom nothing was to be expected, who by tradition had something to give. She was preparing something:

"This from you, Miss, who were too impudent to believe your cousin Elizabeth?" But her eyes were going up and down the delicate angular girl, lifting her gown of dust-coloured cotton, till Mary turned with a small smile and shrug, looked into her lily and out again and noticed that her mother was growing old.

"What's wrong with the lily? I saw white lilies before you were born. Shew it me in the dark?…"

Her mother dragged her out again:

"My girl, tell me about this."

"The angel said I was to become the mother of God now…"

The pattern changed. She heard her mother hurrying out, gone to tell Joseph her fiancé, her cousin Elizabeth, and the others Nehemiah, Hezekiah, Jeremiah, Ezekiel, Nathaniel, Peter-Paul, Uncle Simon-bar-Jonah and Saul. They would be turning round and setting off, exchanging texts. She hugged her lily in fear of the old men, and flung it into a corner and laughed at the old men.

It stood propped in a corner, unbroken, burning, illuminating nothing but itself.

She squeezed out of the window. The "lion coloured" hills were driven through by a road. Her people used the paths, and the Romans the road. She lay among the olives till it was evening.

They had lit the festival lamps, and were sitting around, close together, Uncle Simon-bar-Jonah with the lily, on a mat. She stepped up behind her mother. Her betrothed squatted, sallow, silent. She made him once a beard and hair of curled cedar-shavings. He smelt sweet.

"Let her tell her story."

"There was an angel."

"What was he like?"

"Bright and very tall."

"Had he a beard?"

"He was like—he was young—"

"A female demon, I don't doubt. The angels of the Lord are male."

"His face was hairless, not like you. I know no other man."

"He spake unto you the tidings that you were to bear the redemption of Israel. What answer did you make, daughter of David's house?"

"It's my opinion, Nat, and I'll stick to it as long as I live, that it's not certain what she is. Enquiries don't always follow one's fancy—"

"We had better hear what was said."

"Come along, girl."

"It is my angel, and my lily—"

"They are our evidence."

"Not unless I tell you. You'll know in time, anyhow."

"There is no reason to suppose that the Messiah at birth will be anything but a plain child, such as any man might get with you."

"Abnormally plain," squeaked little Nehemiah, "visage more marred than any man's."

Joseph spoke—"Fathers, I am betrothed to this girl. Personally, I should prefer the Messiah to have a father."

"I have not gathered who is to be its father."

Mary said: "The angel said I need not marry you."

"You know what has happened to Elizabeth," said the Levite. "It makes one not know what to believe."

Mary said: "He had wings," and watched Joseph while they rent the crumb of information.

"In the days of the captivity of Israel—from which forever the Messiah is to deliver us—the heathen had for image an eagle-headed demon, doubtless capable of procreation."

Said Joseph: "The cherubim on the Lord's ark will give us an idea of what Nathaniel means. O, these birds!"

Mary giggled. He was just tolerably mean and amusing, and he did not like her people.

"It's all right, Joseph. Look at the lily."

"How am I to know?"

"The Lord of old spoke plainly by the mouth of His servants the prophets."

"Not plainly," said Joseph. "God is subtle."

He led Mary into a corner and thrust her back into it, speaking very close, his small hard body against hers.

"Little girl, I do not mind. We will call it by a right name and be married at once."

"Then I need do no more work."

"Then the child, whose ever it is, will not be strong."

"How do you know I want to have it?"

Anne shrieked: "Nothing has gone right in this house since Zacchariah had his tipsy dream and the old woman got dropsy."

Mary said: "I'm not old. I've not had dropsy. I've had an angel."

"Angels are incapable of procreation."

Joseph made a face.

"Joseph, why do you still want to marry me?"

"I don't know. It would be better than this noise. These old men don't smell nice."

"Is it because you love me?"

"Yes, perhaps. I don't know—I prefer not to wrangle."

"Joseph, it is all true."

"Quite so."

"Oh, why did it ever happen?"

"Peace, sirs. I am willing to marry her, and let her tale pass and then confirm it."

The air rushed out of seven old lungs.

"Then, son, it is your affair."

The lily fell into dust.

"A question for you, fathers—supposing the lily miraculous, does its change constitute another miracle, and what miraculous element is there in its dust? On this question hangs that of the homogeneity of divine substance. Again—it would be suitable for the mother of Israel's king to make a thanksgiving. I leave it to Nathaniel to prepare. I will teach it her myself. Mary, go into the storeroom and sleep."

He left the house. The dark road was full of lights. His people were about and soldiers. He passed in and out in his clay-coloured gown. His light, cleft beard stuck out. He plaited in his intelligence with his desires. True or untrue the story might be good as true, and so serviceable. To him the divine was an ambiguous element, appearing in life, and occasionally plastic to man. There were two kinds of men necessary, or a man and some men. A man to conceive, and men to execute and adopt in the great *ludus sacer* which is the whole of man's activity, a sport of lions, only subsequently rationalised, whose rule is that every man must win, and every man but one be annihilated.

He tested his positions, while his sensuality grumbled, waiting its turn.

He did not like the moon. He could not follow the stars. In his workshop he lay down and poured the cedar curls on his head and did not reconstruct a glory for Israel, but a future in which God seemed to have let them down again under an ornate construction that resembled the Roman architecture he had observed.

.   .   .   .   .

The next day she cleaned the house. Cleanness attracts light, breaks up a room into point and shine and glitter. Water loosed the colour in the tiles, the mud brushed into dun bubbles, and left moist stone for the sun to suck and polish. At the well the water split and broke like loose glass.

A quick day ran through into night, when the other side of being breathes and wakes. In the morning she had not known how to evade her mother. At night she walked out.

. . . . .

The boy who had thrown the puppy and the date stones and offered the lilies ran after her upon the hillocks.

They argued:

"You can't have the Messiah, you've been about with me."

"They don't suppose you're a man."

"They're marrying you off to Joseph because they do."

"But I saw an angel."

"I guess what it was you saw."

Anyhow, there is going to be a Messiah."

"*I don't believe in the Messiah.*"

"What is going to happen if there isn't going to be a Messiah?"

"There's a man over there who knows everything. They're Romans. They've been after robbers in the hills. They camp down here at night. I am going to Alexandria where there are lots of them. They're soldiers. The officer is called Panthera. You can come, too."

She followed him.

. . . . .

"Brought your sister?"

"No. She's the one I told you about."

"From the family that does miracles?" He cut on his tablets by a clean fire, the brush of his helmet curled beside him.

"She saw one of the angels, and now she says she is going to have the Messiah, and Joseph's marrying her—"

"Shut up. I'll ask her to tell me."

There were the squares of his armour, his small chin, his nut-shaped nails that were like his teeth. She edged in.

"Do you think it happened to me?"

"If you saw an angel, you saw one. Think carefully if you did. And if you did not see an angel, but something else, think what you saw. And if you decide that you saw nothing, think why you thought that you saw anything. There—try that."

"There is another kind of seeing."

"There is not."

"Yes, I saw it."

"You mean you wanted it and thought about your want till you saw?"

"I did not want. I did not think."

"I can believe that, little beauty. Well, what was the angel like?"

"He shone."

"Are your people pleased? Oh, the boy said they're marrying you. Do they want the Romans to go? You don't know about that? Run off, boy, and talk to Psellus. He's been to Alexandria. Were you brought up to expect this?" There, I am schoolmastering again, he thought, and said:

"Let's sit over the fire."

She sat down on a stone, straight up, the night passing behind her head. By the centurion's hard fire there was another arrangement of life, like a bass scale played firmly. A long time ago she had seen brightness in a dark room.

She sat slackly.

"Well, little lady?"—is she really a virgin?—"Have you heard of Rome?"

"Yes!"

"It was founded by the son of a mother like you."

"What happened to her?"

"She was numbered among the immortals. A she-wolf looked after her baby. There were two of them. One killed the other, and founded the city."

"What are the immortals?"

"The Gods who are supposed to look after us. Like the one you have at Jerusalem. Dionysos-of-the-vine."

"We have only one God."

"So I have heard. Anyhow, Rhea Silvia became a goddess. Would you like that?"

"No."

"What would you like?"

She thought. The interesting tranquility in whose circle she sat. Not to marry Joseph. Things to wear and eat. She said:

"Not to go home. Not to go back."

"No one goes back."

"Then I shall be the mother of God."

"What do you think of what I have told you, that every country has its heroes, and most heroes have had for a mother a girl like yourself?"

"What happened to them?"

"Some die: some are married to kings: some join the stars."

"Is God ever good to them?"

"Well, I don't know quite what you expect of God. They had what God gives when he comes personally. Good reveries they must have had.... God is like undiluted wine. We'll have a cup, but not like that."—Jove, she's a pretty girl.—"Of one of them, it was said: *and she bore a blameless child.* Do you know what a man is? Was it a bird? You'll sit on my knee and I'll tell you the story of stories, of Leda who bore two men, saviours of men, and two women who were their enemies, who was married to a swan."

He rocked her but she stared. On a great breath she sailed out on his knee, her sight on the blue hangings above the world. The pool of hot wood rose with them and the next seat was the moon.

"Have I made you familiar with these ladies?"

"Yes."

She began to cry to herself, slid off his knees and squatted by the fire.

"I forgot. This was all for my satisfaction, not yours. But tell me, after all this, do you insist that you saw anything at all?"

"Yes." She plaited her hair.

"Don't you know that the thing which cannot be said is the thing that is not true?"

"No."

"So you'll take your chance with God and man?"

"How do you know I want to have it?"

"How would you like me for its father?"

"Not now."

She became the peasant girl running home to a community of theological peasants. She had come to the point of her cycle when their nature was expressed in hers, and she was ashamed to be where she was. She saw the map of her cycle, the blind round of nature and emotion, fear, a little blessedness, ennui and shame.

"Tell me what will happen to me."

"I think anything may happen, and I don't suppose your people are up to good." He thought: She would have her God in peace, or else no God. That is exactly what will not happen. Life is not like that. There never will be a clear run. If something remarkable gets born, it will be more and less than a man. The fire wants making up. And when she is old she will be lucky if she can look back and notice a coherency. She won't want to. It will either have happened or not. Or another set of events will be insisting. She is ready to run away.

He looked round for wood. The moon had set. That ended it. She hung on quiet, holding herself. He made a sign for wood. And to herself she said: "*Let it go, my beauty, let it go.*" A new word. A blessing. She saw only the grey tent and its gilt bird. Not even that. She got up.

"Nico!"

"We march at dawn," said Panthera.

"I have to take her back," said Nico. "I don't want to. I want to come to Alexandria with you."

"You can't do both."

He scowled at her. "Come along."

"Cheer up, little lady, You'll be the mother of a hero."

They went away.

. . . . .

"They would never have taken me to Alexandria."

"Panthera would have."

"It is your fault."

"It's not. Cowardly. No, no, no—you can go when you're older."

The sky, emptied of the moon, had the night to itself. It covered them, a witch's mantle, untender, observant.

"It's lucky Joseph will have you."

"His luck you mean."

"No, yours. I wouldn't. If it is the Messiah, no one will know till it's grown up. You don't suppose there will be any more angels?"

"Why not? Yes. I do."

"Bet you there won't be."

"Why won't you let me have anything?"

"You spoilt my chance of going to Alexandria."

"You were afraid to go."

"I shall say how you got your baby, I shall say it's the soldiers. I shall say it's Captain Panthera. They'll believe that."

It seemed that there was no more room in space for her to occupy. Every inch, a spear-point turned. She sighed, the malice gone out of her, the baby pride, the amusement, valour, grace.

"They mustn't say that. He must have his chance."

"You sing all the way back, then, while I'm pinching your arm. It'll get you into practise to sing old Nathaniel's song."

"If I do, you will not keep your promise."

"God isn't the only person who can keep a promise."

"Then you believe in my angel?"

"You might do it, if those old brutes don't spoil it. But I don't let you off, either. You sing, or I tell."

She drew two heavy sobs and, as his finger and thumb tightened, stared with running cheeks and cried: "*I will think upon Rahab and Babylon, Tyre and the Morians also, lo, there was he born. The Lord shall rehearse it when he writeth up the peoples that he was born there. The singers also and the trumpeters shall he rehearse....*"

His hand went on pinching. The sky went on watching. The centurian's fire had gone out and the moon. Near home he stopped pinching and sang after her. "*All my fresh springs are in thee.*"

.   .   .   .   .

He led her in, his finger on his lips.

"She went out among the olives to pray. I watched over her and have brought her back."

Nathaniel followed her into the storeroom. Presently he came out.

"She has learned my psalm. The third verse is her own. She will come out now."

Joseph rose to fetch her.

"My dear. Speak to me. I believe. I will worship him and take care of you." She turned from him.

"When you smile like that. I cannot bear it—I am exalted. There is so much pain about. Go through, Mother of God."

The old faces turned to her.

And Mary said.

❖ ❖

Several Occasions

Widdershins
Scylla and Charybdis
The Dinner Party
Brightness Falls
The Later Life of Theseus, King of Athens
In Bloomsbury
Friendship's Garland
Green
The House Party

1932

Widdershins

EVERY DAY HE WOKE to the desire to take the world by the throat, and choke it. He had no illusion that the world wanted to be saved; still less that it was ready to be saved by him. Ready!—it was punching at him with agonising blows, to be rid of him, once and for all. He woke up. Even that was not true now. It had been true once, but now the world was getting over any slight alarm he might have caused it. It was leaving him alone, to realise the wounds it had given him. Sometimes it was even tolerant and trying to patch him up.

Oh, God!

He was in the middle of London, in a dull hotel bedroom, stale with travelling from the Shap moors, where two years before he had gone away to think. He had called it thinking, but he had gone there to lick his wounds and dream. He was just intelligent enough to notice that he had not thought, and that what he remembered was certain moments of action. Certainly he did not understand that what he wanted was magic.

He lay, and remembered something about himself: that he was called Dick Tressider, that he was a mystic; and that among the people he met the word meant a snub, a cliché, an insult, or very occasionally, a distinction: that he knew a great many people who almost realised his plan, and yet did not: that he was a gentleman. He had not thought of that for a long time. London had reminded him. He damned the place and ordered his bath. He shaved, and put on his good, worn, country clothes, his heavy boots, his raincoat and leather gloves, all without pride in his strength or tonic from his unconventionality. He ate a country breakfast, and looked up his appointments. He felt that he was held from behind by the short hair on his skull, and cursed the city. But what he needed was magic.

It is doubtful if he understood the idea of progress, but whether he did or not, he disliked it. It may be certain, but it is obviously slow. He had his immediate reasons too. He had tried every association which tries to speed man's progress; labour and revolution, agriculture and religion. In each, it was the soundest point in his perception, he had seen one thing and the same thing, which was the essential thing and, at the same time, did not come off. Meanwhile, labour and revolution, agriculture and religion were entirely sick of him. He knew, if any man living knew he knew, that sometimes things were improved, or rather that they were changed; and that in individual action there were moments of a peculiar quality that expressed the state in which he knew the whole earth could live all the time, and settle the hash of time, progress and morality once and for ever. What he wanted to happen was for some man to say a word of power which should evoke this state, everywhere, not by any process, but in the twinkling of an eye. This is magic. Lovers did it, especially his lovers; and saints, when he and one or two men he knew were being saints, with a woman or so about to encourage them, at night, in a smoky room. There were moments, too, under the hills, breaking-in horses, when it came, the moment of pure being, the co-ordination of power.

But the universal word did not come off. He was over forty now, and he was losing his nerve. He was beginning to spit and sneer; and, since he could not find his word, he was beginning to grin, and hope for the world to ruin itself; and rub his hands, and tell his friends in their moments of pleasure that they were damned, not exactly because they had not listened to him, but for something rather like it. And, as very often they had listened to him, in reason, they were hurt.

Because he had not mastered the earth, he was beginning to hate it. Hate takes the grace out of a spiritual man, even his grace of body. As he left the hotel and walked west through the park, and saw the trees coming, he drew in one of his animal breaths that showed the canines under his moustache, bright like a dog. *Grin like a dog, and run about the city*; but then he understood that this was one of his empty days, which might be filled with anything or nothing.

"I must fill it," he said, and he meant that on this day he must have a revelation and a blessing; which is a difficult thing to get to order. He went on to the grass, in among the trees, which are a proper setting for almost every kind of beauty. Their green displayed his tan and harmonized his dress. Their trunks drew attention to his height, the grass gave distinction to his walk. It was early, and there were no pretty women about to make his eyes turn this away and that, greedily, with vanity, with appeal for pity, but too scornfully for success. The trees went on growing. He looked at them and remembered Daphne, and that she had said once: "Stop fussing, Dick. Why can't you let things alone for a bit? Think of trees." "Silly fool of a girl. Wanted me to make love to her, I suppose." He had said that at the time, and still said it, but he added Daphne to the list of people he was to see that day. Like men of his kind, at cross-purposes with their purpose, there could be nothing fortuitous that happened to him. Everything was a leading, a signature of the reality whose martyr he was; for he could never allow that he had made a fool of himself, and only occasionally that reality had made a fool of him. So he pinned the universe down to a revelation from Daphne, and took a bus to Holborn to get on with the business of the day.

It is much easier for a man to lose his self-consciousness in Holborn than in the female world of South Kensington. He went first to see a friend who was teaching a kind of Christian anarchism made dramatic by the use of Catholic ritual. He was a good man, patient with Dick, who trusted him. It was one of the things that made Dick uneasy that the works of sanctity and illumination are now distributed through offices, and he saw himself a terror to such places. His friend Eden was out. The typist was a very childish one, with short hair and a chintz overall, and she did not suggest the Sophia, the Redeemed Virgin, Dick was looking for. He shifted his expectation and saw her as the unredeemed and improbable virgin, which is the same thing as the soul of the world, and prepared to treat her for the part. He was hungry by now.

"I'm Dick Tressider," he said, "and I'll wait for Mr. Eden." He dropped his stick, picked it up, lit a cigarette, and walked once or twice up and down the room. "D'you know about me?"

"I can't say that I do," she said. "So many gentlemen come here for Mr. Eden."

"D'you know Mr. Eden well? Are you conscious of what he is doing here? I mean that it's an expression of what is happening everywhere, of what is bound to happen everywhere, man's consciousness becoming part of the cosmic consciousness?"

"Mr. Eden never says anything about it."

"D'you know this whole damned earth is going to smash any moment?"

"Mr. Eden says that if there are any more wars we shall starve. He's trying to stop it."

He grinned, and showed his wolf's teeth.

"I tell you. It'll make precious little difference what he does. You look as if you might understand. Come out and have some lunch."

She got up obediently. She remembered that she had heard of Dick, that he had been a soldier of some family and some service. Also he was a tall figure of a man, not like the pale, ecstatic townsmen who came there.

He took her to a restaurant and ordered red wine and steak. He crammed his food down and asked her what she thought about love. Immediately she was frightened. She was not frightened of seduction or of a scene. It was pure fear. He saw that it would not do, and sulked at her, pouring down his wine.

"I don't want to waste time. I've got to get down to reality. Tell Eden I'll call in later."

He took her out, and left her at the door of the restaurant, without a word.

He walked about London, through the streets round the British Museum, on a cool still afternoon without rain, past the interesting shops and the students, and the great building of stone. He wanted to persuade men that they were only there to illustrate the worth of the land. He did not want to see Eden, who would be busy trying to stop the next war, and getting people to dress up. He knew what war was and how it would stop these games, more power to it. It was all up with the world, and the world didn't know it. He would go to tea with Daphne now. It would be too early, but that didn't matter.

At the Museum gates he saw a man he had known who said: "Is that you, Tressider? I didn't know you were in town."

"I came up last night."

"Wishing you were back?"

"Wishing I could smash these lumps of stone or get men to see their cosmic significance."

The civilised man winced. The idea might be tolerable, but one should not say it like that.

"I am going into the Museum. Come along."

"What are you going to do?"

"Look at things."

"Some earth-shaking new cooking-pot?"

"It's not a question of size, is it? Come along."

He had to run beside Dick, who flung himself over the courtyard and up the steps.

"I read a jolly fairy-story about this place," he said. "Some children got a magic amulet and wished the things home, and they all flew out. Those stone bull things, and all the crocks and necklaces."

"I remember. They found a queen from Babylon, and she said they belonged to her, and wished them all home, and home they went."

Dick looked at him with a sideways, ugly stare.

"I know. You like me, don't you, when you think I'm a fairy-boy. A kind of grown-up Puck? You like me to like rot."

"But I do," said his friend. "I like that story myself, and was glad when you recalled it."

"Do you know that the only thing we've said that meant anything was a bit of your talk— 'She said they all belonged to her.' That's the cursed property-sense that keeps this world a hell."

"Oh damn the property-sense! I was going to look at the casts from Yucatan, and I always forget the way."

Dick was staring at a case of bronze weapons. He put his hand easily on the man's shoulder. "Don't you understand that that fairy-story is true? They could all fly away out of here. It's as easy as changing your collar."

"Do it for us then, Tressider. I'll come along and applaud."

"My God! You people will find a man who can do it for you, and worse things, and soon. Someone you've treated as you treat all people. Take it from me, Brooks."

Madder than ever, thought Brooks. Won't think, and can't play. "All right. The room's at the end. Come along."

It is not easy to get on terms with a cast the size of a house, whose close decorations mean nothing to anyone except to an archaeologist or an artist. Dick lounged and stared, and leant up against the central plaster lump.

"What are all these things for? I suppose you think you've done something when you've dug 'em up out of the earth."

It is exceedingly difficult to explain why a thing is useful when you like it.

Dick smote it with his hand.

"A lot of good those'll do you when the world busts up."

But Brooks was thinking what a type was there, leaning on a sacred mayan monster, a fair, ruling, fighting, riding man, and what twist of breeding had turned him prophet *à la* Semite, "sad when he held the harp." And that the harp that once—etc.—was now completely cracked.

"All right," he said, "we'll leave antiquities for the moment. But it's a speculation worth following: Where did that civilisation come from, and did it have any contact with Egypt?"

"Egypt? They knew about the soul there, and I don't care where their jim-jam decorations came from. Civilisation's going. The world wants a man whose contact is primeval."

"Oh does it?" said Brooks. "I suppose you mean yourself. You're about as primeval as a card-index. Come and have some tea."

And at tea Dick asked him sweetly about his children, and sent messages to his wife, and told the story of his uncle's funeral with point and wit, and left Brooks, to go up to Daphne, with his affection intact, and his doubts.

Now it was evening. The 'bus climbed up the side of London, and above the screaming children and the crowd going home from work, it rolled like an animal ship; and from every contact Dick sighed and withdrew himself, until at the five roads at Camden Town he felt something coming to him which had come before. "This place is not here," he said. "I can lift myself out of it, in my body. So!" He sank down a little as he said it, and answered himself. "The things you hate are only your body being knocked about by phenomena." Then the place disappeared, especially a public-house with a plaster tower; but there had crept up through it tall, perpendicular folds, which looked like dark grey rubber, which rose and passed in from all sides. But he was free, both of the houses and of what had replaced them. He lifted himself like a clean man out of the sea, and rested in his mind, which was now full of order and peace. He wondered that he had ever minded anything, and at the end of the ride stood several men drinks in a public-house and roared with laughter with them.

Before dinner he came to Daphne's house and rang the bell. There was some time before anyone answered it. Then her old nurse came, and looked at him without knowing who he was. He came in, and took off his raincoat before he said: "Is Miss Daphne in?"

"I'll see, sir," she said, and led him into the living room, which had tall windows and a balcony on to a garden full of trees. The wind, a new thing, was moving in them. It was almost night. Next door was Daphne's room. He heard the door open and shut several times, and brief voices. The room was very empty. He stumbled over a rug, and saw the shining boards and a gramophone gaping with the lid up, and records on the divan among the cushions. He did not make himself at ease by the fire. He understood that they had been dancing. He walked up and down the room, wondering what they would give him to eat.

It was all right. The peace was there. He would tell Daphne about it. Daphne would give it back to him with assent and vivid words. Perhaps he would take Daphne out to dinner. Her youngest sister came in.

"Please forgive us. We're in such a hurry. We've been dressing Daphne. Would you mind coming to see her in her room?"

He remembered Daphne's room, rows of books and glass balls and chinese pictures of birds and windows that stepped out into the air. He followed her sister, and as he came in, heard Daphne's cry, "Hullo, Dick!" that was like a battle yell. In a minute he was treading into a sea of tissue paper that rustled like snakes. The shutters were closed. All the lights were on. Here was night, suddenly and strongly lit. As Daphne came to meet him, her sister fell on her knees, and followed her over the carpet, pinning something at her hips.

A woman he did not know was sitting on the couch looking at Daphne. The old nurse was somewhere beside him, by the door.

"Shall I ring for a taxi, dearie?"

"In a minute, Nurse, I've a few moments to spare." Then he trod on the paper like a man and saw her. She had on a green and white dress, and crystal earrings that touched her shoulders, and a crystal at her waist, slung round her neck with a green cord. Dick remembered enough to know that it was a dress that is not seen in shops, but is shown, *like an ear of corn reaped in silence* to certain women on certain occasions. He saw her feet in silver sandals, her hair like a black, painted doll's, a curve drawn out over each cheek. On the dressing-table, white with powder, there was a bouquet in a frill.

"Dick, I'm going out to have a glorious time." She did not look at him twice to see what his heavy eyes said.

"Val, my dear, is my back even?" Valentine got up and took a powder-puff and dusted her sister's white back. She sat down again at her mirror, and called at him into the glass where she could see him. "Dick, sit down. You know my cousin, Mrs. Lee?" He would not know her, but sat down and stared, and saw that Daphne was like a tree in glory. And that the colour of her mouth was due to art. It was not trying to be anything else. If it was kissed, it would come off so much sticky paint. The room was warm, full of scent and whirling with powder-dust. He tried to hear the wind rising. He wanted to swear at Daphne and hit her. In the mirror, he saw her little head sink an instant. He knew her. She was thinking, "Oh, Dick, don't spoil my pleasure." Well, he would. Then she whipped round and smiled at him, deliberately, brutally, and he knew that he could not.

She was pulling on gloves like curd, picked up her flowers, and moved across the room.

"Nurse, ring for a taxi. Angry, Dick? I'm going to dance all night. Oh, it's good to get into decent clothes—"

He said vulgarly: "It seems to me that you've got out of them," and she looked at him exactly as she would look at a man of his kind who said a thing like that.

As he waited and hated her, she forgot even who he was.

"Say you like my dress. I must hear everyone say it."

"I suppose it's fashionable, but I remember you in the shrubberies at Pharrs in a cotton dress. You came for a walk with me."

"Oh yes. I remember Pharrs—that reminds me—"

It had not reminded her of him. She turned and went quickly to the glass again, and spoke to her cousin beside him.

"Terry. I'm not certain, but I think it wants a headdress." She pulled out a wreath of bright green leaves and set it on her head.

They were like the leaves of no earthly laurel. He shuddered and called, "Daphne!" Her cousin agreed with her.

Her taxi came. She said: "Dick, I'm sorry I've had no time tonight. Can I give you a lift down town?"

She flung on a silver cloak, and he followed her down the steps into the cab. The wind was rising, and drummed on the window-glass. They ran in silence down London. It was very cold. He saw where she was going; into a high square house, and down to dinner with a black and white man, down golden stairs.

She looked at him again.

"Cheer up, Dick. Don't you like to get back to it all when you come to town?"

She had won. He had not known how to express his disgust; now he did not know if he felt it.

"I suppose I miss it sometimes."

"Look here. We've a party at the Savoy on Saturday, and we want another man. Will you come?"

He would not come. Anything might happen in the world, but he would not come.

"I'm afraid I should be out of place. You would find my change of values too complete."

"Should we indeed! There are several Paradises, Dick. Me for this Paradise."

She had known all the time. He must say something destructive, inimical, quickly. Only she had forgotten him again.

"Oh," she said, "it's cold," and drew her silver stuff round her. Without concern he put his oily rough raincoat over the silver, the white and green, the milky back that came off a little. She made a little face, said, "Thank you" and forgot.

The wind roared through the square. She opened the door, two half-crowns in her hand.

"Here's my share. Goodnight, Dick. Come and see me some time. Goodnight, Dick."

He did not want the taxi any more. He only wanted to meet the wind, and let Nature knock the nonsense out of him and the memories. He took the half-crowns from her, and she was out into the street before he could find his stick. He did not help her. She was gone. The wind roared past. He paid the man, and at the last instant before night, saw her run up the steps, and the wind take her cloak and open it. He saw her bend like a full sail, and balance to the wind. He saw her head go down, and her silver shoes run up. The door opened; he saw her run into a tall yellow arch, and the black door immediately close on her again.

❖ ❖

Scylla and Charybdis

CLAUDE STIRRED THE cushions and laid me down on the divan beside him, as though he was afraid we both might break. The exquisite room, the exquisite day stretched long and empty before us. I asked him if both his friends would be staying with him at once. He admitted it, painfully.

"You see," he said, "Boris is here already. I don't know how to ask him how to go." Knowing Russians, it did not seem to me to matter much. He would not have gone, anyhow.

"Who is the other one?"

"He telegraphed," said Claude. "Wants to come to Paris to meet people. I suppose I invited him. He's called Crane. He tells wonderful stories."

"What about?"

"Himself mostly. He really is remarkable. Got a complex about something at the moment, and I didn't see how I could get out of it. You know how it was. I thought I rather wanted to have him, and I do. I could manage him without Boris, or Boris without him. It's together—"

I reflected on Boris' habits. Claude went on:

"Boris goes to bed just after I've had my bath—always. That was why you didn't realise he was here. Crane's day will end when he begins—about midnight. He's like that."

"But won't that do?" I said. "Boris goes out all night, and sleeps all day. Crane'll go out all day and sleep all night. They'll never meet; it's a perfect arrangement."

Claude said: "My hours are between the two. It doesn't suit me at all."

"Language difficulties?" I asked.

"Cut both ways, as usual. Crane doesn't speak French, and Boris no other known language. That may prevent them from quarrelling, and will keep them from being friends."

Knowing Russians, I saw Boris making strategic use of this. I asked: "Is Crane a snob?"

"I don't know. If he is, it wouldn't be the same sort as Boris."

It occurred to me that, in any case, Crane had not had his place burned down; nor were what remained of his people expiring in prisons, or existing in the Crimea on the sale of the family plate. Crane might have a complex, but behind him extended a reasonably stable background, not the sordid, film-scene of a penniless russian boy living in Paris on his wits. Drawing the moral that penniless russian boys were to be forgiven much.

"Telegraph to Crane," I said, "and say that you can't do it." But Claude, who had been nursing a cushion on his breast, suddenly sat up and spoke over it solemnly.

"I've told you it wrong," he said. "There is something rather tremendous about Crane. I think some day the world will hear of that young man. One is rather proud to know him; at least, I feel that some day I shall be proud to have known him."

This surprised me. Enthusiasm was not Claude's métier. A long way off, an unknown young man was hurrying towards us in a train. Claude lay back quietly.

Then a vase, top heavy with double lilacs, tipped over, and the water streamed. We dealt with that, and returned to the cushions, and lay and watched a plane-tree, a roof, and the sky. A puff of cloud ran up and skimmed across the sun who, reappearing, winked. I understood that, whoever came, it was not going to be possible to lie there with Claude and watch the tops of things. A something was hurrying up to put a stop to that. Set us all on our feet, and make us earnest with our lives. I hoped not. The touch of idealism in Claude was new to me. At that instant we passed one another each an extra cushion, and sinking into them, became aware again of the leaves streaming outside, the speed of the wind, the quality of the light.

Next day, I dined across the river, and did not go to our café till after ten. What was going to happen would have only too much time to happen in. The windows were up, the tables were out. The Paris air of crushed gold and violets filled the place.

At the bar I saw Claude's friend Boris, elevated, but not drunk. No one else. "My dear," he said, and rattled through his compliments. I climbed up the bar-stool.

"Where's Claude?" I asked.

"In bed."

I thought that it was exactly like him to solve the difficulties of his friends' hours by getting neither up nor down, and I waited.

Boris jumped up beside me, like a little dark horse. I studied again the chinese white face, the oblique set of the cheek-bones, the wired black hair and unspoiled child's eyes used for a parade of innocence and sorrow which might exist, which ought to exist. Did it? I knew and he knew that I should act as if it existed. Automatically I calculated how much drink I should have to afford him.

"Claude," said Boris, swallowing hastily, "is naturally much preoccupied with his friend."

"So much so that he retires to bed," I suggested. Boris spun a silver bracelet round his small white wrist.

"Mr. Crane is very interesting, very remarkable," he said, "he has been telling me about his life among the Arabs. It is extraordinary how much you English manage to see of the world. Almost as much as Russians." He cocked his little head sideways at me. "Of course, we make different use of our experiences. Is that not so?"

"What d'you mean, Boris?"

"I explain it badly. I do not quite understand—it is difficult—" he leaned his elbows on the bar and grinned round at me. "I know I can tell you this and you'll understand—I must express myself—" It is possible to yell in a whisper. What followed I felt through my skull.

Boris said, "*Enfin, c'est un type qui m'interesse peu.* Excuse me a moment. I see a friend over there."

I saw him fall on the bosom, not actually, but with a greeting like it, of a man trimmed in soiled astrakhan. His drink saucers were before me. I paid them, and looked round for the third person, any third person, who, crossing the affair from outside, might tell me more. I saw a café gossip, but he was talking about a row the night before with the police and some american sailors. Then, outside in the black movement of the street, I saw a group detach itself, about to come in. Claude and a stranger, Lionel and George. One's own family party. The stranger was Crane.

They surrounded me, introduced him, and faded out as quickly as they had come in. Boris gave them a quick look. Crane sat down beside me.

"My first evening," he said. "Let's have some champagne. I'm so glad to meet you. I've been following your work." For the first moment one hates the person who follows one's work, and can do nothing but grunt. I took a good look at him.

'In too hard condition,' I thought. 'Ugly. Bold eyes like metal. A very tough nut. No, not exactly. Above all things, not easy. Not the sort that lies, flirts, flatters, or asks for tangible things. What a change.' He went on about my work, until it was only decent to pretend I knew something about it. Then, in the bar mirror, between the bottles, I saw a group out on the terrace. George and Boris, Lionel and Claude. My nearest and dearest, and I wished I was with them. They were listening to Boris, and grinning; but Claude looked as if he would be pleased to die at any moment. "Of course, Boris is busy helping them dislike this Crane man. How sweetly he is doing it." I nearly said it aloud. Crane said suddenly: "You don't know how glad I am to be with your people. I've been alone too much, doing damned hard things I didn't really want to—now I'm free to do what I like with my life, and you people are just what I need to start me again."

I nearly said: "How nice."

"—Someone to talk to after all these years in Syria." He began to talk about the place, and I was interested at once. What he said had character, like good art, significant but never over-produced.

"There was a man there called Muhammad Ibn Hassan." He was worked in, character and habits, into Crane's story, into an elaborate description of a young man's natural preoccupation with administration and war.

He gave me his hard, intelligent look, that changed sometimes into a rather blind stare. "My whole life's been hard. Much too hard for anybody. Left me too hard with everyone else. I'm trying to realise that. I want to use what I've been through."

"Not be subtly smashed by it," I tried.

"It's just that. My health's perfect. I can work at anything, and I do. I don't mean to leave anything out. But there is somebody that comes between me and people."

In the mirror I saw Boris, softly laughing, answered by two laughs and a smile from George, Lionel, and Claude. And I was thinking: 'They needn't plant their new friend on me for half the night.' Then I was sorry for Crane. He was saying:

"I married once on leave and my wife died. I realised I had never known her. I don't want to be unable to use what it has cost me a lot to learn. I have to loosen myself up—people are my difficulty—I want them to become one of my own sort, not always carrying on by myself."

I liked him, but I noticed myself being afraid that he was going to say it all over again. Too soon. I said, quite untruthfully: "I'm glad you're staying at Claude's."

"D'you know," he said, "I think Claude has the most beautiful personality. I only wish he'd look after himself and take his work more seriously."

"He's young," I said, "he'll grow. But he should take more care of himself."

"I'm trying to make him see that." I hoped that Crane would see the first part of my sentence. But he added: "And not be so easy to take advantage of."

"Everyone is in this quarter, by everyone else," I said hastily, and looked back at the terrace table. George made gestures at me, and they joined us. Boris fidgeted up beside us and said:

"Claude, I'm going across the river. Can I have the flat key? I mayn't be back till late." "Back till late" being an euphemism for a return some time next day, drunk, soiled, obstinate, gay, even when he was plaintively gay. Possibly accompanied by friends of whom the less said the better.

Claude felt vaguely in his pocket. "But there is only one," he said, "and Crane and I won't be able to get in."

"Oh, well, perhaps one of you will let me in."

Claude said: "Couldn't you come back with us," but completely without insistence. Boris deprecated.

Crane said: "Boris understands English, doesn't he? Don't you see that we can't get back if you have the key. I sleep like a pig, and shouldn't hear you knock. And it's bad for Claude who doesn't sleep well to be dragged up at any hour."

Boris raised his eyebrows, hesitated a moment, and ran off. I thought of the child's eyes, and the slight indignity to the penniless (but not friendless).

"Anyhow," said Crane, "we've got the key." Claude looked as though he would rather have been without it. George frowned out at the streaming boulevard, where Boris had disappeared. We got up to go. I leaned against the bar, while they settled the bill outside. Lionel came back to speak to someone. Passing me, he turned, his mouth shooting up at the corners into his wild animal smile. I saw the bright teeth, the insolent, joyful look.

He said, "It's beginning."

II

The beginning was an end in itself. Next day I met Boris and paid with lunch for the news. He had left Claude's for ever.

"And why? I had no key. I came back—it was about six. It was raining. I sat on the steps and knocked. No one came; so I went round the back into the yard. There was one of those place with a glass roof under Claude's balcony. I was drunk, you know. I climbed up into it, and I fell through. There was a noise. Claude came out—he let me in, and he was angry. He said—I could not imagine that Claude would say such things. And my position makes it difficult."

The delicate, hurt dignity was incomparably done. I had to imagine the weeks of this sort of behaviour that had moved our gentle Claude—probably into saying too much. I reflected. This left Crane in possession at Claude's, and Boris on our hands. Of course he would be on our hands. Already he was suggesting that in my flat there were many mansions. I thought of my own salvation.

"Lionel's away," I said. "Go and stay with George." Then I saw what I had done. Lionel would not be away long. Boris would be there when he returned, and would never leave. George, if only to be one up on Claude, would never send him away. Lionel would be angry and quarrel with George. Boris, planted even deeper in the heart of the family, would play everyone up, and make George and Lionel, who would only quarrel about him, not with him, a reproach to Claude. Crane, in possession at Claude's, would have plenty to say about his second impressions of Claude's friends. I saw Crane, so vigorous among our delicacies, so competent, so hard. What would he think of us? We had been at ease together, shut away on the top of Paris, so that we had forgotten to question ourselves; adjusted not ethically, but harmoniously. Now Crane had come, and Boris had gone. Goodness only knew what would go next, but peace was on the wing, our tolerance of each other's little ways, and of our own. I prickled; uneasy sentences for future use framed themselves and were discarded. Like a slug with pins in it, the sense of broken rhythm, now called the inferiority complex, was on its way.

III

Of course, Boris went to stay with George. And didn't say I'd sent him. And stayed. George was very good to him. George gets kick out of things like that. Claude fell ill. Lionel was cross. The next thing I saw was Crane drunk too. He was asking Lionel why a man who had controlled a piece of desert half as large as France, a town of people thirsting for his blood, several desert tribes and some brigands (between whom the distinctions seemed inexact) should miss all contact, which he earnestly desired, with us.

I told him it was because he desired it earnestly, and was cross-examined. I left him to go and see Claude, walking out into the Paris street, into the thin triangle of our world, whose base was a strip of the Boulevard Montparnasse. A grey and green map, of stone and trams and trees, whose noises were american voice noises and street cars and wind; crossed its base, from our café to Claude's little tower, full of flowers and glass, where Crane came out. I thought of the star-pointing apex, over the fortifications, above the Lion, where lived Boris and Lionel and George.

I stayed with Claude. His spirits were out of order. We called it liver. I sat with his dark gold head on my knees, and we sympathised.

Crane came in, sober. He made the bed and gave Claude medicine, and an interesting account of the treatment of snake-bite in Arabia. The way that he had, impromptu, handled a case. I remember that the man died later, because they would not keep Crane's incisions clean. He was perfectly happy, tidying us up, making us feel his strength. Asking us to understand his weakness. That was implied. That also exhausted. I didn't believe in his weakness. I did. I did not care about it. A man you never wanted to forgive and bless. He lit his pipe. Claude did not seem to want me to go. The bell sounded, as if it had been rung by a cat. I answered it. It was Boris, come to fetch something he had left. His rapid French, the deftness of his body, were like a little tune.

"You have some of my shirts," said Claude.

"They are in the laundry; I am bringing them."

More laundry bills for George? On second thoughts, no.

Boris said: "I must go and meet a friend who has just got out of Russia."

"I haven't seen George for days," said Claude. I knew why. George thought Claude had been unkind. He was all for Boris now. It was exquisite the way Boris ignored Crane. He ran over and stood at the foot of Claude's bed.

"*Soignez vous bien, mon amie,*" he said. In that was all forgiveness, delicate affection, well-bred indifference. He vanished. Later Crane saw me out.

"Poor Boris," I said.

"Why poor?"

"Well, he is."

Crane answered, in his cold, ringing voice, "Why, when you put up with his cadging and exploitation and disgusting behaviour, I don't understand what you people are sentimental about."

"It's because he doesn't take us in," I said, defensive as though I was hiding a secret. "Besides, we must help each other."

"Doesn't it occur to you that there are people who need help more and who ask for it less?"

"Surely," I said, and could not keep the essential indifference out of my voice.

Crane said: "Well, I've got Claude to see it. He agreed with me that night before he turned Boris out."

But I remembered a tranquillity which had fallen on Claude as his eyes had followed Boris out of the room. Not my company or Crane's management; Boris' forgiveness had worked like a charm.

After that, nothing worked at all. Boris flew like a bluebottle over Paris, and like a bluebottle returned to the meat to lay its eggs. Crane said very little, but he took us out to meals, in reason, to keep us out of Boris' way. While I saw Boris give the barman twenty francs for fifty francs' credit, and Crane give him one franc and fifty on twenty-five francs he had paid.

Lionel had a song:

> *We keep Boris*
> *Crane keeps us*
> *God keeps Crane*
> *So we might do wuss.*

But when I told Crane that he was supporting Boris Sarantchoff after all, his mouth changed shape, until I was glad that my hand, no, the bridge of my nose, was not between those level teeth. Then George called me a bitch for trailing my coat; and I said that he'd take that back or I'd not see Boris get his dinner that night. And George said it was a privilege to do it, and I said he should be thankful to get his pet lambs minded, without camping about it like a virgin aunt. And George said he had got Boris a job he would like, and we said we should see, and George sulked.

Indeed, I suppose I have the best of it, for Boris at least called my taxis, fetched me to my parties, and told my lies. I had only to pay to be praised. With the others he took a more manly line.

Presently Claude rose again, and we passed the afternoon in cinemas, hiding from all we loved. One or the other, the two were always with us. I was only safe in bed, the others not even there. Scylla and Charybdis we called them, falling alternately into their power. And Claude wanted a Crane to get rid of Crane, as Crane had got rid of Boris, and there was no successor to Crane. Certainly not Boris. He was perfectly well-off working up George. And George, it was the way affliction took him, got thinner and more malicious every day. More sentimental, too, in justification of our uneasy feeling that we needed justification.

One night we were out with Crane, whom we had so far managed not to call Charybdis to his face, and Scylla in the Champs Élysées, spending more money than we had ever spent on him. Crane said moderately that it was absurd of George to think we could make a self-respecting Englishman out of a russian *émigré*. And George said that he was out to save Boris from what he was doing that night. And we reminded George of the job he had got him, and that Boris had never once turned up at, and we laughed at George.

IV

So it went on, until one night Claude and I returned after a theatre to meet the others at my flat. The last days, with their suspensions and repeats, had been rather like poetry, but what we found there was not. Or perhaps it was. Poetry is some sort of a shock, usually displeasing at first, and this was.

First we heard a noise, a gay, rowdy noise, at a pitch which could not have been the others speaking, or even laughing or crying. There was something soft in the dark on the floor. Claude picked it up. A dark thing to wear with a collar of some other stuff. I could see a faint line of white.

Claude said: "D'you wear this?" as I said: "I don't wear that."

Then a body, white above and dark below, bounded at us out of a door. We dodged. A moment later we were in the salon. There was Boris, and there were five american sailors with him, and one of his little russian friends. I have seen the place disordered, orgiastic, a disgrace— I have seen my clothes on the wrong bodies, the floor bright with glass splinters. But always as a moment of play, sport before renewed attention to business, never as though that state of things was going on forever. There was Boris, bubbling explanations based on the perfections of my character. Also, left to ourselves, we might have played too. At least I would. There was really nothing else to do. On the other hand, Crane would be there any minute, and the sailors looked a god-almighty set of toughs. Claude was more scared than shocked. We looked at each other. There was something that appealed, and it was interesting to notice that Boris must know a lot more English than he pretended that he did to us.

"All right," I said tentatively.

"Have some champagne, ma'am," said an enormous Yank, the one who had leapt out on us in the dark. I could not see how we should ever get rid of them. The little russian friend might be going to pick their pockets. And how had Boris got in? Had he picked mine? I was turning the corner of adjustment, which I suppose is the test, if there is a test, of civilisation, when I heard outside the ascending steps of Crane and Lionel and George.

Again, it would have been all right if they hadn't brought Crane. To him I could not pretend that I had given Boris permission for this; that I could endure this; that I was even amused by this; not to Crane with his years of despotism behind him.

I stepped back to stand among them.

"Good God!" Crane said.

Lionel giggled.

"Boris!" said George.

About me were the subtle, beloved faces, that were too subtle to be of use; and Boris' face most subtle of all. And about him were the five baby faces of sailors, virile, without modelling; and behind them the little russian friend, a piece of perfect corruption; all sprawled under the lights, among my properties—as unimportant to them as arabian magic had been to Crane!

I said: "I don't know. We've just found them here." They were taking no notice of us as they banged the bottles, and tried to make noises like a russian chorus, which ended with the word "Da."

Among our diversions and hesitations, Crane stepped out.

"What are you doing here," he said to them, "uninvited, making this filthy scene?"

I would have protested, but a sailor staggered up, steadied himself by a carpet on the wall, and pulled it down. It fell on him and on the little Russian, who bit him as they struggled beneath it. Crane went on: "You know how you had to leave Claude's. You'd better leave this place, and quicker."

Boris answered at once, with extreme propriety, that it was for me to say.

I said: "Your friend can't bite people in my house."

Crane grew ten feet high. He knew about gendarmes and naval police. And on that night of nights I knew the telephone would work. The man who had been bitten had blood on his cheek.

Then I saw that they were only mischievous drunk; the man who had been bitten explaining that he did not speak French. They began to play catch with the cushions and other loose objects. Presently it would be the glasses. It was. I saw Lionel, his sainted head thrown up; heard him giggle and say, "It's begun."

Then Crane had a few words, man to man, with the petty officer. That my flat was not a brothel. That Boris was a shark, and no friend for good Americans. That he must take his men away. Whitewashing me. I suppose he was used to doing that sort of thing. Anyhow, they went. The little Russian went with them. Two of them thanked me for a pleasant evening. Was it necessary to thank Crane for the deliverance?

Boris surveyed me. "I'm afraid," he said, "one or two of them have broken things."

That worked me up, but his candid eyes turned on penitence.

"Hadn't you better follow them?" said Crane. His voice was like an ice wind to blow the boy out of the house.

Boris only pointed out again that that was for me to say.

I said: "If you weren't too drunk to help me clear up, you could stay." Trying to be just.

Crane almost pouted at me. He said, with that terrible concentration of manner and emotion which made him so hard to deal with: "I don't understand why you people waste your lives on this." A remark to which there was no answer which could be given.

George pulled himself together.

"I'm taking you home with me, Boris. You're so drunk, you'll be sending up the police next. Come along."

Boris said he'd never drink again unless he was sure I'd forgiven him. I told him we were enemies for life, and he left the field, tight in George's arm, with most of the honours of war.

Crane excused himself. Claude and Lionel helped me with the house.

The sobriety of next morning reunited us to Crane, not because we loved him, but because of what he would be thinking of us. George joined us, crestfallen, after lunch.

"How's Scylla," was whispered down the bar.

"Don't know," said George. "I'd nearly got him home, when he kicked off his shoes at a policeman. I tried to hold him, but he fought like a horse. He's as strong as one. Kicked my shins—I let him go, and he ran off."

"Arrested by now," I said. "Let's leave it at that." But George said with patience and bitterness that were somehow both a little false: "I shall have to get him out."

Later Crane selected me as the victim of a party of depraved young men, and asked me to dine alone. Boris ran round as I was changing, and said pretty things, and brought me to him. He was wearing George's shoes. Claude had gone to bed again. We were dazed. Crane took me away.

I kept the meal steady with gossip; but when it was over he said: "You must tell me where I fail."

"If you know you fail, you should be able to find out for yourself."

"If George or Claude or Lionel, last night, had sent those men away, you would have been pleased."

I tried to feel, not think. Then I said: "You haven't the right to send people away."

He turned his steel eyes at me. They hurt me, paralysed me, like the advancing lights of a car. I saw that his body was taut, all of it: also made of steel; that it only worked because it was at an intolerable tension, and that it was our sensation of that tension which had exhausted us, which could no longer be borne. He was the wrong spring which had been put into our machine, that had made Claude ill, George foolish, Boris an anxiety.

Then I found something I wanted to say.

"You're too tight," I said. "I told you that before. Relax. Then it will be all right. Then you'll be able to be what you are without bothering about it. It's the only way."

His shoulders moved at me across the table. "Relax," he said, "why say that to me? You know I can't. If I did, I should be mad. I daren't try. I should all go—" Here was a bad secret, a bad muddle. Some pain. And I did not care. And his whisper to me was a yell, like Boris' opening speech (*"Enfin, c'est un type qui m'interesse peu"*). "What am I to do?" he said again.

I was trying to look at him, feeling that I was being stretched on the same rack as he was. It was against my will. It stupefied me. At last I stammered: "Oh, I don't know. It would take too long to tell you. Try deep breathing or something." Then it was as though I went blind. Until there was something put into my hands and rubbed gently across my nose, and there was Boris, leaning across the table with a sheaf of red roses.

"*Ma petite chérie*, what has happened? You are distressed. You must not be distressed—" I came round. Boris was sitting beside me, rubbing me with the roses, thorns and all. Crane was on his feet, staring at us. Boris said: "Listen, Marie. I have just come from George. His sister had come over, and we are going to dance. You are coming out to dance with us. It is all arranged. You are not to mind anything. I do not think that Monsieur Crane cares to dance."

.   .   .   .   .

Many hours later, tumbling out of one dancing place into another, I wondered what it could have been which had made everything wrong—everything that was all right now—George sane, Claude well, Boris himself again.

The Dinner Party

THERE IS SOMETHING difficult in being asked out to dinner at a house on the top of Hampstead Hill. There is ease in gliding down into London, through parks and blazing light stretches; other suburbs are somehow accessible. Hampstead Hill is not. It is a black peak, black like the barrow that caps it above London. It does not look like that on a contour map; but that is its nature after dark. Perhaps it is that by nightfall one's body is running down into sleep, and would like to run down into the river valley also. But to get to the top of Hampstead Hill in the bleak hour before dinner, one is tilted on one's back as the taxi crawls up, one's face opposite the sky. Or perhaps the changing gears affect an empty stomach, but such occasions are often unpropitious.

They had both avoided the invitation for months. They had said they were ill, said they were in Paris; said every paraphrase for the fact that they did not want to go. Then her husband had insisted. Why, she would not ask. He came into her room that evening, and stood beside her mirror, and let her see that her meticulous dressing maddened him. Then her suggestion that they should go there by Tube,

"One goes up and one goes down," she said—"one might be going anywhere."

"It's ten minutes walk to the house," he said; "the north wind's blowing tonight, and that road is a funnel for it."

"In a taxi the stars will look as if they were hung upside down. Must we go, Angus? I don't want to go at all."

Everything that can be said has been said about the disagreements of husbands and wives, but no one seems to understand their almost insane reluctance at times to be explicit with one another. He watched her at her dressing-table selecting earrings (her appearance would be her only armour, and he didn't want her to want armour); and remembered what she was remembering, and shrugged his shoulders. While she was thinking: "He must remember. I've got over it now, but he must remember that I nearly died of it," she said: "I won't play bridge, and we needn't stay late. Just dine, and never see them again. I wish I could be on a diet so that I needn't touch their salt."

" Julia, are you ready now?" he said.

She turned a carefully arranged face to him. "You see, we have a perfectly good excuse for not going to their house. After that ghastly business they had with the Frazers. Are you sure Jack Frazer won't mind? I won't tear a leaf out of friendship's garland with Jack for anyone in London."

He answered: "Jack's curious. He's sitting up tonight to hear what's happened. I said you'd 'phone."

She said: "I think people who have libel actions brought against them and lose shouldn't be allowed to give dinner-parties for a year."

And Angus answered this sadly, as if his mind also was running back to something different. "I was in the Army with him," speaking of the man who was to be their host.

It was then that her sense prevented her from screaming at him: "I don't forget what you did one night when you were out of the Army. If you were a fool, he was a coward, and you tell me to eat at his house."

Why could she not have said that soberly and quietly, in quite different language? Because, she supposed, he had forgotten that she needed to be comforted for it. She had not been comforted for it, and, because of that, what the two men had done together that night was still alive, part of her relationship with Angus, a little thread of fire burning its way in them.

"I'm coming," she said aggressively. She was thinking that her husband only remembered what they had done as a futile and slightly regrettable business, which had left him without the least rancour against the man, but friendly and indifferent. She thought: "A much better attitude than mine. A much more animal memory. A lot he cares. How awfully wise he is to be able not to care."

"I've rung for a taxi," he said. "You can't walk. It's a filthy night."

The dark way up the hill she lay back in the car, seeing the rain splintering on the panes. The old houses and their trees made the hill road into a black lane. It was too like nature. The countryside was pressing in. She took refuge in spite, in determination to be pleased at nothing, in revenge for Jack Frazer's now triumphantly righted wrongs.

Inside the house there was a great bustle, the only peaceful figure an archæologist she knew, celebrated for his company, preparing to please and be pleased. But his pretty wife had guessed that there was a situation behind a situation, and was ready to notice and be noticed. The room was too small for them, the fire too large. There were too many chairs and too many art properties. And the old stairs were terrifying ladders with their worn, glassy treads.

The cocktails tasted as though they had been shaken in terror, which was nonsense in a hard-drinking house. And what a pretty woman their hostess was, the man's wife. Strange to think that she could have hated Jack Frazer so. Julia saw that she was frightened, and that it must be a difficult occasion for her to entertain Jack's side of the ghastly business, Angus Ruthven's wife, who didn't want to come, who had come because she couldn't help it, and out of curiosity, and because of a dreadful thing their husbands had done a long time ago. She thought.

'Mine's alive. They're both alive. Which is he? Of course, That's him. He's my host. How afraid he is. Strange not to be sure if I knew him, but he has so many brothers. There's one of them here tonight. Why did they ask him? Perhaps I'll be able to talk to Ramsay after dinner about looking for the Green Roads from an aeroplane, and all the fun he had.'

At dinner she sat between the man who had invited them and his brother. Neither of them spoke to her. She saw her little hostess staring at them, imploring; so she looked down and picked the table service to pieces. The table was badly waxed, the mats had crumbs, the glasses had been polished with a fluffy cloth. "Slattern," she thought, and secured a bowl of salted almonds, and talked at an angle like a knight's move with the archæologist's wife. Angus, her husband, was behaving with that extreme lack of grace only a man has the vanity to allow, sitting hunched-up, answering imperfectly, avoiding her eyes.

She sat back, munched her almonds, wondering: 'Why should the man's brother be rude to me?' Then she saw how it was; that he detested the party as much as she; had not wanted it to be given because of the Frazers; and because he was given to hating; and that he hated her especially because she was Jack Frazer's friend. Also that he had come to this dinner to make it impossible that any decent conclusion should be reached; that if drink loosed their tongues, it should be for railing, not for forgiveness. How ugly he was. His bull-neck rolled out over his collar, his ear turned away from her was scarlet and very thick. She saw also that his brother knew this, and was terribly ashamed, because of the secret between her husband and him, because of the Frazers, and for what his brother was doing to the party now. She asked him very gently for some salt. He was so eager to give it to her that his blunt fingers tipped over the little silver shell. All his family were badly finished off; it was their characteristic, she thought, and threw a pinch of glittering dust behind her.

He tried to imitate her, and spilt it on his collar, and was dusted prettily by the archæologist's wife. They began to laugh together, a patch of contact widened. Then an enormous voice spoke on her right. "You must be very fond of salt, Mrs. Ruthven, after all those salted almonds." It was the brother speaking again.

How very funny that was. She laughed because she remembered that she had eaten disproportionately of their salt, who had not wanted to eat it at all. Then she noticed that every soul round the table had withered at his voice, like green spring frills under the north wind. Her pretty hostess's eyes were scared and wet. And her own husband? He had played the lout all the evening, curse him; now he had pushed back his chair, put up his monocle to stare at the brother, and still staring dropped it again. Cad. Useless devil. How funny. Now we may be in for a scene.

There was no such luck. A fourth woman began to talk about psychoanalysis. Julia caught her husband's eye, who immediately began to sulk again. (Never know the middle-classes.)

Somehow after dinner she found herself safe, by the fire, at the archæologist's side, where he could tell her about Karnac in Brittany. These are good men, she thought, a word here and a word there for prompting, and they tell their tale. Only she knew that he knew that there was something going on, and that he was not without the malice to encourage it. But only because of the Frazers. He also was Jack Frazer's friend. She looked round to see if the rest of the room was properly shuffled.

It was not. It was standing about; and, at the back of the group, her husband was almost alone, with the man who had been his friend. They were next to a table with drinks. They were edging back together to the far end of the room. She heard a siphon squirting. Did she care?

No, she did not care. Why couldn't they go and drink in pubs? Angus was almost alone now with the man who had betrayed him. Only she did not want to see. The wind was storming at the house. Might it send in a great wing and hurry her away?

The little hostess ran at them, and unskilfully gathered them in. At last she got them all together by the fire. Plumped down on a hassock at their feet, she insisted that they should talk, like a doll's schoolmistress taking a giant's school. But the two men moved always a little further back.

The archæologist ceased his speculative, benignant stare and helped her. But not with Avebury and the green hills, but with the varieties of the complex, which leads so rapidly to stories about one's friends.

All the women helped them, and slowly Julia crushed out the remembrance of the south country and helped too; and he allowed her to show off and serve the talk in turns. She was glad of that; believing that if she were given any more time to relax, those two men would be off alone outside, remembering what they had to remember. She understood now that the man had made his wife ask them because he wanted to be with her man again. Wanted to defend himself to him and to her, wanted, before the evening was over, to have drunk enough to be able to shout his apologia for what he had done. Reconciliation over the Frazers was a mask, not a skilful mask. He was standing with Angus, a long way behind her chair. Every few minutes she heard the squirt of a siphon. She thought, 'Angus will never tolerate a scene.' Then that Angus' hands were clean. How clean? And then, 'If you don't stop this sort of thinking, woman, and enjoy yourself, you'll get what's coming to you.' She began to talk again.

Then came a *divertissement*. The elder brother, who had gone out, came back into the room, and stood by the fire, looking down on them. She understood that he knew all that she knew, and was afraid of the same thing, only with a change of villains and Angus for that part. A huge, greasy, *entrepreneur* of a man, he was in a fury about her and Angus' presence; because they were the other side of what his brother had done. He came of a family inconspicuous for honour, and was now in a fit about it—a fit that was turning into fury. Julia laughed. At dinner she had eaten three persons' share of salted almonds, and been ticked off for it. That was funny. The elder brother was fidgeting against the corner of the chimney piece, and his voice roared out: "As a mere outside observer of the arts, I wish someone here would explain to me why we are supposed to go to these Elizabethan plays. I know you're all literary, but to me it's a cult of the indecent—"

The archæologist looked up at him. It was his turn to enjoy himself. "Wit," he said, "and poetry. Cultural importance if you like—"

"Culture," the man said, "I don't object to culture." He was trying to shake the end of the marble shelf, his red face was purpling. "The women go there to pick up obscene words." Then he turned on Julia. "Perhaps Mrs. Ruthven can explain. I'm sure she's read *Ulysses*. Tell me, would that make a play?"

She smiled seriously at him. "Have you read *Ulysses*?" trying to look serene and childish. (Never know the middle-classes.) "I know the part you've read," she added, speaking very clearly, so that there would be an instant's pause. There was, while everyone began to laugh; but he switched back.

"What about Ford now? Writes a play called *'Tis Pity she's a Whore*, and you all go to it. I suppose it's the title. I don't see any poetry in that."

This was unbelievable. The man must be crazy. Letters were the profession of everyone there. And Jack Frazer was a good writer. The man was at the bottom of the Frazer libel, of course. What should she do? Defend the classic stage, or recite a list of obscene words not to be found in it? What was he bawling now?

"You're all war neurasthenics." And to his brother at the end of the room: "Richard, come over here."

She looked back at them. They were on the sofa. The brother was talking, his blunt hand on Angus' knee. And Angus was sitting like a cold, black idol, listening, appallingly himself. He stared at the room, but the brother half got up. He was trying to speak, trying to say to her, to the whole room, what they had done, and his defence. But Angus was not giving a damn, anyway, and the elder brother seemed to think that he would now remember his duties as host, and turned to her again.

"Do you drink, Mrs. Ruthven?"

"Yes, a whiskey and soda. Then we must go." She drank it fast, the violent talk passing over her, from one huge bellowing voice. The women were covering scandal, and would not answer back.

"As a business man among all you people, I think I have as much right to be heard—" She found her bag. One moment's idiocy of farewells, and they would be out in the street, in the iron wind which would knock them about. But she must not leave confusedly, she must make some exit speech. The evening's bully followed her across the room. The others also were beginning to get themselves away. She was between the brothers now, her husband looking at her. The elder brother said again: " *'Tis Pity she's a Whore.* Tell me now, Mrs. Ruthven, what you think of that."

"I am thinking," said she, "that I prefer the *Fancies Chaste and Noble.* I don't think you'll know that." She was past him, and now there was the other to face. His small, stony, blue-green eyes looked ready to drop on her out of his red cheeks.

"Sorry I haven't been able to talk to you all the evening. Had to see Angus. You know that. And you mustn't mind the rot my brother talks about poetry. We three know too much about poetry to mind."

She thought, 'We three know too much about too many things.' "I don't mind," she said. "He even reminded me of something I wanted to say." Angus' eyes were turned on her now. She was beginning to frighten him. Because, in this business, he had had no loyalty to her. Because she could make people afraid. She said: "You'll remember. It's also in Ford: *Sigh out, a lamentable tale of things, done long ago, and ill done.* You'll remember."

She saw Angus stare at her and heard him say, "Come now." She went straight out, and put on her cloak. She would not say another word in that house. But they were followed to the foot of the stairs.

She saw her host's face again, cracked like a broken mirror. He would not let her pass. He was saying:

"It's all right now, isn't it? Angus knows what happened. I didn't urge him to put that bullet into himself. And run and leave him to die. He was to do it and I was to do it. And I ran away and left him to do it. You see how it was—he was stronger than I. That's all. You know, don't you? It is all right. You know now that it is all right."

❖ ❖

Brightness Falls

Brightness falls from the air,
Queens have died, young and fair,
Dust has filled Helen's eyes.

THERE IS NO HEAD or tail to this story, except that it happened. On the other hand, how does one know that anything happened? How does one know? How do I know that Max did not invent it? Only, if I invented it that he invented it, it doesn't mean that what he thought he saw happen, happened as he thought he saw it. And I am profoundly suspicious of those two women. They are after something they want, and won't be happy till they get it; too careless to reason or even condescend to describe. Light-hearted minxes or spae-wives or immortals, and on top of that Parmys, I suspect, is a little sorry for herself. What has she got to be sorry about, if the story Max told me is true? And I could not sincerely be sorry for him either; though there I can't precisely say why. Except that we all have to take our chance, and to be married to Parmys must be an adventure.

He came into my rooms "hot and bothered," as our nurses said, obviously with something on his mind he was determined to be truthful about, and indignant that he should have such a truth to tell. I saw at once that it was the kind of truth that slips through the fingers, that is to say, a fishy truth; and that I should have to exercise the virtues of friendship without their reward. Max is not a stupid man, but I knew that night he was going to be stupid, and from the highest motives. And he was in trouble and alone. It was about Parmys, of course. When all's said and done, we do hang together against our women, and not wholly from rational reasons. All one finally discovers is that, when they urge us, the loveliest and wisest become all one with the slut.

He was saying, "I feel I've got to tell someone, and it might as well be you. I won't ask you not to repeat it, because you won't be able to. And no one could injure her reputation over it. Only mine. Either for sanity, or for not being God." It was plain that he was annoyed and surprised that he had not been God.

"I don't believe in a word of it," he said. "The explanation lies in some kind of hypnosis; and it is going rather far if she has come to trying that on me. You see, if I allowed myself to believe what she wanted me to believe, I might credit the whole caboodle."

He threw out the rather naïve argot at me. Slang makes us feel safe. Yes, and by a contact with some sort of reality.

"What sort of caboodle?" said I.

"Witchcraft," he said, "spells, magic; all women's occupations, by the way. Or the whole slush of theosophy: auras and reincarnations. You know I am not the man to stand for that sort of thing. Candidly, my mind is not sufficiently trained to examine and explain."

I told him, with perfect truth, that I could think of no woman than Parmys less likely to practise witchcraft or theosophy.

He said: "I agree. It's one of the things that makes it so impossible."

I reflected on the number of times the impossible turns up in a man's life.

He went on: "I told Parmys to keep out of it. Like I do myself. Whenever the infernal things crop up, I irritate as much as I can. Talk rationalist press stuff, and when that won't do, I try Freud. That's good enough at the moment with the kind of woman you meet out. The truth is, I'm as sensitive as a cat, and as ignorant as we all are. While Parmys—you may know that over our marriage there was some occult link?"

Knowing him, I had supposed that he would think so.

"—I mean—I minded nothing then—but there was some blend of passion, friendship, and wonder which was different from all these. Like a separate quality—detached. It gave us some strange moments, which were perhaps our best. It was like a place, slightly to the right or left of where you are going, that marches with you; that is occasionally lit up from inside. Not quite an ingredient, normally, of the greatest love. But we had it when I married Parmys. Only, gradually, it annoyed me when she said it was the key. Besides, she was wrong. You can't *turn* that key. It is never any good doing that."

"Did she ever tell you to turn it?" He did not answer. I said again:

"Tell me more about this place that moved on your right and left. What did Parmys call it?" Hoping that he would go on talking to himself. He hesitated.

"I don't remember. She loved chinese balls. I can see the living rose of her hands against their dead ivory. And there were witch-balls. She did say that when you looked into them you saw yourself there, and the one who was with you. Yes, and she said once that there were places about like it."

"Like what?"

"I can't explain that till I come to it."

He began to talk to me again.

"I was right to take no notice of it after the first."

It is no use denying that women resent us when we say about our relations with them, "after the first." I mentioned that. He said:

"If they'd only consider what Nature is instead of their own desires. Anyhow, Parmys shut up." I ran through the marriage of Parmys and Max. How we had all blessed it; and if there had been a touch of thankfulness that we hadn't fallen for her, that had probably been sour grapes. We'd said of him: "Max is the only one of us for her. Max is absolutely all right." Because there was a daft touch in him which might carry him through. He was not being daft now. He was going on.

"This story fits nowhere. If our divergence on this one thing had limited our contact, there was so much besides. And I thought that side of her nature would take a proper feminine course; that she'd become an Eastern Star or a Purple Mother and content herself that way."

"Good God," said I, "Parmys a Purple Mother. It's unthinkable, whatever it is."

"It's american," he said. I thought of Parmys with her bright wits and her elaborate "side." Her husband went on:

"She just said no more about it. When I noticed that, I hoped it was because she was beginning to think as I do, not a mask for devilry. I think I found it best not to think at all."

"She did not seem unhappy."

"Not at all. And what is a bruise or so to a woman as supple as Parmys? You know how cynical she is, and how little secretive?" I did, but also how childish. He went on:

"She took more than ever to the world; tore about it in a flurry of clothes and people. Especially with that tall woman who races, Cynthia Montgomery. They were always together. There was no un-happiness between us, just a small parting over a thing which does not exist. We lived as we have always lived, and were no end pleased to see each other at night. And all the time it must have been like an army with banners—"

"Or like water from the reservoir emerging from the bathroom tap," said I—but he was talking to himself again—"or from a fountain in a place that is right and left. I mean in a garden," he said. Now I didn't want him to start to dream again.

"For goodness' sake tell me what has happened—" He licked his lower lip endlessly, trying to rehearse facts, disputing with contempt and fear.

"I tell you those two women, Parmys and Cynthia, went about to-gether. Parmys with Cynthia; and they danced and went to parties and were in the eye of the world. Cynthia had never done anything else, but Parmys took to it again. They'd go out like lacquered idols. Their extravagance was a scandal, only they looked glorious. But they brought their troubles to me. I used to tell Cynthia to trust auntie, and she did. They'd a nice fatiguing taste in mischief."

"You did not feel you had lost Parmys then?"

"No. Her pleasures were mine, in my way."

I did not see how that could be quite true, but it could pass.

He said:

"Now I think I can tell you. It has been difficult to tell you, so as to tell it straight. And keep the quality in it. I took Parmys to a show, some decorative art stunt, because Cynthia wanted to redecorate her bathroom. We saw a man there, and I asked her who he was. Parmys said: 'Oh, that man. Gothic fonts.' It must have been Cynthia's bath we were after, because I remember saying: 'You can't wash Cynthia in a gothic font.' She didn't remember his name, and kept trying to. Then she heard some people talking and said: 'That's his name, of course, Corandel, Dr. Corandel.' She was rude about his exhibits, loudly and inopportunely. Then she forgot his name again, though she was in-troduced to him later on. No, she was reintroduced. I remember she said that she met him once, years before.

"I never heard anything to his discredit. He's a high connoisseur, and makes enamel plaques. Parmys said they were exceedingly bad."

"Sounds innocent," I said.

"It *is* innocent. There was nothing to be said against him. I doubt if there is anything to be said against him now. Then, it was about a week later—I remember, we were dining somewhere, and Parmys ordered a cream caramel, and called it 'Corandel,'—'Caramel, Caramel,' she corrected, staring the way she does. Also, that same evening, we went somewhere, and someone asked what was meant by a Coromandel screen. She started, and went over to the man who had asked, and said that she didn't know and had always wanted to and could anyone tell; and nobody could."

"This story, then, is all in terms of food and the applied arts?" said I.

"It has nothing whatever to do with them. Nothing happened after that. Cynthia was away in Wiltshire. If Parmys missed her, she did not show it. Perhaps about the house there was a sort of winter hush—I mean when one hears things too distinctly, or does not hear them at all. Parmys was in the house a lot, and several times I think I was expecting her to say something important, not about our tabu at all, but about her friendship with Cynthia; or whether she would condescend to have a baby. She did not say anything, but she was loving and gay as ever—oh yes, she once asked: 'Do Corandel and parallel rhyme?' As if anybody couldn't hear, as I told her. 'Oh, it's like that, is it. Assonance, not rhyme. That doesn't make much difference. I must go on with it.' Then I did say, 'Go on with what?' 'Go on listening,' she said. Do you know what she meant? I don't know what she meant."

I didn't know. He went on:

"But the little cat had made me begin to listen. I didn't want to listen, but I found myself attending to noises. In November the third week was still, you remember. A few leaves to fall, and each one I thought was like a little word that you just couldn't catch. Light and brown and so few of them—whispers in the air. I used to stand at the windows and watch, until I thought of coral and pearl and how red and white they are."

I said: "I'm sure Parmys didn't listen like that."

"No," he said. "I did, who didn't want to. With her it was like waiting, though she was distracted and busy, like a flower full out and full of bees. But with me it was the idea of listening, for what I shouldn't hear because it wasn't there. It got on my nerves; and then, one night, I could see she had gone daft on some interest that had nothing to do with anything. Like a fairy child, for all that she's thirty. Staring and inclined to sing. I said something, and then she said: 'There is magic about,' and I said, 'Drop it, can't you,' and she sang, '*Oh no, we never mention it,'* turning away. After that we had the formidable, chic Parmys again."

"After that?" I said, doing my best.

"Nothing for ten days. Yes, there was another word-play I tried to ignore. Only a boy from Dartmouth, who asked me what was meant by the Coromandel Coast. I told him that the name had passed out of use for that part of the indian seaboard; and heard Parmys laugh and say that it didn't seem to be a lucky noise.

"Next morning I came into her room and sat on her bed. I remember thinking that her quilt was like a neat green and gold sea. She was picking feathers out of it, and drowning them in a teacup. I remembered the boy the day before, Peter's nephew, and mad about old voyages; and I told her, I don't know why, what I'd read in an article, that in Lincoln's Inn there was an old map of the Coromandel Coast.

"'Oh, is there,' she said. 'Oh hell,' and when I asked her what hell had to do with it, she said something about a long, long trail winding. I asked her later if she missed Cynthia down at Pharrs, and she answered, 'Oh no, not at lovely Pharrs. Excepting that November is the worst month down there.' Meaning, I knew, that all the ghosts are supposed to be out there then. I ignored that; but then I asked a question, because I felt it was dragged out of me— 'What has Corandel to do with Cynthia?' I said. 'Don't know,' she said, 'don't know. He had a house round the corner from hers once. No good came of it. Now he's staying down there, not at Pharrs, but in the old house at the edge of the wood.' I thought of palladian Pharrs, and the little piece of the earlier house sticking out across the lawn. There was nothing to be made of that, and I said so. Tell me—up to now, do you make anything of all this?"

If there had been one mercy in this infliction, it was that it could hardly be turned into a story of Parmys' infidelity. Once that is out of court, one is free to be interested or bored. I had made nothing of it, but supposed that there was more to come. Some secret between Cynthia and Parmys. It is getting more and more inopportune to suppose that women have no secrets unconnected with sex. I supposed that Parmys was shielding something Cynthia had done; and I remembered that once I had heard her say that we must take care of her, because Cynthia, for all her high manners, was innocent of heart. So I told him to get on with it.

He said: "That was all until the thing happened. How shall I tell it?"

I saw him pause with that look of admiration and fear one can see when a man is greatly moved by something his intellect does not recognise, and he appears half as animal, half as God.

"I was waiting for lunch when Parmys rang up from the Savoy. 'Come down here at once,' she said; 'come down at once. I must have you to trust. Come at once. Come at once.' Even over the 'phone I thought her voice sounded no longer distinct and cool, but like the sea beginning to rise before the wind. I went down at once, very irritated. After all, Parmys had lived freely. Why should I be dragged into a business that was not in common between us, and would necessitate explanations I was not willing to hear?"

"You assumed it was the business, then?"

"Yes, I did; and that it might be a trick to drag me into it. And when I got down, I found a double cocktail of the kind I like waiting for me, and that annoyed me too. It was too simple. 'Listen,' she said, 'drink it, and eat those sandwiches. We'll need them.' I asked her why—and women are maddening—she said: 'Not two, only one now. We must be there before them. I've been hearing those noises again, like a storm rising. Not in my head—people and advertisements. A hawker would sell me caramels, a man at the bookshop was arguing about parallels. There was: "Go to Arundel for architecture" in the tube; and that infernal Coromandel again—'

"'You'd never hear such a word in the street,' I said to her.

" 'Oh yes, I did. Name of a horse. I backed it—out of perversity, I suppose. Such a lot of noises, Max.'

"I wouldn't let her move me, suggested that we should go in to lunch. 'Oh no,' she said. 'I got here half an hour ago. I was coming in anyhow to see the man who sent me the coral links, and I was waiting. Then I saw Cynthia come in with Dr. Corandel. And Cynthia doesn't look like a queen and huntress any more.'

"I thought I saw it then; that Cynthia was having an affair with the man, and that Parmys did not approve. Not out of morality, she'd never condescend to that, but for some reason that was probably a mask of jealousy, and dressed up as psychic. I was going to say this, when she went on: 'They didn't see me. We've got to go to Lincoln's Inn and stay there till they come. He is feeding her now on the wrong things, especially to drink, inside. When they get there, I'll do what I can. But you must be there too, to mind the lot of us.'

"Then I said things: not what I had meant to say, but about the size of Lincoln's Inn and its partial privacy, and why Parmys knew that they were going there, and how we were to find them, and why she drank cocktails; and almost that I'd see her damned first. And her answers were: that it would be in Lincoln's Inn, because in Lincoln's Inn there was a map of the Coromandel Coast. Then, and here she began to entreat me, that Cynthia had a lawyer there, and would certainly have to see him about money directly she got back to town; and that it would be on the green lawn at the back of the hall, 'because that was one of the places, and one had to go through one to get to the other. We have been there together, Cynthia and I.' I cannot tell you with what irritated reluctance I followed her."

After this, I admit I was pleased that I had not married Parmys. Cynthia I hardly knew, but I suspected the high-strung female friendship and the cruel jealousy of Corandel, the amiable connoisseur. Cruel also to play Max up. No, she had not done that consciously. In some way he had failed her—what an over-spiritualised woman calls failing; and it may have been an inevitable reaction to drag him into a mystery he was not to share. But I was all on his side, if ironically.

"What was the anti-climax to this?" I said, confident that he would admit one, once it had been suggested to him.

"None," he said gravely; "but, impossible as it sounds, a real business. Brass tacks of a kind, and I wish I knew the nails. I had better go on telling you straight through.

"We got on to the Benchers' lawn at the back, through a little door Parmys said would be open, and it was. The air was wild and mist-softened, moisture everywhere, but without shine. Like a picture that might easily become another picture, and has to be very good to stay put at all. It was all so dull, a London pool, and not deep enough. Deep enough, God knows, I have found it. Parmys was looking at me with friendship, and that hardened me, until I saw her harden herself. Against me, I suppose, and she had need to, for I was beginning to be afraid. She smoked and we walked about, inside on the grass, always with her eyes—and mine—on the little door. The wind began to pitch about, shifting up from the west. I remember the grit of the gravel, the softness of the turf. I stamped and shivered. 'Patience, oh patience,' she said, 'patience with Cynthia, patience with me.' There seemed nothing to do but be patient, and then with a surprise that was like a sudden note or a sudden light, Cynthia came in with Corandel through the door by which we

had come in. They were walking fast, straight along the path by the
hall. They were going somewhere. Then, from being sick at Cynthia's
name, I was suddenly aware of her extreme distinction and beauty. A
kind of wonder, pity, and admiration. Also I saw that beside her, Parmys looked coarse; and again that that was because Parmys was like
an archaic goddess stored with raw power. Not my wife, not Cynthia's friend and *belle-femme*, but something that is in the foundation
of wise woman and child. Half-moons of black hair crossed Cynthia's
cheeks; she moved like a lost star. I heard Parmys say: 'Mind Corandel for us,' and I followed her as she walked back to meet them
as they came along the path. 'Minding' seemed to mean that I was
to get Corandel out of the way. I was rather knocked sideways. You
see, they had come. Parmys' calculation, I know it was calculation,
had been right. Also I wanted, for the first time, to know why they
had come.

"Parmys walked up to them, and said to him, as though she knew
the answer, 'What are you up to?' There were no greetings between
them. I saw Cynthia shy like a sensitive horse. 'I'm going on,' she
said, 'to the old house.' 'No, you're not,' said Parmys, 'you'll never go
there with him; and he can't take you round the other way.' Then to
Corandel: 'You go.' Now Corandel hardly paused, but came straight
over to me, and we walked away together. I was past embarrassment.
I *knew* the thing had not been prearranged. Apart from what I trust
in Parmys, it would not have happened like that. Now I wanted to
find out what had happened; and, so are we trained, to spare Corandel if possible. And I allowed the second instinct, which did not
matter, to spoil the first, which did. 'I think,' I said, 'that my wife and
her friend have not met for some weeks. Let's leave them while they
talk.' Then I added, 'Perhaps you will show me the map of the Coromandel Coast.' Just that, a kind of equivocal burning of the boats.
But it was a right thing to say, because without embarrassment, annoyance or surprise he said—sleek under his silk hat and umbrella—
'How strange women are. Who would have thought she would have
noticed that. Or the set of the houses.' 'Notice—you mean?' I said,
trying a tone of easy confederacy. 'The map,' he said, 'and, of course,
the houses too. But then, she's been down to Pharrs. I suppose she's
one of them. Which is your house?' Then he understood that I knew
nothing. We were mounting some steps, and it was as though he
were suddenly possessed—made automatic and afraid. For he turned

round and walked away fast in the direction he would have gone with Cynthia, at an oblique angle towards Chancery Lane and, I think, the Strand, without a word, the wind blowing up behind him. There were people about, but I could still pick him out. There was someone following him that I just did not see.

"Then I went back to find them. There was no one about, and they were on the edge of the lawn, a little apart from each other. There was a tear running down Cynthia's face, but as if it did not belong to her. Parmys was staring ahead into the empty, rising level of turf. Being full of curiosity, and now of love, I went up beside them. Parmys nodded to me, and went up to Cynthia. I saw her take her left wrist, putting her arm round her, holding in her right hand Cynthia's right hand. 'Look now,' she said, 'look again. It is here.' Her voice was like strings of gold and silver, love and something detached, or even matter of fact. A sort of jade dark cloud blew up, and it began to rain. They took a step forward; indeed, through all of this we were walking very slowly across the grass, into the wind, I beside them. But this is true also, that I couldn't stay beside them, because they were half in, half out of another world. Also, they changed. Before there had been Parmys resolute, and Cynthia distressed; now there were two shapes, abstractions of women. The cloud was right over us and the wind lulled. I saw Parmys press down on Cynthia's wrist, and Cynthia steady herself on Parmys' hands.

"After all this detail I'm trying to come to it. They were walking up to and along with a place that I could see in flashes. Up to and along with. They never seemed to me to be quite inside. What I got was the changed quality of the old London scene. How shall I describe it? Say that everything was enhanced to fantasy and to breaking-point. I was peering at it, when a large drop of rain fell, and I did see. They were beneath a fountain like a tower, on long terraces divided by strips of water clear as glass or driven like plumes into the air. Beyond that there was some kind of wooded country, coloured like spring. I heard Parmys say to Cynthia: 'Here it is again. But what happened to you, my dear, when he followed you to Pharrs?' Then the answer: 'I knew that I was hunted, there and back here again. I couldn't get into the cedar-house, let alone out here. There was always the white house and its copy at Pharrs. I was to go there with him, to where it is, away to the right behind us.' I remembered that was the way Corandel had gone, and heard Cynthia saying: 'But if he has gone there, he's inside it now; I told him too much, and what'll I do.' Then the tune of *What'll I Do* came into my head and annoyed me. I was seeing the place they were almost inside all the time, but not always clearly. Parmys must have caught the air too, because she went about afterwards humming it, but cheerfully. She answered Cynthia by showing love for her, not by speaking, but tightening her hold on her wrists.

"'After all,' I heard Cythia say, 'we have to go there some time.' 'Not yet,' Parmys said. 'It's the place, but it's bad and small. We're not ready yet to be able to get in, and take away what has been lost there, and watch the house fall. Corandel went there on his own business and much good may it do him. Look into our own place again.'

"I stared with them, and saw again the fountains and terraces, the unobtainable blue air. Not perfectly. At one time they were in a hall of dark red wood, and there may have been music. I knew too that we were wandering along over the common grass at the back of Lincoln's Inn, away from the hall. There was a bell noise, and then whatever was there was not to be seen any more. We three were standing alone, out there in the wet and the wind."

I wondered what on earth they had done then. The first question after a thing is over is often revealing. I asked Max. He said:

"They turned to me, discreet and sweetly smiling. Triumphant, I thought, and a little sad. I said nothing. In a minute we had got a taxi, and went home."

I asked him what happened then.

"Nothing. You see, I didn't ask, and if they wanted to tell me, they didn't. They were charming to me, but they were like children, enchanted, drenched with some abnormal radiance, and inclined to giggle at the same time."

I could not believe that he had not tried to find out more, but he explained:

"I was annoyed again. You see, I had helped them, and I thought I had earned their confidence, and to be given credit for what I had done. After all, I did not fail them, and I saw part of what they saw."

I asked him if he had behaved as if he had.

"No," he said. "No. That would have been going too far. I'd been scared, which was more than they had been. And it may have been hypnotism, and hypnotism may be anything. I was speechless too with trying to make up my mind. And they were simply enjoying themselves. Yes, and I was proud of Parmys too."

"And jealous?"

"Yes, that too. But not of Cynthia. But of the way their folly had been rewarded. Ignorance, credulity, dangerous practises turned into imagination and love."

I could never see why they shouldn't. The world seems annoyed that any sort of hand can win. And I was sorry for him, who seemed as if he could not be judicial, indifferent or all in. I asked him again what the end had been.

"At first they were delightful. I think they were a little shy. But they began to cheer up by the time they wanted their tea. When they'd had it one could feel something new coming along."

"What sort of thing?"

"An enormous lark. Physically they were so refreshed and lovely, they would have been bound to do something. Anyhow, they got livelier and livelier; out of their clothes and into them again, telephones, taxis, dancing somewhere; more mischief—"

"Did you go out with them?"

"No, I would not do that."

The Later Life of Theseus, King of Athens

From the *Memoirs of Menestheus, the Erechthid*

W E WERE ALL WITHOUT illusion that any good was to be expected from these affairs. From the first they appeared deplorable; now that the worst has happened, I can only repeat that it was expected, foreseen, foretold; and that, as so often occurs, now it is over, the situation is left much as it was before.

Now that the government in Athens has changed, as it was bound to change, it can be seen that the activities of the late king were no more than the wind ruffling the unstirred baths of ocean. Wherein exist those dumb and flexible powers who reigned before him, and have been shown to survive him. I mean that I, after these years of exile and observation, have come back into my place. Or, it would be more prudent and more cautious to say, that a place has come back and been filled by me.

Theseus has gone. He was not legitimate. Not one of those earth-sprung princes created to rule because, in some sense, he *is* this piece of earth. He had no business here in Athens at all, though he might have done well enough in Trozên. When he chose to come and lord it here, he should not have been surprised if, though the people applauded him, the air and the stones did not accept him; and that in time the people of this ancient situation were repersuaded, not by him, but by the stones and the air.

Theseus went. During his reign I watched his efforts. I and others, and knew that all we had to do was wait and watch the spending of his energy, and even admire its furious turns. It passed. When it was over, I returned and took my place. The land sighed, turned over, and now sleeps again.

But what a time we had! New laws, new drains, new wives. I remember as if it were yesterday the morning that Phædra arrived in her cretan ship. The daughter of Minos and of Pasiphæ, she seemed a staring, silly maid. A little subnormal, I thought, a freak of over-breeding. She was very quiet in the palace, though I was rather pleased at the shrine she built to a featureless, but peculiar, Aphrodite.

There is nothing I deplore more than the effort made by men like Theseus to abstract and beautify the Gods. At the same time to make them into men. I and my friends know that they are neither abstract, human, nor necessarily beautiful. So I welcomed the gesture of Theseus' wife; but, again, I may have idealised it. She was probably homesick for some uncertain cretan daimon, a furtive goddess-of-woman-indoors.

Well, the cretan neurosis soon found its expression. As is usual in these affairs, it was the talk of the place before the actors and sufferers were aware of their own passion.

What no one foresaw was the appeal to Poseidon. Nor the immediate response, in circumstances when a god such as Theseus conceived, might well have counted seven. In half an hour the matter would have been explained. Artemis should have seen to that. Personally, I wish Poseidon had let Hippolytos be, promise or no promise. Only I knew that the divine element must always work like that. It is an automatic quality, and the Gods, when they act, are so much stored power released. In the same manner, Artemis did not come until Hippolytos' extremity compelled her. A racing Goddess, but a woman!

But it is entirely inopportune to speculate on what ought to have happened. Theseus, our late showman, gave us an exhibition that will not soon be forgotten. It was not the first. It proved not to be the last.

In the first months of his widowhood, his energy in passing new laws is impossible to describe. It became difficult, before the feast of Anthesteria, to catch sprats: to draw water between sunset and midnight from the public fountains. And forbidden to invoke Poseidon on any account at all.

It became impossible to marry one's aunt; and there were regulations as to the destruction of fish-heads in hot weather, for which I think there is something to be said. At the same time, the war he made almost immediately on the Lapiths was plain evidence that his character was weakening.

We did not oppose it. There are worse things than a small war, fought in one's own place, so as not to interfere with the harvest. I was not curious about the Lapiths, but when a community is ruled by a man like Theseus, kept in a constant state of excitement, with nothing to do but neglect its business to talk, not even about his ideas, but about him, I considered that their arrival was reasonably well timed.

Personally, I believe he invited them, but I will describe, as I saw it, the result of the first and only battle in the campaign.

Indeed, it is well known how they met, Theseus and that old scoundrel Perithoös. How they craned over their chariots to observe each other and Theseus countermanded the charge; and how they walked out between the lines and examined one another until Theseus kissed him.

The city know how they came back, arm in arm, both sides straggling behind them; and the noise they made opening up the palace for the foreign army to get at the wine. It had always been more of an inn than a gentleman's residence. The little Queen Phædra tried to introduce cretan formality. Theseus had played at that, but not for long. There was no ceremony that night, when they roared their songs and rang their cups, and lit cressets, whose light danced in the wind on the marble and lit the palace right out to sea.

At dawn they went roaring down to the Piræus, and I thought of the wonderful luck of the man, to whom the next event was always kind. There is a kind of compensation for the man who uses life, who gets into trouble and into pleasure as a boat runs from tack to tack. He had better remember though that he is used, and not honourably, as the man who submits to life's using of him. I might have been a Theseus.

But there they were that night, Theseus and Perithoös, the heroes. He sent his Lapiths home, but he stayed; and they went riding together, went drinking, went talking, until the town began to say: "The end of this will be a new Queen."

It must be remembered that he was not a man to act upon design, and one who would as lightly have offended the Dioscuri as he would have taken Heracles into his own house, when that hero had gone mad and murdered his own children. The fool never knew that blood will do more than out; that blood will have blood. He has been praised for what he did then, for his friendship with a man so close to him in temperament that he could despise his madness and the pollution of his blood; keeping him with him till his wits came back, and telling him that the sole evil in his act was his terror of it.

I heard that said, and saw Heracles comforted at last. I smiled. I do not know what blood is, but it is not so easily got rid of. The earth wins at last. We shall go down to the house of Hades, and there will be no more of these swaggering Olympians, and the heroes they have so jovially begot. And I mean to be on the side that must win, if it means a lifetime of quiet.

Besides, I saw Perithoös chewing a twig of buckthorn last March; for a purge, I suppose, not uneasiness—before they began the scandalous entertainment we witnessed when they stole the immortal sister of the Dioscuri, Helen-of-the-Egg, the daughter of Leda and the Swan.

I do not doubt that people were right when they said that the suggestion came from Perithoös. He would have done anything for Theseus, who, I suppose, said something like this: "Those neurotic cretan sisters were both a mistake. One to hang herself, the other to go off with a god. Hippolyta was too much the other way. We were too alike; I was unfair to her, and I'm sorry for it now. I did not treat her as I would have been treated, and it is a shame to me. There are only Phædra's children left; I don't like the breed. I must have another choice of heirs; and a fine Greek, this time, Perithoös."

Then Perithoös suggested, without an idea but to get his friend what he wanted: "Why not a goddess this time, Theseus?"

I suppose they discussed it a little, but I am sure that after a hundred words they were asking: "Which one?" And when I consider their difficulties, I do not wholly reject their choice.

Every far-seeing and observant man has had his eye on the nursery of King Tyndareus. The girls were born to be queens in Hellas. Queens have come to no good lately in this city, but there was no harm in Theseus asking. Only, when he asked for her, he was refused on the count that she was a child.

The reason was not only sufficient, it was true. But Theseus and Perithoös left the city at once. A month later they came back arm in arm and told the town they had stolen her.

To marry her? No! For ransom? Not at all. But to live with his mother for three years till she should be old enough for marriage. Anyone could see that this would not do. What did he suppose her brothers would have to say about it? The Dioscuri are a notable pair of young men. Far better to have married her at once, child or no child; but that is the sort of things Theseus would not do.

I immediately retired to my country estate, where they would know where to find me.

Theseus made no excuses. I cannot suppose that he had any. He is reported to have said that the marriage would make for peace in Hellas, and one of the Fates would cut her throat when she heard about it; but that he could not touch a child. His position seemed contradictory. I suppose he was vain enough to want her conspicuous beauty. At his age, who had had Ariadne, Phædra, and Hippolyta! I waited with impatience for her brothers, hoping to hear a piece of the divine mind and watch a contest between an old hero and the young. I am not a hero. I and my house were before this fashion for lawgivers and deliverers and unfortunate husbands; and I shall be here when some funeral games, getting cheaper every year, are all that is left of them. I should not be surprised if it is we who will insist on some small decencies being preserved, and an offering of at least a minimum of honey and hair. All the same, since ceremonies round holy graves are a part of public life, why not have the body in the grave practically anonymous and the Sacred Snake? It is known what the Sacred Snake is there for. At the same time it is not known. Certainly I would have Theseus forgotten as Theseus.

I will not describe what happened. There was an attempt made to hide the girl. Theseus had brought her to his mother; but this was not generally known. I was looking for her myself, in a strange place, when I came upon the brothers, Castor and Polydeuces, doing the same thing. I offered them my reflections, nothing more. They were too innocent to use and too proud to influence. One is a king's son and the other the son of Zeus; but my position is less equivocal than theirs. Not that they recognized it, blown as they were with these new splendours; but they were boys enough to be glad of any company, and to explain why they were found among the cliffs at Scyros in a cave.

Their objections to the marriage were obscure and mostly untrue. They said that Theseus was too old; which did not matter. They said his former marriages had been unfortunate; which is immaterial. Then they implied that Theseus had foreknowledge, and was deliberately doing what was bound not to happen; which is impossible.

They showed no love for their sister, but an acceptance of her as though she were a part of nature. Not as men speak from pride of race.

They took her away, I was told, in silence. Afterwards Theseus and Perithoös were seen on the terrace, looking out to sea, for a long time, together and also silent.

I did not pretend to understand. The life of the girl Helen has been worth attention. I felt that she was of the same stuff as myself, put to the uses of those new heroes. The uses to which she had put them we are beginning to learn. They have forgotten that there were potencies here before Zeus. But this affair began with a jovial theft of a pretty child and some inconsistent behaviour. It ended with the return of the child, and it was plain to see that Theseus did not think that he had lost one scruple of his dignity.

Knowing that he was soon likely to attempt an even more conspicuous adventure, I had a time of indecision, when I questioned myself, not for the first time, as to what I had gained by the part in life that I had played.

Before the Argo's voyage and the hunt of the calydonian boar, life moved quietly in this land, arranged on certain antique forms. These I have upheld against the innovating heroes. There are dark spots in nature; let them stay dark. Men need not try to illuminate them. His business is to keep harmony by due propitiatory sacrifices to the infernal powers. I would offend no Sacred Snake. Omit no libation of honey, milk, or blood. Especially not blood. It is, when you think of it, the cheapest of the three.

That there are powers propitious to men I do not deny. That the unpropitious can be disregarded I hold to be the belief of an idiot child, or to deny that man is man's wolf. Hard, pliant, and astute he must be, observant of birds and the prohibitions of his folk.

That is what these men are not doing. In the place of nature they have put their own wills. The Minotaur died, but the cretan curse returned. I was sorry for Hippolytos, the son of a virago, our hero king made a martyr of.

What has the Golden Fleece done for us? Gold will go back the way it came. I have seen this in the sky.

·   ·   ·   ·

With three queens under the earth and one refused him, with heirs of kind to succeed him, the ruler of a people who cheered him and twittered at him, but who were really waiting for me; in the late middle years of his life, Theseus decided that he had not dared enough, and that the time had come for a yet more outrageous enterprise. He had lost the young Helen. Well and good! This time he would have a goddess.

It was said that Pallas Athene was his first choice. I wondered mildly what she would have thought of Phædra's small white palace after her olympian house. Of course I remembered that in earlier days her life had been simple, and she had exacted from us no more tendance than was customary when our lives were simple too. That was before these goddesses had gone up in the world, and all became daft on heroes.

Jealous, also, of each other. Artemis attended Hippolytos' death and swore to Aphrodite that she would kill Adonis for it. That, I suppose, is going on somewhere. But would they allow themselves to be stolen? Anyhow, Theseus changed his mind. He and Perithoös went away, side by side, in two small chariots, and no one knew where they were going. They did not return, and slowly the tale came round that two handsome men of middle age had been seen going down to the House of Death and Persephone. They went through the mountain. They came to the place. They crossed Acheron, Cocytos, Styx; I do not know how they managed Cerberos. To end it, they got inside.

They had come to steal Persephone.

They stole Persephone. I am telling you what happened. I do not know how they did it. Nor what they said to her. It is a long time since she lost her habit of reappearing among us in the spring. Also, there is something about the house of Hades that is agreeable to women. Most of the conspicuous ones there are men, but a woman sits on the throne of that house and distributes its poppies. It is all Persephone, and Eurydice who a man put back. Only, it seems certain that she was willing to go with them. Here on the earth one may guess what will happen, but there may be more chances in the house of Hades. It is a terror to me to admit it, but certainly, since those two went there, the place has also lost much of its prestige. I can no longer see it, half lit, smelling of dark flowers and blood. I wish I knew how they had persuaded her. Unless he was lying, and Theseus did not lie, she said she would come and live with him in his athenian house and be a queen to this city. What did they offer her? What did she ask? It happened quickly, I imagine, but she came away between them.

Then Cerberos caught them at the door, and all I heard was that Persephone herself was turned back, and Theseus' bottom stuck to a rock, and of Perithoös nothing was said.

It was then that opportunity found me, and I became king in Athens, and did something to restore old ways and discourage conversation. I was in the full interest of my negative experiments when they returned, first Perithoös, then Theseus.

They seemed to take more pleasure in my society than they had done, and were good enough to say that they found me unchanged. I could not say that of them. They were older. They were fatigued. There is one thing certain about these heroes, that they wear themselves into their graves. And they do not wear well. However, I thought it becoming to give up the kingship at once.

We were back where we had started, nearly a lifetime ago; and time was now our common enemy. If I had realized it then, I should have grieved to have given up that which I had waited for so long. But it had always seemed to me that Theseus was mortal, and I the immortal; for I come of the life that rises and flowers and passes down into the earth again. From uncountable ages my fathers were the earth-kings of this place, and for them the earth's luck held, and they were reborn in their sons forever. Only I have no son. In me, to the last in direct line, Athens has returned to her kings, seed of the Erecthidæ, sprung of the soil. So I conquered Theseus, the hero who did not understand these things.

I have striven to alter nothing.

It was not I who threw him over the cliff. We were walking one day and talking, and I noticed how he was ageing, though proud and angry like a king bull. The thought of bulls recalled my mind to Crete, and Crete to Minos; to a square throne, tight-waisted women, pinched Phædra, ropes, a grinning black Aprodite-at-home, the north wind that comes ruffling our sea, loud voices, men with gold hair.

Then, as I was thinking, his foot slipped, and he was over the edge; and if I trod on his hand as it clung, well I was king again, like a tree that reclothes itself, year out, year in.

Only, to quiet all tumult in the city, I established his young children by Phædra at Scyros, and have given him the mound, the games, the libations, and cut tresses for a hero, even the Sacred Snake.

But it was I that put them there. Things may be equal between us. I leave it at that, as I have left other things.

In Bloomsbury

IN ABOUT 1850 there were once two brothers. The elder brother disliked the world in which he found himself and went away to India where he did not stay long; to Cochin China where even less was heard of him; to South Africa where he finally disappeared. The younger brother stayed in London and became a solicitor of repute. He had a son. The son became a barrister, took silk, and married a daughter of a famous man at the British Museum, who left her his magnificent collection of jade. They were a good and useful and delightful family, and lived in three houses between them, two in Bloomsbury and one in Hampstead, until the fathers died, and one house, in Bloomsbury, was enough. There were seven children in the third generation. The War accounted for the two eldest, leaving four boys and a girl almost grown up.

When something is known of two generations, the third is worth watching. Families like this are of the stuff of England, of the stuff of any distinct civilisation. They have moderate direct and great indirect power. They come naturally to high positions of trust, and their exceeding security often makes them generous and kind, even to their children. Having lost two sons they were quite determined that those who remained should enjoy themselves. In the best kind of way. And so they did.

There are no people who know less about the War or what life was like before it than the people who were just too young to play any part in it. And with their fathers and mothers it is a point of honour not to speak of it, not to try to explain. Nor did their children encourage them, but politely ignored the occurrence. Of this family, whose name was Curtin, the eldest was at the Museum; one wrote; one took it out in elaborate dissipation; the girl, Clarissa, painted; one had a fashionable taste in sex. All had received an admirable education, talked the current psychology, dressed in the admired disorder of their world; had a true and just, if rather *faisandé*, understanding of the arts. Each of them moved, without knowing it, in as rigid a convention as any other. Each of them cultivated an over life-size ego. No one had ever seen them enjoying themselves. None of them were in the least grateful for their blessings. None of them were fools. Not very long ago it was time for something to happen to them. In reality they had all been marking time, are still marking time, until something shall happen in the world; something sufficiently vital—that is to say, strange and oblique—to catch their whole attention, exercise them, use them. For when a pinch of credulity would have served them, they were taken in by nothing. Not sex or by the arts even. Secretly each one was ambitious, with nothing, that they acknowledged, to be ambitious about. Five steel blades used to cut butter—the best butter, the worst, any butter. In the low voices they took care should not sound harmonious they insisted on quality. It was their keynote. Quality in learning or lust or priggishness or the refinements of pride. In this they were infinitely correct. In their early thirties, though exasperating, they were sufferable.

While at that time, over the flank of a planet, the twin branch of that family had been growing, working, reproducing, dying, re-stating itself. The son of the grand-uncle had left three sons by two mothers, three men, their cousins, whom they had never seen, of whom they knew nothing, though two had served in the War in the East, and had come back to South Africa to find the youngest, their half-brother, a man.

It was by chance that I met them in Paris, the two elder come to Europe for the first time, on their way to England in search of the relations they had heard of and had equally never seen. They were in a café in the heart of Paris, set back opposite a bridge, outside which, in a wide space, the traffic flew, parting at the bridge-head to meet five other streams. In the open space their arcs swung and intersected freely, so that their flights were never interrupted, and sitting outside on the terrace one had the illusion of flying also.

I saw them lope in like powerful animals, a glint in their eyes, not a light. Not tranquil or steadfast, but aware. Wary, I thought, and what were they, with their tanned faces and great bones, their clothes new but practical, as if, once in the green woods outside Paris, there was a desert with wild beasts? For that was the landscape they carried with them, as each person carries his landscape; and at any moment they might step off into their own business. War and hunting business, without doubt. "Guerilla," "gorilla" said the subconscious in its helpful way. Then I knew I should meet them. Very soon after I did, for they sat next to me and my brother, and could not make the café understand what they wanted, and intended that their wants should be understood. We translated. They wanted cold chicken and whisky, and when the leg bones cracked under their knives it sounded like teeth. Then we talked. I was not sorry. One has one's Kipling side. "South Africa," the subconscious completed. They did not talk about it, or much about themselves—not as we talk about ourselves; and I do not know how it was done, not by words, the picture of them completed itself, image by image, as we sat. Picture, it was a cinema, an *actualité*, infinitely prosaic; and not until I had listened for some time with the minimum of polite interrogation and response, did I notice that it was creepy. Wary beasts were padding about in the moonlight, identifying themselves with shadows and sand. To them the gracious amenities of Paris were no more than traps. I spoke in praise of it. They did not believe me. My brother was not amused.

But they were very helpless, and we were English. They asked shrewd questions, and gave up our directions in despair.

"Are you going to England?" I said, implying that they'd better. There was the shortest possible hesitation. Then they said that they might, that they supposed they should, that they had heard that they had relations there. In London, by name of Curtin, legal folk once. I saw a father and a mother, infinitely courteous and intelligent and formed. Five offspring, more intelligent, run into more extravagant moulds and hardly courteous at all. A critical extravaganza of five. I said boldly: "I know them." The two men backed like wild animals when a flare is thrust in front of their eyes. For an instant. Then they circled round. "Was that so?" I repeated it. "Well, we might meet there." And then (they were not used to the light), did I know their address? I gave it because I could not think of a reason not to give it. Then we said goodnight. From the step of our taxi I looked back, and saw them in conversation under an arc lamp.

The next day I ran into Julian Curtin on the Boulevard Saint Germain, and as we walked along the gay antique street I told him. "How *most* eccentric," he said; "they might be great-uncle Francis' progeny."

I remembered where they were staying; and the next thing I saw was Julian and his sister Clarissa sitting outside the Deux Magots with the two men I had been calling the Wolves.

. . . . .

The next scene took place on the steps of the British Museum. I had been staring at the Easter Island enigma, turned away from it to look down the calm terrace, and saw the men from South Africa walking up the gravel drive from the gates. In the same belted raincoats and crêpe-soled shoes and bashed hats; on the same stride that might side-step at any moment. In they went. To see what, I wondered. Culture to face their new relations? The night we had met I had seen that they were not nice people, but they had power. Not pleasant power. How was the power working? It was a raw, delicate thing, easily got out of gear. Had it been used yet for anything more than immediate ends? Did they know they had it? Had they? Or was I doped with talk about Empire builders?

Pigeons clattered down. In the mild gold air an antique charm was captured by that terrace and its courtyard and stabilized there. Chord of a classic circle dropped in London, a memory of that preoccupation of our race. Inside were the mysterious treasures of the world, separate, almost sterilized, but *there*. And all the books which have ever been written. What had they gone in to look at? They had entered like pirates who dare not swagger, who would loot if they could. Loot was their property and they'd collect it. Up-country? In war? Heartened by the thought of a smash-and-grab raid in the British Museum, I followed them inside.

They had not gone far. Down the narrow lit shaft of the Assyrian Room I saw them, looking at the lions arrow-pierced and stabbed. Their eyes were on the glance backwards. For what might be coming up behind? An animal or a man? One drew the attention of the other to points about lions. Neither was greatly interested. (Were the stone panels of the Assyrian Room a wall without ears?) There was nothing for the Museum authorities to fear. I left them and went to see if Julian and Clarissa Curtin were at their flat.

There I explained without pretence that I wanted to know what their cousins were really like.

"*Too* extraordinary." "*Most* peculiar," said the sister and the brother. "Clinton agrees with them best." Clinton was the one who took it out in stylised excess.

"But how d'you know they are your cousins?" I looked at the pale olive faces, the brown crystal eyes and cropped black heads. Clarissa answered: "Father is quite convinced. Says that he has known *all* along about his great-uncle. He got out a series of daguerreotypes, and is quite positive. Altogether fascinating and obscenely like—"

"You say there's a third brother. Why didn't they all three come?" I wanted to know that.

Julian said: "That's the marvellous bit, and such a pity. The youngest was *quite* legitimate and *half* Bantu. And he's *just* dead."

"Careless of him to die now."

"The way they told us about it was charming," said Clarissa. "I don't think they would have told us if Father hadn't been so certain that there had been a second marriage, and that they were three. Then Clinton said to them: 'I suppose he was a native. Your father must have done *something* with his opportunities.' They gave a sort of snarl and glanced at each other. One could see Lewis telling Peter—that's their names—with his eyes to make the best of it. I suppose they thought we knew more than we did. But they actually showed us their stepmother's marriage-lines. Clinton said: 'What's that for?' And they said: 'It's genuine, I tell you.' And Julian said: 'Don't you think he'd have *better* been a bastard?' 'Maybe,' they said, 'but he wasn't.'"

The brother and sister said nothing more for a moment, and I knew that silence had fallen in Mrs. Curtin's long drawing-room also, where the jade was, and the Veronese, and the *petit point* chairs. I tried again: "How d'you get on with them?"

Julian answered: "*Each* member of *our* family seems to have a *different* point of view—"

That surprised me, for they usually formed a league, a tacit league, for offence and defense.

"Father and Mother" (they were usually Gillian and George to their children, so I judged the situation had reached full tribal significance) "seem quite disturbed. We had always assumed they must have known about some previous skeleton. But no. Mother went so far as to say that she was so sorry for the little nigger-boy who could not come. So were we all. *Most* intriguing. Father spends almost *all* his time with the jade and a *new* burglar alarm. Lewis has actually been in Asia with some *mongol* tribes whose business it is to find it and sell it to the Chinese to be carved."

Genghis Khan's men: out of Karakorum in High Asia: the Golden

Horde. Jade hunters in Kurdistan: to Bloomsbury: to gentlefolk in an eighteenth-century house. How long a trail? Men to find, and men to love and make, and men to keep and love. The becoming, the *durée* of a work of art. Jade lasts: jade you cannot destroy or make or unmake. Jade is secure. Jade is loot.

Clarissa went on: "I found I couldn't possibly have an affair with one or both of them, as was suggested. When I'd seen them, I felt quite positive about civilisation—"

Good for Clarissa. Women invent good reasons for their sense.

"Fabian does not seem able to make up his mind which he likes best. He complains that once you know them well they're practically interchangeable. John says that he is quite afraid of them, and that he'll explain it all in a book he is writing—" (After the delicate classicism of Julian, Fabian, Clarissa, why had the Curtins run short on names and called their youngest John?) I was harassed that day with irrelevant speculations.

"Clinton takes them out on the most protracted parties. Down to the docks. He finds the places and they find the way back."

"Then you, Julian?" I said.

"I find that I spend as *much* of my time at the Museum as possible, and there I spend it trying to *make* up my mind. *Most* disturbing."

It was. I said: "Are they here for good?"

"They're not going to back to *South* Africa. When they've spent their money, they seem to be thinking of *South* America. They staying in a *temperance* hotel, but we see them every day."

"They may be coming now," I said, and told them about the Museum and the lions. There was a light ring at the door. They came in, and were exceedingly restless and heavy in hand. Yet I saw them impose their weight, the weight of kinsfolk who, without help from God or man, have kept on their feet; whose hands have kept their heads; who are hardy, unencumbered, and, within their sequence, adaptable. Figures of stone and running water and wind-drawn trees. Of the forces, strong, subtle, delicate, and pure, which had shaped their english cousins, they had no conception. They were not awed by such things, or envious, or even interested; but were they trying to impose or trade, except through necessity or native awkwardness, upon them? What did they want? I could not make it out. Not even money, it seemed. A good time? Yes, but not permanent adoption. They would be off again. Why were they standing about like visiting mountains in a delicate landscape, mountains that were even careful where they put their feet? "Horrible people!" The words nearly came out on a sigh. They'd strip the Curtins bare if they could, go off with the pictures and the jade in sacks, mixed with their skulls and their chopped-off arms and feet. Only for reasons and for one reason they could not. If they were not always on their guard, their movements would be beautiful, like animals are beautiful. Then, on a look from Clarissa, I saw Julian come to a decision. "Father wants us all to come down to Ashways before the weather gets too bad. We usually all go down there for a month at *this* time of year. Won't you come too?" A bold move to concentrate the situation in a country house. After their usual, just perceptible swerve at a proposal, they accepted.

. . . .

Three weeks passed. It was late, and again a bell, this time a telephone bell, rang gently. I heard the accurate italicised voice of Julian asking me if I, too, would come down to Ashways for the week-end. As I said I would (I had never been there before), I added distinctly: "But I'm no good with them," and gathered that it didn't matter, and understood that strange things must have happened before that family made to a rather barbarous person like myself the suggestion of an appeal for help. And I wondered why the powers who arrange things had picked me out to sort that family, and resented it, and was amused and rather afraid.

. . . .

Harvest at Ashways, radiant, serene. We picked hanging apples and bit on hot peel and sweet ice within. Seven people, parents and their children, secure, intelligent, assured, against two wolves. Before I came there had been situations, a series of them, but no quarrels. They do not quarrel in that set. Not among themselves. Outsiders are pursued in fantastic vendettas. Outsiders stand no chance. I had just begun to decide that the brothers had some claim on the whole family estate and were waiting their chance to spring the news, when Clarissa came into my room, and went, as was her reasonable habit, straight to the point.

"It seems to me," she said, "that like any other primitive persons they might be more understandable if we knew their tabus. So we each decided to keep notes on anything we observed and report."

They would and they had, and they'd find out a lot. "Well?" I said.

"The obvious ones first. Lavatories. The usual reserve of people who generally don't have them, and are only too thankful to use them when they get the chance. No particular inhibitions. Sex. It seems more what they expected us to have than what they've got themselves. Fabian and Clinton both say that they're never so drunk with the people they pick up on their nocturnal expeditions that they can't tell whether the police are likely to arrive or not. Which does not seem to indicate a repression. On the other hand, they don't seem able to put up with people of colour."

"That's the half-brother," I said.

"Do you really think so? Then that does seem to be definite."

We did not get any further because there was to be a lunch-party. The Chief Constable was coming, and in the library I heard John Curtin telling them what a Chief Constable was.

"But don't you ever read crime books? You really should. When anyone is murdered in a *country* house, it is always the *Chief* Constable who arrives and makes up his mind *who* has done it. Either that or else the Inspector from *Scotland* Yard finds out he has done it *him*self."

"Be accurate," said Clarissa. "Don't mislead them. It's almost always a guest in the house."

I watched them say nothing, noticed that there was something, a fatigue perhaps, in their silence. Later I had an idea, and was able to say to all five cousins before dinner: "I've spotted a tabu. It's police."

"*Most*," said Julian, and before he could add "peculiar" was silent. We all were. Until I caught myself babbling:

"Of course, they've always lived up-country, in places where there aren't any, and it may be just the idea. Or perhaps they got across the military police in the War." As an idea it lacked vitality. Suggestions like that mean nothing to the Curtins, but it passed without comment. I felt that something more was expected of me.

"It seems to me," I said, "that it's time someone forced their hands. Curiosity like ours has no business to be wasted." The Curtins did not like this. Perfectly courageous within their sphere of courage, they did not admit people whose hands have to be forced. Then we all turned round. They came in, and I saw the two men, rather splendid in their black and white, formalized as they could not be in their easy clothes. I said:

"If they were several centuries back in time, poetry could be written about them."

Clarissa nodded: "Edom o' Gordon and his men." She had a pretty step and a delicate perception of her own. Her training had made what was natural, choice. She looked up coolly at her cousins, one stared at her for a moment, then both looked away. Oh the fine brutes among the small, dark, lean creatures! While she had nothing to fear, who should have had everything to fear—in Edom o' Gordon's time. Was she woman enough to lead them a dance? The youngest would be led. Was she up to it? It seemed as if we were the hunters now. Was that the truth of it? Had we been all along their hunters who were their natural prey? Were the Curtins up to it? I was, if I had to make them.

As the Chief Constable's lunch had passed without incident, the evening went soberly enough.

In the library after dinner, Clarissa played Corelli on the harpsichord. Her mother embroidered, her father listened. Of the rest of us, one played a crossword puzzle, two chess. One talked to me. The cousins sat together, pulling at their pipes. I noticed that they reduced people to domestic life or tribal occupations. In that house conversation was the exercise and the sport, and the brothers were bad for one's conversation—so non-committal that one never could be certain if they were stupid. Non-committal and pent-up, and by that time we were become the last. It was then that Mrs. Curtin said: "Did anyone ring up?"

"Only the Constable," said Mr. Curin. "He says he wants to see me again tonight. I can't think why. It's most unusual."

John looked up from his puzzle: "Could EGPA, by any exercise of imaginative phonetics, be the name of a central african tribe?" He asked this of his cousins.

"Can't think of one," they answered, hastily for them.

"What a pity," said Clinton, "that your brother isn't here. He might have known. And we really do regret him. Where is he buried? We were wondering if you'd like a really *good* fetish to put on his grave."

"I guess he's all right." Then, after another silence, "What does your Chief Constable fellow want?"

"He wouldn't say. I gathered that it was to ask me something. Has anyone heard lately of any petty crime?"

"What a bore," said Fabian, "the police are."

Clarissa played on, delicately, deliberately, accompanying her brother.

John said: "You know you never really told us much about him, and he was, after all, as much our cousin as you. And the *natural* result has been that we want to know *all* about him. *How* he died and what you thought of his mother. I suppose she is *dead* too. And *what* you thought about him, and what the neighbours said, and how you got on with your *nice* bantu relations; and whether he was like them *or* your father—And whether"—the requests were becoming a chorus— "he wanted to be *like* a white man or a black man. You needn't think it will make *any* difference to us."

"And I must go and see about the Chief Constable's room," said Mrs. Curtin, "in case he wants to stay the night." Perhaps she was a little sorry for them, but equally intended to give her family a free hand.

It went on: "Was he married?" "And which kind?" "Or *half* and half?" Having made our modest inquiries, we turned round in a half-circle, ten eyes interrogating four.

Again they backed and blinked, and I saw what I had always suspected, and knew that I had been blind not to have known, their ferocity of hate and fear.

"He was a pretty poor lot," the elder said.

"What particular kind?" came the chorus, getting into full cry —"reversion to the bush or to victorian England?"

"Not the sort," said the younger this time, "that a white man wants for a brother. It's as well he's dead. We couldn't have brought him to you people over here."

"But why not? Why didn't you bring him?"

"I tell you he's dead." (Unconsciously they had insisted that he was alive.) "You can't bring over dead men—"

Then Julian said soberly and gaily: "Then you must do your best and give him a kind of vicarious *after*-life. These fascinating hints are *not* enough."

"Are you sure," I said, "that he is dead?"

Clarissa stopped playing and turned round on the harpsichord seat.

"Are you *quite* sure," said Julian, "that you didn't *murder* him yourselves when he was tiresome? It might happen *so* easily. One is so *apt* to be prejudiced—"

There was the noise of a car outside, steps and voices. Mr. Curtin went out. "I'll see him in my study," he said.

Seized by my idea that they had lied about their brother's death, my impression had been blurred for a moment. I looked again. Julian, pitiless, was pleased. So were they all.

"I thought from the beginning," said Clarissa, "that it was that. You've murdered him. Now didn't you?"

Above the slight rustle of excitement and lightly moved chairs, I heard a sound like a low howl escaping and immediately lost on the air.

The elder was snarling: "What d'you mean by saying such things?" They had half risen. It was too tense to be true.

Julian went on: "But that is what we have been thinking. *All* the time. Do tell us *how* you did it—"

Mr. Curtin and the Chief Constable came back. "Another of these extraordinary cases of cattle-maiming. Colonel Thornleigh wants to borrow some people to watch the farm tonight. I wonder if you have had any experience."

Two falling bodies under whom an angel's hand has been slipped. I heard the proposal—heard, understood, accepted, complied with all in one movement, and the two brothers were out with the Constable's men in the night.

Five Curtins beamed on one another until I said: "If that's that, it explains why they're shy of the police."

"Were they?" I was asked, and again saw the suggestion miss fire.

"They'd be *sure* to understand about cattle-maiming, that's why they went off," the Curtins explained.

I persisted: "Yes, and weren't they thankful that he'd come about that?"

"I'm quite positive," said Clarissa, "that he's not dead at all. The only thing to do is go on till we get them to admit it, and send for him to come over here."

.　　.　　.　　.　　.

It was just before dawn, dim, spiritless, not yet lit, as though night's pure dark had given out, never to be replaced, and I was aware of Clarissa and Fabian at the foot of my bed. I was to come downstairs. In the library a fire had been kept up for the cattle-watchers, and there were thermos flasks and food. The brothers had gone up to bed. All the Curtins were down. The police left.

"*Where* are they?" I said, falling into the family italics. Did *they* maim the cattle?"

But Julian broke out shrilly, a cry in his voice: "It appears it was true—that there is something in—in the *preposterous* pleasantry that they killed him. We were told to move quietly and separately along the edge of the wood, past the farm. I came up and they were *behind* a tree, and I heard one of them say, "We needn't have done it." And *complain* of the fright Thornleigh had given them. And ask if we re-

ally believed it; and if we were safe; and if they thought we should try to blackmail them. Then they laughed. I nearly came round the tree and said I should speak to the Chief Constable *at* once. Then I realised what they were and what they might do, and I had to go on *watching* the cows till we *came* back and they went to bed—"

"Essential daylight, colourless and clean" filled the room. The fire sulked. The hour was unpropitious for the turn of the event. Besides, what were we to do? Julian went on: "I made an *under*-statement. They spoke of their victims in the plural; referred to "them." The woman, I suppose, their stepmother." Situations which sink in. All their little peculiarities which had hitherto delighted us, reseen in this light. Revision at dawn. Of murder; of blood on black ivory skins. Polished boxwood and scarlet; two bodies who would stay dead. Two men upstairs, sleeping, who had made corpses of their own flesh, a brown stain out of bright blood. *After such knowledge, what forgiveness?*

"Futile beasts," I said.

"That won't punish them," said Clarissa, "—they're not clever enough."

At the same time, everything now was in its place, everything they had said and not said, everything they had done and not done. The worst in coming to the worst had made order, proportion, light. We knew now how ignorance and cruelty had bred fear, and fear murder, and murder more fear, so that the desire to further which they had killed twice had never since run free. Prisoners? What need to make them prisoners who had walked into their own trap?

Curiously enough, this was not the line the Curtins were taking. The debate, getting actually shrill, was whether or not to wake the Chief Constable up at once, or wait till he had had breakfast. Their reactions were as much on time as those of the wretched brutes upstairs. Who were, after all, upstairs? Who were asleep—or talking? What would they be saying to one another? After all, were we quite sure? I asked that; held up Julian Curtin's disgust and alarm with what seemed to me to be a reasonable question. Repeated it, while five sets of mixed statements reiterated their point of view.

A blank, absurd hour for such an awakening. Reluctantly they went back to bed. I went back to bed and had only just fallen again into the exquisite sleep that follows shock, when I was called to face the real day. Breakfast came and went; the Curtins came and went; and it felt as though in every room in the house there was a pair of them, each proposing to do the same thing in a different way. Colonel Thornleigh left unenlightened. Mrs. Curtin had not come down. Only Mr. Curtin and I sat at our meal, asking each other no questions.

It was then that the two cousins came down, and in their walk and voice there was a new unrestraint, in the way they ate and used their hands. Something assured, raw and lewd, a relief and a new assurance that would bawl at us, now they thought they had found out that what they had done would serve their turn. Not as they had meant it to do, but enough. In fact they had been sharp enough to see how their supposed crime had enhanced them. "Meet our cousins, the murderers," as they thought the Curtins would say, and to profit by it, not adroitly, but with a sufficiently ugly swagger. That it was all an utter miscalculation did not spoil it as a spectacle, as they snapped down a sausage at a bite; and when they stood up, stared insolently, feet apart, pitching their huge bodies from their hips. It was their hour of satisfaction. Like all hardy and adaptable men, they cared little for the nature of the event, so long as it could be made serviceable. In this case, a crime had been proved to have been unnecessary, and now it seemed that instead of losing by its discovery they had profited by it. They were in no danger from these cousins: they feared them, these cousins. The poor little fish. It had worked out all right, the murder they needn't have done. It had *worked*.

Behind shut doors the Curtins were fluttering. A thousand delicacies of intellectual perception and interesting angles of approach to life coming together like puzzle-pieces—to make a quite different picture. Not a picture anything like the Curtins' picture, the gallery of significant forms they hung in their front windows. Called into their council, I thought they looked smaller, and more alert; the blood-rhythm of one generation of a family almost audible.

Julian was repeating: "I heard it *last* night, *standing* behind *a* tree. They actually murdered him—and his mother."

"Hardy sons of the great open spaces," said I. "What are you going to do about it? Their half-brother and their stepmother and probably several others—"

"Do?" Five voices intoned the word— "Do? Go to the police *at* once."

"Absurd as it may seem," said Julian, "we are accessories *after* the fact."

"This isn't a detective book," I said unkindly—"the Chief Constable's gone."

"I am going over," said Julian, "*on* my bicycle—*at* once."

Leaving two women, a father and a mother, who, presumably, did not know what had happened, to the care of three young men who had two murderers to deal with, who might try it again.

"It's absolutely necessary," said Clinton. "Not a moment's delay."

Fabian squealed: "Thornleigh will cable to the Cape police at once. They must be quite upset looking for them, and that's why they left."

"To come over here and hide with us," said John venomously.

I am not sure whether Clarissa intended to catch my eye. I asked: "Who's going to break it to them? They're bucking about in the dining-room, entirely convinced they're masters of the situation."

Fabian said quite simply, "Why?"

I explained.

"It's quite impossible," they all said. Then Clarissa:

"The best thing to do would be to ask them in here and tell them what we know, and tell them to go away. In which case, I think, they should have a start of the police. You know, they may only have been bragging—"

"In the *middle* of the night; *behind* a tree," said Julian. I remembered that it was not my family.

"You always had a way with them," said Clarissa unkindly. "Will you go and fetch them? This must be settled."

I have not forgotten how difficult it was to make my mouth smile, nor what it feels like to walk off somewhere on an errand of that sort. I put my head round the dining-room door and said: "Come into the library, you two, for a moment."

"What about?" said the eldest lazily, yawning in my face, a beast's stretch to his jaw.

"Plans for tonight about the cattle."

Damn them! They were murderers, and they might murder me. They shouldn't find the whiphand so easy. It *was* fair.

I went back and heard them following me, strides that could overtake me down the dark corridor, quiet to the feet. One stride would catch me up; one spring bear me down. I put away imagination as I opened the library door and faced the Curtins. Turned into a comedy that was rather over-strident, a little over-seasoned with false excuses, the true truth of the situation was on us.

How could the Curtins handle it? It had not occurred to one of them to run away. Excess of imagination or defect?

All irritable alarm, Julian was on his feet, saying: "Now I know. I heard you last night, behind a tree, actually admitting that our preposterous supposition *was* true. That you are *both* murderers. *More* than once. And we asked you *in* here to *tell* you to *go* away–immediately. After twenty-four hours we shall go to the *po*lice. If you refuse to go, we shall do it *at* once. The twenty-four hours are to give you time to leave the country. It's most astonishing that the police in *South* Africa have not been here *al*ready."

I felt embarrassed for them. Painfully and unnecessarily. I did not want to see what they looked like.

"What in hell d'you mean?" the eldest said.

"What I have *just* been telling you. I am speaking for us all. It is *not* possible for Clarissa to see *any* more of you. While, until the police know, we are in the *po*sition of accomplices *after* the fact. Most unusual. *Quite* impossible—"

I do not know why the youngest of the wolves looked at me. Then I said: "You'd better get out. They mean it."

"You are murderers," said Clarissa severely. "The only thing for you to do is to go away at once."

"Parasites on us, and a disgusting prey on society; d'you want to leave here in handcuffs or your car?" Fabian fluted at them —"and don't try to kill any of us. You won't get away with that."

"That means you go when the going's good," I interpreted.

Now I was able to watch their faces. Insolence at first augmenting their surprise; then immediate watchfulness; and then, as the seconds passed, a veil over the watch, a fade-out of all contact between us and them. They got up, narrowed eyes half closed, their shoulders loose, feet that backed nearer and nearer towards the door. Mouths that said: "Fine way to treat your own kith and kin," and "lousy bastards," and more curious endearments, but on the whole a brutal collapse, a poor savage show, and a complete ability to disappear. Something to laugh at, nothing to cry about, and only to be feared in a lonely place.

"You've got twenty-four hours," Clarissa cried after them. We waited. By general agreement the library door was locked. A quarter of an hour passed. The front door was invisible from the windows, but it was then we heard the particular shriek and bang of their fast, dilapidated car.

"Contact with the criminal classes," said Julian. "Disgusting. *Most* peculiar."

❖ ❖

Friendship's Garland

THERE ARE DAYS when the worst happens so completely that the whole consciousness is dyed to the particular colour of the abomination, when escape is impossible, and one plays rabbit to the world's weasel with just a little bravado, no courage, and no sense of style.

We were caught that day in Zoe's bedroom full of flowers, arranging our hair. We had forgotten that we were the hunted and innocent. They had been after us for a long time. We knew that they were after us; but we were younger, quicker, and more impudent; only too young. We could not believe that, in the end, they would not come and eat out of our hand. Perhaps they will, but only by exhaustion, not by persuasion, and that will not be good enough.

Among other things, they wanted to take away our lovers, not because they wanted them themselves, but because they could not love themselves, and naturally disliked it that we could; and there was money in it, and fear of us. At least, we liked to think there was fear. But chiefly it was virtuosity in the creation of pain, and that we did not understand. "What do they do it for?" said Zoe. "Never mind. I know they've got their knife into us. The great thing to do is to keep them in a good temper, and never trust them at all." You see, we could not get rid of them; they had seen to that.

Then we began to laugh, and make little traps to annoy the blind animals who were following us. Keen noses and no eyes. Intelligences without imagination. Zoe arranged a little bribe of flowers. I could see them smell it—and soon it would be out on the dustbin. They were not people who burn their dead flowers. "It will look pretty and civil. It will keep them quiet a little," she said; "but they don't know how strong I am when I mean to get my own way."

Indeed, I hoped they would find her strong. She was a better fighter than I, but she could not make herself invisible. That is my long suit.

In Zoe's room we could see trees waving over a wall. The summer wind was moving them, and below us there would be tea, and great, silent cars moving so pleasantly in the street. The white staircase of the house was like the easy stairs you fall down in dreams.

The telephone rang by Zoe's bed. I heard a man's voice speaking from any distance, from no distance, from a place outside the world. He spoke a great deal. I heard Zoe say: "Yes, Carlo, of course we'll come," but his voice went on, and I was reading a book when she said to me:

"They want us to meet them, and I said we would. Who says we're afraid?"

"Where?" said I.

"At the Craven. Where Carlo can pretend that he's a man of the world." That made us laugh. We ran about Zoe's room, taking alternate turns at the mirror, and calling "Carlo" and "Craven" to one another till the door opened and his sister ran in. We could not think how she had got there. It was like an annunciation or a burglary. I felt she would be followed by the servants she had run past. She wanted to do her hair and show us her hat. It was a tight, evil hat of scarlet leather. I re-set my sombrero, and Zoe got into the car. Carlo was repeating, "The Craven. We'd better go to the Craven. I've got some news for you, Zoe." I lay back and watched the streets slip past.

We stood about the steps while Carlo fidgeted with the car and tried to make the commissionaire recognize him. He tipped him a wink, he was haughty, he confided in him, he gave him half a crown. He was attended to with the others, but still Carlo hung on, and would not be done with it. His sister was impatient: "Oh, Carlo," she said, "let's go in and leave him to it." Willing enough we were to leave him to it, and wasted no embarrassment on her.

Through the noise and the iron streets, even through the racing wind the sun poured, roaring its heat through the wind at the huge buildings and the crowd. Those are the hours when the city pays for being a city, and is delivered over to the wind and the sun and their jackal the dust. All the earth pays, but principally the city. On the other hand, inside the Craven there is no nature at all. These things are not natural, marble like cheese, red velvet, and plaster gilt.

We sat down. Carlo was a long time seeing about his car, and when

he came he was petulant because we had not waited for him, and had
ordered tea. Only for a moment. He never thought of anything for
more than a moment. He was quite safe to forget. Only he always
remembered again, and a little differently, so that he could always escape on a misunderstanding, and pick up the line again and again and
again. He bounded across to us, and flung himself into a cane chair,
petulant, pretty, and artful, and his sister deprecated him while they
were both hunting. I knew. It was Zoe they were after today, and they
had not expected to find me at her house. I could lean back and watch
and eat éclairs. They were too sweet, and I got sticky. Then I could
smoke in the rich, stale quiet whose murmur was like the tuning-up of
birds that never would begin to sing.

Zoe wore a pearl, hung from a piece of jade, on a chain spaced with
small pearls. Cosmo had given it to her. Carlo saw it: "I say, Zoe, d'you
know you're wearing Celia's pearl?" Celia had been Cosmo's first wife,
and we had hoped she was now reincarnating as something reasonably
intelligent and plain.

Zoe answered in her small, distinct voice:

"Yes, his father brought it back when they looted the Summer
Palace."

The brother glanced at the sister, who looked as though she could
eat it, and Carlo said: "I only mean—you don't mind my saying this,
Zoe?—that I don't think Cosmo thinks it's worth much. I was going
through some papers from him the other day, and he hasn't insured it.
Of course, it suits you." His sister laughed, and lifted it off Zoe's breast
with her pink paws whose dimples felt like rubber. She said:

"I expect he's left it to his daughter. Anyhow, I'm afraid she'll think
it ought to be hers. I don't envy you, Zoe, once you're married, with
that young lady."

"She shall have it as soon as she's old enough to wear it," said Zoe.

"You are quite right. But you know in seven years—she'll be eighteen then—will you want to give it to her? We always mean to behave
well. But jewels are jewels, and flappers are flappers. It becomes you
perfectly."

Zoe lifted her small, apricot-brown head. "In seven years we shall be
so rich that I shall have all the jewels I want."

I sorted this. First of all, the thing wasn't real, and later there was
going to be a row about an artificial gem. Of course those two, I added to comfort myself, hadn't the wit to choose or the money to buy

an ornament like that. It had been left to Cosmo's daughter, who was preparing—who was being prepared—to hate Zoe, who was to be her stepmother. Wasn't it real? It looked real. I wanted to lick the pearl to try it—I did not like to do it then and there.

Carlo's sister said: "I don't know if you've thought of it yet, my dear, but I should send that child off to school. A good convent would be about the best. If you keep her there most of the year, she won't see so much of the Travers. She spends all her time with them now, and they don't like you—"

I protested—"Oh, not convents. They save you the trouble of teaching it manners, and that's all."

"Manners maketh man," said Carlo, who had not been to Winchester. I looked away spitefully, and saw his sister register both slips.

"What did Mrs Travers say about me?" said Zoe steadily.

"You know what she is," Carlo hurried up, all anxious friendliness. (His attack was to dance up and down and give tongue, while his sister hunted soundless, ready to spring.) "They want to keep Cosmo for themselves. They make a lot of money out of him. Travers thinks his wife had an affair with him once. Anyhow, you know how people are jealous. She's awfully attractive, Zoe, and she'd like to do you in."

In the mirror in her bag Zoe looked at her face, brown, painted, celestial, a mask to set dark crystal eyes and hyacinth-curled hair.

"Yes," she said stubbornly, "but what did she say?"

A remark like that is pure science, the investigation of a fact. I was pleased.

Carlo answered: "Only that Cosmo's a bit older than you."

"Oh, be quiet, Carlo," said his sister; "it's not as serious as that. At any rate you can be sure of one thing, the Travers would sooner die than fall out with Cosmo. It would lose them half their business. People in their position can't afford to say what they think. That's a very effective check."

And admiration and honour and affection? One has heard of these as reasons. Only today we have to find out what is the reality for which these words are the correspondents. It was tolerable when we used to say the words and go ahead on the emotion they evoked, but now one has not the courage to say them any more.

"Come off it, Carlo," said I; "you're inventing the whole thing." If Cosmo quarrelled with them, would Carlo get the business? To be put away for future observation.

His sister said: "Don't you think that the test of success is to be in a position not to know people? After all, like all the arts, the art of life ought to consist of a series of eliminations—the Farrells, for instance. I am always telling Carlo not to know the Farrells. People like that do one harm. You never know what harm people will do." Carlo fidgeted.

"I tell you I've dropped them." And then—"Don't you see, Zoe, that one has to be careful? The world's a rum place, and people do such impossible things."

Zoe, who should certainly have learned something about science, said: "Which of my friends do you mean, Carlo?"

"Who d'you want to be rid of now?" said I.

Carlo tapped my knee. "You know, Cesca, some of our set are impossible. Dennis, for instance, and his brother. It does one no good to be seen with them. They are *mal vus*, you know."

"One can't afford it," said his sister. "Things get about, you know."

"What things?" said Zoe.

"It is very difficult. Of course that is not their real name. My cousins are furious about it. It is not quite right to trade upon other people's position."

Dear me, those boys were my cousins too. They'd always been called that. Acquitted, after a gasp—the dears! "Really," I said, but still feeling shame, and too proud to defend them. They were my dear friends, but I suspected them of needing defence. And did not know how to defend them. Then I remembered that Carlo and his sister hardly knew them at all.

"Cosmo adores them," said Zoe, "and helping Cosmo is my job."

"You'll have your work cut out," cried Carlo, pulling one of her curls with his rapid familiarity. "And talking of Dennis, Cesca, guess who I saw him with last night?"

"My husband, I suppose," I said.

"That's it. They were at the Pomme d'Or, and I can tell you they were getting on with the brandy. Pippa was with them." Carlo's sister laughed.

"Young wives like us have to put up with that, I suppose."

And why shouldn't they go to the Pomme d'Or and stand each other drinks? I saw my life through a dingy glass. These people had made me ashamed and afraid. They were also my kin. I must lose them and could not. The effect of shame and fear was to rearrange every physical object that I could see. The Craven turned into a temple built of cane and plaster, oily marble and velvet, and I observed the cult there. To be rich—to be *rangé*—to be cute; to cut your friends—to suffer for nothing—to be a cad. Carlo and his sister suffer. They were priests there, and I hoped a sacrifice.

All the same, I was afraid of their temple. Zoe was chattering about where she and Cosmo would live when they were married.

"There's a lovely house in Lower Seymour Street—we could just afford it. It has such a room to dance in. Anyhow, I'm to have it."

Carlo shouted: "I advise Cosmo not to touch it! Doesn't he know that Van Buren has bought all the houses along there to pull them down in two years? That's why they're going cheap."

"Don't bring down the walls," said his sister with her good humour.

But I became suddenly afraid of a pillar with a gilt mask on it that might be coming at us, while Zoe and I were being fattened on éclairs and listening to this and burning our mouths out with cigarettes.

Zoe rubbed out of the stump of hers and refused another. So did I, thinking I must find a gesture of my own. Well, I was out of gestures. I wanted to hide. I wondered what religion would do for Carlo and his sister. Then I reflected on what it had done, and saw religion like an anæmic girl, like Peace in a foreign post-War cartoon, not attempting to keep this cretinous juggernaut on a lead. I thought of the Polis, which appeared clean but feeble. I wanted a sanctity to turn on like a tap. I felt myself growing old, my face greasy and stretching under its make-up. Then we left.

Outside, the wind knocked us about. It blew me into a Tube, and up north on the back of a shrieking noise. At the end of the Tube the trees were rocking in a wind that wrapped itself round me and flung me down a steep road.

"So that is what happened down there," I said, "and I am running home to hide." That is life. That is the world. The wind is doing its best for me. Home is good enough, but a little austere, because one is always at work there.

I noticed that it was evening. Then I heard the old trees. I crossed the wide road and saw it was empty, and came alongside the house, and went into its dull, dark porch and let myself in.

In an instant I knew the house was empty. "They" were all out. "They" never troubled me, but they had gone away. I went into my room and saw the trees. The afternoon had gone over its crest, and was falling downhill into evening. In my room the walls were white, and went up to the ceiling like a pure sky. I saw my own things, coloured wood and polished wood, a Persian duck painted gold and scarlet, a green quicksilver ball.

I saw my face in a mirror, grown old. I had not chosen that. I stripped my face of its make-up, and combed my hair into a straight short piece. The wind marched in from the balcony, and dying in the room, it died outside, until there was no sound but that of the oldest of the trees turning. Then it was renewed. Not a cat came in. I lay on a bright shawl and listened to the tunes of the house. Every room had a tune we had taught them, and under our tunes was their tune, which I had sometimes heard, but could not learn; though I think I moved to it when I did not think at all. I did not think of us, nor of the mummy upstairs, nor of the wireless set or the flute, nor that in the room next mine lived the most beautiful child in the world, nor of the seven glass balls for the seven planets that hung in the room downstairs. Or of the cat that threaded the rooms, or the green bath-salt in a jar upstairs.

I listened a long time to a song like the noise made by the footfall of cats, and when I came out of listening to it, I saw the room take fire. Point and point and point that could reflect took light. The low sun covered my face with fire. Outside the leaves were fiery green tongues. The white walls soaked it in and waved it back, so that, when there were not steady points, there were cloths of fire. It was cool. I pulled a fur over me. The fire took the colour of each object, and presently they began to move, and I swung with them. Out we sailed, and I knew that I was conscious of the movement of the earth through space.

I got up and crossed the room and went out onto the balcony that ran round the wall of the house, above the garden where the dandelions were in seed and in flower. There came a roar of wind that flattened me against the walls, and I knew the house was a ship plunging through the sea. The trees were racing us, and a small moon beat up against us up the sky.

When I came back, and looked in the glass again, my face was half old, like a child's recovering from a sickness. I lay down again, and turned on the light beside my bed, and read a book about the greek Polis which now sounded like a fine folk-tale.

But almost at once I went to sleep. When I woke, the wind had gone again. It was night. Houses at the end of two gardens were pure gold inside. I saw them through black leaves. My light was out. But the great tree had come in and stood on the threshold of my balcony. It did not menace me. It was absolutely silent. But it said: "I guard your door. This place is tabu. Keep tabu." When I saw the branches pass in and point at me, I did reverence to the tree and its precinct; and when I could have knelt on the floor in awe of the tree's sanctity, I saw that it was also myself; and when I got up and looked into the glass again, I looked like a child that has been dipped in dew.

❖ ❖

Green

"Don't you think, Madonna Loring, that it would be better if I went down to see?"

"I'll think of it," she said quickly, and he noticed a slight hauteur in her voice.

"We are sure, alas! that she takes too much to drink, and we know that my son does not. And you have heard what people say about her friends. Nick would never allow me to know the Taverners, so is it likely that he will have them to his house unless she insists? And if she does and he refuses, as he certainly should, she will fall out of her own set, and most of his friends will have nothing to do with her. The Derings have hinted to me that they might have to drop Nick. I hardly like to tell you, Ambrose, but they said—" A paraphrase followed for several sexual and social irregularities.

"Don't you think I might go?" Ambrose Alexander said this with loving earnestness, with whimsical adoration, leaning over a narrow space towards an old woman, upright by the fire in a dull-gold London room. Inside her tight silver wig and her mask of paint, she was yielding to treatment. In one hollow centimeter of her mind she knew she was, and that she would send Ambrose, because he would bring back an exciting story, a story that would justify malice and moral indignation: that could also be repudiated without strain. He owed her a good deal, she thought. He was a Jew. His function was to please. He did please. A slim, supple young man to run about was essential: to confide in: to reassure her.

For his part he was willing to oblige her. There were good pickings in that family, and benefits apart, she was giving him what he wanted—a chance to get his own back on her son and his wife. For the six months before, for the six months since, their marriage, she had been ravenous for its discredit. The discredit it was for him to supply. But a full meal, this time, and more than a meal, a provision, on which she would never satiate, of the wife's blood and sap. What she wanted would serve his turn; but when he thought about her, and he preferred not to think about her too much, he misunderstood her degrees of consciousness, the balance of her scruples, her ignorance, her appetite, and her fears.

"If you are to go down and see her, how can it be arranged? It mustn't look—"

"They had better not expect me. If I could have a car and it should break down, then I could simply be there, and they would put me up for the night."

"That's a good idea. I'll pay for it. But, mind you, Ambrose, it must be a real break-down. I won't have any lies."

"Madonna Loring, it shall go up in flames to make my word, since it is really your word, good."

She looked away from him, a little sentimental smile disturbing the corners of the old thin mouth. If only in her life she had heard more men say things like that. He meant it. Ambrose was a good and noble man. Of course he would not have to burn the car. That would be too extravagant. Even for the most disgusting news of her daughter-in-law.

Splendid that Ambrose was going. Her son might be in agonies about his wife: her son might be wanting his home again. She would give Ambrose messages to make it easy for him to come home for help. She foresaw decent divorce, and when Ambrose was gone, walked up and down the long room between the azaleas and the inlaid chairs, rehearsing a long, hideous, and wholly satisfactory scene with his wife.

Until the nature of the interview from being a source of pleasure became a kind of pain, and she noticed that she was not sure how far she wanted to be able to trust Ambrose there. Later she rang him up.

"Of course I'll pay all your expenses, but don't be too extravagant. I've just thought we may need all our money later."

She had said "our money" out of romantic delicacy. Ambrose relished it differently. It had been share and share alike with Nicholas, who usually forgot about his own share. Then, a year ago, Nicholas had found out that intermittent rebellion is exhausting, and had conducted an entire revolution instead. Six months later he was married. Now his landmarks were off both their maps. Only their débris re-

mained—nothing but skeletons and broken boards where his places
had been. A devastating escape, but Nick's mother had herself to
thank. And hatred of his wife, which had been her refuge, was to become her revenge. Against Nancy Loring, Ambrose knew nothing—
had not heard much—"*Le dossier accusateur de toute jolie femme.*" But
to be kept by Mrs. Loring; he must keep Mrs. Loring; give Mrs. Loring what she wanted, a daughter-in-law unkind, unchaste, and, so
far as possible, unkissed. It seemed that he might have to rely on his
imagination. After six months they were still living out of London,
in that small, remote house, where no one that he knew ever went.
Without a car, a telephone or a horse. With cats and an old boat
and books. That did not promise disillusion yet unless the girl was
bored. What was there to find out? Could he return and report bliss?
A spring wind filled the curtains of his room; coal-dust from the unlit
fire charged its delicate touch. With his eyes on the tree-tops breaking
leaf he could only smell London. He did not particularly mind, but at
night with the fire burning he could feel Mrs. Loring behind his chair.
Boards cracked before and after her tread, step of a bully with small
feet and ankles swollen a little with age, and there was a sound of gob-
bling already, and appetite unglutted, and punishment for Nick shaping once she had got him back. Once they had got him back.

Need he go at all? Could he go in theory, or, if he went, in theory
provoke Nancy to behaviour whose character could be decided on later, and Nick actually into appropriate disgust? There is nothing more
difficult to deny than a casual event whose importance rests on its
implications. It is said that you have been to Biarritz with friends of
doubtful character.

You do not know the people.

You have not been to Biarritz at all.

Prove it, if you have not been conspicuously with other people anywhere else. The force of your denial will fly loose, attach itself, and
strengthen the accusation. You will have been at St. Jean de Luz, where
you met, and were notorious with them there. It is this fact that lies at
the base of all non-resistance to evil, that the resistance becomes a neutral agent, equally able to strengthen what it attacks.

Ambrose felt that he need not be too anxious. There is always something wrong. If it were not yet conscious he had only to give the unconscious a name. While it was equally possible that the girl was bored,
loose or a slut. If not, she was going to be. The elegantly set problem

absorbed him, in whose solution he ignored himself, his emotion for Nick, his curiosity about Nancy, his fear of the mother—about whom he assumed himself to be particularly cynical and gay.

Two days later he ran out of petrol on a remote road a mile from their house.

. . . . .

Nancy Loring asked her husband: "Who was it called the sea the 'very green'?"

"The Egyptians, I think. The Red Sea and the Mediterranean. What about green wine?"

They were looking out at a green plain which lay as far as the horizon on their left, and their house stood on the shelf of a grass hill beside the plain, tilted in the sunlight to another green. High trees stood about the hill, and a short way outside, across a lawn, a copse crested its last bank. The plain had once been the sea, an estuary savage with tides, now narrowed to a river, tearing at its flow and ebb; where all winter, for every hundred yards, a heron watched its pitch. There was no dust: no sound but birds and air; no colour but green. There was every green.

In late April the top greens were of gold. Across the plain there was a march of elms, open hands with blood inside them, tipped with saffron fire. The copse was a stuff woven out of the same green.

They went out. On the small lawn were cats, black and white enamel in fur. One watched its lover; the lover watched a bird; the third, bow-stretched and upright, ripped the bark off a tree. Two kittens tumbled over like black and white flowers.

They followed one another through the copse. Each willow trunk was a separate man and woman. They came down the farther side to where, when it had been sea, the plain had worn a little bay under the hill. There was long wet grass where the tide-mark had been. They came to a dyke and an old house. There were willows along the glass water, very tall; along it and over it, one flung across and an elm tree drowned in it, its root out of the ground in a flat earth-cake. The house was a deserted farm. An orchard reached it, down a small valley between the rising of another hill. There was no path. They went up through the apple-trees, through a place wholly sheltered, where no wind came but only sun; where, when there was no sun, there was always light; so that in mid-winter, in the stripped world, the seasons did not exist there. They called it the Apple Land, remembering there something which they could not recall, that seemed to have the importance of a just-escaped dream. The orchard ended sharply in an overhanging quickset, and a sharp climb to the top of the hill. To follow the valley to its head there was a glen on the left, sickly with flies and thin shoots and a scummed choked stream up to a short fall, almost in the dark, which was not quite wholesome, whose pool was without stir or light. The way out of that was also sharp and steep but quite different—to a shut cottage on top and a garden with tansy in it, and herbs used in magic.

Through lambs running in the up-fields they came to their village, and bought a morning paper, cheese, apples, and cigarettes. They came back another way, by a highroad, by a lane, over the open grass along a ribbon their feet had printed, green upon green.

. . . . .

Ambrose Alexander reached the house as they had entered the copse. A shy country servant left him alone. He was pleased that they were out; he stood back by the door from where he could see the whole length of the room.

Across the table an open ordnance map hung like a cloth askew. There was a chessboard beside it, and men half tumbled out of a box, and a wide bowl of small mixed flowers. There was a stone bottle of ink and a dish with sticks of sealing-wax and stamps, pencils, and a seal. There was a dog's lead and a pair of leather gloves. A red handkerchief was knotted up full of needles and wool. When he handled it one ran into his palm. There was an oil painting of Mount Soracte and steel prints of forgotten gentlemen; and on the black chimney-shelf a fishing-rod crossed with a gun. There were books of poems, and on murder, the roman occupation of Britain, chinese art.

Mr. Hunca Munca, the mouse, climbed to the top of the kitchen chimney and looked out. There was no soot. Up to the age of five every child laughs at this version of that joke; but to Ambrose it was as if the room was calling him, very plainly and in another language, an outsider. It was not what he had come to hear. He stared out of the window and up the hill. There was no one. Then he went upstairs. Under his feet the old boards had no friendly squeak. Like old servants who might talk.

Their bedroom had a rose-brick fireplace and a line of persian prints. Under the mirror, piled in a shell, were strings of glass flowers and fruit. Everything was in order, polished and very still, and the bathroom full of things to wash with. He went back to the bedroom, supposed that in one of the shut drawers there was a shameful secret among soiled linen, persuaded himself, opened it, and in it there were folded silks, bedroom books: two more murders, a County History, *Per Amica Silentia Lunae*, Sterne. A cat looked in at the door and yawned before it went away. Under a scent-flask was a receipted bill. He looked out of the window at the very green.

There they had been all winter long. They did not seem to want to go away. Told nothing, saw no one who would tell anything, asked for nothing. He was discouraged. Propriety, simplicity, the routine of country-house life. The house went on talking out loud; not without passion but with directness that annihilated. Down any passage there might be met a wall of fire. He looked at the bed over whose foot-rail hung a bright shawl and a fur.

The persian pictures were perfectly proper. In the dining-room cupboard there had been two bottles of beer. He went downstairs, heard no approach on the soundless turf, so that they were on him in an instant, as instantly recoiled, and a moment later were overwhelmed in his cordiality and excuse.

Disentangling themselves from him, they exchanged a word together, out of the house. "What has he come for? Car broken down? Whose car? Who's given him a car?"

Nicholas Loring was annoyed; his wife uneasy. There was nothing to do but feed him, and not to go after the swan's nest that day. Swans stay put, but are more interesting than a townsman ill at ease, vocal and supple and full of admiration that did not try to be more than a display. Voluble and mobile, Ambrose had a trick of statement, one to each sentence, followed by a denial, a reversal of it in the next. So that which seemed, sentence by sentence, to be a vivid reaction to life, cancelled out to nothing. To no belief at all. Nicholas, folded-up in country quiet, was now without illusion and irritated by what had once stimulated him. Ambrose had no belief at all. And Nancy saw that everything Ambrose said would mean nothing, and felt giddy in her mind until she felt sick. They were his hosts and they must stomach him, feed him, and endure him to an hour they had not fixed. They were saved from spiritless irritation, and she from fear, by curiosity and the involuntary hosts' calculation of the time when they would be able to lose him. Ambrose understood this, and that he must stay the night, and that at the present no mere breakdown of his car would get him the invitation. He saw himself after lunch led by Nick, grim, courteous and embarrassed, to restart it at the top of the hill.

.   .   .   .   .

They came to the end of lunch. Nicholas was listening to Ambrose, to what he had once heard, year in and year out, and now had not heard for a year. And after a year there was no more pleasure in it or surprise at the changes. It was as if he knew it by heart, for the first time at last.

Ambrose was trying hard with a parade of emotion, trying to praise marriage, their withdrawal, the serene country; displaying himself as the neurotic townsman, the alien, whose pride it was to humble himself, to look into paradise through bars. A peep he owed to them: "Is that safe, Nancy?" turning to her from Nicholas.

"I think so," she answered civilly, not at all sure. 'He is trying not to cancel out,' she thought. 'Why? He can't do it for long. Why is he here? He does not like me. Would like me to be vile so as to hurt Nick. Nick he loves and hates. Then that he had once loved Nick and then hated him, probably for his marriage and now did neither, or in different proportions. What was he there for?'

He said: "Suppose me at my rôle again—the old serpent. You used, Nick, to call me that, and any variation that struck you from 'you dirty devil' to 'Lucifer.'"

"Lord of lies," she murmured.

He heard her. She was ashamed. He looked steadily at her and smiled. "You're right, my dear. I'm just as much that variation of the fiend. Only neither you nor Nick need the serpent in me any more. Serpents"—he added—"are not sentimental. That was useful once to Nick. While who has ever heard of a mother-snake?" They took that in.

"There was a time when Nick needed an old, contradictory bloke like me to leave all doors open and let a spot of reality in. His mother" (the pause which left her unqualified perfected suggestion) "she would have shut the lot, and everything open is the only answer to everything shut. But now—" He went on to explain that Nicholas, now he had welcomed the reality Ambrose had provided, had made his own freedom and been given love. It was true. But Nicholas must be repersuaded that he owed it to him. Doors that have been opened can be shut. One implies the other. They could begin on him again, he and Mrs. Loring, and Nick would be well retrapped. The doors would be shut and the wife outside. Only it would take logner than he thought, and Mrs. Loring would not see the delicacy of it. He must find out how to persuade her that the cup of deferred blood is richer.

Rapt in these thoughts he started smiling at them. Nick was moved, but remembered that once he would only have been moved. Ambrose had opened doors once, or he had thought so. Until he had noticed that he had only slammed them to and fro, chasing him between draughts. Until he had stuck open a certain number that he needed for himself. (Who wants to live with every door open?) His exits and entrances were now his own, and by one of them Nancy had come in: helped to fix open a few more, and, by one of these, first Ambrose, then his mother, had gone out. That was what had happened in terms of doors. He softened, feeling that he could afford to. Old Ambrose had come down for some sort of thanks. Or perhaps for a share. Share of the rich strength which made things easy with Nancy: easy to give and take: easy to go in and out: to live: like music, all the musics. Ambrose was by himself as he'd always been. Nancy was thinking the same thing, that here was a man alone all his life and always would be alone; and thought of him on a toadstool and with people round him on toadstools, and that he spent his time picking their stalks from underneath them and his own stalk.

Then, the strength mounting in her also, she wondered if Ambrose had been necessary to Nicholas, to that woman's only son. Was it possible that they had shaken Ambrose off his fence? Was this visit, after all, a no mean congratulation and praise; one of the mysterious triumphs of love? She forgot his subtle opposition to their marriage. Was this old Mrs. Loring's last defeat? She judged it most improbable and forgot her judgment. Only remembered that it would be good if it were true. If it were true, they might some day be able to forgive. She looked at Ambrose, very simply. It seemed a far cry to "mother's gigolo." He observed her, went to the piano and played the letter-song from *Figaro*. Whistling softly. *And the sounds of beauty flowed and trembled until they seemed to triumph…over the hard hearts of men.*

She brought him over his coffee. There was not a cruel animal behind Nick, only a vexed old woman, who had been lovely, who would never feed on her son again, or with septic finger-nails scratch at the bloom of her own youth. She had been ungenerous about Ambrose. How hateful is the wife who does injustice to her husband's people, to her husband's friends.

She lit his cigarette, and stood by Nicholas' shoulder, wholly herself and part of him and part of the very green. Part of Ambrose? Yes, for this moment, if this were true.

.   .   .   .   .

They took him out, a tramp across green, from green to green, entertained him with birds' nests set deep in thorned twigs and split light. There had been tea and toast and chess, an evening to get through and a night. He stood between them at evening at the door of the house. Now in the sky there was a bar of the green that has no name. He was standing on grass darkening beside dark green. She had said, "*It is all Hermes, all Aphrodite.*"

He had been bored and concealed it, with the night before him, becoming unsure of himself. Dinner, chess, music, country-talk. A drink? They had filled up his car and put her away in the village and refused to let him go.

They gave him a drink and a rabbit cooked in onions. He had gained nothing but the fooling of them, and, if they did not know it, they were slightly bored. The worst thing that can happen to a liar is to be believed. If he did not notice that, he suffered, as Nick indicated in intimate outline, his serene and final detachment from his mother. Confident, they told him their plans, about excavations and gardening, and Nick's new book, which was not about himself or even about people. He had to listen, and by that time it was night, grey, windless, with a squeak in it. The great chimney flared. Standing inside it one could follow the sparks up its square tower to a square patch of sky. Innocent as wine, as dew. He sneered. Outside was it innocent? Innocent for them and strong. His room was away from theirs. On that side of the house the night could do what it liked with him. The night would have him to itself. Nick and Nancy would have themselves to themselves. He would have nothing to himself but himself and night. Oh! there was someone who might come in and sit beside his bed. Madame Nick might come in and talk, smile, and suck in her thin, red lips. Keep him awake because she was hungry. She would not mind dark green night.

He would have nothing but lies to feed her on: have to invent her a meal because her sort of food wasn't in the house. He was getting childish. With their stupid innocence they were doing him down. What did Nancy want? To give him another drink: be sure that he was comfortable: a game of chess before bed. "Glorious game" he must say, but it took longer to play than he reckoned. A shy woman, what she did was better than her promise. Later she said: "It is good for your complexes, Ambrose, to win things and be praised." For that he should have let her win. God! But he could not bear to evade the game. And it put off bed, and whatever it was that tapped outside on the windows its peculiar code.

But when he went up, the soft air surging in put him instantly to sleep.

. . . . .

They woke next morning with a distaste for him in the house. He was to go after lunch, and the morning seemed an hour-series that could not be lived through. There was no reason for it, only that they did not care now if his visit marked a triumph. They wanted him out of the way. There were interesting things to do and he would not do them. Nancy decided that she would disappear, on the excuse of leaving Nicholas alone with his friend, and came downstairs first to see that Ambrose had his breakfast in bed. There was a letter for her from Nick's mother. That hardly ever happened. She went outside to read it, barefoot on the cat-printed dew: split it open and read:

> My Dear Child,
> I wish this to be entirely between ourselves, but I have an idea that Nicholas' old friend Ambrose intends to come down and see you. Please be very nice to him. You know how it is—he was so fond of my son and has suffered the break since his marriage. Of course it couldn't be helped, and I am so afraid of emotional friendships between young men, but I am sure you have nothing to fear now. Don't tell Nicholas anything about this—and also what I meant to say is—don't be upset or offended if he should try and flirt with you. It means absolutely nothing. He has a very fine nature really, and is not at all interested in women. I just want there to be no misunderstanding, not that Nicholas is likely to think anything as long as you are careful, only I do not wish you for your part to be led away. I explain this badly, but I am sure you will understand. I hope you are both as well as possible.
> Your loving Mother,
> Angela Loring

The crisp dew melted between her toes, and their colour changed from pink to red. One hand held on to her curled, cropped hair. There was a moment when nothing happened at all, neither image nor concept nor sense impression. She came-to, first to the small bustling wind, then to a bird. Then to a draught of other life-like voices, shrieking from London, recorded on a square of thick white paper. It was mad; it was comic; it was dangerous. She ate a light breakfast in silence. Anyhow it was tiresome.

She said: "You will want the morning with Ambrose. I'm off." But Nicholas had his plans also.

"Look here" he said. "I forgot that I said I'd see that man about—"

"Take him with you."

"It's a trudge. I got mud to my knees last—"

"Am I to keep Ambrose?"

"I mean, if you be that sort of spirit—I'll be back before lunch."

"Very well. Do you mind what happens to him?"

"I'm leaving him with you—" He grinned, and there began to be less of him, a hand or an ear or a foot left, and the rest out of sight, and then the whole of him out of reach.

After she had been alone for ten minutes she began to feel holy, and inside herself an immense preoccupation with power. She went upstairs, put on a gayer sweater, and delicately painted her face. So Ambrose had come down to see if there was anything to be done about Nick. Through her. If she had been easy, to have her; easy or discontented or jealous of Nick. Very likely Mrs. Loring, mère Angélique, had sent him herself and repented, and so written. She had thought such a thing possible? Wanted such a thing? Wanted her son's wife a slut and had not wanted it. Wanted Ambrose back? In her mind there was the old woman's name written-up and scored through. Then she went out and called lightly up at his window from the cool lawn.

"Come down, Ambrose, it's a perfect day."

With sweet animation and pretty phrases she made Nick's excuses, and took him the plain way up the hill to the village for a drink.

He had better go, he thought, there was nothing doing here. He was separated after the night's deep sleep, cut off already from what had been yesterday's preoccupations, and those of weeks and years and even of a life past. Indifferent for the moment to their reassertion, like a man drugged, but not as though it was well with him there. So that the only thing was to get away. Go before lunch and cut its pointless coda. God! was Nancy, the woman beside him, talking, running a primrose through his coat, trying to flirt with him at last? The gentle admiration of last night turned pert with a grin behind it. She went on like that all the way to the village inn. He had a drink. He needed it. He was imagining things. She was a gay baggage after all, and he'd interested her. She wanted to know about himself, did she? She'd got rid of Nick. What was she saying?

"It's good of you to tolerate me, Ambrose. After you and Nick. What a marvellous friendship we might have. But oh, my dear—!"

"What do you do me the honour of thinking about me, wife of Nicholas?" There was another drink before him. Put it down. It was quick work following this up.

"This visit has cleared up so much, made almost anything possible. And now we are friends, I feel I must say anything to you that I think."

"Go on."

"Anything? You mean it? Then, Ambrose, I shall begin about yourself; and first of all I'm going to tell you something you're to do and that you are not to do."

"I'll obey you." Her voice had light music in it.

Now she leaned across the inn table, *dulce ridentem*, a shadow in her smile, making him aware of her awareness of him.

"You are a great man, Ambrose, but oh, *mon ami*, love Nicholas, love me, but don't, don't—"

"What am I not to do, lady of the place?"

"You should not, you must not. Ambrose, you are not to let people call you—you are not to be so mixed up—with old women who exploit you. I'm a woman, and I'm not an old woman, but do you know what some old women are like? They adore your looks and your sweet manners, and," she added rudely, "how? They want you physically, of course, but not simply physically; and they've their own way of getting that. And when they've got what they want, or not got what they want, then they make comparisons."

What was this? She was serious, she was smiling. There was a smile set against him and eyes lit with cold fun.

"Whatever dowager takes such an interest in me?"

"Oh, my dear, with so many about, and you so liked and hard-up. Why, this morning I had a letter from Nick's mother, for you to be returned intact. A perfectly wolfish howl. How did she know you were here?" The smiles were working easily on her lips, but her eyes were steady. Steady as two carved stones on rock.

"I think you should be kind to her; kind as you are to Nick; kind as you are to me."

She was making a sing-song of it, her head drawn up, her throat strained a little under the high collar of bright wool. Then relaxing: "Forgive this candour," she said; "I know how they can be useful, these women. Only if you can't do without them, you must learn how to keep them in order. Nick was a little annoyed that his mother should write such a letter. Keep her in hand. You remember about Peter Carmin and how his friends got him out of the country—"

If she had been alone down there with him at the house she would not have been safe, in spite of the green.

"May I see the letter?" (He must say that.)

"Nick has it." That was what she must say. She could say what she liked. She was in her own land. It was then that she heard his surrender.

"Tell Nick I will write to him. I think I had better go up now since the car is here."

Its noise drowned her light farewells and excuses.

$$\cdot \qquad \cdot \qquad \cdot \qquad \cdot$$

She dropped back softly between the hills, by the first way, through the Apple Land. Round the green bay, through the copse, until outside the house she was looking at the plain and the trees' open hands. Her husband came suddenly round a corner of the house and saw that she was alone.

"Gone," she said; "and before I come in take this letter into the house and read it."

❖ ❖

The House Party

To *Jean Cocteau*

H E WANTED TO GO and stay with them, in the sea-washed, fly-blown, scorched hotel along the coast, whose walls were washed primrose above the blue lapping water, where one mounted to bed by a plaster stair outside above the shifting sea, under the stars shaken out in handfuls.

There might be peace there. Under Vincent's wing a man could stand up a bit. Vincent was English, tender, serious, older than he. Vincent wanted him to come. Was no doubt cajoling, hypnotising away certain objections. Objections that were always made about him, especially by his own countrymen, the Americans who made a cult of Europe, a cult and a career, not quite perfect in their transplanting, and conscious of it. As he was conscious of the virgin energy and high intelligence which made them a reproach to him. Also, that in certain directions, his adventures outnumbered theirs as the stars the dim electric-light bulbs of the hotel. No they would not want him, and Vincent, poor fish, would sweat blood to fix it so as not to annoy them. And at the same time risk his old friendships on his behalf. A fool, but a sort of glorious one. Glorious fools pay. Meanwhile he would go—and not be a nuisance to Vincent. Take a back seat all right. Give Vincent what he had to give. An audience, someone to *play* with. Worship carefully disguised. If Vincent bored him—. An essential meanness in the boy reminded him how he could take it out of Vincent, Vincent who was standing by him; not out of Vincent's friends. A cracked little specimen of a gigolo, after a year in prison for something he had not done, his comfort was to be revenged on the good. Vincent should pay.

Great André also was staying there; the silver hill, the lance-point of the boy's world. Vincent would present him. He would have something to worship as well as Vincent. Make Vincent jealous? No, no, no. Perhaps he'd find out how to behave as they behaved. No, no, no. God help him, he'd play no joy-boy tricks.

He had met Vincent at the Casino of the great town, and had heard about the fun they were having, the harmonious, mischievous house party ten miles along the coast.

"International relations going strong. I'm still on speaking terms with Dudley and Stretton, Winkelman and Marjorie, Edouard and Clarice; with America, Mittel-Europa, England and France. And since André came I've never had such a time or known such a chap. Like lightning and Mozart."

Not a word about the social lift André's presence implied. Only response to his longing to be there, and a little diffidence.

"Dudley and Stretton are difficult, Paul. Tastes very definite and standards unaccountably high. It works out that they don't like anyone who isn't in the arts, or pickled in New York, or else extremely important socially—"

Paul said: "I'm a pickled New Englander. That's to say that I'm of much better family. But you can tell them I won't interfere. They won't even see me except across a room at meals. I suppose they can stand that. If I come, it's to see you—I know what's due to people who have been kind to me."

Vincent smiled. "I see a good deal of André. I expect you'll meet him too. I'll take you a room for tomorrow, and when the high cultural atmosphere of Dudley and Stretton gets a bit too much we'll amuse each other—"

Paul saw him leave the Casino and shoot across the bright gardens to find his car—a young man whose large bones the flesh covered delicately, who, even indoors, set the air stirring. Not noisy at all, but easy, as if his life was nourished by a fountain, whose very deep waters rose and sunned and spread themselves evenly, and mounting kept everything they touched astir. Paul, shooting craps at a bar, remembered a sentence Vincent had quoted, "The generosity of strength," supposed Vincent had it, and his heart felt the little nick of pain which was his form of worship; he knew that he did not mind saying, even to Vincent's face, that Vincent was his superior.

A moment later he began to reflect on his simplicity. These scrupulous Englishmen were easy to make. Because of their innocence, because of the insolence implied in "the generosity of strength." He counted the knuckles of his small, rosy, gold-wired hands, tried the pointed nails, jerked up the arm to feel the bicep, who had once been an athlete, looked in the mirror at his pretty clothes and handsome childish head, spoke to the barman in faultless French. To reassure himself. It was all he had to take over there to people disorderly with treasure of mind and spirit. Of bodies also, but he knew how to exploit his—

Vincent, rushing his car along the hill coastline, was saying that the ill-used brat should have his treat.

He had acquired Paul in a moment of occupation with human wrongs. The boy had been handed over to him by another man as a hopeless case. It had seemed to him that Paul's life of dissipation, malice and despair, occasionally touched by a kind of nipped sweetness which flowered only into unwilling loyalty, was one form of a universal condition, a rot nibbling at a generation. This gave him the power to illustrate the particular by the general, translate the boy into boys, and take valuable notes. His feebleness lay in an observation he had shirked: that all Paul's qualities, his vices, his sincerity, his aspirations, and his affection had been steeped, as though his body in filth, in some essence of the sordid which made him repellent. Apart from the blindness of generosity, a connoisseur in bad smells might have accepted the handsome lad, courteous when he liked, ravenously grateful for scraps, rather chic.

Vincent looked out to sea, over jade dancing, called it a drawing-room ocean after the Atlantic, and kicked himself mildly for ingratitude. If only Paul could be dipped in it and brought out clean. He knew that what he needed was purification, from what corruption he did not quite understand. He concentrated too closely on the horror spot of the story. The boy's imprisonment for folly; his desertion by his friend. The savage sentence; the appalling illness that had released him; the details of his third degree. Little Paul naked and terrified, and beaten up. Questioned to insanity; flung for weeks into a filthy cell; chained to a black murderer running with sores. He had infinite pleasure when Paul responded, told him how peace of heart and self-respect ran in like small tides "into the mess it has made of me. Don't suppose that when I'm with a person like yourself, it doesn't do good to my character—"

Vincent knew that behind the small admission there was a continent of waste land and reserve. Also that it was sincere. Paul brought him presents, a cigarette holder in almost good bad taste; popular fiction that had impressed him; once, God knew how acquired, a lapis snuff-bottle stoppered with coral, the most gentlemanly chinoiserie, full of oily, permanent eastern scent. Paul loved to give, loved himself for giving. Vincent was touched. He enjoyed presents too. They played with them together. Vincent was persuaded that Paul did him good, not by exercising him in charity, but by taking him out of his group intensities. Paul had lively adventures, good because they were ordinary debaucheries. Yet in each there was something distasteful, as though the prison and the hospital had left a taint and a sepsis. The sea racing below on Vincent's right was the sign of purification. For purification was necessary. A saturation—in what? Vincent did not exactly know. He only knew an essence that washed his spirit daily as the sea his body, the wine in his throat, music in his ears. What was it? He resisted the easy race-temptation to call it by old names, religion, God's grace, because they had once been counters for it, possibly were so still. But observing great André with his crowd of lads, who came for an hour, for a day, flashing in and out of the Frenchman's darkened room, a word had crystallized out for such activities. Kourotrophos, a bringer-up of boys. Not much more than one himself, Vincent brooded its meaning, half ashamed of its emotional charge, the humility and elation it brought him. If he could not show Paul the Good, he would bring him samples, rub his nose in them if necessary, pitch him, kick him into it, scrub him. Hold him up a glass to see his restored cleanliness. For the spiritual-sensual reward: to hear Paul say that it was good, clean and on his knees. And see the little thing run off translated, his small gifts liberated, reasonably at peace.

Beside the classic sea, the classic title took form: Kourotrophos. He saw Cheiron, Pallas. In the same land, built of gold and violet rock, barren, but "*a good nurse for boys,*" André; the dead scots officer who had licked him into shape. He meant to try a practise hand on Paul; for someone in the future, the friend of friends, who at the start would need that. Paul was just a try-out, with a dash of affection in his sentiment towards him, and a slight kick.

Vincent was an english type, mutely convinced that he was there for a purpose, accepting the discipline of the virtues as preparation for an unknown. A particularly unknown unknown at this time, with religion and love and pride of land and race off the map, and the unconscious the cheerless substitute. Meanwhile he had to be observant, study the iron puritanism in which Paul had been raised. Was that the soil which had grown his corruption? He decided finally that it had only set the stubborn will that resisted catharsis. They had read together the story of the Butcher of Hanover, and he had noticed that the horrible fairy-tale had struck Paul with terror. Also that it had excited him. Which suggested a Hoffman in Paul? Really, really. But Vincent had spent an hour or so of his imaginative life in the old quarter of Hanover, in and out the over-hung, cobbled passages and crazed buildings, greased and glazed with old blood; still alive, this time with painted, emotional boys, followers of men's oldest profession. Current hysteria, gossip, intrigue, on a mediæval stage. Mystery of stairs that lead nowhere and doors that do not shut, and round the corner to Augustus' Live Wire Bar.

Throw fire, crystal, salt between little Paul and that place, where Vincent could have strolled and picked up wisdom; where the absence implied the presence of his lord. He left his car at the hill garage and ran down the terrace stairs of the small town, past gay, plaster houses roofed with round tiles, along slots of cooled, highly seasoned air; a ribbon of liquid sky on top; and at the end of each stair a patch of still water, divided by masts, the basin of the little, prehistoric port, till he reached the hotel on the quay. He had Dudley and Stretton to appease, where, from his point of view, appeasement should not have been necessary; and it is hard to entreat those we love. He could foresee the iron stare at Paul's name, the lip-twitch of contempt, and, incidentally, the glance of apprehension.

He ran up the white, sea-cracked stair and knocked at André's door. In bed, God bless him, in a room where the sea-light sifted through wooden slats; the red silk of his pyjama coat falling back up dark ivory arms. Ready for any emergency. Ready always to talk. As by magic, he spoke immediately of Dudley and Stretton. "Any news from the Upper House, *mon cher?*"

"I've news for them," said Vincent. "Listen, André, I've a *déclassé* little friend—"

"You always have—so have I. Well?"

"—I put it to you, André, the boy ought to come. You'd think that, after his past, his countrymen would be hunting him round with bouquets—" He tried to find the French for scapegoat.

"*Bouc émissaire,*" said André. "I don't suppose they chose a valuable beast."

Then it was like a ride on a wave, repose on the sea's back, when the Frenchman said: "I will arrange it—he has a right to stay where he pleases—Dudley and Stretton can't have everything their own way. Leave it to me."

They embraced, and Vincent felt as if the sea had lifted him gently onto a firm beach.

. . . . .

In another room of the hotel Dudley and Stretton's sails emptied a moment and flapped in a pocket of the rising gale they were running before to well-earned fame. Vincent had said "check" when he had gone straight to André to sponsor this deplorable specimen of their native land. In their sun-steeped rooms, filled with objects of comfort, utility and impeccable taste, they yielded to distress. Dudley picked at the typewriter, Stretton sat on the edge of the bed. The sea danced at them. They were saying that no European ever could or ever would understand the way rumour reached New York, and booked its passage by return of liner under new and horrible disguises. That people would talk; that people might say they were friends with the boy if they were seen in the same place. It was all very well for André, a prince of the arts, and for Vincent with his shameless english indifference to public opinion; they had extra cats to whip. Stretton was tall, fragile, ageless, beautiful. Dudley was handsome, quick, serviceable. The pair two formidable hunters, out for the lion's share. In the civilisation of Europe, kind, ruthless, observant pioneers. Neither aware of the power of their arms, the prestige of their fresh strength. Both aware that Vincent had put their queen in danger, intentionally or not.

Dudley clattered off a letter on the typewriter. Stretton put on a record. *"I Ain't Nobody's Darling"* pointed the situation. He took it off and substituted Mozart. Perhaps not perfectly appreciated, the lovely air flowed out above "the hard hearts of men."

The day after, while André took a cat-nap after two hours' unbroken lunch conversation, Vincent hurried along the sea-bordered rock-path to the station. In the train Paul soiled his hands, clinging to the black-dusted rod in the corridor on his way. The train ran into a tunnel, into the mountain that rushed down to the edge of the dancing beach. In an instant he had passed out of flashing air into brownness, into hell's neck, after a paradise of blue stone-pines. The boy suffered in it, and from more than fear that its filth would soil his smartness. To his literal, primitive fancy it was like what hell would be, hell where he'd been before, hell where he belonged. Only this tunnel had an end, which ran full into a station, where Vincent was waiting for him beside more sea.

Together they left hell's mouth, Paul trotting a little behind Vincent's stride, and glad to run to earth in his sunny room and arrange his pretty properties. It occurred to Vincent, as he watched him displaying trifles, that there were people without house or land, with a dressing-case and a photograph frame for anchor. Paul said: "I suppose you couldn't get me a window table downstairs? I can promise you not to look at Dudley and Stretton. Or rather I shall leave it to them. They can cut me or not as they please."

"I've fixed that for tomorrow—André asked you to dine with us tonight." He saw Paul start, harden, and then sitting on his bed drop backwards, his forearm over his eyes.

"What is it, lad?"

"I don't know; but you take me out of hell into heaven. It's all you. I know that. I'll kiss Dudley and Stretton if you like."

Vincent jumped. That wouldn't do. Keep 'em apart. Quite simply, because he was ashamed of Paul. Also he remembered their iced politeness when they had seen him once before, the night he had taken Paul to one of their parties, when he had been at fault, and Paul had acted in character. "Let them be," he said; "you can make friends with them later."

"You mean," said Paul, "that I may be fit to know them later?"

"I mean that if you clean up and cheer up you can meet them later on your own ground."

· · · · ·

At dinner Paul sat by André, at the head of the table, opposite Vincent. Beside him an Englishwoman, neither ugly nor old, who had Dudley beside her; and by Vincent, Stretton; and by him a pretty, watchful french girl. The long table, with a Frenchman at the head of it, which was the hotel's show-piece and alarm. An annoyance and bewilderment for the old soldiers and older maids who filled the *salle à manger*, when the conversation rose above the clash of plates and the shifting of the sea.

> "*J'ai du commerce sexuelle*
> *Avec mon colonel*
> *J'ai connu, charnellement, mon commandant—*"

seven gay voices sang when the courses were late. The Englishwoman
was teasing André, who was whittling green olives into improprieties.
As Paul passed a carafe he was nodded to by Stretton, and asked where
he had been, as though his address had been a public lavatory, and he
given a chance to conceal it. It was like being let out on parole. No, it
was not parole, it was freedom. He told them all a story, suggested by
André's anatomical reconstructions of the olives, and they were silent.

He felt walls closing on him again. Like the walls of his prison that
his body had somehow got out of and left the rest behind. He was listening now to their talk. About the same thing as his story, but excused
because the words were different, and mixed up with implications he
didn't understand. That was cleverness: that was hypocrisy. They were
like bright flies hatched out of dung, and he the beetle content to roll
its ball. He thought about that until he caught André's voice again,
half-way through a tirade on the theatre. He'd seen the play. Coolly
Stretton asked for his opinion. Again, what he said was not *like* what
they said. He flushed. André sheltered him. Stretton illustrated André's
criticism with a New York production. He was analytic, weighty. By
chance, wrong on detail. Paul corrected him eagerly. Silence. With a
pinch of assurance gained, he invited André and Vincent to the café on
the quay. André refused gently. Vincent carried him off.

The little town was built on terraces chipped out of the mountain
flank, between two precipices, round whose base even the Mediterranean flung itself in spray. It was very still in the little port, white docks
ran in sideways along stale emerald water, an utter security for little
boats. The quay stones, salt-bleached and fretted smooth, where the
cables rubbed, were laid with rust-coloured nets. Eternally torn, eternally repaired, untidy girls in black gowns, with black-brown necks
and dusty, dark curls, mended them. But at this season, at night, the
open bay looked as if it were divided by a wall, pierced with round
holes, blazing with circular light, behind which could be heard voices
and music; the space between the wall and the quay shot across by
launches turning and tearing, ripping the water's green back; and little
ceremonies of recommitment to land or sea took place on the quay,
as the commander of the battleship welcomed or was welcomed. And
every room along the front or up the terraces roared with sailors, their
pockets full of money; and the town girls out with them to supply the
honey; and nine months later, after the christening of too many grey-
eyed, flax-haired babies, the curé would get out his annual sermon on

the sin of fornication, until the next season brought more ships from newer and richer lands.

But from the day the ships arrived one could observe the girls' black overalls and dingy espadrilles shed, to be replaced by wall-paper cretonnes and shoes whose high heels turned over unaccustomed ankles; and shiny, pink wood-fibre stockings over olive legs. While the gramophones worked to death, and the tin pianos beat out jazz, and the cars of arriving and departing officers swept light paths on the bent road up the hill.

Much later the noise became more concentrated by the water's edge, more expressive of the emotions of drunk men struggling with a foreign tongue. Finally the ship police would load them into boats, groaning; the last cargo would shoot out, to be replaced at dawn by men with fresh leave and stragglers returning from the great town where Vincent had refound Paul. It had not occurred to him that it might be more than a spectacle for an american *deraciné* to see the men of his fleet out on a spree. Only he noticed a difference in the quality of their pleasure. He was at a play of which Paul had seen the rehearsals. Might at any moment run off behind the scenes. For Vincent the play was just sufficiently amusing; but Paul had imported something with him from the great town, where half the earth swarmed up and down an esplanade, where each vice had its location, and even the lamp-posts and bicycles were over-sexed. Sailors talked of the swell joints and the swell girls they had found there. Paul stood the drinks. He was sparkling with excitement. The somber child, alternating at dinner between timidity and impertinence, changed into a sharp-eyed lad in the know.

For some days before, as well as for some nights, Vincent had observed a shadow about the quays. First because it had tried to sell him an obscene book, then because it tried to sell André an obscene book, then because it tried to sell everybody an obscene book. Then because it was obscene. Of no race or of any; grey, green, greasy, with a few horned teeth and black nails; its clothes a patchwork of hotel leavings, its speech a kind of American, pronounced with a lisp, the chi-chi of the East. Referred to as the Pimp. No name, no associates, it would appear and be gone. It knew a whore-house, a cinema. Lived by finding the people who wanted those places. Found them. Of no age. Probably an immortal. Vincent composed of west wind and tree sap, the wine, beef, apples and classic literature of an english country house, was affected by him as by a bad smell. In the café he went over to speak to Stretton, escorting the little french girl. Danced with her once, introduced her to a sober, charming sailor, turned and saw Paul, leaning along the bar with the Pimp. Stretton must have seen him. Anyhow, he pulled the boy's shoulder round, surprised at the shock inside himself.

"What d'you mean—speaking to that filth here with us?"

Surprise from Paul might have cut his fury; defiance justified it— but the boy said: "No, no. Please take me away. It was not my fault. He spoke to me. I'm afraid of him."

The man glanced, cringing at them, and began to melt away, merging into the crowd at the door.

"Don't play into Stretton's hand then." Thoroughly cross he replaced him at the table.

Timidly Paul looked up at him. "I couldn't help it, Vincent. I saw him once or twice about before. I don't quite know what he is—" Then as "All right. Tell me why you're afraid of him" framed in Vincent's throat, the child's notes went out of Paul's voice, and the self-conscious, self-righteous debauché spoke: "Why should I mind what Stretton sees? If you're ashamed of me, you've only got to say so and I'll go—"

"Say go," said a guardian angel tartly to Vincent. As generally happens, he told it to shut up. In fact, "Shut up" was all he said aloud to Paul.

. . . . . .

"Pan," said Vincent, on a terrace on the top of the world, overlooking the sea in which some day Solomon is supposed to drown it, "what's Pan to you?"

"I guess," said Paul, "he's my god."

He seemed to want to hear something about him. Vincent sketched the varieties of his cult. He did not neglect him as a god of sex, but down the gulf below them a yacht race was standing in, on blue-roughened water, the true wine-dark, a handful of silver slips. And as he watched them, all that was natural in his training and imagination made him breathless with love. Inattentive and unprepared later to meet reserved sarcasm from Paul—"That's all I know about Pan— what's your idea?"

Paul's answer was the smile of contemptuous pity a novice might get from a nasty old priest.

"I could show you a bit more about him if you came with me up the back streets at night."

"Only drunks and drunks and more drunks. Like the Prince Regent's waistcoats."

"There's more than that—you'd see how people get away with it— what I can do—" The dark blue stone eyes were shining again; his smile to himself, an acute sensuality outside the romantic attitude to sex. Vincent whisked the car back down the hair-pin bends and wished it would grow wings, fly away with Paul and punish him, and show him a life so different that back streets or high hills would be Tom Tiddler's ground to him. And it felt as though he had exchanged a cake of soap stuck with nails for a crystal ball when he joined André after dinner, alone.

Then Stretton came in. He said, "Where's your interesting experiment, Paul Martyn?"

"Out somewhere, I suppose. I'm not his nurse."

Then they listened to André, brought their lives to illustrate his. They loved him.

Dudley knocked. "I've seen your Paul below. He asked me why I was ashamed to be an American. I didn't know that I was."

Vincent did not understand their problem. The hag of unspecified bad conscience hobbled in. André was tactless.

"He will not make a scandal for us here, will he?"

"Of course not. And he asks rude questions out of defence. Let the boy enjoy himself his own way. What reason is there to turn him into a bad copy of us?"

"By all means," said Stretton. "A glimpse into the mentality of the Pimp at second hand might be useful."

Vincent felt an impulse to go down, fetch Paul, and beat him. Both ways Dudley and Stretton cramped his impulses. And for nothing would he miss an evening of André's magic mind.

Very much later he looked out his bedroom window, high up over the slip of cobbled square. Dancing was over and carouse and rows. On the other side of the hotel the sea lifted quietly up. Here and there a window of the old town showed a square, rose or orange. Somewhere a concertina gasped a dying breath. A line of plane trees rustled, and drew a delicate shadow on moon-whitened stones. Out of the house shadows an occasional cat slipped. He washed himself in the moon-quiet. Then saw that there were two people about, presently visible in the open square—Paul and the Pimp. At the foot of a stair they turned and mounted quietly together up the town. Vincent stayed still. So that was what Paul did when he went out to play. Follow him out and ask to be taken to see Pan? The shadows seemed to be coarsening and thickening. He remembered the smell of thyme—sweet, rank, classic grossness. He cleaned his teeth a long time. The stuff was called euthymol. A whiff of magic about; great indifference to Paul. He slept.

Paul woke late next morning, and with the nervous anxiety common to his race began to feel for symptoms of disease. Throat sore, mouth "like the bottom of a parrot's cage," nerves no worse than usual, but outside scrutiny. Normal awakening under abnormal circumstances. He should have been rather pleased with himself, but part of his conscience was raw and in raving protest. He hadn't come to Vincent to behave like that. Hated Vincent for the stab of remorse which made it necessary to suppress tears. The spasm passed and he smacked his lips. Stretton wouldn't have dared to go where he'd been, and Vincent wouldn't have cared. And André. He bet André knew more about it than he'd let on. All the same, he hadn't meant to keep the rendezvous he had made with the Pimp at the bar before Vincent had turned him away. Why in hell had he? Why in hell shouldn't he?

He got up, groomed himself with concentrated attention, and went out. At the tip of the breakwater, under the pepper-box pharos, André and Stretton were sunning themselves. Paul had on the coat he had worn the night before. A pocket crackled. He pulled out a sheaf of dirty drawings and sat down to reperuse them. The breeze blew one along. Stretton retrieved it, glanced at it and rose politely to return it. Impudence seized Paul. He walked back with him and showed the whole lot to André then and there. André laughed; but both were embarrassed by Stretton. High intelligence and boundless information uncorrected by wide experience takes all comfort out of criticism. But because André laughed and chattered, Paul thought he had triumphed. Would not let his sexual curiosities drop. Again he bored them. André finally let him see it, and was told in French too rapid for Stretton that there was no need for him to play the prude. He lay sprawling by André, his tight, smart looks displayed beside the worn seraph, laid out, light as blown steel, along the stones. Blind with need for response he became reckless, using *"tu"* and calling the Frenchman by his first name. Knew himself further and further separated from him, until he yelped from his starved little heart:

"D'you know, André, you seem a hypocrite to me. When you were younger you raised enough hell. You're getting affected."

André, infinitely wise and unwise, whose memories were of Paris, poetry, the adventure and passions of a unique personality, did not want to be reminded of his incomparable adolescence. How it could be visualized by this little animal. He raised himself on his elbows and began an apostrophe on aeroplanes, men, birds, bird-priestesses and the hawk of Horus. On wings. Stretton tossed back the thread as it wove over Paul's fair head laid comfortless on his small, clasped hands. He held hard to the belief that all they said was only his own life dressed up. It was because they weren't honest and had read things. Suddenly he got up and almost shrieked at André: "If you'll excuse me, I'm going. I can't stand any more. *Ta voix m'agace.*" Stretton made a gesture. André carried on, his voice the minutest division of a tone higher.

He lunched with Vincent. It had been agreed that Vincent should leave the long table, to which he had not been reinvited, and join him for one meal each day. His outburst at André, his failure with André, had let loose a storm of sensibility and a need to confess. Vincent was cold. Paul began to explain how good Vincent was for his character. It was a dreary shock when the Englishman said: "Then what were you doing out last night with the Pimp?"

He saw the boy retreat into himself, trapped. Then plaintively: "I can't speak to you now, Vincent. Leave me alone, please." He saw Vincent shrug his shoulders, unaware of the pity which could have won him forgiveness.

Vincent went to fetch André, Dudley and Stretton for a run in the car. Found André on his bed talking, supported on his elbows, and morally by Stretton. After Paul's small, musical drawl, French tired his ears. He was oddly unstrung. Paul's presence, which could not separate him from André, divided him from Stretton. All three whom he loved, and differently.

Stretton said: "Paul has told André that his voice gets on his nerves."

The pit of Vincent's stomach made itself noticeable. "What's it been about?" A few careful sentences, terrible in their scrupulous avoidance of condemnation, gave the meeting on the quay. Stretton holding his mirror up to nature. A superb mirror, reflector also for his petulant, stern beauty. He might as well have struck Vincent when he left the room to tell Dudley the car was ready. Vincent looked at André, to watch his mouth set in its divine smile. It did not. He turned over nervously.

"Vincent, let me speak frankly. Before your *protégé* came, and Dudley and Stretton were so perturbed, I had thought them unjust. I meant, in fact, to take the boy up. To give him the run of this room. See if one could help him. Teach them a lesson in kindness. I see now that it is impossible. To begin with, he is a bore. Bores are unhelpable. Then he is corrupt. Not on account of his life or his taste in art. And I rather liked him when he said that my voice got on his nerves. It gets on mine. I am speaking of the quality of qualities."

Bitter-crystal waters of lucidity. Vincent nodded. "But, André," he said, "I had him here on trial. I know now it is no good. I'll send him away."

"Not at all on my account. It is you I am considering. You let your heart run away with you. The boy adores you, but some day he will play you a dirty trick. You don't know these little boys as I do. And you English play the *grands seigneurs* in a world that does not admit their existence. And—" (the clause was flashed in) "I do not want any scandal here."

Very well punished, Vincent said: "All right, André, I'll clip his poor little claws. I shan't cut him myself because of what happened to him in prison when he was a child. I hold that because of that a lot should be forgiven him. We'll run up into the mountains. I'm going for the car."

"Nasty pill," said Vincent, stopping in the corridor to feel his wounds. So much for the Kourotrophos. He had risked André and Stretton on that piece of swank, and had been very properly put in his place. Was it for that he was nearly weeping? Not at all, he observed, sufficiently a pupil of the french mind; but because his little kouros could not be brought up. Would never *put off the old man like a garment.* The filth had gone too deep, he was dyed in it. Vincent knocked at Stretton's door.

"Coming?" There was discussion in the further room.

"Dudley wants to know if there will be room."

"Yes, for the four of us." Dudley appeared, perfect, neat, complete, hands in pockets, his look pitched straight at Vincent. He did not mean to come if Paul were asked. And he was perfectly right.

Worse luck. They were perfectly right.

"Only us four. Are you coming?"

"Yep."

They dined on another terrace-rock, hung over space; a cloud hiding the gardens and vineyards of men. All that was visible was other stones, staring like animals at the shifting, glittering sea. They sat until the sun turned its dancing-floor into a lacquered parquet, a gold path for his dip into the ocean baths.

Vincent told them the memories of Atlantis, Hy-Brasil, the Apple Land. André told them about Basques. A Basque and what had happened to him swimming in the basque country. A story which would have pleased Paul.

The boy spent an afternoon chewing the cud of stale excess. Inclined for company, he went down to the hotel front, on the quay; and there, as though newly risen from the dead, was the Pimp, pestering a tourist. And when he had pestered him, he made straight for Paul, sat down beside him, and carried on, as though it had never been interrupted, their conversation of the night before, held in a dim-lit maroon-hung brothel of the old town. There followed suggestions how they might be useful one to the other.

"You gotta pull on plentee smart guys. You bringa them to me."

In bright gold daylight. The only creature who wanted to speak to him. Misery rose in Paul. The man became a spectre of his imprisonment: of all that cut him off from other men. He was a louse out of his filthy cell, who had crossed the water on his body: fattened on his secretions. The rich pleasure he had taken in the man became a fearful punishment to him, who believed in punishment: who had been punished. As he stared away from him, the green harbour water plaqued with gold, the old stones tufted with wild flowers, the fringed mountains against the low sun, all the shapely, brilliant beauties of Europe's cradle became alive with obscenity; neutral forms for the foul to make plastic. His very precious ring, the gold snake with the diamond sunk in its head, was a small fiend in command. A late fisherman landed a net of flapping, dying, sea-people; snatched a small squid from the salt-running pile and held it up. Once Vincent had caught one—Vincent so easy and happy out in boats—and had told him how they were motifs for decoration on cretan jars. An awful people they must have been. Between the squid, the Pimp and his little ring he was being damned alive. He could not tell him to go. He must go where he was bid, as before he had gone to prison. A calvinist ancestor appeared.

"My great-great-grandson, it pleased the Lord to damn you before you entered your mother's womb. It is so, even though you should learn humility and bless Him for it." The squid's arms writhed. The fisherman, young, gay, beautiful, held it up; flashed his white teeth at the small crowd round him, lowered his head and bit till the eight arms fell limp. Lifted his slimed face and laughed. Paul, now nearly mad, shrieked.

The Englishwoman walked along the quay, looking for friends. She saw Paul and smiled at him. He staggered up, agonisedly produced the pretty manners of his upbringing.

"Come and have a drink with me," she said; "are Vincent and André back yet? You didn't go with them?" The Pimp faded.

"No," he said; "I'm afraid I've offended them."

"English people ain't easy to offend. It's your american nerves." He looked to her also like a child. "What have you been up to?" she said.

"Vincent is angry because I spoke to that man. I didn't mean to. I'd give anything to get away—"

"You've only to cut him and he'll run."

"But you didn't know. I can't." She saw that it was serious.

"Vincent told me something. If you want to live differently, you have only to tell Vincent. He's patient—"

"God knows I am sorry, but what's the good?" All the same, when he looked round, the harbour was again a place for ships. "Thank you," he said, "most people are decent to me now. And when they aren't, I dare say it's my fault."

They dined together, waiting for Vincent. But by the time he returned, Paul disintegrated again. The Englishwoman spoke to Vincent: "Go and look after that kid." Vincent, only half-willing, found him in his room; heard only a petulant, self-righteous harangue on Vincent's misconceptions about him—which he answered grimly enough with André's sentence: "You could have been adopted, given the freedom Stretton and I have: to teach them charity, and you something more about life. And André, who is infinitely merciful, saw it was no good."

Paul said, "Yes, for a Frenchman, he is merciful. But he would never understand. I think that man below is the devil and that he is following me."

The agony in his eyes, blue stones, glazed and burning, convinced Vincent. "Let's look at it clearly," he said. "Why did you go off with that man?"

"I don't quite know. You see, I'm more accustomed than you to that sort."

"Sort of swank then?"

"Perhaps. You've had such luck, you people. I was just as well raised. And if I'd had your education—"

"Cut that out. If you want education, you'll get it. I'll tell you this, Paul—" The countryman of Blake took a long breath, lifted the apricot-tanned head, darker than his hair. His eyes counted paint-flaws on the wall, his imagination aware but sightless. He said: "That man is an ambulatory, mediterranean sore, living on the viciousness of our vices. But I think he's a shadow, d'you see—the image, the signature of a very living thing that is your torment. He is nothing, a corpse, a nuisance; but he may be under orders. Orders he knows even."

Paul amazed him, breaking into sobs, the unfathomable hysteria of the damned. He took him by the shoulders, almost to his heart, and said: "You have only to summon your courage. It'll come: and he'll melt."

But Paul sobbed on, racked noises leaving his body, as a man might spew up formless evil spirits. Vincent hitched him into the crook of his arm, each jerk of the slight shoulders registered against his heart. Was this the beginning of purification? He caressed, careful not to talk. Paul at last lay still; then sat up suddenly, slung his fine ankles to the floor, went to the *lavabo* and washed his face with hot water, with cold, with cologne. Drew a wet comb through his hair, worked on his cheeks with a powder-wad.

"Thank you for letting me cry. It did me a lot of good."

"Where are you going now?"

"Down to the lounge. I don't think he'll come there. I've got a book."

"What sort of book?"

"I like it. It is about the sort of gentlemen my people were; like yours. The sort I might have been." Vincent was conscious of the whine, the sniff, mixed with the utter truth. He sat on the side of the bed, pensive and fatigued.

He went down to the garage and saw to his car; and there, among its intricacies, anchored himself against flights on to planes of suffering which produced the phenomena of one fair boy weeping on his bed, and one green, gap-toothed figure dodging on the quays. Also distaste, division, and disgust among a band of friends. He ate up his car's insides like cake; here was something precise to *do*, for people who were dependents on his car's flights for pleasure. He had worked himself into a serenity, a little too ardent to be sane, when, rising from his knees he saw the Pimp, looking in at the garage door, pulling something out of his loose pocket, a book or a box.

"Get out!" he cried. The man's mouth moved; it sounded like whistling. Something flapped. He went off. Up the moonlight-stair Vincent had watched on the last night.

He left the garage and crossed the square to the hotel. It was getting late. In a corner of the empty salon he found Paul with his book. A child sent to Coventry, in the arid, frivolous, depressing room, his face was still scorched with crying.

"Vincent, for pity's sake, don't give me up. It is true what you said; there are evil spirits around me. I've been too kicked to fight them alone. You invited me out of hell into heaven, and it seems I brought my own hell with me. For pity's sake—"

And pity like a naked, new-born babe striding the blast. Vincent flung himself off down the corridor to André's room, and found him alone. "André, I've sent that child sky-high, and it seems to have kicked him permanently off his legs. I'm out of power; I can't handle him."

The passionate sentences, thrust into literal French, intrigued André: "Oh these little boys with more sensibility than wits! I know them. Send him up to me."

He went back. "André says you're to go to him."

"I'm ashamed."

"Do as he tells you."

"I'll try."

Vincent sat on the foot of André's bed. All lights were out but the reading-lamp that lit the Frenchman's hands, the gay, dark, imagination-worn head in rose-gold shadows. Paul drew up a stool to the bed and sat between them, leaning against it, his hands on the sheets.

"*Mon gosse,* what is this trouble about? Vincent tells me that you are afraid of the Pimp. But Stretton says that he saw you talking to him last night."

"I did worse than that. I went with him up to the old town, with the sailors. Today I saw him again. He would speak to me. Today I saw that there were evil things all round me. And I see the man everywhere. In places where I know he can't be. He is a devil. I am being punished again. I am always being punished—"

André scribbled a note and gave it to Vincent. "Take that down to the *patron*. It is to say that if that man is seen round the hotel again I and my friends leave. That should settle it. Will that do, boy?"

When Vincent returned to his place Paul had drawn closer to the bed, and André's hands were invisible, the boy's face laid on them.

"My little one, you are young and handsome. Clever at some things, Vincent says, and neither poor nor sick. What is it that spoils your life?"

Paul answered in a low voice: "It has always been the same, André. When I was at school. People were unjust to me. I hadn't laughed much in years till I knew Vincent. He can make me giggle. And in spite of his friends, who hate me, he brought me here and introduced me to you. And my filth's followed me just the same. I'm in prison like I was before. Then something that separates me from you. Dudley and Stretton are quite justified. I shall never hold it against them that they won't know me. But I'm sorry I was rude to you today."

"It isn't that," said André, looking out as Vincent had done, summoning his angel. "It is your attitude to life, to people, that is wrong. Don't you know that the kind of general insolence in which you take pleasure makes people your enemies—separates you, as you say? When your charm is all you have, you ruin it, and wonder that you are ruined. If you used it, you would have friends, and your devils would vanish, and your life fill with pleasantness."

"But I am better, much better, much more moral since Vincent—"

"When did Vincent preach morals to you? Morals are an excuse for a boy of your sort, to justify your tempers. Or hags to ride you to hell. Leave your little virtues alone, and attend to the virtue which gave you Vincent. Don't you know that God does not like us for the things we think good. For the rest, courage—" He pulled a silver ring down his arm and slipped it on the boy's wrist. "Wear that tonight if you're afraid." The lovely, tired voice ran on, with passion fatigue seemed to strengthen, and all the vicissitudes of man. Paul kept his face laid on the hand he clung to, the bracelet that had changed wrists lighting the sheets. "Remember the old woman who had been pious, at heaven's gate, who was secretly afraid because when she was a child she had stolen cherries from a tree. She told Peter all the good she had done, and while he called up God the Father, prayed that the cherry-tree had been forgotten. Until God answered, 'Let her in. After all, it's the woman who robbed the cherry-tree.' It is a sin to wear thorns when God meant you to wear roses."

Vincent, silent, curled-up, heard Paul's rare, short, flute laugh. Knew he was listening to the Kourotrophos, the bringer-up of boys. André, the peacock of the world, who had borne the cross. Paul was smiling at him, and now he had lifted his head, Vincent saw André's hand wet with tears.

It was late. It seemed as if there was a huge balance in this room, a scale filling up and up against the other which had been filled. Paul's face was hidden again, this time on his knees. André spoke on; but Vincent dreamed that the scales held the life and death of Paul. If the high one sank, a cup would sail in down a light ray (he imagined it through a hole in the shutter slats). There would be a lance with it and an aureole for the boy. If it did not, well, he could only see a seedy man with green teeth following them about.

There was a knock at the door. Without waiting Stretton came in and stood for a moment against André's bathrobes. André said: "A moment, Stretton."

Paul sat up, but both he and Vincent had time to see Stretton's face, set like the Lucifer of the english imagination, in blasting pride and contempt. A son of the morning, visiting a son of the morning, his eyes were on Paul, the scorn in them a thing to cross dreams.

André said: "Come back in a quarter of an hour." He went out. The high scale stayed in air.

Paul got up. "Thank you very much, André. You've done me a lot of good. I'll say goodnight now. I'm very tired. Goodnight."

Vincent followed him. "Well," he said, "now can you have a little faith?" and saw Paul look at him with lost sweetness that hardened again through misery past comprehension to a coarse denial that would never leave him again.

"Almost," he said, "I had. It was like music that you could see. Till Stretton knocked. Then it turned not real, flat, a bit of pretence. Stretton did it. He meant it too. He's in with the man on the quays." And at Vincent's agonised laugh: "I'm not so frightened now. I reckon I can get along. But not as André meant. Or you. Not after the way Stretton looked at me. He's put me back in my place. I know now that the filthy can never mix with the clean. He won't forgive you in a hurry either. Or André, when he's thought it over. D'you think I need give him back his bracelet? The boys in Paris will make a fine story out of it. Sorry, Vincent. I hope, I hope— Oh, only that Stretton will never be able to bitch you as he's bitched me."

Vincent felt very cold—utterly tired. He took Paul's wrist and slipped off André's silver ring. "If you ever want it back, you will only have to ask for it."

"Thanks, but I shan't. I'm off tomorrow. Run in to you sometime if you care to remember me. I should like that— Vincent, you're a poor fish to take it so hard. It's my business. I shall be gone before the rest of you are up. Goodnight."

❖ ❖

Last Stories

Look Homeward, Angel
The Guest
A Roman Speaks
The Warning
Mappa Mundi
A Lover
From Altar to Chimney Piece
With and Without Buttons
After the Funeral
The House
Honey, Get your Gun
In the House
Lettres Imaginaires

1938

❖ ❖

Look Homeward, Angel

THE LOVERS SAT, side by side, building up their fire; and Julian laid across it a bleached log of driftwood, to burn with a white flame and spitting blue sparks, charring to a silk ash over a core of rose. Contented, they sat together in the old house in the secret valley above the sea. Outside the stream ran, singing its full-throated mid-winter song; outside the night was blind with sea-fog, windless mist, made visible by the light streaming from the windows as made of myriad of diamond points.

Since dusk it had entered their valley, rising off the sea, brimming the tiny cove, rising past the mill to their house enclosed in its trees and its garden where the flowers bloomed the whole year long. Past them, it had risen across the moors, to the dreadful hills with their standing stones. Avenues and circles and huts and stones of sacrifice—of a race which has by no means died out in the extreme West.

Cynthia took up her sewing: "*Still she sat, and still she span*'—and had no wish for company—" They smiled at one another. Julian poured out a glass of wine and settled himself again before the fire.

They sat for a time in silence while the fire played its flickering air. Outside the house the quiet was absolute, "*Not a mouse stirring.*" Not a sigh of air from off the Four Winds' Playground; even the sea beat inaudible for once. This with one exception: for each alternate minute the stillness was not so much broken as underlined by man's answer to the day and night terrors of fog at sea, when the siren at Pendeen answered the gun on the Longships Lighthouse, muffled thunder alternating with a strangled moan. For even these huge voices the fog had by the throat; and men heard them as you might imagine voices from the other side of death.

"Queer," said Julian, "millions of drops of water a reason why large iron ships should pile up on rocks, and be ground to pieces on equally hard stones. All by more water, lots of water, pulled about by the moon. It's a queer universe."

"And we live in one of its queerest patches. That's why we love it: and it is well with us here."

"It would be well with *us* anywhere," he said. Again they smiled. Cynthia put aside her work and lit a cigarette:

"Here's another queerness for you. Here we are at Nanquidno, almost as far away from people as it is possible for people on this island to be. Yet the Atlantic at our door is an Oxford Circus of the sea. All the great liners, *Berengarias* and *Aquitanias*, pass us on their stately way to America and back. Pick up our lights, the Longships and the Wolf and the Parson and his Clerks. First sight of home for us, or of a new land for them, as they go by, blazing at nights as if they were carved out of fire. These and the others, nosing their way round to the Irish ports—My word!" She stopped. "So it is," he said. "Time slips past here. Fergus," he ended, "will be home now any day."

They were waiting for Fergus, their friend, the third part of their lives, whose lives were part of a theme, lines that have found their meeting place at the point of the plane. Or, in the place where parallels meet their three lives were one. The united life they were waiting for, to begin again once Fergus should have done with his travels. Travels now so nearly over that they might expect him from day to day.

"Let's see—he sailed on Saturday. That makes it five days. They berth at Southampton, tomorrow morning. That's it. Julian, do you realize that he's passing us now, tonight? There's been nothing to set them back. Oh, can't we go out, climb up Aire Point and wave a light for him to see?" Julian grinned, pointing out that, on a night when the garden gate even was invisible, the chance of Fergus seeing them, several miles out to sea, might be considered remote. Cynthia's crest fell a little. Her husband laid his hand on her cap of gold curls:

"It's our friend the subconscious again. Though I'd forgotten the days, yet I've so felt he might have news for us that every night I've nearly gone out and tramped up to the Post." She nodded:

"I've been the same. For two days now or three I've felt he had something special he wanted us to know." "Something," she went on happily, "tremendous: that we'd know for ourselves if we weren't such sillies. Something he's too Scots-prudent to wire: and he didn't want to spoil it, but he's panting to tell us."

Silence fell. She looked at her husband, but the smile of joyful understanding she waited for did not flash out from Julian's eyes and back again. Again a little checked, she queried: "Nothing, sweetheart," he said. Then it crossed her mind that he came from the north, from the outmost islands; and irrelevantly, that he was far more a part of this land than she, who had been bred in the true south, in the chalk and turf country, where the great civilizations meet. Not from the ultimate west, where, day by day, men watch the sun stepping into the Baths of Ocean. Into his mystery which is death and resurrection, a play enacted daily, with the Sun for hero and the Moon for heroine. She herself was called after the moon. What was Julian doing? He was standing now by the window, in one of his "dawms," staring out down the candle shafts at the myriad crystals spinning in the air. Talking to himself, as he was wont to do, muttering bits out of great poems, as if their words had come out of their place in their own heavenly country and entered the ordinary world. Something about: *"The shores and sounding seas Wash far away, where're thy bones are hurled."* Who was hurling Fergus's bones? Still the murmur continued and she too good a wife to interrupt: *"Whether beyond the stormy Hebrides."* But ships didn't get blown out of their courses like that now; that was what longitude was for. *"To our moist vows denied."* But why moist and why denied? Who was denying Fergus anything? *"Visitest the bottom of the monstrous World."* What *did* he suppose Fergus was up to? "Monstrous world." Indeed. Fergus was coming home, to be with them. "Till death parts us, and it won't." *"Look homeward, Angel,"* Julian's voice gathered strength and she heard him clearly. That was more like it. The sea must just have raised glorious words in Julian's head. He would tell her later. Perhaps, in a day or so, Fergus would be telling them himself how he nearly fell overboard; or, when he saw the Longships lights, felt he must jump off and swim straight for land....

It was ten o'clock. Their maid slept out, and Cynthia began to put the house away to bed. The cats mewed themselves out and in. She lit their bedroom fire, the candles beside their bed. Julian went to his bath. When all was ready, she went to their room, changed her frock for a dressing gown and sat by the young fire, combing her curls to silk, reading from a book Fergus had given her.

From the lighthouse where, six miles off, the last stone in England stands up out of the sea like a black tooth, the thunder roared. Broke in this time as if it were at their door. A minute later, this time to the east, the dreadful moan answered, like a vast cry of pain. What had brought them nearer? A thinning of the mist? The curtains were drawn over the open windows. Not a fold stirred; nor could she, listening for a moment, for once be sensible of the tide-lap, even in that world of eternally angry seas.

Nor were there any footsteps outside in the lane. Only the garden gate must have swung open, for its hinge creaked. She almost thought, too, that she heard the latch fall.

In the bathroom Julian gave a sudden slow splash. A tap roared and was shut off. She opened her book again, at a song she had first heard Fergus sing—about a mother who sat waiting for her sons, who came back suddenly in the middle of the night in bark hats. Bark that only grew at the gates of Paradise. Paradise hats. Paris. Paradise. Paris—she must be falling asleep. She remembered Fergus in a play, with a huge hat slung across his back. Apollo he had been, and her name was the moon. Their Apollo—and he had gone the sun's way west, doubled back on it. Like the wanderings of Apollo, who for a part of his time on earth kept sheep for a king.

The sun in service, wearing a Paradise hat; and to make the pattern quite perfect, that was what Fergus looked like. One of those early statues of the god they had been digging up, with a neck all wide and grand, and your eyes travelled up to a great forehead under curls, and staring, inscrutable eyes. He and the sun and the six sons in the song all got their hats from the same place. It was most important that she should remember that…she sat up with a start, her curls fallen each side of her cheek…falling asleep in her chair, dreaming of Fergus, bee-lining about with the sun. The sun that was now blazing away thousands of miles under their feet. Would it ever be possible to fly so fast as to overtake? Catch up with the sun and race with him. Have no night? No, it was the earth that did the racing. Anyhow it was adorable to think that in a few hours he would be back, streaming, with any luck, in gold ribbons over Carn Brea. As it was adorable to think of Fergus, now safe in-Channel, ploughing stately across from Cherbourg to Southampton, and back, following the sun again, across Carn Brea to their arms.

The sun has a bath every night. What a long time Julian was taking over his. Strange—like the garden gate, she would have thought that the front door had opened and shut. She must stop falling asleep. Soon she would be asleep, by Julian, glowing, damp and sweet-scented. Sleep softly, with the mist streaming in and the fire leaping up, and between them, at their feet, curled Fergus's cat.

Had she closed the sitting-room for the night? It looked as though there was a light still burning there. Not the fire-glow. Nor the moon in such weather unless the fog had lifted. She got up and stepped softly along the passage. It must come from outside, the head-lamps of some car, stationary, a long way off on the moor.

She reached the door. And, oh! sitting there, waiting for them was Fergus. They must have made a record passage, and he had torn himself back. Walked home that night, over the Penzance hills, and slipped in to surprise them. He was sitting there, in his high red chair—it was his grave glorious bearing. Home at last, but very tired. Bare-headed— dear Apollo. But—but—it must be the light—there was a curl of light round his hair, half a disk of it; which would do for a Paradise hat.

What was it—he was wet. How wet he was. The mist beads laid all over high and shining. Dark water even, running on the floor. So dark it might be blood. It was she who must be asleep, in a cold dream. Else why had she not flown to embrace him? The air round her was like ice. Fergus was getting up. He must be got to bed. Perhaps he was ill from exposure, from the night, from the evil road that crosses Carn Brea, where the stones hide the drowned men who have crept there up from the sea.

Else why had she not flown to his arms, the moon in transit with the sun, the top of whose head could reach up to his breast?

Out into the warm corridor, on whose panels the fire from their bedroom leaped, she ran and beat upon the bathroom door. Julian opened instantly and drew her in.

"Julian, Fergus is here. I found him in the sitting-room. So tired he could not speak. Only smile at me. He was getting up but he is wet and icy cold, and there's a queer light, and I ran and fetched you—" Her husband said:

"I'll go. I see. Go to your room, Cynthia, for a moment. We shan't be long." And the authority there is between husband and young wife, between man and woman, between lover and lover, was so clear in his voice, that she obeyed him gladly.

"Shut your door." Shut it, shut out the fire's warm play. Shut in profoundest night. Now he knew himself to be standing, alone with night. He turned towards the room, where, now risen to his feet, his friend would be standing, his height outlined in that light that shines or grows:

> "in dyke or ditch
> Nor yet in any sheugh—
> But at the gates of Paradise—"

Who had dragged his bones together out of the flood, from the darkness that lies at the roots of the mountains, to be the first with his news.

At the doorway Julian forced his eyes to obey him. The room was empty. While through the windows, scattering the mist, a dazzle of moonlight poured; and the great red chair that had been Fergus's was drawn out; and, as he touched it, he felt on it a gauze, a skin of mist.

He went over to the window and leaned out, looking across the garden to the wide lane, at a world moon-struck with a pure, blinding light. Then, with another of those small sounds he heard the house door shut.

"Thank you, Fergus," he said: and a moment later found Cynthia standing by his side. Thus, for an instant, at the window their arms went out, as though to embrace what stood there, outside in the white air. But as they fell empty at their sides, they smiled, and when Cynthia spoke it was with a cry of gladness:

"Look homeward, Angel." The garden gate clicked.

. . . . .

Now it was spring, the spring Fergus would not see; and they sat together in the garden, side by side.

"We will have it cut on the memorial: 'Lost at Sea.' "

"I suppose," said Cynthia, "they would not let us add where he was found?"

✧ ✧

The Guest

H E CAME DOWN FROM London to meet a wife prepared by her husband to receive him, by reminiscence, by anecdote, strung together, as essentially unrelated as the rough stones of a primitive necklace—tales of what he and her husband had done when they had been in the army. Both on the same staff, temporarily out of danger, two very young men, taking their first look at the world under circumstances favourable to swift friendship.

"Erskine-Browne's the name, and more Browne than Erskine; but damned good-looking he was, and money he just could not bear to spend."

"The Browne part turned up when he got engaged. We all came along to do our bit. I had the girl's mother in tow—the Cheltenham *haut monde* touch. I did a drawing of her, poking her lorgnette in our faces. Then there was *his* father, and the point was to keep him quiet—like a war-memorial before the unveiling, in a sheet. But the string broke at tea, when he tipped his cup out into the saucer and sucked it in through his false teeth. I tell you the lorgnette broke, and next day they all came round to explain to me."

"All the same, on a horse you might have taken Archie for a god."

Scraps of this sort of enlightenment. While for recent data the fact that the two men had not met for years, that Archie was richer than ever, unmarried—rather suspiciously so. Nor could she determine the link which seemed still to remain, unbreakable, between them. Not long training or breeding or gift or grace. One overwhelming common experience? In part. Admiration? Not on her husband's part, who seemed to consider Archie a rich, slightly sinister, and wholly private joke. Perhaps a little envy, a little compassion mixed?

231

There it was, and Julian a little emotional about it as well. Amused, too, and expectant, as though in some final way he would always have Archibald Erskine where he wanted him. This in spite of Archibald's wealth and consciousness of his wealth, his apparent social ambitions, his still formidable good looks.

She had just done the flowers in their small house, perched like a wart on an eyebrow of flowery cliff 300 feet up from the Atlantic, when a long car, streamlined in black and scarlet, with glittering head-lamps for eyes, tore down the ruts in their lane, and with a touch of gentle magic stopped at the gate.

There followed a most peculiar set of days. At first a very large, very handsome man, particularly fearful of women who play the fine lady, reassured, was amiable from excess of relief.

So far, so good, yet that delicate sense was active that tells us there is something just ahead, an event all ready, waiting till time shall catch up with it. Once in that state of perception, there is nothing to do but fill in the time gracefully.

After the second day reminiscence and courtesies began to wear thin, characters began to adjust; and she waited for Archibald Erskine-Browne, after a header into strange waters, to come up again with his catch.

He came up shaking himself, like a diver more than a dog. Out of their sea, which, in its visible body, lay below the house. Below the stream-cleft, bog-patched, bush-picked, flower-scattered decline of huge rocks and moist earth it lay. From headland to headland, the gold crescent of coast, filled in with the sea, chord of that pure circle where the sea meets the sky. All under the June sun, pure colour saturated with light; and up the green walls of the shore an overpainting of rose, the rose of the wild campion following the streams. Placed there, as Archibald Erskine seemed to think, by God, for Julian to paint. When it came to Julian's painting he was respectful and rather irritable. He countered, as Julian's wife noticed, any allusion to it with reference to his own wealth. Not quite vulgarly or obviously, but as though it was the natural, the inevitable remark to make. As though one was the an-swer to the other.

Late in the evening she left them and went out by herself. Came back with the flowers she had gathered and laid them on the *salon* table. At the further end of the room the two men were sitting, oppo-site one another, in intimacy, in comfort; yet about them hung a sense that all was not well, that there was something coming out which had always lain in wait. She began to fill a jar, to stand on the table of the tiny entrance, where the gloves were flung and the caps, the torches, and the garden scissors and the letters piled for the post. Little implements of country life; and laid beside theirs, his, more showy, more costly, and always, as if by intent, for display.

"What have you got there?" Archibald Erskine asked.

"Wild flowers," she said—"fox-gloves and mallow and that campion that's growing everywhere. All the pinks and purples. Here you need not strip your garden to have enough flowers."

He began to explain how it was his custom to send an order to Solomon's. She answered politely that it must be pleasant to be able to do that,

"Yes," he said—"it's always a satisfaction to know that you are getting the best."

"A best," she corrected, sticking up a tower, bell-hung thick as bees.

"I suppose that wild stuff is as good in its way."

"*As* good—lilies-of-the-field *and* Solomon in all his glory. I'd like," she added wistfully, "both. While one gets as much fun out of either. Different fun." He continued to stare at her garden-tanned hands, sorting, thrusting, lifting, loosening.

"What do you call that pink one?"

"Campion," she answered—"one of the old flowers that turn up in letters as well as in life, and gave a name once to a martyr and to a poet. One of the plants that have made a place for themselves." She said something about the Campion who was a priest and the Campion who was a lutenist; and then, from the shadows among the cushions at the end of the couch, Julian spoke :

"And there's Cynthia's friend, Jack Campion. He said he was coming down. Round, I mean, round the coast in his yacht."

Instantly in Erskine-Browne's unfed imagination there rose the image of a ship. A hull lifting over the horizon, standing in like a swan to lie reflected in the cove's blue cup. Image of a serene ease and a sport he had never mastered. One with a high prestige value as well, slow, a mystery, and to be showy, expensive. In all, unsatisfactory for a man who wanted quick and striking results, without more cost than his Scots good sense told him he could afford, without loss attaching to the other methods by which Archibald Erskine-Browne imposed himself upon the world. Not to score off other men, or to win himself women—least of all to enjoy himself. But to reassure himself, make certain that he was one with other men, for the sake of participation. To be sure that the small dreadful hole within him was filled. A hollow he had been sensible of from his first consciousness. At mess, on parade, dictating letters at his business, it would open within him, like a bubble whose tough skin resisted whatever was thrust into it. A hungry hole he knew for an abyss; and his life a search to find what would fill it—something that would take root in it and spring up; and springing, complete his manhood. That was why he had sought out again Julian's company. If in that company he lived all the time in anguish on the hole's brink, yet in that company food that the hole would neither absorb nor vomit up never seemed so near. Now there was a sound, a word hanging about—campion. What did it mean? It had gone instantly into the hole, and the hole had spat it out, yet seemed that it asked for it again. What was it—a flower and a saint and an unknown man? He was afraid of unknown men. He was beginning to be at ease with these people, and now someone was coming who shared their lives, linked up with theirs at a score of points where his attachments were no more than threads waving about in air. Julian was saying:

"We shall now see Cynthia behaving like the moon, clear off down the Atlantic in Campion's infernal boat. Have you ever tried, Archie, the motion of the cradle of the deep off here, and can you see Menelaus sick when he went to fetch Helen from Troy?"

"I can," said Cynthia. "I believe that's how half of it happened." What they were talking about was just inside the range of his knowledge, only just. Yet one thing at least seemed clear—that Julian did not wholly approve of his wife's friendship for this image of a man known as Campion. Name of a flower and a man, with a whiff to it of rather special slang. A lounge-lizard? Yet "infernal boat" did not sound like a regatta yacht, white sails and white decks and white ducks and fancy brass-work. In which first suspicion he was entirely wrong; Cynthia was a woman to whom disloyalty appeared as a lapse in good-breeding, a lapse in taste, only Archibald Erskine-Browne was one of those men whose response to the word "marriage" is "adultery," to whom love has to be illicit before he can begin to think of it as "love."

"We've crawled about in boats, Campion and I, all our lives." Her flowers done she set back the rough-glazed jar, her eyes out to the evening sea, her voice tuning-in until it was on the edge of music, saying :

This was the man I saw,
He had been in England as long as dove and daw,
Calling the wild cherry tree, the merry tree.
The rose campion—

She broke off. The lovely words, one of the flower-pieces that match with Lycidas' strewings, the Winter's Tale Pastoral roused no echoes in him. Just sufficiently imaginative, and contemptuous of it, he felt them as a nail picking at a raw surface, ignoring the *daimon* who, with infinite patience, told him to throw them into his hole.

Yet that night, undressing, and in and out of sleep, and next morning, shaving, the delicate step of those lines picked their way in his brain. *Ionic a minore*, with Four and Twenty Blackbirds—*This was the man I saw.* With *Quinquereme of Nineveh*—*As long as dove and daw.* And with the Lake Isle—*alone in the bee-loud!* He had heard it as far as the Blackbirds and that had made it worse. *Calling the wild cherry tree....* He had heard her singing the rest of it as she went to bed: *The rose campion Bridget-in-her-bravery....* By the next evening all that it had come to mean in his mind was that a strange man was coming out of the sea, to spoil his visit and his renewed contact with Julian; also that the woman, Julian's wife, was about to leave her husband; and, as Archibald Erskine put it "have an affair with him on his boat"; and ought he to tell Julian ; and how was he to tell Julian?

The next day a bank of fog lay round their world in a ring. *As near a ring to a magic ring....* A cloud wall hung across the high moors, the pastures, crossing the bay a short way out to sea, enclosing it so as to make it into a pond, a toy, a cup of blue glass where the fishing-boats rode like ducks. "Pride of the morning"—soon the sun would suck it up, restore their width of hill and sky and sea. From the terrace they looked down on it, Cynthia and Julian remembering stories of one mist: how, when a certain fog-bank lay, making a bar across from point to point of the coast, in relation with one rock and another, with certain tides and the moon, then the fog was called the Hooper, and the boat that sailed out into it never came back. Either it met the local mermaid or ran into the ferry of souls that runs between their waters and the Scillies, but, there it was, it never came back. A piece of folklore they handed on politely. To hear it received with a snort of aggressive incredulity, as the sun struck the bank, sending the sea-cloud spinning into blue, and disclosing a small yawl, standing-in from the outer sea. On she came, as if asleep on the tide. Cynthia swept her with her glasses, and with hardly a word ran down the hill to meet him.

Actually she went alone, Julian remaining out of mere politeness since his friend showed no inclination to follow his wife. He glanced thoughtfully at him, standing beside a jar of cactus on the terrace wall, his eyes fixed on the sturdy sea-going boat now coming busily to anchor.

"Campion works him alone with his man, unless he has Cynthia to help him." There were two figures discernible, running down sail; and there was Cynthia, rowing herself out violently on a thing that looked like a water-beetle. She reached the yacht, and Archibald Erskine-Browne still stared at her—to see a tall man in a white sweater lean over the side and almost lift her on board.

"Your friend with the flowery name seems pleased to see her." Even Julian's marital obtuseness noticed this, and registered faint annoyance. Archie was going to be difficult and he wanted to go off sketching. Why was Archie going to be difficult? What was biting him? Like all artists checked at their job, Julian began to distil the magic by which, delicately, by degrees, yet very fast, they disappear. The Cheshire Cat's trick, which is an actual process, observable wherever such people are. Archie was aware of a series of faint sounds, which are the excuses proper to the ritual, suggesting that Julian might go down and join them; that he might not; that he would be there later: not here. That lunch would be as usual, unless they all lunched on board: that light changes very fast when there is mist about, and something about it being no good writing down blue unless you knew which blue: that blue and green fairly follow you about behind your back; which means that you have to follow them. By the time Archibald Erskine had done staring and had some sort of a response ready, there did not seem to be any more Julian to respond to. Alone, he picked up the glasses again and focussed them on the little ship. A sailor's boat—so much he saw at once. He saw Cynthia and Campion go below. The other man was busying himself on deck. The blind feeling was rising in him again—of being on the edge of the void, of looking down into his hole. It had begun the night before, in the pattern, by which as even he knew, these things make themselves known. In the trippery trip of those words the woman who had married Julian had said. Julian was married to a song. Damn nonsense—if he'd a wife, he wouldn't let her vanish with another man inside ships. A ship was a female thing, and women and ships meant trouble. *This was the man I saw.* Candour! That was damned cheek, and by God! he'd stand by Julian. Show him what a man's friendship meant....

Suppose Julian didn't care two hoots? Had parked his wife on her friend? Suppose Julian cared like hell and hated him for telling? No matter, one way or another he saw himself caught again in his early ambition, getting Julian where he wanted him.

Where did he want Julian?

Another sweep of the glasses. There was Cynthia's head in the hatchway. He saw her tumble up on deck and Campion after her. In bathing suits, by God; and an instant after he saw their two bodies curve over and part the green water; and, as it often does, sight stimulated hearing, and from a quarter of a mile below he would have sworn that he heard voices and laughter and endearments travelling up the hot blue quiet to his burning ears.

The two men dined alone. Campion had left his man on shore-leave and gone to sea with Cynthia. After fish. Sitting opposite Archibald Erskine-Browne was a poor fish called Julian. Fish that didn't seem to know it was a fish: a fish that must be told that it was a fish. The sun had long heeled over into the baths of ocean. Julian had made him look at Campion's ship, poised like a black butterfly on its gold track. Now the slow-gathering night had come, night still saturated with the reflection of the sun though the earth turned its back on it. If you were to hurry fast enough over the Atlantic plain would you catch it up?

Half an hour before midnight, and still pale in the West. In the terrace room the two men had fallen silent. Then from the lane came the mingled noise of two voices, two sets of feet; and Archibald Erskine got up to glare at the shameless wife, returning with her paramour, to fill with insolent laughter the house of the man she had betrayed.

For by then it had worked up to that. His very inability, at the moment, to tell Julian had strengthened the idea as a piece of secret knowledge, revealed to give him power. At the same time he feared to meet this Campion, a man who whatever he did would feed his uncertainty, make unknown calls and demand unknown adjustments. Unwillingly he stared at him, while Cynthia lit candles in tall glass sticks.

A very tall man, and shadowy in that light; a man with the sea in his eyes, and with that an air of fastidiousness that goes with interest only in quintessences, in people or possessions or experiences: that distils them out of the common forms of things. A man so secret in his private relation to the universe as to have no other secrets; who was his own secret. And Cynthia, now bending over Julian, was singing :

> "He shall have a fish,
> He shall have a fin,
> He shall have a haddock
> When the boats come in."

Song of the faithless wife? But women, he had heard, were very clever when they had a thing of this sort to conceal. The three of them were talking together like persons to whom months of separation are no more than yesterday.

Quite blind with his emptiness, he left them and went to bed.

.　　.　　.　　.　　.

By the next day everyone knew that he was unhappy. He took them out in his car, and drove so slowly and so furiously that the men were uneasy and annoyed. But to Cynthia it seemed that through the furious vibration a communication came to her, of rage and will to destroy—and incidentally power to do so. The *daimon* of secret knowledge asked her the question: "Do accidents happen like this?" And with it the answer: "At this moment, this man would not care if it did; but why?" Actually, a sheep was killed on the way back, and they had to watch Archibald Erskine throw money at the farmer without a word of grace. "I never argue with these people," he said; but it was they, in the man's small secret black eyes, who had to face the contempt. The Bentley started again with a roar; and then Campion saw Cynthia shut her eyes and make a little blind movement towards him. He leaned over: "D'you mind driving a bit slower—or it'll be a cow next time?" To see the driver's face turn for a second with a look that left him too astonished for protest. It was Julian who settled it by saying: "Slow up, Archie. This is where I'm making my big picture, and I want to see it in this light"—and kept them creeping along a winding moor road under the hills.

"Curious," thought Campion, "say 'painting' and he goes tame at once." Tame but hardly agreeable, for at tea he began that strange entertainment with which some persons divert themselves; for each object that was mentioned, extolling his own, and especially the price that he had paid for it.

"Blast him and his tea-service and his driving gloves and his rain-gauge and his spoons," Cynthia cried, when for a moment he left them. On his return his opening was different:

"Like Julian, I'm a Scot. Campion, Campion, what sort of a name is that?"

"From the south-west," he said.

"Accent invariably on the 'camp'?"

"Refer to my song," said Cynthia, quietly. He thought. (*He has been in England—as long*—as Lindsays have been in Scotland… as that bitch-faced wife, as long as either of them, in the south. I don't belong to these people, and they sit, quiet, watching me not being part of them. They'd sooner have his boat than my Bentley.) Like a huge handsome child, pretending he had no one to play with, he turned suddenly and strode out of the house.

"Julian, what's the matter with your friend? Julian, what are you laughing at?"

"I'm not laughing, but I like to see things happening all over again. Archie was always like that."

"All the same," said Campion soberly, "this afternoon he was up to murder point."

"Did you get him down here to annihilate the lot of us?" Cynthia asked. Then: "After all, I think I do understand. Julian, you're amusing yourself with him. *You* have power over him and like to see it working. You are a connoisseur in devilry like that."

"Not at all," said Julian piously. "I only wish he didn't make such a fool of himself." He laid his painter's hands together, like a man regarding an instrument. Cynthia sighed and shivered a little. Campion mused on the motion of a ship in the water, the minute response, widening to power, of the rudder-touch and the under-sea streams, and pitied this man who had no hands on the tiller of his soul.

The next day Cynthia and Campion went out to sea and stayed out. Before breakfast Archibald Erskine had said: "I think I ought to go away," and Julian had said: "Why?" and Cynthia had said to him privately: "Won't it do if we go away all day? Then he can have you to himself." And Julian had said: "But I want to paint." To which they had both said: "But you got him here," and all at once saw Julian begin to fade out.

With the result that for the next three days Archibald Erskine-Browne was left pretty much to himself.

·   ·   ·   ·   ·

It was the day after that something went wrong with Campion's boat, and pending the arrival of spare parts her crew had to remain on shore. Cynthia made an attempt to devote herself to Archibald, but, as she soon understood, he was by now past amusing. Yet he showed no sign of leaving them. While Julian contributed to the entertainment of his wife and his friend by suddenly losing his temper, telling them no matter where he vanished along the cliffs to paint, Archibald Erskine managed to follow him:

"I get away and suppose he has done what he said—gone over to the Penzance links to golf—and no sooner have I got down to it than he pops up. Yesterday I told him to go away, and this morning found he'd been watching me from behind a rock. As if I was a bird. Talk about the wings of the morning. Finally I had to give him a brush and a drawing block and let him try and do it too."

"Can he?"

"What d'you suppose? As a matter of fact, he has got some frightful sketching-club tricks." Lovingly they invited Julian to come with them on the yacht, and paint the cliffs sliding up and down between the Atlantic hollows. He answered them rudely. It was late evening, the lucent weather still holding, when Archibald Erskine strode in to join them out of the crystal night.

A little elevated by drink, he began to tell them of the golf he had abandoned, and the state of his handicap, in order to be taught by Julian to paint; of the picture he had done, of the pictures he was about to do. Depressed, they went to bed. By the smile on Julian's face, Cynthia perhaps rather more than depressed.

It went on. For each of the days that followed he watched Julian, interrupted Julian, annoyed Julian, tried to copy Julian. Yet not yet had he succeeded in enlightening Julian about his wife, alternately fretted and enchanted by the effortless ease in which Julian brushed over blank paper with colour and light. Why he ought to be worshipped for it—and that damned woman—he began to think that probably Julian would not believe it of her; had never thought of his wife as a wanton and wouldn't make the effort. It had always been difficult to get Julian to see what he did not wish to see.

The next day the weather broke, and there was no question of sailing or of painting out of doors. Instead the rain blew in grey squalls, and, to his feverish mind, Cynthia and Campion, no longer able to be alone, must be in torment. Must be making plans for getting out of torment and meeting one another secretly. At sea they had the universe. On land it was different. If only he was not such a bad sailor, he'd have spoiled their game. Suppose now he could catch them, come back to Julian with evidence of things seen with his eyes. Then he imagined a Bella Donna exit for them, out into the night, driven on board and out to sea in the deadly night of the storm.

Then he would be alone with Julian. Julian bound to him by a deadly tie. Julian vanquished. Julian restored. Julian bound. Julian his wife had never bound or any mortal....

By tea-time he had made himself so thoroughly and bewilderingly disagreeable, that the others could think of nothing but escape. Julian was the first; shut himself up, and the intricate design of a Bach fugue filled the house, enclosing him. Then he saw Cynthia get up, suggest vaguely a walk. To be refused by Campion, then belt herself into a raincoat and go out alone. The wind-born rain wove its music round the house. Below the turquoise cup had become a ragged grey fleece, ravelled at its edge, tearing at the earth's belt, no longer gold but a wet brown. Campion thought of thousands of tons of sand, each grain a star-miniature and of the distances of outer space, and gave thanks for these, and for each drop of water and each sun. It was Sunday, and earlier they had all taken Archibald Erskine to Church. Utterly bewildered, he had let Cynthia find his psalms for him and the hymns; and he had seen Julian's eyes fixed on the altar and Campion praying and Julian, one on each side of him, and shuddered at their vileness. A hatred which, though he did not notice it, filled his abyss up to the lip.

Half an hour later Campion also rose, said he had changed his mind. Archibald Erskine from a window watched him take the same high hill-track as Cynthia. She also had let fall a word—Nan-dreath. That was for Campion. Five minutes later he had looked up Nan-dreath on the map and went out also. Round the corner of the house he met the wind, the Bach-pattern still threaded, faint, but infinitely distinct.

He knew now how to find Nan-dreath and where they would hide there. Across Sarscathian Moor to the black wood where the pigeons call and the wind cannot come, in whose centre is a clearing and a log hut, and cut wood beside it for a resting-place.

He plunged across Sarscathian, into a bunch of horses out to grass, who wheeled and scattered. Along the grass causeway, between thickets of bramble and thorn, broken by bog patches, knee-high in yellow flag and swarmed with iridescent flies; earth and water patches, savage moor upon which man has never yet laid his hand, primeval waste.

The wood rose before him, shutting out the dim sea plains and the soft air he had breasted like a deep water. At that instant a hunter, but of a quarry gone to ground in no green-wood, but in the black heart of the haunted wood on Sarscathian Moor, where there are three woods and a *daimon* in each, but in this one a devil.

He vaulted the stone hedge, and in the sudden quiet heard his own breath. "Rook—kook—kook—kook," said a pigeon, and there was a clattering up in the tree-tops. He strode on millions of red needles, scented, springing and soft. At the entrance of the clearing he stepped behind a tree. There he would see Cynthia in Campion's arms. The rain had filled the warm windless clearing with every scent. Would he see her, stripped like a nymph? Or both of them, playing dryad and oread, playing at the powers they had told him haunt such places. Fine fools they would look, getting into the clothes again. Unless he drove them off, naked. No, he wouldn't do that because of Julian. Fine thing it would be to drive Campion's harlot naked over Sarscathian Moor....

He saw her, sitting on a log, looking into her lap which was full of plants. A wilder thought entered his mind—that she had come there to gather plants by which to poison Julian. She had told them rare plants were to be found there. She had come for the means to put Julian away underground, and soon her paramour would join her.

He saw her get up and walk round the hut. He crossed the open space, swiftly, after her. She must have heard his coming, for he heard her call: "Jack, is that you? I've found it"; then turn and see him, and from her face instantly realize her danger. Huge he knew himself to appear to her, full of anger and brute power, and not of her kind: looking down at her, raving against her, who was holding her flowers to her breast as she might a child.

"I am sorry to disappoint you, Mrs. Lindsay. But I may as well tell you for Julian's sake, if not for yours, I do not intend to leave you alone in this wood." She stared at him:

"Do you mean that you've come to see me home from the ghost?" (There *was* something wrong with the wood. She had been afraid all the time she had been looking for flowers—always afraid, more or less, in that wood.) She saw him looking at her with contempt; understood even before he spoke:

"When your friend Campion comes you'll not be able to pretend. One or the other of you will give it away, and I shall see then what I know and have it to tell Julian." (Contempt and something more. What was it called? Lust.)

"Campion?" Instantly she understood the whole business, and what the man had in his mind.

"Campion—but he is not coming here; not if we sit here all night. Don't be ridiculous, Captain Browne. If we were betraying Julian, as you seem to think, do you think we should do it so clumsily? There is always the yacht."

"With your damned boat laid up, yon hut's not such a bad place for lecheries."

("I must hold him off. I must get away. I can't get past him, and off the path I'd tumble and get caught in the undergrowth. Be tumbled on those red needles, all soft. What a bed.") She could see his short red moustache, two teeth below it pressing on his underlip. It would be like a red fox.

"This is intolerably silly. I am going home at once to tell Julian—I bet—" she added, critical and suddenly inspired—"that you have not dared to say any such thing to him. Preferring instead to bore us all with your hysteria, and then spy on me. Man, you're making an awful fool of yourself."

She made a movement to pass him. Unfortunately, Archibald Erskine had burned his boats. How was he to go back and tell Julian that he'd found his wife alone in a wood, and he had said she was unfaithful, and she said she wasn't? "Make it true, anyhow," said a demon, popping its head up over the rim of his abyss. "I've so much I can't tell him, she may as well have something too, the stuck-up trollop."

She made a movement to go serenely by. The wood in its silence, enclosing within a flying world, seemed more than usually equivocal; the clearing, the trees standing in, even the one-eyed hut and a pair of saplings whispering together as though they were all watching them. Closing in on them to hear better? To trap them? It would be a horrible walk away from this lunatic across the clearing, down the dark tunnel and over the stone hedge out onto Sarscathian.

("That's the walk I have to take, and *not* look behind me. Even though there's a fearful fiend—two fearful fiends—for goodness knows what lives in this wood. I have always been afraid, going in or coming out. I've found the plant anyhow, I mustn't lose that.")

Then his arm shot out and dragged her round.

"You came here for kisses, my fine madame; you shan't go without."

The reek of tobacco and whiskey met her quick breath; his chin rasped hers as she thrust it back. He had hold of her, loose as a puppet swinging, and as she shut her eyes in primitive terror it seemed that the trees took another step forward to look. Her feet could not make the ground; this was not a strength you could resist, thrust off, and double away from. He had her swinging like a doll, like a corpse on the arm of a tree. This was rape. This was what he was doing for the love of his Julian. This was what she was enduring for being Julian's wife. The trees were keeping the ring—not her trees. Black trees. *Calling the wild cherry tree....* Upsey-daisy—what on earth has happened? She must have passed out. She was sitting on a log and Campion this time had his arm round her.

"How did you come?"

"Archibald Erskine and I must have had the same thought. Two minds, you know, but still—thought you might be frightened out here. I was on the cliffs, and suddenly it seemed important. So round I came, and what I saw looked like him catching you as you fell. He handed you over without a word. I supposed he was frightened at your faint. He had a queer look on his face, and now he seems to have gone."

"Altered his plans quickly."

"He's gone home to find Julian and tell his story first." Then she explained.

.   .   .   .   .

"And now what do we do about it? Go home, too, and protest our virtue? How you found me, struggling in his loathsome embraces?" Campion meditated.

"Julian will be so bored."

("Will he? Does one ever know? He'll put some filthy idea into his head if it isn't that one, and some day it will come out, like an egg that's hatched a spider; and I shall remember his friend, mouthing down at me in this wood.

"Should I be the happier if Campion were my lover? I had never thought of that. When he came through the trees today, he was like a lover. Only a lover comes like that—even on the movies.... This thing has taught me already to sneer like that—at this most lovely deliverance. How much more will Archibald Erskine do to us?

"And does Julian care enough to believe that he came—not like my lover but like our friend?")

Cruel thoughts; and now she knew that she was longing for Campion to take her in his arms. She stole him a glance. Then, surprisingly in that wood where there were no birds:" "Cuckoo," a voice said. Campion was now looking at her, with such a look as a tree would give if a tree were ever in love—a tree like the great World Ash or, in Dodona, the mouth of the gods.

"Is there nothing," she said, "to take away that man's filthy kiss?" She spoke piteously. Campion thought a moment or seemed to think. Thinking what she was thinking.

He put desire where it belonged.

"Try this," he said, pulling up from between two stones a bunch of thyme and balm-in-Gilead. She held it to her face, bruising it; and as the pure scent poured out, scrubbed her mouth and cheek. He watched her, his face one of those made flesh who "smile in the niches of Chartres." After this she heard him say:

"The great thing is for no one of us to get like Archibald Erskine-Browne. When one does, that's the real result. Not the immediate antics."

"Rape and little things like that."

"That's the idea. No use hurrying either. Let's go to the pub and have a drink."

.   .   .   .   .

They returned to the house to find Julian alone, sharpening pencils delicately; and when he spoke, it was with an air of fretfulness:

"What *is* all this about? I've had Archie, stamping all over the place, saying so far as I could make out, Cynthia, you don't love me any more; that you and Campion had gone off to that wood to pick plants to poison my tea; that he'd seen you.

"Did you? I mean—don't you care for me any more? I mean, I mean, you needn't, but it's all rather sudden, isn't it? Archie's batty, of course; but you know, if you do, I do hope it'll be a quick one.... *Has* anything happened?"

"Only," said Cynthia, coldly, "that he has just tried to rape me, and—"

"You?"

"Who else?" It was Campion who added: "You're not the only charmer in St. Enys." Julian looked at him with an air of gentle reproach:

"Do you mind telling me what it is all about?"

Campion told him, ending with: "He's your friend, Julian. Isn't it up to you, just a bit, to deal with this?"

"What on earth do you want me to do—kick him out of the house when he gets back?"

"If you like—though that won't settle anything. While Cynthia has had an ugly shock."

"I've had one too—I mean, I'm having it."

Cynthia cried out suddenly: "Julian means he doesn't care enough to care either way."

"Why, what is it you want me to do?" She did not answer. It was Campion who said:

"I know—let him return, and find us all sitting here round something better than tea, and tell him to pull himself together and have it out with what has been the matter. I don't know what it is with these men—it is not simply what they do, it is what they brood on, until they distil something deadly out of their silence; and we breathe it; and before we know what we have done, we have drawn it into us."

Cynthia blushed. Out in the wood she had wanted to implement the treachery suggested. Campion had kept her from it. Now she was glad; that when Julian's eyes smiled at her she could smile back.

Once more, outside the house, there came the single noise of boots. Steps with a trip in them, their minds' eyes translated instantly into the steps of a drunk man.

"Archibald Erskine's come home tight," they said. This time Julian concealed a giggle. He had. When he appeared in the doorway, it would have been hard to associate him with the avenger of the wood.

For from head to foot he was covered with dust and scratches and bits and pieces, and drops of rain and smears of blood; and it occurred to each of them to wonder what the village had made of it, the sharp remote eyes of an alien race, watching the arrogant foreigner on his way back from the inn. Cynthia and Campion had not seen him there. He must have gone off somewhere with a bottle. Returning along the car-strung high road and paths divided by stiles built up out of stone bars, six feet in air. Down lanes and across streams, tracking from left to right; stumbling, kneeling, falling, rising, going backwards, talking out loud and certainly singing, like a ship carrying too much sail in a heavy sea.

From his coat pocket a goggle-eyed bass stuck out its head. He, too, stared down at them with glazed eyes. "Beautiful fish," he said: "dam' cheap in London. I'd have—had—'ad—pad—paid—for Cynthia." He lurched up the room, tried to get his feet together, tried to present it, tried to bow—and threw it into her lap.

"Poor fish," said Julian.

"Meaning me—?" And Archibald Erskine-Browne burst into tears. There was nothing to do but to get him to bed.

"Call it a day," said Cynthia, faintly.

Julian said ;"I'd rather we could call it a night."

. . . . .

Next morning he told them he must go away; and before Julian could give signs of the Cheshire Cat, it was Cynthia who answered:

"You can't, you know, until we've come to some better understanding." Archibald Erskine answered, simply:

"I think we have. I mean I have. I wasn't so drunk last night that I couldn't see you three sitting there by the fire, so quiet, so sure of yourselves and of one another."

Cynthia paused, wishing to spare him, anxious to question him. Until it was Campion who broke the silence, saying:

"You see now that you saw us through a kind of fake glass of your own?" Archibald Erskine answered, almost humbly:

"I see now that I've been off the deep end. It's the way it takes me when I can't get my bearings. Nothing like lost bearings to send you blind." Cynthia was beginning to ask if he was sure of them now, when Julian said:

"What I want to know is—why you thought that I didn't love you any more. I'm just what I've always been."

"Yes, I see that now." Again he spoke bitterly. It was clear to the others that he had better go—leave them, probably for good; call the whole affair off. If Julian wanted more amusement out of the spectacle, he could go and have it with him, by himself. Julian was saying again:

"D'you remember the portrait I did of you?"

"The one you never finished?"

"I was going to ask you to sit for it again while they were on the yacht; only what with one thing and another, one gets about as much privacy in this house as a goldfish."

"One thing," said Cynthia, "that I must know is: what actual thing was it that made you see things in a better light?" After a long effort, he replied:

"I don't understand—it was the way Campion came, looking for you in the wood. Out of those black trees. As if it were a green tree coming— it sounds awfully poetical—a tree in spring.

"It was that song of yours that started me off. Then it was as if I'd learned that song was true; and so everything that I had been thinking was beside the mark." His voice trailed off: "*The...wild tree...the merry tree....*"

A little later they heard Campion say prosaically: "She'll be ready for sea by the afternoon tide. I won't suggest it to either of you with this sea running." Archibald Erskine said obstinately:

"I'll say good-bye now."

There was no protest; only a feeling, a certainty that that was the only thing that could happen; that however good it might be, complete reconciliation and understanding was impossible. Something destructive had been at least neutralized; something complex and useless, dangerous and incurable had been examined and its dangers deflected from them. They had, as so often happens, saved themselves, and Archibald Erskine they could not save. Or Julian would not save.

After lunch, after the last farewells had been said, he followed Cynthia into the studio. "Show me Julian's picture," he said. Rather hurriedly she got it out. Together they looked at it—at the handsome head, in profile against a wall covered with trophies and a disarray of manly junk. The petulance was there, the stressed virility, the extreme good looks.

As they left the room, half to her, half to himself, she heard him say: "I too might have been a great painter."

❖ ❖

A Roman Speaks

S O MY FATHER KNEW your father well. Come inside the hut, boy, and let's shiver over the fire. We have an hour, haven't we, before we sail?"

"Let me mend it, sir,"

"That's right, do. I've just had my nails fixed and I'm no good with fires, anyhow." The centurion knelt by the hearth on one knee working delicately from beneath at the smoking wood, till a ribbon of fire blew out, followed by another and another, streamers the draught gathered up, towards which Caesar stretched out his small transparent hands. Hard hands, pure muscle strung over bone, but not harsh, and beautifully kept. The young man rose to hang a cloak of fox-skins over the back of his general's chair, and at a sign sat down on a stool beside him.

"Tomorrow then," Caesar said, "we leave this island; if it is an island. The Greeks said it was, if they meant the same place; but I'm wondering how to make it go down in Rome, where they don't believe it is here at all. Or if it is, that it's been taken over by the dead, sleeping round old Chronos in his tomb." The centurion said something about its belonging to the dead all right if they had any more trouble with the tribes.

"You would say that," said Caesar plaintively, "and I suppose the only thing to do is to bring a few of them back to show, as blue as possible all over. Are the shipmasters clear what time these tides will allow us to sail?"

"I gave you, sir, their report and their calculations."

"Of course you did. It is something also I want to talk about. There are nights when I must talk, when I must answer the questions others ask me; the questions I ask myself." The young man hardly paused to consider. Caesar had given his officers enough to think about. (Then I will ask him this.) "Why is it, sir, that you chose the People and the Assembly rather than the Senate?"

"Of which my ancestors were the ornament. It's charming of you to want to know…" Florus gathered confidence:

"One only knows what great men do. So rarely why they do it." Caesar did not answer at once. Florus looked at the exquisite figure beside him. A man from whose body everything but the essentials had been purged, sweated, worked out. Everything that would hamper or clog the workings of a unique mind. A mind essentially social, a dealer with men and women each by each and in their packs and cliques and clubs, their deep unconscious groupings. Body of an ascetic of the intelligence, supreme in every physical activity because they served mind. A body mind had made transparent, a crystal for its thought; that activity had trained down to its essentials, bone and muscle and racing blood. A quintessence of these, as though each centimeter of the man were an essence of pure power, terrible but exquisite and fit for human use. While the skin over the body graced it, white, transparent, clean; the clothes over the skin a repetition in other terms as cleanly, elegant, and fine. The same with the last external, the beaten leaves of gold laurel over the curled red thinning hair, the polished skull.

"Why I chose the people. That's a long story. You can't say that I went about banging workmen on the back or that I liked their sweaty stink. No, I talked to them as though they were Senators. It's that that puts them in a good temper. It's the old trick.

"I see I haven't satisfied you. You're saying to yourself: 'After all, Caesar's no Tiberius Gracchus, who did what he did for something like love; whom the Gods persuaded that the plain roman citizen should inherit the earth. (They let him down in the end, and he died cursing them, don't forget that.) But this Caius Julius men now call Caesar was not born to be a song in men's ears, but a fact. A call to order; the man who when Necessity was brought to bed, delivered the child.'

"The Senate, Florus, is played out. I don't know why. Only that they are not replacing themselves in their children any more. But the Assembly is not the alternative, nor the Populares. Only the people directed will give power to the man who can control our state.

"Don't shy, boy, I'm not proposing to be a king. What your question meant was 'What do I, Caesar, mean by Rome?' and exactly why I backed the people; and I was saying that it wasn't for love, and as I said it, I knew that answer was not quite true; and if you will listen I have a story to tell—you and myself. Something that happened when I was a boy: something I have never been able to forget.

"Since then you see how it has gone. Without the people I should not have got my offices, nor that one hungry legion that tramped after me to Gaul. It came to loot and stayed to conquer. And conquering was transformed—until we come to be sitting on the edge of this island, waiting to leave it, where as yet no Roman has been. A nice job for the men who come after me." Florus nodded:

"Aren't you saying, sir, that your Rome is the whole roman people plus one man? And what would that man be but a king?"

"The one thing that man must not be is a king. That is the problem. But the answer is not the story; and the story is my first adventure, when I was a boy, at the end of Sulla's day.

"It is the glory and the strength of our City that her history has been singularly free from the bloody spans we call civil war. It was my father's fortune that his life should coincide with such a time; that he should have been on the losing side, when the solution was the acts by which Sulla re-established the Senate with doubled powers. Or thought he had. A victory which left the Senate with powers it has never dared claim. And could not—cannot—use. Florus, do you, a soldier, think to go home and stand for office, alternating your jobs? Once you'd have done it as you breathed. The roman soldier and the roman Senator are becoming two different men; and soldiers are impatient of stout gentlemen without military experience. One reason why I came away.

"Still, Sulla thought he'd put them back where they were when they knew how to save Rome both in debate and in the field. Only, as even a boy will remember, before he left office and went down to the country to give parties, he thought it well to knock off a few last poppyheads on his enemies' estate.

"Yes, your uncle went in that last effort. All the roman gentlemen who had backed the wrong horse; and what are the people worth with their Tribuneships and their Assembly that so many of us should have gone against our own order and died for them? As the Gracchi died. It was the People who betrayed them when Opimius and his cretan archers had done their work and Gaius stood alone by the Tiber, and the Romans huddled together like cattle and not a man of them dared cross that space to bring him the horse he prayed for—Gaius Gracchus, their saviour. So his last prayer was that such a people should never be free. A lesson every roman patrician learns and does not learn. Whenever the Senate weakens, we are at it again—bribe, bully, cajole, persuade, teach, preach, shove them there and hold them here. In my case, at least, for a little touch of something more than my own ambition. As this story I am trying to reach will show. While Necessity, too, had her part in it.

"Where was I? Sulla and his parties. Well, as I said, he left office and went off to the country with all the people he had never before had time for, painters and players and philosophers for *patres conscripti*....

"Three hundred skulls left in Rome behind him. Three hundred skulls for three hundred heads. Three hundred heads of the best brains in Rome emptied out for worm-food. Price we paid for the brains in Sulla's head. High price for one man's wits. Your uncle and my father's head. Young Antony's father, too, the throat that held the beautiful voice. Used it to hold up the swordsmen, talking against the steel. Till someone like you, boy, who hadn't heard a word of it, ran up the stairs and asked them what they were waiting for. Cut off that voice as the head went rolling; a Roman cut down by a Roman in cold blood. It hadn't happened for centuries. Prelude to the picnics and the water-parties and the ballets of Lucius Cornelius Sulla who called himself Felix in retirement.

"And here I come in."

Two hours before the tide would lift the galleys, send them softly out to sea into the warm white summer fog. Receive them gently on their passage from Britain to Gaul, leaving behind them a population its fingers on its nose and its heart in its mouth. On the smooth white rocks, chalk, rounded by the sea into eggs and platters, cups to hold scarlet weed and ice green water, the tide talked pleasantly. Red, green, and white, the three colours of right magic. To these Italians, un-Mediterranean Sea. Sea that drew away with the night and came back with the dawn from the secret places of Ocean. The Gods knew where, the Gods and a few Phoenicians; and they were all dead, with their log books and their shipmasters' secrets. What power withdrew it to its fountains while its ebb left bare the mountain's roots and the bases of ocean, left naked the underwater world? Caesar's men went scrambling

in the tide pools after lobsters, lobster he had had for supper, lobster
that had helped banish sleep.

"My mother saw what was coming, that Sulla had not done with us
yet. One night we heard her litter coming down the lane to the little
house outside the city where I was living, *en garçon*, with young Catalina. We thought it was Claudius Pulcher, coming to see us like that
because he'd been ill, and waited inside to rag him. Instead the curtain
parted, and there was Antonia, my mother, standing in the arch. I see
now what a moment it was. Then we were boys who didn't want to be
called to order.

"'My son,' she said, 'I know that it pleases you to live by night,
nor shall I complain about it any more. For now you will have to do
it if you want to go on living at all.' Then she explained: that I was to
leave instantly, in her litter, for a certain house where I was to pass the
night. House after house I was to visit, all the way down to the coast
in the south, travelling by night, sleeping by day, showing myself by
night only.

"'They will do it for your father's sake. Your name is on Sulla's list as
one not to be left alive.'

"I was not pleased. But, as Catalina said after: 'It was Rome speaking.' So, off I went. My mother sat up with Catalina half the night,
till the slave came back to say that I had arrived safe at my first lodg-
ing. Sat up and told him stories about the private life of the eliminator
of our house Catalina said he would never have thought possible. Sat
until I was watching my first compulsory dawn. In those months I became quite a specialist on sunrises. I even began a poem on ten different kinds. 'Ten Tips of the Rosy-Fingered'—I'd the sense to leave off. I
saw as much of south Italy as one can by night, that is to say I saw stars,
the whole host of heaven; and as the weeks passed, the changes in their
positions, like minute adjustments on the battlefield of a host of men.
Principally I remember Sagittarius, standing in the south heavens, his
bow drawn on the vault. From day on I was bored stiff by a number of
pious hosts and hostesses, who thought little of me and a great deal of
my father and mother.

"This, till I came to the last house, right down on the toe of Italy,
in a remote place where it was supposed I should be safe; and when I
could think of nothing more polite to say to them, I went boating. It
was then that the pirates got me.

"I suppose it was the first important thing that had happened to

me. Sulla I'd taken as a boy does. But here I was, quite alone and responsible for myself. After all the trouble my mother had taken, I felt
that I couldn't just perish. While I had never imagined men such as
these existed.

"All that I knew was of men working within the law, seeking to
formulate the more perfect forms under which community is possible. Man's common task, and the Julii what you might call profes-
sionals at it.

"But these men! For the first time I saw a community without law.
You are saying to yourself: 'Rather as we began,' and the answer is 'yes'
and 'no.' For from the first we sought law, for the fun of it, not at the
expense of other men but at our own. The men who were rowing me
off to their island had no purpose except to live on others; yet even to
do that were constrained—as I found out later—to a measure of discipline, a self-imposed law."

Outside the hut in the dark came a rustle and squeak, a scatter in
the parted bushes and grass. The night life of the earth running on its
business, and below the single note of a trumpet, and voices to mark
the return of the sea.

"Well, there I was; a gift to them in my fine wool and gold sandal
straps. A foraging party had caught me, back from burning some miserable village for its goats and some stinking wine. I had to use my
mind. 'And now you'll know, Caius,' I said, 'if you've a mind to make
up.' Risking one thing—that Sulla was tired of looking for me—and
said who I was. Piled it on, I, Caius, last of the Julian Gens; and from
the look on their violent vulgar faces, saw I'd guessed right.

"So when they sent off their official negotiator to collect my ransom, I abused them for not knowing a gentleman when they saw one
and told them to double it. Watched them nudge one another and
whisper and agree, and knew again that I had guessed right.

"Then we settled down to it. On the sort of island where Philoc-
têtês must have brooded his wound. Remember it was all new to me,
straight from the city and our great roman households, which in some
ways are so many mirrors of our State. I knew a little of life on farms
and in villages and our military colonies, but never this thing—units
of civilisation flung together outside civilisation. A parasite on it and a
wolf at its door mixed.

"Cured me of any tendency to boyish romance about life on the
ocean main. Yet I remembered to remember that men are men, and

that I had been given a unique chance of contact. One of the fountains of knowledge unsealed for me, and I should have to drink it though it tasted of blood.

"I knew I was safe for the moment. The money would come and probably before Sulla did, and I was far too valuable even to ill-treat. A few wanted to for the fun of it, but their leader said 'No.' Had one scourged for insisting. I was already rather pleased about the ransom, and sat up the first night, listening to them drinking themselves unconscious and asking myself the philosopher's question: 'How far is slavery a state justified by nature?'

"The answer seems to be that some men are born slaves and some men are made slaves, and the difficulty is that these categories sometimes overlap. It is also a question we find it hard to consider clearly. To us a roman citizen enslaved is an indecency which ought not to exist, a horrid distortion of nature. While one of his captors is our natural property. This bias allowed for in the unreflecting mind, where are we? Very much where I was when I came to consider my captors.

"It was a very curious unit to which I was delivered; which was delivered also to my inspection. Not men who would ordinarily live by piracy—an occupation only too liable to become an organized business—among whom may be found many freemen out for adventure; but a bunch of men, each of the same kind from a different place. Runaway slaves, all tired of the position, and taken to hold up such ships as they were not afraid to attack by way of revenge on society. (I've known a man equip his slaves and turn to that to collect enough money to start a boot factory. Got an army contract, made a fortune and indemnified the people he'd robbed.) These were not like that. A scum—just that sort of sea-fluff that collects in a tide-corner, full of sticks and chips, dirty brown with foul lights in it. All born slaves; of all races, with a common hatred of the world as they found it and a passion to do it violence. But neither the patience nor the wits to alter their position.

"Get inside the rules and the protection—that's what our slave must work for. His freedom by the process of law. Instead they'd put themselves outside all rules. Done such things that they could never go back on what they'd done. Doubly now outside the law and yet expecting it would work out all right. Had a mythology of their own of the slaves who had become kings.

"What they wanted worked out in practise to no more than enough women and enough drink. Have you ever realized, boy, that to want the earth is one way to lose one's share of it? Yet in wanting no more than the satisfaction of the belly's double itch, there is something ill-bred, something that the Gods pass by. Why, with my ransom alone they'd have had enough to live decently, but they didn't want that. Wanted excitement and risk and killing and oblivion and the dream of revenge. A sort of cheap ecstasy—I'm no expert on ecstasy, but the cheap sort you get in crowds and among men with a grievance seems to me about the nastiest emotion to which man is subject.

"Women were scarce among them, which gave them one of their chief excitements. Betting on the father when one was got with child; when it was born, trying to settle it. Then they'd fight to the death for the privilege of fathering some lousy crimson brat. Sacrifice to some godling a jewish prostitute they had with them invented—a god-who-takes-pity-on-poor-men. Still, as there weren't enough women, they went in for the love of one another—ghastly parodies of husbands and wives. A forest barbarian from the north and a thing from a harem out Syria way told them all about that, complete with conquests, separations, tears, infidelities—and the eternal, senseless scrappings and blood.

"Looking back, sitting in my tent, the successful general, all clean and tidy, I can see it all. A life that was a quite dreadful parody of our lives, who have passed under the yoke, the great arch we call the Law.

"One hears certain philosophers talk of a beautiful age before men had thought of it. Implying that we were once so innocent that we had no need of it. Nor have I ever understood their justification; for if we were ever thus innocent, it was with the innocence of beasts.

"Look at it another way—those creatures were as we were once except that they founded no city. Content to live, each day for each night on what other men had gathered, more or less fairly, and been forced to hazard at sea." Raising himself in his chair Caesar spoke with his white passion:

"Oh they howled about liberty, that, if Gryphon, their chief scoundrel, a Greek of sorts, he always is, didn't obey the common will they'd teach him his place; while he by sharper cunning scourged and drove and tricked them, feeding them with lies and whips, and words which were themselves a parody of those a man who is first among his equals speaks.

"Until—it was very curious—there had grown up a whole structure of mimes, parodies, of the forms under which men live together in their cities. Assembly, debates, officers, elections, contracts—with penalties attached.

"It reminded me of those little beasts from Upper Egypt that are so much the fashion among our roman ladies. Little animals who have a look of us and the trick of copying our ways; and it is all very amusing until suddenly they forget what they are doing; and relieve nature all over the fruit.

"Gryphon was great on the proper exercises: 'We must keep fit,' he would say. 'When we pirates meet the legions.' (Yet he called things by their proper names; the others would say 'free adventurers.') Their idea was that quite soon he and his lot and all other slaves and outlaws would join up, and, by a sort of magic, become invincible and march on the lands and kill off their defenders; and it would all become theirs; and Gryphon would be king of the world, and Kezia, his jewish wife, queen. Not a man of them, except perhaps Gryphon and one other, who did not believe this. Told it to me as children tell one another a fairy-tale, making it into the songs they sang in the evening when the drinking began.

"So he had 'em all out and exercised them, running and leaping, work with the javehn and the bow and the sword. I watched all this, and on the third day, after a great pretence of shaving which I hardly need yet, turned up on their parade ground, all clean and curled and scented, and said I needed to keep fit as much as anyone else and that I'd show them a thing or two. For they were quite hopeless—the sort of fighter who'd prod or slash at a man's parts, and when they'd got him down, cut bits off him or gouge out his eyes. So I showed them a little decent point work with the sword and the legion's rip and slash.

"Then they all started crying out why in hell I should want to keep fit, and something about currying favour with them when my turn came. So I jumped on the hillock, where Gryphon used to bawl his orders, and called for silence.

"'My friends,' said I, 'I'm showing you something about fighting so that when Rome sends along a few men to finish you off it won't be too like killing cattle. And I'm keeping fit because when she does, I shall be in charge.'

"'You mean,' one of them cried, a skinny little Syrian, called Taris, a hoppety louse of a man, all covered with the marks of branding irons, 'that if we let you do as you like, you'll spare our lives, you cock-a-whoop roman bastard, you.'

"'Bastard,' said I. 'Father, I didn't know you were here. Spare your lives, nothing! I give you my word here and now to have you crucified, every man jack of you.'

"It had never occurred to them that such a thing was possible, great is the power of a fairy-tale. They took it good-humouredly, roared with laughter. Let me in on all their doings. Being my family priest I married them; explained the laws of contract when it came to sharing out. Went pirating with them once; heard all the filthy things they were going to do when they got on board, the instalment of the revenge. All the rape and castration and general torture and unpleasant ways of leaving this earth which were their idea of justice. Very serious they were, arguing the pros and cons of cannibalism—until I ran short of logic and told them it was bad magic, that, once eaten, the evil of their enemies would enter into them and make them give at the knees. So they swallowed that rather than the next batch of prisoners.

"While the time I went with them, the galleys were prepared, drove us off with more than we bargained for. Ships belonging to a most respectable man. I met him later—the time I was Pontifex Maximus—he'd been on board and told me all about it. Afterwards it was Taris who came sneaking up to me and asked if they were ever smoked out, to put in a good word for him. 'He'd been driven to this sort of life. He'd run away because they said he'd poisoned his master and he hadn't.' The thing they all say. 'He'd have been a different man if he'd had a real roman gentleman like myself for master.' I repeated what I'd do and he didn't believe it. (Here we come to a point about human nature I've often observed, and now accept without pretending to understand. These devils—sparks, bubbles—what you will, of violent and generally hideous feeling, living on robbery with torture of the robbed for sauce, thought they were fulfilling some moral law. Avenging themselves on society they were about to replace by *their* society, and that thereby an essential balance would be maintained. Showing at least that even the vilest man cannot live without some such concept. What they did not notice was Divine Justice having a joke on them when it sent me.)

"Yet here was I, in their power, only just too valuable not to kill; my money-scale—it went to the wrong island and was late—just tipping my agony-scale. While without my bluff it mightn't. That's odd, too. Some god whispered in the ear of the boy who was Caesar to dance on these people. Dance on them and with them.

"Yet it did not occur to them that society, the moment it had time or they made themselves too much of a nuisance, would turn and treat them as it has been treated. Let alone that it is also part of necessity, society *must*. It could not have been that they expected mercy—they just couldn't see it happening. Which made my promise of the cross the cream of wit. '*It's the slaves' turn coming*,' they sang. Perhaps, for a few hours, it did. For, will you believe it, there were times when the boy Caesar danced with them, and we forgot what we were doing or why it was we were there.

"For the rest he watched. I wonder sometimes where that boy is. For when I look at you, Florus, I don't quite see him. It's not that I regret him; on the whole I prefer the Caesar I am taking about with me now." The young officer thought that this man had kept everything that was essential in himself, perfect and entire; that the query was only sentimental. Modestly, he suggested this. Caesar scratched his head:

"Perhaps you're right. These men, at any rate, packed him away inside an enlarged Caesar. Up to then he'd met only pleasant people or great, and they're often both. Even Sulla was a statesman, thinking it might benefit, not only his ambition but the Roman State, if the last of the Julii were to join his ancestors. But down there on our island on the raw yellow sand, I saw something that was like a final opposite statement of mankind. For the Roman Senator and the Matron, this bloody stuff of all races, camped out there on the blood-drinking sand; stained brown, I noticed, where it had drunk. It was their habit to drag what was left of their prisoners' bodies—the men and women for whom no ransom came—to the shore and throw them in. Where no tide draws in and out to wash the shore clean.

"Do you hear it now? It pleases me, that slowly-gathering voice; that the girdle between sea and land should be cleansed each day. Cestus of Aphrodite it was the Hellenes saw rising out of the sea. Not the kind of story we Romans tell of the Gods. A pity, too, that Homer knew nothing of these seas, except by repute. The song the Sirens sang goes to their beat; can't you hear it? 'Come, come hither. Far-Wandering Odysseus, great glory of the Achaeans.'"

The young soldier nodded, aware that there was sitting beside him another Odysseus; that he was hearing of adventures, equally famous, equally secret. Caesar felt encouraged to go on.

"It was round, our island. As I used to think, round like a wheel of pain. On which these men were bound as much as the men they captured, and let out of their bodies so slowly and unpleasantly there. In the centre there was a hillock with three trees. There they sometimes hung them; or, their shape being convenient, finished them off on the cross. Hub of our wheel that little hill; and only I not conditioned by its turning. I, a lad, fleering and posturing and balancing on the felloe. Doing that, I'd somehow made myself master of the wheel. The difficulty was to keep it up. Keep them scared and fascinated—while the money didn't come. It was not an easy plan all the time. There were nights when I was afraid. You see, I couldn't let it drop for an instant. Always I must be mocking, bullying, showing off.

"It was then that I learned that Caius Julius was not to perish. Tied fast to human vileness, bound to it face to face. Thrown with it onto that island, as into a river, to swim or sink.

"There was one of them, Amynthus of Alexandria, a man of some education, secretary to some court official in the service of Aulêtês, the Piper. Helped him get up his serio-comic orgies in honour of Dionysus. You've heard of it—when His Majesty of Egypt assumed the God? It had been their business to find new spices to keep their Crowned Fool happy; not seeing how he dished us all in the end because he knew how to laugh at himself. This blown-off blow-fly from the Palace sink, tall, grey and greasy, horribly thin, used to come up and sit beside me on the beach. I remember one evening he tried to fasten a red brooch round my wrist, and told me of a Nothing, like a worm, that was found at the bottom of a place he called the Abyss; that all human valour and the things men have done were incited by the worm to illustrate, by some form of opposite, itself. That was what it sounded like. If it hadn't been so silly, rather horrible for a young man to be told, with sacred conviction, that was what lay behind the Athenians, for instance, chasing their delicate truth. Foul concept really; and when we got him on the cross, a worm dropped out of him, and he spoke in a thin voice to something that had not the name of any of the Gods.

"I remember this to show you what a strange lot they were. While he wanted only one little thing of me—that I should perform a little act of homage to his worm or whatever it was, and then I'd be sure to get out of my troubles. I mention this because, of all the strange beliefs of men, I have never met anything to equal it. Nor ever met it again; though, here and there, and the odd thing is, *anywhere*, you come across—a sensation, a taste in your mouth and a bad one, that that worm has its worshippers yet. Amynthus, too, came out of Egypt, out of which most things come.

"You know my favourite saying: *homines libenter credunt quod volunt**—but how could desire enter into that? Yet I have always felt that it was just as well that I wouldn't wear his bracelet. Still less, though there I was a point curious, take the little stroll round the bay he was always urging and meet his friend. To which my invariable reply was that I'd had quite enough of meeting my social inferiors, with a low class demon thrown in. At that he used to sigh, and I gathered that not many even of that gang were keen on accompanying him.

"For the rest, he was humble and obliging, and devised some quite atrocious tortures for their wretched prisoners. Did them as if he were praying, which he undoubtedly was. *Tantum religio*—for it was religion. It is possible that it is this that has prevented me from making any closer inquiry into the ultimate nature of the Gods.

"Then there was Taris, the little black African, and Matta, the thing he called his wife. They couldn't have a baby, and *that* was their late-owner's fault. Matta'd had one, and her mistress had made her nurse her own instead, and her own died, and it had never happened again. Secretly she used to try other men—I know this because she came and asked me. I suppose that laugh means 'Did you, Caesar?' My dear boy!

"I tell you, I had a full time, marrying them and divorcing them and teaching them to fight, and how to box and wrestle and not use their teeth at a fall.

"There was one night—the night before the money came, and it makes me wonder, worm or no worm, if the Gods are not weaving their own pattern we are not usually intelligent enough to see—that night our carouse turned into a dance. A regular ballet it was. I was drunk, I admit, and the money was overdue, and some of them were getting restive, and Amynthus was always trotting off to his little cove to meet whoever was there and get hints as to the painfullest way to dispatch me. I admit that used to worry me, till I began to look back over my shoulder to see whether or not he'd come back alone. Amynthus was the man behind all their doings at their filthiest. Gryphon was a Gracchus by comparison.

"You want to hear about the dance? You are now one of the few

***Men believe what they want to.*

men who have seen Caesar blush. That night I did my usual leap back into Gryphon's good graces. Chaffed him as the thieves' Jove and the kind of statue he'd get in *his* Capitol; showed them all how to balance their wine cups, the satyrs' trick. So, when it came to the dance, I was Ganymede. I said, boy, to the *dance*.

"Next day I was going through my morning's private exercises, which consisted first in cleaning my teeth, then setting them. And praying—what does one in extremity pray to? That I should get through the day with my feathers still in air: that if the money came too late, I should die decently a most un-roman death. Oh yes, and a trick I first discovered then, that helped, that always helps. Especially when one's life has been passed, as mine has been, continually in the stream of humanity. A kind of gesture of withdrawal into oneself, as though one had stepped inside a ring; and from within that circle moved as though invisible.

"Hints for you, my dear, if you come to rule the State.

"Where was I? Next morning I had flung this circle of mine like a hoop round my neck, as though I saw it, lying perfect like a gold ring at my feet, when the money came. I watched them count it out. Mother was taking no chances—there was a bonus extra for good measure, and as they began to quarrel over it, I hopped onto the ship that brought it and we shot off.... I stood in the stern, waving good-bye for the present and repeating my promises how soon I should be back and finish them.

"I believe if I hadn't taken that line they'd never have let me go. It was my bluff, and their fairy-tale about themselves that did it; and I'm not sure that at the dance the night before they hadn't thought that I might not be some kind of an immortal. Anyhow, off I went; and there on the mainland were my father's old friends to meet me. Husband and wife—both crying with relief, because they'd sworn an oath, if they failed my mother, to kill themselves; and since they were old-fashioned people, it must have been a relief when I turned up, safe and impudent and polite and very full of plans.

"That evening I went for a stroll in the gardens with the Domina Flavia, telling her as much about it as I thought she should know, and my mother's old friend said:

"'For all that you've come back a man, Caius, you've left something behind you with your pirates.'

"'Flavia, Domina,' said I, and told her what I have told you, the reverse of society I had seen. I remember I likened it to the side of a coin, the other side of the disk to the one that carries the roman image and superscription. The good face we turn on the world, and that it had somehow a wider circumference.

"'Do numbers then matter so much?' she said, 'so long as we rule. The fewest are ever the best.' To which I answered that it may take one man or ten or fifty to destroy one ruling man, but that he can be so destroyed and that those people meant to.

"'They have all had bad luck,' she said. 'It is with them as it was in Sicily when I was a girl and a cheapjack made himself into King Typhon. They carved their mistress up piecemeal and sent her daughters, who had been merciful to them, away to safety for the very short time in Syracuse that Typhon was king. I have never so ruled my household.' That I knew.

"'Yes,' she sighed. 'You must go and clear them out. You are too young for pity and I too old for indignation, and neither of us will be surprised at anything any more. You are a statesman shaping, and I an old lady, a roman woman, old enough now to see behind the moving pattern the forms that rule its varieties. But if there are any decent ones there, Caius, or any fit for honest use, give them to me here.' I had to assure her that in this case there were none. I regretted—above all not to please her—but how was I to send such people to service on a roman manor?

"It took me a fortnight to get the men I wanted and take command. It was then again that I found out that when I assumed myself to be leader, men let themselves be led.

"Then Rome sprang. For the first time I saw that. I see it still, our galley-line, the oar-beat falling in a single stroke, the spring we made across the sea to that island and back, a business of one day and one night.

"They tried to do me credit, some of them. Formed up in a kind of order, gave each other some part of a backing. Our numbers were pretty equal—I was taking no chances. I pranced up the beach, leading the charge. Before, we'd asked them formally to surrender. (I wanted to do for the Domina Flavia anything I could.) They refused with a roar—the fairy-tale mounting to their heads in songs, filling them with a supernatural knowledge that we should soon be asking them the same thing. Also because they did not trust us, being, as they were, creatures long given over to their destruction.

"It was all over in an hour, and my men chasing them over the place; and in the rough and tumble when it came to taking prisoners, my pirates forgot my orders and bit. Some of them had rubbed their teeth with a poison gum, deadly if it gets into the blood, and from that we had five casualties.

"They brought Gryphon to me. 'I've kept my promise,' I said. All his answer was, 'I never said it would come in my time. There's plenty more to take our places. Now get us onto the crosses and finish it.'

"I've seen many a chief turn heavier on his heel than that Greek off to his death. Reckoning the hours, I could see, before it would come and take him. What he thought would happen after—though he'd been an initiate of some sort, I suspect. I can see the group of them, facing me now, their faces quite secure in their dream. I have no comment. *Magna est Delusio et praevalebit.**

"So we did. Put the rest to the sword; but those three. Gryphon, Amynthus, and Taris—we crucified on the three trees on the hillock, where Gryphon used to play at being a king, on a carved seat he'd looted from somewhere, for a curule chair, on which I sat myself to watch. After we had taken down and burned the bodies of the last men, roman citizens, they had nailed there.

"Matta sat at the foot of the cross on the sand, on the needles whose scents, I noticed, struggled till they drowned it with the smell of blood, howling: 'I'm going to have one, after all. Just as I was going to have one after all,' and telling the men it was mine!

"We threw the bodies of those we'd finished off decently with the sword into the sea, to keep the place sweet. Weighted them with stones so that they would not wash up in a place that has not this place's advantages of a tide.

"Gryphon hung between Taris and Amynthus. But I'd told the men to make a quick job of it. I wanted to stay and see the end of them, get away by nightfall and never set eyes on the place again. They were strong men, and there was something I disliked in the idea of leaving them to hang there indefinitely, with the days and nights fading out in an even bloodier haze, dissolving with them, with their dream. They had deserved that and anything, but I prefer roman justice sharp. It is easy to condescend to the level of one's enemies.

"So I told them to spear them and dope them well up and break their legs. Amynthus died first, talking all the time in a low submissive voice. (It was evening by then and the shadows were stretching,

**Delusion is mighty and will prevail.*

gathered over him, I thought, with a curious suggestion of what I can only describe as stale darkness, night neither transparent or coloured or deep.) Then he screamed: 'Worms—Worms. They are turning.' Then 'No. I can't get back. My Lord! My Lord!' Then, as I said, something like a grey worm fell out of his hair and down his body. Vanished into his loin cloth, and he was dead and began to corrupt immediately.

"Gryphon and Taris were cheering each other up. 'There'll be a good world some day,' they said, 'where we'll get our own back.' Telling Matta to cheer up, and she was saying: 'Of course it isn't his. I said that to make his men laugh at him.' (I was standing by, but they took no notice of me.) They were getting so friendly that I stepped forward, and before I knew what I was thinking heard myself say: 'Maybe we'll manage to get a world where none of these things happen.' They stared down at me and Gryphon said: 'Do *you* want that?' and I found myself speaking to them, as if I were justifying myself. Reminded them that I'd played fair. Paid my ransom *and* told them what would happen. Cried out that law has no other punishment for such things as they had done: that if they hadn't been such vile brutes, I'd have done what I could to spare them. They didn't answer that. Then Taris said: 'Come away. We're best out of this.' And to me: 'You'll kill her, sir, won't you, first? Not leave her alone on here when you're gone.' 'I'm taking her where she'll be all right,' I said. Then he turned his head away and died.

"I was alone with Gryphon. Then I felt as I have felt more than once; in the hour when my falling sickness comes upon me, as though from within I was lit up with a single white light. I knew his eyes were looking down on me, looked up at him and he was saying:

"'The god is within you now, Julian lord. He will tell you how it will be.' And for once I answered, not as I bid myself answer, but as I was bidden. Yes, an oracle—a real oracle, Florus—*on earth as it is in heaven.* Seven words, as though they came out of other known but not remembered words.

"After that there came an instant for which I can give you no rational account at all, unless it be true that divine powers exist and at certain moments can enter in and possess a man. But this is true that, for a few seconds after this I could not have told you whether it was Caesar or Gryphon who was hanging there. Make what you like of it, at that moment I had taken his place, the place of them all, and they mine—young Caesar become the slave, the ruffian and the outcast. The crucifier had become the crucified, the crucified the roman lord. And this also was of the nature of law.

"Gryphon died instantly. I saw his spirit pass swiftly out from the cross, and with that I fell down on the scented earth at the foot of the crosses the three trees had provided for us there.

"A sergeant picked me up and brought me wine. 'You're young to this, sir. It's got to be done and it's well over—we've made a clean job of it.' Whether it was all that death hanging round those trees I don't know, but I walked straight down to the shore, and it seemed important that I should not once look back."

Caesar sprang up, and with him the fire leapt, shining on his white mask and remote brilliant eyes. Far down below at the water's edge a trumpet sounded, and on the full tide the galleys rocked which were to take them back to Gaul. For a moment he stood staring with lifted head, till a smile broke. He stooped and twitched up his mantle, fallen over the back of the chair.

"There! That might be called my entrance onto the stage of our affairs. To tidy the story up. I left behind a detachment, ordered them to cut down the trees with the bodies, and to throw them, all weighted, into the sea. That for purification. I learned later that Amynthus was so far gone that they feared for the salt and had him burned. Nothing can de-purify fire. So you see what I mean, that my leadership of the party which, in its inception at least, stood for the common man, has not been without some slight measure of contact with that man at his worst.

"Anything else? Matta? Yes, I took her and any children there were about and gave them to the Domina Flavia for her farm. Got ragged for my pains. She had her baby, and not a soul would believe that it wasn't mine. So much for our works of mercy. Shall we go?"

The Warning

THIS HAPPENED IN the kind of house people live in who used not to live in that kind of house, who were taught to have very distinct opinions about the kind of people who lived in them. Yet, now that they have gone to live in them, they are rather different than when the other sort of person lived there.

Difference between the architecture of one generation and another? Or a kind of spiritual modification? Both, without doubt.

So it was not on ancient stones that the sun shone, nor chimneys warmed by generations of fires that the sea salted with spray. Only in situation the house might have been built by a king, a Ludwig of Bavaria, with the sea for play-boy, whose imagination had led him to make his palace of art, instead of perched up on mountains, under the sea:

> ...*bowers*
> *Where the ocean powers*
> *Sit on their pearlèd thrones*
> *Through the coral woods.*

It is strange that none of the world's play-boys have ever thought to do that; yet this house was set in such a place where the most enterprising of them might have meditated it. There, three hundred feet below, the full Atlantic poured its waters in and out of a cup. There you enjoyed night and day the entire conversation of the sea. There it sang, swore, snored, shouted, whispered, yelled. "Dancing floor of the sun" there, on a reef where contending waters met, it leaped in seven waves, whose hair shook out the prisms of seven rainbows. There, round that reef, the pattern the tide draws in a white line takes on the shape of the Bull, the one beast off a cattle-boat that staggered up onto its black back and bellowing, faced the raving of the green water beasts; and there in the still seething his outline rises before a storm.

There, at the pull of the moon, the tides draw out half a mile. Draw back across lion-bright sand, a delicate flat-race, sea babies at the water's lip, coral and crimson weed and a starring of shells, pearl beads and glass and yellow stone. In every colour but the sea colours. Each one smaller than the last. A perfectness.

There, in a world jutting with empty stones and airy as though you stood everywhere at a great height, the cliffs have clothed themselves; and you look down or you look up into a cross-work of gorse and bracken, blackberry and bryony, threaded with the drip of streams. There, all summer the rose-campion waves a scarf in its face exactly the opposite in colour to the sea. There in the middle of the bay the sand has blown itself together into one place, a dune thrust out from the land, a child carried upright in the belly of the earth; dunes the couch-grass has covered, the grass that never stands close enough together, so that between each blade you can see the skin-pale sand.

And there, round about the house at night the hedgehogs squeak; and night and day, in every tone of voice, the sea says out loud its stupendous secret which is the meaning of everything, the tuning-in for the music of the spheres; and men often listen attentively, understand, and instantly forget all about it; while a foot above their heads the gulls mew like cats.

There, it was only natural that with the summer the friends of the two friends, the husband and wife who lived in the house, should come down to see them. Inevitable, too, that they should arrive all at once and spread themselves about the village, in the tar-and-whitewash cottages of the fishermen; or at the ancient Inn, now pretending to be a hotel; or plant themselves under canvas in the corners of a field, under a stone hedge beside a planting of willows, whose green wands, cut in autumn to weave crab-pots, quivered "upon the wild sea-banks" in summer cat's-paws off the sea.

Equally the husband and wife were glad that they should come. But with the pleasure went the knowledge that there was friendship and friendship, friends and friends. Their intimacy with each had been a separate act, a special creation, extended over time. Would they all instantly harmonize with each other? They would not. It was a question for delicate arrangement, for judicious pairing. The naval officer and one of the painters. Not the other. The stage-and-hunting woman with the sailor and the tow-haired politician whose job it was to restore ruins, rebuilt for a very different habitation the ruins of past West Country life. She would think his opinions a boy's barbarities; know his strength and his kindness for a man's. The journalist was for all the pretty women. There were not quite enough to go round.

"Except," said Marcia, the wife, nibbling at her pen, "Caroline, with two babies in tow, and the divorce she doesn't want in the least."

Julian, her husband, said: "Why doesn't she bring a nurse?"

"It's the new idea of mother-love. Besides the expense. You can't get one here..." There rose before their eyes the picture of Caroline, slender and very young, her wide tormented eyes, her tangle of curls, the delicate coltishness of movement young maternity was turning into grace, desertion and sorrow had made a little wild. A creature made to adore and be adored—now torn defenceless from such petty shelter as the graceful scamp had afforded her when he made her his wife. The graceful scamp would end the graceless scoundrel, as the wise Frenchman had prophesied. The lovely lass—what distressed both husband and wife was the stamp he had left already on the girl's delicate wax. Along with the innocence that made them weep was an ignorance that appalled. Corrupted innocence can turn ignorance, a damnable state of the soul.

While the immediate question was how to blend a grown child and two babies with a number of people who were strangers to her; and the men strange to children of any form. Men are rarely conscious of exquisiteness in the young, shapes of delight that seem to them to combine the dangers of a live bomb with the disadvantage that it cannot be throw over the cliff and has no pin to take out. No, Caroline must have her special hours, a separate play-time.

This arrangement broke down. Not wholly, not disastrously; but since the same plan had to be followed with most of the rest of their friends, the summer became more and more a service of time-spans, conditioned by a constant and vigilant effort to bring people together and to keep people apart; and inevitably the last became the more important, and separation the chief term of hospitality. The wide porch up the steps with the green benches and deck chairs, the summer's outdoor room, where the earth turned over on its side and fell away down to the sea through flowers—half cocktail bar, half restaurant—now seemed the place where everyone else was happy and they were not.

In their bedroom, in candle-light and midsummer dusk, Julian said: "I don't see where our fun comes in. They are all right, with the view and the tea and the drinks or whatever it is, while we keep wondering whether someone who doesn't get on with somebody else'll take it into their heads to call; and if they do I have to take them along to admire the stream. And now that eldest of Caroline's found its way here by itself and its mother will come and look for it, just when Toby and Violaine have settled down side by side, telling each other about their operations."

Toby was the sailor. And Violaine. It was not quite easy for either of them to speak temperately about Violaine—the tall woman, who had been brought there a month before by another friend, who had gone away and left her there. Much as a pretty launch, dressed for a regatta, might give tow to a racing yacht, its mast stripped, rising to the heavens, in that building for speed inside the winds that makes such a ship the tallest thing in nature.

Together they were sure of one thing—that here was a gift, a peculiar finding of treasure. Jar out of some rare earth, and inside it something at once familiar and rare. While frienship was in its second state of crystallisation. The first recognition over—would it harden out into its pure shape? Was it a late frost crystal? Or a superb flower in a cut glass, to be hurried onto the fire, so as not to shame it with the miserable change in its beauty? Too early to tell, but not if they could help it. For with her went, more than an ambience or a memory, a statement that was the opposite, among other things, of the outside of the house. Forms that had once "composed the beauties" of all three, forms like lost moulds, dies for their stamp, and to have Violaine near them like a new mint; who were all three exiles and from a life that it seems is more and more passing away. To build a Civitas Dei in such minds as theirs, lay up its pattern for itself. Until such time as it will return, and stamp itself again upon its outward images.

Another thing that was perfectly plain was the gulf fixed between Caroline and Violaine, a gulf they had made no attempt to bridge. Why not? For reasons that made them blush. And then blush for blushing. So hard it is for one kind of person to enter with the inward being into the life of another order of society. Yet that was what Violaine herself had done when she left her Border castles and the dark ruins of her house, her salmon rods and her horses to plunge into the world of the stage-world, not as actor but as spectator; and her friends

half great persons of the world, half women players with their lovers
and their sorrows. A world of which the wife knew little and husband
much. As he knew less of what his wife knew well, the world of what is
called the Young Intellectuals, the Intelligentsia. A name that has given
itself away. Yet she had lived it once, lived through it very thoroughly.
Was in a position to judge young entry—the kind of lad Caroline had
married—as Violaine the puppy she was walking, her husband the
quality of his own art.

So, with so much enlightenment about, it should not have been
hard to adjust, and tactless of La Bruyère to wake up his little platitude,
asleep in the attics of memory, and send it sauntering through their
heads: *Rien n'est aussi difficile que le commerce des hommes*— What was
to be done about Caroline? When surely the only question should be:
What was to be done for Caroline? Caroline, ardent and sweet, quick-
witted and true, a lass with a delicate air? What also had been done to
Caroline—taken, a child from some awful home in the middle of God
knew where, from a place not marked on any of their maps. There
Arthur had found her, enchanted her, married her; led her a dreadful
life. It was pure Prunella. Made her the mother of two lovely children;
spent too much. Was unfaithful to her; encouraged her to be unfaithful to him. Left her penniless. Taught her the fashionable immoralities
and the slang of cheap intellect, the formula of bolshevized behaviour.
Substitution for such simple faiths she had not believed in much. Deserted her, forcing her through the prospect of starvation to the divorce
she loathed.

Quick-witted, such education had not made of her an utter mess,
held by such simple loyalties as duty to her children and love of him.
Grief also at the harm he was doing to himself. Not bad, but not
enough for a *credo* in the world in which she found herself. Had she in
herself sufficient to develop and enlarge?

The husband and the wife listening to all this believed that she had.

Yet, like a term from another series suddenly intruded, star-dust
from the tail of a very different comet, they still observed that there
could be no introduction of Caroline to Violaine.

Reasons presented themselves. Violaine's health, her trigger-set
nerves. Her unawareness of the existence of small children, too young
to sit a pony or throw a fly. Still less of children whose parents had
lived in the fear of that new disease, the Repressions, more dreaded
than ever the smallpox, for which the prophylactic was behaviour

which would have sent their parents off to learn the habits of civilisation in disgrace. Nurse's business, only there were now no nurses
to do the rough work of licking into shape. (How far has economic
pressure given point to the theory which banished nurse, to replace
her by over-strung young parents, whose fatigue their young, with
the demon perception of infancy, know instantly how to play up?)

This took them some of the way. But what about the starry evenings, when the babies were in bed, and the terrace room hummed
with voices and the clink of glasses, and three hundred feet below to
the purring sea? Waiting for the moon to rise, watching the stars come
out, when "the sounds of beauty flowed and trembled" as from inside
the house Julian played Mozart. Hour of the moth, when they brushed
by, each with a lion's head, black eyes and white fur. A mystery. Or a
baby snail, his still transparent house in black and coral rings. A young
hedgehog, tender-quilled. The toad. These were night-callers, the faint
coloured stocks giving out their perfume in little floods born on the
night breeze off the sea.

No, she had better not come if Violaine was there. Was it because
they were all so much older, the War-generation with its unspoken secrets, that complete assumption of a common experience? In part. Because they were all such old friends? Not all of them were.

"You can't go on feeling sorry for a person all the time," said Julian.

"She loves us too much," said his wife suddenly.

"She kisses me too often," he answered simply, "outside the Post Office with all the garage men grinning. Hangs round my neck…"

"That's true," she said, "she twines." Reflecting on the counsel handed down from mother to daughter through the ages, how only to pretend to be a vine.

"It's not *natural*…"

His wife said: "It's Arthur. You don't realise—husbands train their
young wives. And when I first met him his chief asset was the way he
sank on to the floor at your feet, and looked up through his eyelashes.
The way every woman from a matron's size down was encouraged to
lean against him like Leighton's 'Wedded.' I did. He never forgave me
when I told him to stop when he put on weight and the bump of his
derrière could be heard on the floor."

"What I mean is," said Julian, "someone ought to tell her *when* to
do these things. Not with a village watching. Or," he added candidly,
"anyone."

This did not take them much further, though agreeable in itself. Then, little by little, there became perceptible a certain restlessness in Caroline at the mention of Violaine. A touch of curiosity; eyes that once or twice implored. With that the other pan of the balance moved a little when one day Violaine asked:

"Who's that pretty little woman with the children I saw coming out of your gate?"

It is easy to answer a question one has waited to hear, easy to draw a picture for her of Caroline; try to elicit interest, sympathy. Violaine without doubt could be useful to the child. Violaine was saying:

"Of course it's pretty hopeless looking after these young things who've got their lives into a mess. Besides, they always turn in the end and blame you." Easy to protest that, for once, this was impossible. Easy, too, to bore Violaine. It was dropped. Easiest of all, when the wistful look came again into Caroline's eyes, to explain how useful Violaine might be, with introductions to designers—and, privately, to a world more seemly than Arthur had ever chosen to show his wife. Part of their broader plan came in there—to lift the child out of the intellectual slum, the mental house of ill fame this young pioneer of our future society had offered her for home.

"And when her life is settled again, I shall tell her about her bearing…" Which done—and accepted—they saw the pretty ship set sail again, dressed for a blue day and a following breeze. *Départ pour Cythère*, as they both prayed.

It was two days later that the wife was led to the indiscretion which brought the delicate structure of their lives crashing down, with a harsher sound than a card-house toppling. Or compare it to a lid lifted off a simmering pot, showing under the bubbles a stew not designed for human food. Caterpillars out of the garden or inedible snails. Slugs even, and for herbs a few rank weeds. (Lately a fleet of henbanes had sprung up on the waste land outside the garden gate. A sending from Pan knew where, set on empty soil, as though even the weeds feared them, henbane from whose grey leaves the hyoscine is distilled that Doctor Crippen gave to Mrs. Crippen. Henbanes, on which and on no other plants, a swarm of black caterpillars were riddling to rags. A cycle in nature which struck them as sinister, no matter to what scientific terms it could be reduced.)

It was late afternoon when she turned to Caroline and said:

"My angel, you are passing Violaine Standish's house. Would you leave this note?" And saw her up the garden path, a lovely child in each hand.

"It's only to say I'll be down tomorrow for a cocktail at six."

This to her husband. Twenty-four hours later she heard the latch of Violaine's gate click behind her. She walked lightly, whistling, the hostess dropped and the housewife, the mother, the wife, and the apprentice british matron. A guest mounted the path, a guest come home to a meeting sweet with tradition. To a friend in the making. Over the edge of the ring of Violaine's high bearing, into air it gave power to breathe. The door of Mrs. Penrose's house stood open, the best rooms in St. Enys. In Violaine's sitting-room in the low window, two armchairs were drawn up. Twenty yards off the sea broke in a light thunder. Flood tide after a Biscay storm, its backwash sweeping the Atlantic coast, line upon line of breakers marching in under the lightest breeze, a limpid sky.

She sat down and opened a book. Upstairs Violaine would be changing shorts for trousers, dinner-dress at St. Enys if you are slight as a larch and as tall. Casing her tanned legs in grey flannel, cut and creased like a man's. Running a heavy comb through her hair, brushed back in short waves, the tiny sea of brass she carried on her head. The arms in her checked shirt would be bare, arms that matched her legs, the wrists so turned to make the senses ache. Only the tips of the fingers cut perhaps too short, a thought too square.

She heard her enter the room. Half-turned to the sight of something that instantly cut her smile, held it half-shaped. For what after seemed for a very long time. For Violaine at first did not come and sit down beside her. It was she who turned, slewed half-way round, while Violaine stood beside the table piled with glasses and books and records, her eyes on the high seas, her brown nostrils wide.

She was saying:

"Who in hell was that little woman you sent to see me last night?" Marcia knew instantly catastrophe when it arrives, crashes out of the invisible into the visible world like the clown out of the cupboard or the pantomime cat down the chimney; or at the play, the hidden witness to all impossible secrets when he knocks over the screen.

"I sent no one. I asked the little Caroline Adams to leave a note on you about this evening. That was all."

"That doesn't interest me. Perhaps you would like to hear what she did. She chose to come late last night as I was going to bed. Yes, then, with a howling child on each hand. Asked to see me. Got past Mrs. Penrose, who knows my orders. Gave me your note and sat down un-asked. Yes, stayed. A friend of yours I had in decency to receive.

"Sat where you are sitting now. What could I do? Took hold of my hand and stroked it. Said she'd been longing to know me; had watched me from the beach. Told me she admired my hair, the way I moved. Told me she thought me beautiful. Asked me about my health—inti-mate questions; and was I doing this for myself, and did I know how to do that?

"And all this time the children were whining and yelling: 'Mother, we want to go home. Mother, who is this lady? Mother, can't we go home to tea?' and running round the room and spilling my cigarettes and messing about the records, and falling down and shrieking, and starting to play and starting to shriek. First one and then the other. Then one got hold of the back of my chair and the other little brute hurled itself on me, and they both grabbed and pushed and fell about and kept asking questions. And one got hold of my jade figurines and the crystal and threw them down; and all their mother did was to tell me that *you* said children should be allowed to handle precious things to get the feel of them young. I can see you allowing anyone's brats to paw your things.

"And all this time she was cooing and stroking, and I had to sit still, knowing the next second I should insult her. How should I know how to control such people? A friend of yours, I could hardly kick her out of the house. But, my God, I shall if she tries it again. The slut! I'm not surprised that her husband left her. How did he ever come to marry her? Got her in the family way, I suppose, and she whined him into it. And, Marcia, I warn you if she tries it again, there will be trouble. I'll not answer for myself if I have any more of that insolence. And I can't help wanting to know what you mean by knowing such people and letting them loose on people who are defenceless because they are your friends–"

Defenceless? The storm went on, not shrill, high and clear, deadly with its steel edge. An edge to which Marcia's own brow was exposed, bare. Or was it her eyes?

And "Steady, Violaine," was all she found to say. "I was a fool to send her with that note. For that I apologise." ('I am paying too much for this—for that child's folly. We guessed Violaine capable of this. Yes, be a little formal—') "If I had dreamed she was so foolish I would never have let—" ('All perfectly useless. That's not Violaine's point. What is? That she must whip herself into a fury, ultimately to punish herself. Long-tortured body, long-thwarted pride. Called nerves. A contact she loathed. We know all that. Oh damn and blast the little fool!—What is she saying?')

"I can't see why you waste your time on such people. A mother! Fine sort of a mother, keeping those wretched kids up to all hours, howling in other people's rooms. Poor little devils—fine chance they'll have.

"And she's not the innocent little sweetness you both think. She had her reasons for coming. Those morons have. I only want to warn you she'll get nothing out of me; that if she tries it again, I'll not answer for my temper."

"Is she answering for it?"

('It's no good my repeating and repeating. What am I listening to now?') Violaine was sitting beside her, visible only in profile, her hard brown hands making gestures of tearing and destruction. Exhibiting something destroyed to scorn. Now she was asking how well Caroline knew the other men of the party; men she had referred to by their nicknames; and who had asked her to call Commander Norton "Nibs" and give details about his inside? Marcia writhed. These "imposings" which are more deadly than vice, the want of training that hustled youth and sorrow behind a screen.

Violaine was perfectly right. Perfectly wrong also; only her wrongness did not matter in comparison; her rightness was essential. The subtle contract broken on which human association depends. What is implied when you say: "People do not do these things." And where was Friendship's Garland, the wreath she and Julian had made with such splendid flowers and nailed up over Violaine's door? Or the posy of gentle blossoms with which they would have comforted Caroline? Not the roses and bays for Violaine's proud head, but such plants as columbine and love-in-a-mist. Love-lies-bleeding—oh damn love. —Stop protesting, however coolly, to her. Walk out over the scattered wreath as lightly as you can. Don't stop to pick it up.

Marcia was on her feet now, making—not excuses—but sincere and aloof apologies to a stranger. A tall bony woman, dressed as a man, flung now in a deep chair, her face lined with long endured atrocities of the body and spirit. Cause or effect? Eternal nagging problem. Her body was like a sword used for stabbing—ultimately herself.

"I can let myself out." Only half an hour before she had heard the garden gate click behind her, advancing towards that house with joy. Now she was walking up the cliff road in strong sunshine, in light become a burden as it does when the interior light has been turned off; quenched in another's darkness.

. . . . .

She sat beside her husband, in the terrace-room. Aghast they looked down onto the roof of the house below, where Mrs. Penrose kept the best lodgings in St. Enys; the house with its strip of lawn the road divided from the sea. Up through the gulf of air the sea-thunder rose. He said:

"When you got back so soon, I could see that something was wrong. From the way you walked up the road—"

"Two perfectly good garlands gone west. We shall doubtless make fresh ones, but—" He finished for her:

"C'est toujours moins involontaire."

Later, in his evening bath, she heard him singing, the theme-song of their household, of marriage, in times of stress:

"Never mind if things look glum
You're sure to find there's worse to come—
Every silver lining has a dark cloud inside—"

Smelling agreeably of violet salts, he sat up in bed, again the candle light crossing the last midsummer light, reflection of the sun on the Atlantic disk, as the planet rolled over, along with Mercury and Arcturus and the rest.

"Find me the bright side of this," she asked.

"What's the bright side of a hollow tooth?" he said, finishing the quotation. Suddenly she sat up also, clasping her knees: "You are angriest with Violaine and I with Caroline."

"Well, haven't we agreed it was stupidity made her do it, and curiosity and Arthur; that Violaine's forgotten more about manners than she ever knew; and hasn't Violaine got bats in her belfry and haven't we always known that?"

"Agreed, but don't you see—you can have Caroline for yours—but Violaine was one of my Muses, and in this life you want the Muses to be their very selves, not turning on a little hedge-sparrow for singing out of tune?

"And what are we going to do about it?" A question one partner does not always like to be asked. Julian said nothing. There was silence. She sat still straighter up:

"I know. One thing is true—this that has happened is the greatest of all cautionary tales. I shall make it into part of our saga and our children's children shall tell it, and the awfulness of its warning shall go with them from the very first time they go out into the world."

"So, like a good housekeeper, you'll not let any of it be wasted."

He drew her down beside him.

Mappa Mundi

Paris is not a safe city. It is never supposed to be, but so often for the wrong reasons. Perhaps the only place in the world that is really and truly both a sink of iniquity and a fountain of life at one and the same time; in the same quarter, in the same place, at the same hour, with the same properties—to even the same person.

It is no use, or not much use, to know it only as a spree, or as an aesthetic jolt, returning very sophisticated about it. Like all the great feminine places, behind its first dazzling free display, you come quickly upon profound reserves. After the spree a veil is drawn, a sober, *noli me tangere* veil. Isis, whose face on a first swift initiation you think you have seen, even to the colour of her eyes, Isis you believe you have kissed, withdraws, well wrapped-up, grown instantly to her own height—as is the property of a Goddess. Colossal, as Apuleius saw Hecate, and made of stone which is goddess's material; and for lover and mistress you are left with an image, remote as St. Geneviève where she stands looking upstream, an inviolable city behind her.

Properly snubbed, or enchanted, if you remain, above all if you live there, you learn that the delights of that first spree are repeated and confirmed as pleasure does not often repeat itself. Not only these, you find that there are others, possibilities of thrilling ways of life that do not depend on wealth or sex or the excitements between midnight and dawn; vistas of well-being that touch the commonest acts with the service of the goddess and her law, the quality of sheer living, sufficient in itself, as Tamar Karsavina tells in her book.

That is as far as most people get. Wise men stay there; more than the ghosts of good Americans settle down to the bliss of it. Only remember we are dealing with the goddess Isis. Her forbidding veil is off and not for a long time replaced. She moves now in transparencies. Only do not pretend to yourself that you have seen her eyes. Still less her smile. Least of all perhaps, do not ask what she is smiling about.

If you do you must be prepared for other things to happen.

There are people who do. That is how I account for what became of Currer Mileson, the american boy I met outside the Café des Deux Magots. Who was seen, who was seen less, who was not seen. Until he was never seen again. It was a business people explained in various ways—so far as it was explained at all. Until they gave it up. For he had come to Europe, so I gathered, all by himself out of the Middle West; and there one supposes were a few people who said: "that wicked Paris got him." Which about sums up, perhaps omitting the adjective, all that was ever said.

Yet American boys usually take some killing—if Currer Mileson is dead. As nuts they are tough, and as eggs hard-boiled. Their imaginations having less historic exercise than ones over here, they are inclined to be superficial—that is, romantic. Or, their national culture not yet achieved, when they do not despise they gobble. Or, anxious to assert their capacity, become culture-fans.

Enough about american boys. As rare and no rarer than rarity the world over, there are some of them who do not fit into any convention of their land.

I knew he was a rare one when I saw him, sitting alone on the round-the-corner part of the *terrasse*. The beautiful lean body, immense strength the generations had fined, even to over-fineness. All length that old age would make gaunt, and wild bright hunter's eyes. Eyes that were looking east, towards the shabby end of the Boulevard St. Germain where behind the Boul' Miche rises the Sorbonne, and behind the Sorbonne, the Rue du Cardinal Lemoine, where Strindberg ran away from two crossed sticks when he was finding the philosopher's stone.

We had met before. I sat down beside him and we each looked. The spring sun made one's senses ache as they ache nowhere but in Paris.

"Have you ever thought?" we both began at once. Both meaning the same question, but it was he who explained.

"Have you ever thought what lies behind this city—above all behind the ancient part we're sitting looking at? What, if you go at it long enough, comes through, comes *out*, what you walk into when you're awake and when you're asleep?" I stared at him. He went on:

"It's easiest on the Quai Notre-Dame, by the little old shop where they sell books on how to raise the devil. There it's pretty well done for you."

"What about when you're asleep?" said I.

He turned half round to have a good look at me, as though to be sure of my face for the first time:

"So you go there too?" he said. I nodded.

"Here? In Paris? But I might have seen you."

"Here and other places—places I have really known, got inside of, worked into myself."

Like him I sat, my face lifted towards the quarter which is the womb of Paris, where her young still go and her secret poor. Down the street where the broken bits of Julian's baths lie about, which he built when the legions occupied the little city of the Parisii called Lutetia. Stones cluttering the grass railed off from the pavement, round the house full of symbols of the real story, the Cluny Museum. All the Parises were about us, behind us, on our right and our left. Only before me, invisible behind the high roofs, stood the matrix of Isis' temple, the darkened shrine. He went on suddenly:—

"What do you think is the meaning of it? What do you see there when you go? What is it, that kind of sleep?"

"Well," I said, "I think, I'm nearly sure, that then, in *that* way, we are seeing, or even being shown, as much as we can see of what is really there."

"Why do you say 'sometimes'?" I hesitated.

"You know what dreams are—even these sometimes begin and sometimes fade away into quite ordinary dreamstuff."

"Mine don't. They're as sharp and separate as two kinds of being alive. But this other thing that happens when we're awake, that we're watching here right now, sitting on the edge of the Boulevard St. Germain—that's different, that's another thing, isn't it?"

"Yes," I answered slowly, "I'm pretty well sure by now that it's not the same thing at all; that these two experiences are different. If your sleep and mine are a pair, then we are moving about in places we know, and we can recognise this place or that. Only more real. Only in splendour. Great houses and courts and terraces climbing the sky from squares and steps and streets. A perfectness.

"When we're awake, as we are now, sitting together, it is much more like ordinary living, extended in time." He interrupted: "That's it. Trailers for half the films that have made Paris, or a hundred and one ways of Queer Street."

I agreed. I have a weakness for Queer Street, and people who have that are soon past being astonished at anything. So I did not ask him the questions I might have asked, but took it as I found it that a boy from the other side of the world should have walked straight up one of my own particular streets. A long way further up than I had ever gone.

I followed his eyes again, pitched high on the roofs on the other side of the street beyond the trams.

"It's there it all begins," he said. "Every corner you turn will be the next and the last. How'd you describe that?"

I tried again: "An extraordinary, a unique sense of all sorts of mixed pasts, a sense of the ancient city and all the fury of life that went to make it. Especially for me, in Villon's time and in the seventeenth century. That and"—he gave me a quick look—"that and something else. Like something out of which they *all* came. A matrix, which is Paris and the secret of Paris."

"The pot-boiling," he said, "and the bubbles coming off the stew."

"You can go home," I said, "when you've prowled enough, and pick it over and make plans and patterns. Even maps. But I think we're right to be careful, to keep this wholly separate from what we see in sleep. For there is nothing glorified about it." The look in his eyes troubled me, the look of a hunter of his race at a terrible quarry approaching from a long way off, a quarry that made him the hunted as much as the hunter.

"'Glorified' is the word," he said. "Alone there in a light of a finer quality than day. Funny I didn't meet you. D'you know the white cliffs with the poplars and the fountains, east of the city near the old fortifications?" (I did, it was one of my "places," and I knew the Orphic tablet too.)

"No one to speak to—just a few lovely quiet people about on their own blessed business. All Edens man's been working on. But what are the great birds?"

"Of course you're right. It *is* two different things. But what luck on my first trip to have walked back straight into the lot. History by day and Plato's patterns by night—*Garçon!*" He ordered two long, golden, starry drinks.

Like two travellers we compared notes. Yes, any time of day did, but a misty dusk was propitious in the broken hill-country at the back of the Sorbonne. Yes, and we both knew the ancient church at the foot of the wicked slum, called after Port Royal; and I had broken new country in the three great parallels along the river, of which the lowest was the Rue de l'Université and the highest the Rue de Grenelle. To us both had come the moment when walls slid in and out, to reveal others; both understood *crains dans le mur aveugle un regard qui t'épie.* Pure past or pasts, with their mystery and their passion; and as it were *through* them, the over-powering sense of one energy roaring through each, the crucible, the power-house in which each was formed.

After such wandering you could go home, turn over in your mind what you had walked through. That was why I had spoken of maps. For by now I had in my mind a chart of the place, of a Paris upon which the city of our time was no more than superimposed. One aspect of a central fire, or the womb of Isis, eternally fertile, eternally bringing forth. An activity of which we were the latest *eidola.* Admitted perhaps to this knowledge because we had not been content with her carnal gifts, had never boasted that we had seen her face.

Not even in our dreams, though there was no intellectual work, remembering or researching. There we strayed. Into the courts of her perfected work, the threshold of the completion of her labours; within and beyond the *simulacra* which were all we, in our bodies, could share.

It is one of the curious things about such experiences, whatever their reality, their ultimate significance or insignificance, that no one can discuss them for long. (It has been years before I could bring myself to write this.) After that morning we saw a good deal of one another, Currer and I; and though we knew perfectly what each was doing, what each was thinking about, we never spoke of it again.

Yet I thought of him as well, this young man, strayed round the side of a planet, carried across an ocean to stray again, awake or asleep, in two wholly new forms of experience.

The dreams, so I concluded after some meditation, were safe. So long as you woke up in time. Nor could you prevent them, nor had I ever come to harm in that country. Rather I loved them, as a promise and an exquisite reassurance; knowing too that like the "sensible fervours" of prayer, they were not to be sought or asked for or even longed after, but, like the grace of God, only to be enjoyed.

So much for the Goddess's more legitimate work. No, it was the other business, this waking awareness of what one could only describe as the "goings-on," the furies of dark energy, for which our Paris, with its brilliance, its exquisite sobrieties, was the mere shell—it was there that I felt less happy about him.

He did not know (for one instance) that along the line of my three glorious streets was once the waste place where the witches met—*quartier des Sorciers*; that when it was known what had happened in the little church by the river, the judge ordered a cloth to be hung over the crucifix, in sign that man if he could would spare God the knowledge of what had been done there.

He did not know, and I shied at my own guess, why the Tour St. Jacques stands alone as it does, or who the Child is who visited there.

He did not know the things Strindberg did not tell—even less than the things Joris Karl Huysmans told—in part.

He did not know that it is a curious fact that Madame de Montespan could not even get buried properly.

He did not know that the work of Isis implies the opposite of its own activity, that the Courts of the Morning stand on ground won from the Waste Land. He did not know that there was a were-wolf in Paris as late as the Franco-Prussian War.

He did not know what Hugo meant when he wrote about the Wicked Poor.

Any more than he knew what the Surréalistes were up to.

He did not even know the Song of Paris, how every century she had taken civilisation and made it dance to her tune. Built it and sung it and dressed it, prepared it for the table, for the assembly, for the bed. For prayer, for wit, for treachery, for rhetoric, for devotion; for its life and for its death.

Nor understand what goes with this and what must go; until the ἀνακατάστασις, the renewal of all things, which Paris will be the last place to notice.

Puis ça, puis là, comme le vent varie—that most dreadful line of a terrible poet, the most dreadful line in French literature of the dead men rotting on Montfaucon, might have been written about a girl's scarf, fluttering in the Tuileries in a spring gale. Might be said of the Goddess, flirting with her admirers.

I went across the river, to the Paris of the Empire and the Third Republic, but only depressed myself by the sight of women buying lovely things I should never be able to afford.

Across the Seine, still high, still racing last winter's rains, ancient Paris sat watching the light splendours that had risen across her stream. So that it seemed that a giant, straddling the river, would have one foot in time and one foot out of it; and little doubt, for all the contrast and the easy splendours, on which side the Bird-Priestess who under Isis is the city's *daimon* has her nest and lays her eggs.

Anyhow all mine were in that basket, and I walked home across one of the bridges that have a spring to them like a bent bow.

II

The next time we met was in the Rue de l'Happe—this was in the days before the playground of the Wicked Poor had become one of those spots for vice without tears in which Isis specialises the first time you meet.

I had not thought to find him there, "on the zinc," and the centime-in-the-slot jazz, among the youth in their coloured linen and skimpy suits.

It appeared that he was expecting someone. A friend just over and calling loudly for adventure? He did not want to tell me about it and he did. It was an exquisite night. I suggested a cooling walk along the quays, away from, not towards, the Tour St. Jacques.

We strolled west under the moon. The Paris moon, of all moons the most nostalgic. For what? For everything. Love-in-a-mist at eighteen; for a night spent with a vampire in a vault; for a court ball; for an adventure at sea. For staying in Paris forever; for running away from it at once. For delicate vice, for sanctity, for a great laugh—the moon who creates out of all these longings the final mood of divine high spirits, for which again only Paris has the receipt. The laughter no other city can evoke—except Vienna before we murdered her—the joy and daring she distils out of one like a dance, a running up and down between the alcove and the stars.

Shadows on the moon-candied stones, cat-black and sharp. It was late. Spring night or no spring night, the city was indoors at its play. My companion in his tuxedo was black and white too, the stones not paler than his young cheeks nor the night brighter than his eyes. Nor any hunter moved on a lighter step—I thought of great woods, and of his forbears' watching in the woods for the feathered, silent warriors of the Five Nations, stepping, score by score, on the war-trail in the night.

Then noticed him (we were silent) glancing right and left, checking his step as if to listen. For this friend?

With my mind on secular things, "Who *are* you looking for?" I said.

As though already I was not there, and his question to the wide world (as our questions often are), to *anyone* who would answer:

"Have they never spoken to you in sleep?"

As I have said, you cannot dwell for long on these things. My active mind was on the Boeuf sur le Toit and the friends I had left. "No," I said, was suddenly glad, now I came to think of it, that they had not. Even if they were the souls of just men made perfect (as one hoped).

"No, they never speak—Why?"

"Well," he said, with again that flash across his shoulder—"believe it or not, when it happens in the other way, there are some about who do."

"They're *not* the same thing—" I began, pedantically. Then suddenly felt as if I were pulled up short. By an intense cold. As though the little perfumed breeze that rose across the river were iced. Blown off some glacier—a breath, but a more than polar chill. And if you are to believe Dante, there is ice in hell. Then from behind a shadow I could not account for all but caught me up. Came up and dropped back into an angle in the walls. A little dark that had been following us, catching up and falling back, all the way, a thing that I had noticed and I had not noticed. A shadow thrown from one tree to another, traveling with them as they bent in the night airs on the embankment over our heads? I did not think so. Somehow I was wanted away. Instantly I wanted myself away also.

An interesting adventure, a perception to play with from time to time, wet one's toes in that sea. This man by my side had plunged straight in, with more intuition and even less knowledge, was already past hailing distance from the shore.

Argument and near-panic raced up me together.

"Don't," I managed to cry, "come away. It's not safe. Come tomorrow, and I will tell you everything I know about it"—I caught his arm and it felt as if it was something a long way—an infinite distance—off, and cold, and made of something else; and between us something that was not space, and cold from where cold comes from, was separating us. I heard myself saying:

"Ariadne it's like. You can't go without your thread." Hearing his answer:

"He's got it. He's past the Minotaur he said. Round the next corner he'll wait."

We had been standing facing one another. Now we began to walk again, and into my mind flashed images of men who had been too far. The young publisher who vanished on Olympus; the man in Buchan's story who discovered the corridors and that space, like murder, is "full of holes." We hurried as though driven. Already our feet were on the incline that leads up to street level again; as with the tail of my eye I saw the shadow dart out of its hiding-place.

Just at that moment a taxi drew to the curb at the top.

He did not follow even so far as to put me in; nor the taxi wait so long as for me to see what happened to the American left alone on the white moon road below the street, beside the stream.

It was an hour later, at the Boeuf, that I remembered to wonder who had paid that taxi, and how he had known that he was to bring me there.

I was with friends. But not to one of them could I say: "I've been out with a man who was followed by a ghost, and I left them making friends; and because I was upsetting its vibrations, it drove me away."

Next day this dumbness Montagu James describes as "common form" still held me; and it was three days before a mixture of conscience, curiosity and Paris high spirits sent me out to try if I could find him again.

I learned nothing at all; or rather that he had been seen, and that he had not been seen; alone and not alone (or possibly with a friend beside him, or with a bad character at his heels) by the concierge of his hotel, the *dame du bureau*, a waiter at the Deux Magots and one or two of his acquaintances.

Pensive, I left them, and walked east towards Notre-Dame along the Quai Voltaire.

Oh but the place was sweet! On the Quai des Fleurs I bought some. Country flowers, larkspurs and *giroflées*, and the orange marigolds the French call *soucis*. Looking up at the towers of Our Lady of Paris, thinking of Our Lady at Chartres, who could believe—in the demon who from her roofs looks down upon the city of Paris? That ubiquitous demon they can make into a door-knocker and the simple tourist's

288 ❖ *The Complete Stories of Mary Butts*

souvenir; who may even be a fake, a restorer's idea for a devil. Who, set in the crown of Our Lady in Paris, is yet the best known portrait of the Evil One that exists.

On my way back I passed again by the very dirty deserted house, beside which an alley runs back into the web of old streets at the wrong end of the Boulevard St. Germain. A house that saw the Musketeers in and the Revolution out, high-pitched, crazy, the kind of house etchers love, rat-worn, with something abominable about it. On my secret map a black spot and a question-mark—*crains dans le mur aveugle*—and the alley beside it is filthy. If you could not see the far end nothing would make you walk up it. You never meet anyone in it, and from the river end I was half-way up when I saw him cross the mouth of it; and I could not be sure if the figure at his heels was accompanying him or not.

I hurried up, to find myself in a street market, in a crowd walking round in circles, and on the Boulevard a knot of trams, all starting at once.

It was clearly, perfectly Currer Mileson, seen with something of the small perfection of a figure seen down the wrong end of a glass.

Reassured, I walked back to the Café des Deux Magots.

It began to get about that he was gone, to get about and be contradicted. I said nothing, and as I have told, he was new to Paris and he had no close friends. No one to start the inquiries which set the machinery of society in action. It was some time after that a man from the *Sûreté* came to see me; and I suggested, which did not please him, that Paris was a city in which one might easily be lost.

"Have a look round here," I said at last, "and see if I'm hiding him." It was the quietest of still days. The turquoise and gold dust of early summer—*maquillage d'Isis*—lay upon the city. Yet a picture, a map of old Paris, suddenly clattered on the wall, the *agent* turned his head, and a curious silence fell between us, like a shutter between his incredulity and my reserve.

You can only really give to people the kind of truth that is serviceable to them. I dined early, and when dusk came shut myself in to consider very carefully what I knew that I could be sure I knew, in the policeman's sense, in any sense, and possibly in another.

I ought to be able to believe that Currer Mileson was doing no more than wander about, neglectful of his meals or the people he knew or his bed. That overwhelmed by his discoveries, by the release of certain imaginative and intuitive faculties, he was working off a crisis in himself. That in time he would either snap out of it or be picked up by the police. "Partial loss of memory" was the phrase that rose—until I considered the sense of it and began to laugh rather shakily.

Yet it was the obvious way to approach it. It was what I should ordinarily have believed, even in the face of far stranger-seeming evidence. Only this time I did not believe it, I could not believe it, a single image recurring to my mind continually—of a young man to whom an order had been given: "step out of your body." An order he would obey (the means given, the means would certainly be given) as lightly as he would change his shoes.

Swept up, hurried off into an extension of that knowledge we both shared. Only an extension I had the sense to keep out of or the inability to pursue. "*Something far more deeply interfused.*" That was it. So far that he would never return.

It was after this that people came to see me. Americans mostly. People I had met and people I had not met. Few, or very few, with the idea that I had harmed him or even had some private knowledge, but (as I did not at first understand) as if some of them, at least, had a question to ask me they could not ask themselves. They came for help, and I had no help to give that would have helped them. Yet they seemed to feel that I felt something, and would one day produce it on a plate. One of them got so far as to hint about "vibrations"—but they none of them knew Paris.

Now and then I would try them out. "In the Rue Férou—did they remember who had lodged there?" Or did they know Jean Goujon's fountain, in a panel of which the inner genius of water is shown in stone? Or who had died on the Pont Henri-Quatre, calling upon a Pope and a King to meet him within a year before the Court of God? (A point which taken only provoked a reaction about the Templars and homosexuality.)

Or at Versailles even—had they noticed the silver birch that stands alone in the rough field beside the choked tank between Petit Trianon and Hameau?

Or that in the Bibliothèque de l'Arsenal there is the manuscript with the squares, and the receipts for letting out what, as Montagu James says, most certainly ought to be kept in? Or the emptiness of Boulevard Arago where, for all its broad leafiness the horses shy because of the work that the guillotine does there? Or? Or?

It was during this time, too, more than once, as I had seen it that night on the quays, a shadow would follow me home. A slip of dark I could not account for; and like Punch hiding behind the curtains, so it used my windows. Hanging half in, half out when my back was turned, as though keeping an eye on me to see if I knew enough either to be drawn in or to interfere. One evening it leaned out, shamelessly stretched up over my shoulder, as though to follow the page on which I had been writing down my helplessness. An eye it had on me, but I did not know and I could do nothing; and that was what it wanted, what it had come to find out. And all the time I was aware of this also; that there was a step I could take, simple and obvious, that I was a person with a key in one hand, a box in the other, without the wits to make them fit. Like Punch it sniggered at me, like Punch it was somehow annoyed.

Until one night it gave it up; and this time I was so certain of it that I hurried to the window, to see what appeared like a thin blackness swarming down the face of the house, dart across the moon bar in the narrow street, to be swallowed up in the dark of the opposite wall.

"Goddess," said I, "keep an eye on your servants."

But it seemed, too, that she was laughing at my ignorance; and as the summer drew to its height began to be bored with me, having given me, and in more ways than this, of her best and of her worst.

.   .   .   .   .

The *agent* came once more. This time he was more amiable. It seemed that Authority was still asking questions. Strange as it seemed, even the most insignificant of Americans were not allowed to vanish utterly. As one European to another, he implied that I would see the point. As if one of them, supposing they came from the place they said, supposing there was such a place for them to come from, mattered more or less.

Especially, as I pointed out, the object of his inquiries did not seem to have made a good job of it. There always seemed—just to be a little ghost of evidence that he was still occasionally seen. Then, for the sake of trying to say something, I added:

"Last time, Monsieur, you would not admit that your city was a bad place to be lost in. Yet would you admit that it is a place where you might make a bad friend?"

His answer surprised me:

"I entreat you, Madame, to tell me what you mean."

"I have told you all I can tell you, and you know that." Again there was silence, again our eyes met, and this time it was his eyes led mine to the map on the wall.

Then he surprised me even more. He crossed himself:

"I am not of Paris—I am from Corsica, I; and I do not mean its brothels or its criminals, but I say there are parts of this city that were better burned to the ground."

I nodded: "That is why I do not think you will ever see him again. Can you not get a corpse, any corpse, and satisfy them as to its identity?"

"That," he said simply, "will no doubt be done." Then surprisingly: "It is not you, Madame, who could bring him back?"

"No," said I, "then there would only be two of us. Besides, I assure you that if I could I would have done so long ago."

He stood there, no longer the Paris policeman but a tall man from the pure mountains in the South. And he believed me.

"He met then?"

"A shadow. Who has drawn him into the shadows. But remember, he was good. He may come to no harm there."

"How is that possible?"

"I mean that on the other side of the shadows there is another country, the Courts of the Morning that lie only just outside the gates of Paradise. When you are off duty, pray for him."

The map on the wall was still.

❖ ❖

A Lover

THE TWO FRIENDS sat together, talking over the last night's party and particularly one man who had been there.

They were very old friends, the young actor and the woman who had given the party, who had come up from the remote country to find out what London was like; and because she knew how to give parties, people came to her house; and she had already seen a great deal of what happens in London.

They talked of the people who had got off at the party or changed partners when it had got to its riotous stage: of the two men from the Ballet who had danced: of the punch it had taken three days to make and three hours to drink. Going through it all carefully, she with an eye for failures as well as for successes; for people to ask again: for people to forget about as soon as possible.

All this cleared away, she came to what she had been waiting to ask and her friend to answer—the amiable, fussy man, something of a match-maker and rather concerned for this woman who lived alone in the white victorian house with tall rooms good for parties and a balcony over a walled garden ending in trees. (This happened some years ago, when parties were still gay, before they took their agonised, bitter, debauched twist.) Perhaps it had something to do with her, though she never interfered, only people who came to the house at their worst sometimes left at their best.

"Now tell me, Alec," she said, "about your new friend." She noticed at once how his voice changed, charged as he spoke with unaffected grief.

"Alan, Alan Courcy—that's his name in case you didn't get it. French—not Huguenot—Revolution, I believe. I'd rather like to tell you about him."

"I'm listening. Go ahead."

"I got to know him because he's a great actor gone wrong. Met him on tour—in another company. He'd understudied Richard III and went on suddenly. I saw it by accident. He played him like a flame out of hell. White, too, and piteous, something I shall never forget."

"Reading the character? I don't quite see it. Or just touching up his own personality?"

"The last, I suppose. But it was thrilling. Finished work too: no raw edges. Then I got to know him."

So it all came out. The family behind this Alan Courcy, a mother he adored and quarrelled with and could not do without; a stepfather he played up against her so abominably that the hapless man periodically kicked his stepson out the house. Some money. No need to work. Badly knocked about in the War. An equal gift for painting; for quarrelling with managers; for destroying his work unfinished. For believing in himself: for disbelieving in himself. All of which meant in Alec's simple mind that it was a case for his dear Anne, with her trick of harmonising people. She must take Alan up, persuade him what a wonderful fellow he really was; what a wonderful world it is. Get him to become his promises, some of his promises, all of his promises. Alec was a sentimental optimist about human beings. Though when he saw the pair of them together on the stage of his own mind, his actor's eye hesitated. It was not quite so easy to see them playing opposite. Anne, tree-tall, calm and light. Alan—a conceit formed in his mind, surréaliste image of a dachshund and a serpent. Heavens! how the man did wriggle about. He could see the small, pale, nervous body flinging itself from side to side in an agony of self-assertion and self-depreciation and viperish verbal depreciation of others. It would take all Anne's earth-power to restore that to its original well-being. It was Alec's article of faith that there had been well-being once. Besides—besides— there rose in his mind the essential of Alan Courcy's history, the shattering, appalling fact round which his murdered youth was impaled; and he turned again to Anne, she saw his kind eyes full of tears.

"Besides, Anne, besides—there is the thing that happened to him. That it should have happened to him of all people." It passed quickly through her mind that this Alan did not look the man to be the victim of one annihilating fact, a man too flexible, too diverse. But Alec was an honest creature and not stupid when you discounted the sentiment.

"Go on," she said.

294 ❖ *The Complete Stories of Mary Butts*

"He told me when we first met—he was all to pieces after playing Richard. He has never told me not to tell. It was this. He was in Vienna before they ruined it. Just-before-the-War Vienna." The sigh passed their lips without which the name of that city is never said. Alec went on: "It was there he got engaged to a girl, a proper engagement, family and all. When the War happened he wrote and wrote. Heard she and her people were in difficulties. Brother after brother killed. Then there was the famine and he sent money. Money, you know, and love and hope. After a time he got no more answers, but he went on. Then, directly it was over, he dashed across. And couldn't find them. Utter strangers in their house. Jews. Went to their country house and found it in ruins. There had been some local fighting, and he says they must have left it in a hurry; that in a fallen-in summer house he found her handkerchief and a book; and the beginning, only the beginning, of a dreadful letter to him. I saw that. He carries it about and he read it to me. She had never had one of his letters. Nor the money. She knew nothing. Except that he did not care for her any more.

"At last he got on her track. They'd been driven, her mother and one sister, away to some other town. Became beggars together. Till she died—of starvation, really. A quick illness and no heart left. The woman who had tried to nurse her told him. 'Alan,' she said, 'I'd have seen it out if you had. But you've gone and I'd better go too.' Then she died. By the time he got there they were all dead. He says he died, too, for a bit. Perhaps he's never come back. Lots of us haven't. Only one feels that we all ought to be damned decent—to see if we can help him pull through. I can't help feeling it's a bit up to us."

By the time he had finished speaking, tears were running down both their cheeks.

Half an hour later Anne saw Alec, on and off the stage the eternal *compère*, out of the house. That he had just filled his role she saw laughing; but she was not laughing when she turned to her desk and wrote to ask Alan Courcy to dinner.

.   .   .   .   .

"Anne Clavel, dear, I suppose you'll be saying that I must take the job with a lowly and thankful heart and work up the part, and not tell the producer that a cockney accent goes badly with iambic pentameter; and that Shakespeare talked a nice country accent with a burr—warm, like a woolly caterpillar. How tiresome and moral and athletic, and how very good for me.

"Yes, I will. You're the only being on earth I would do it for. You are making things different. Taken a fool, trying to have a private life as much like des Esseintes as possible, out of his dark room. Opened *all* the windows, let out the musk and amber and let in garden smells. Only why did you do it? Why? Why? Why? Why in hell or out of it should anyone bother about me, licking perfectly disgusting sores in the dark?"

"I don't know," said Anne peacefully, but gratified, "I don't like septic wounds. And I couldn't stand the tortoise."

"The tortoise?"

"Don't you remember? He had its shell set with carbuncles to watch it glow as it crept round, and it killed it; and he could see the stones still shining in the dark of his infernal flat until it occurred to him where the stink came from. Some of your memories were too like that tortoise for me." Alan had left the deck chair and was lying on the grass in the garden at her feet. At this he dropped a moment, his face hidden resting on his arms. She could see the slight shoulders quiver.

"*Mon vieux,*" she called after a moment, very gently. The ravaged, petulant head turned up to her again.

"Witty, searching beast of a woman. I didn't know whether to laugh or cry. But I won't be like a tortoise gone bad—even a tortoise with jewels stuck in it."

"I never said you; only some of the things you think about."

"If you weren't so utterly right, and didn't make it rather funny, I'd lose my temper and show you what sort of a nasty, catty, self-pitying, little martyr I am. But oh, Anne, what put it into your head to see through me so comfortingly? When I came to your party, I actually found myself behaving like a human being. I'm usually rather awful at parties. Drink too much and either cry or else insult my hostess; and instead I found myself indulging in an innocent frolic." Anne thought: 'It had better come now.' She was more and more moved as by something that seemed rather exquisite, wild and young and wounded, that had stopped fidgeting and lay on the grass at her feet, still and appeased, as if waiting for some word which would come from her to make him stand up and let fall a great burden and then move—swiftly and harmoniously and with joy. Like a man delivered from the hell of his own mind. And from more than his mind. From what had been done to him. Like many women after the War, she had been busy patching up; spending herself on it, still young enough to expect too much, old enough to suffer, but not wholly break her heart.

"It was Alec," she said slowly, "he told me."

"Dear old Alec! Such a—*comprimé* of all the best traditions of the stage. So good"—his voice was gentle—"that I bore it the other day when he put his hand on my shoulder and called me a priceless old fruit."

"Be thankful it wasn't 'laddie.'"

"You always have an answer—the sort that puts things in a better light. It would be intolerable if it wasn't true. Anne, Anne, Annette—Anna Perenna, the moon-in-an-out. Which shall I call you?" He twisted round suddenly and sat staring up at her. A dreadful change came over his face, the eyes staring, the body taut; the bright restless eyes, brown-irised, the whites shaded with blue, starting out of his head. Anne thought she had never seen eyes so haunted, so crazed with hopeless escape. Flight down the corridors of the mind, each one that ended with a door, and nailed to it the same dreadful bleeding god. We each have one to meet, but this man's was Eros crucified. The girl he loved, dying out there so slowly, one victim out of millions. Out in Central Europe where the folk-wanderings meet and cross and destroy. A long time ago… Heavens! what had ancient history to do with it? But man had thought he had made himself a reasonably safe place out there in the heart of those lands, where Dacia once stood with its chain of towers. Till Trajan came and took the Red Tower and the city of Smaragethusa, and there Rome had made for herself Vindobonda, and for us Vienna. One of the Holy Places Cities, last seat of the Roman Empire. In place of so many crucifixions, a place of delight. A fountain of wit and sweet laughter. Anatol's town…. He was saying:

"So you know? Of course you know. Why shouldn't you know? She died. She died. Now you know all there is to know, Anna Perenna. I'm glad you know. For now you know all there is to know about me. For her agony hasn't redeemed me—it's made me a maimed cat. A spiteful liar. A man too hurt to use his gifts, who takes his shame out in miscalling other men. I'm not a man. I couldn't protect her; I was caught in the Army with the rest. I was so sure as I went strutting about, and though I call myself a Christian and a Catholic, all the time I see another god, something very old, with a filthy leer, who likes hurting people. He's had his joke—he's still having his joke with me.

"But you are not laughing, Anne…." He flung himself forward and laid his head down on her knees. Her fingers touched the little drakes' tails of the soft hair along the cleft of his neck.

．　．　．　．　．

This time it was Alec who sat at Anne's feet, looking up like an affectionate and enthusiastic dog.

"Wonderful the change you've made in Alan. We're doing a Sunday show and you ought to have seen him at rehearsal. Understudied Biron, and had to go on again at the last minute. His body doesn't fit, but he made it. The sword and ruff did what they should and often don't and helped him, and forgot what he does when he's nervous and goes all stagey—took a flying leap into the part, and you saw little Alan Courcy turn Renaissance lord. It went as though it had been sung—you get what I mean? The young Shakespeare, working up to a hell of a climax—stuck in the rest of the play as an excuse for that speech—and Alan was his rocket. Going up and bursting out on top with stars. You should have heard him, mounting his part:

> 'But love, first learnèd in a lady's eyes,
> Lives not alone immurèd in the brain—
> In valour is not love a Hercules,
> Still climbing trees in the Hesperides?'

"And when he came to the persuasive solemn bit at the end: *'For woman's sake by whom these men are men'* he spoke it like a gay prayer. His English is naturally very pure. A little pernickety—after all he's part French; but when it comes to a show like that and the classic stage, he's got it where he wants it."

"I wish," said Anne, "I'd heard."

"I wish," said Alec, "you had. For at the end, my dear, he was praying to you."

"Not to his memories?"

"Well, it's been you who've treated them so as to make them fit to pray to," said Alec sturdily. "Besides, he's told me as much."

．　．　．　．　．

Again Anne was very pleased. It was the appeasement of nerves that pleases many women, aware that through them has come consolation, a certain order and proportion, virtue set free. Pleasure that, when Alan came to call and tell her about it himself, came with a sensual stab.

The spring came too with its wave of green fire, and they became lovers. Even, at his suggestion, marriage crossed her mind. His family encouraged her. His mother especially, his half-french mother, the elegant old lady, anxious, ironical, profoundly observant and attached to her son. Exhausted too, as Anne noticed, with a lifetime of dealing with him. Did she understand him? Did she not? Was she, *au fond*, wise, or did she suffer from that vanity, that essential blindness of the parent that seems to the lover so shocking and so hopeless? Anne asked herself that, when she noticed old Madame Courcy to be as much amused as impressed. Impressed she certainly was and thankful, with even a touch of hope that in itself sounded like a warning. For every time she heard her say: "Anne, child, what wonders are you doing with my son," Anne could hear, undertone and overtone, fear and something like derision concealed. A little afraid for herself, she summoned the lover's faith. Again, whatever he was, Alan had the trick to make her passionate and to make her laugh, two things sufficient to fly away with judgment and again she knew it.

She was the fountain at which he drank, bathed, adorned himself. With altered step he had begun—she saw it and his mother endorsed it—to "*move about the house with joy.*" Yet she soon noticed one thing—that he never bought her anything but cheap flowers, and these with excuses she did not expect, about poverty which she knew, within that range of expenditure, did not exist. And, though he was always at her house, he rarely took her out, and then with the same excuses. It was queer. Then one evening he told her that he was on the track of a sister of the Austrian girl who might still be alive, and putting aside every penny to help her. Well and good, but it occurred to Anne that a possible wife could hardly be asked to share forever such an excess of charity.

And when he spoke of this his voice grew shrill, the small lithe body flinging itself about, and he would wander about the room from chair to chair, find nowhere to rest. This progress she knew and that it ended in quiet, his body laid down again at her feet, his head with its soft blown hair come to rest on her lap.

But that evening, after trying the fourth chair, he got up again and, apropos of nothing, cried out: "Why should I bring you presents? I know I'm supposed to bring you presents. Convention demands it. I sent her presents, money, all I had. I went without the decencies of other men in my mess and she never got them. They never did her any good. You've got everything you need. What can I give you? My rotten life to pick up. Fine gift that, my Anna—"

She took this quietly. It seemed to her inevitable that it would come to a struggle between the dead girl and herself. A struggle that, for both their sakes, she must win. That it was fair for her to win. The little Elizabeth would not mind. Was not going to be allowed to mind. She waited till he had done and said:

"I wish, Alan, that your french mind would run through what you've been saying. What *are* the parallels? And when did I ask you to give me presents? Only there comes a time—a way—when the dead must bury the dead. It's the only way to keep them properly alive. Otherwise they're apt to stink. You say you're a Christian and a Catholic, and you know our authority for that. Only just look at the sense of what you're saying. You're not to give me presents (for which I've never asked) because once (under tragic circumstances) you gave them to someone else who didn't get them; all bolstered up with camp about convention and lies about me. Alan, dear—"

"Anna Perenna sits there, the Moon-Woman, and talks about logic to the Man in the Moon! But I earned that, I admit. Oh, I'm a nasty bit of work. No one knows how nasty—" He came across, took her by the throat and began to kiss her:

"Doesn't she know I must punish her for being so lovely and so wise and for purging the cad out of me?" As he thrust her back among the cushions, her body began to relax, and he lay beside her, nibbling her lips—"Best french logic"—and heard her laugh from her throat. Then silence close together for the lovely words, murmured but distinct:

> "*A la très chère, à la très belle*
> *Qui remplit nos âmes de clarté—*"

And a moment later, as if to himself: "Go away, Elizabeth, my dear, your time's over." "To Paradise," she whispered, drowsed and trembling at his touch. The long couch in the room where the spring wind stirred held them easily, and his presence shut out everything but the wandering airs and high up in the trees the talk of doves.

. . . . .

A few days later he said: "Let's go to the Ballet. We must tonight. I've got the seats." Anne agreed. Before she started she looked at the programme. There was to be one called "Le Beau Danube" they had not seen. She remembered what she had heard about it, that it was written round the Danube waltz, with one heart-breaking *pas de deux* for Lopokova and Massine. (Critics had called it a return to sentimentality, but those two knew what they were about.) Then that Alan must know: that he meant them to see it together for a kind of adieu, a last salute to the dead.

She met him and they went to their seats. They were not very good seats. While a little worm of observation coiled in her mind suggested to her that, if she offered to pay for them, he would be pleased. So, preparing for some sort of crisis, hoping for a finale or some revision of their relations, she sat still until the curtain rose.

There is still power in that sweet tune to make the shattered children of the after-War world weep. Not because they love like that, or that they would like to love like that. One of the recurrent love-moods of humanity that our society at the moment has no use for and no response. Only, as presented by the two great dancers, one of tears. In that ballet there is nothing but their dance, when the passionate modulation before the end is worked out by their bodies, in a rapture based on sweetness based on grief. A voiceless song accompanied their movements across the empty stage. They were dancing the death of their love, but the song said: "This is Vienna's death." As he lifted her and she mounted in his arms to the passionate air, the heart of the youngest of all ancient cities was broken with their hearts. A dance that lasted ten minutes. It took several years to kill Vienna; several centuries to make Vienna. And all these three times were the same time. Nor are we used, like the ancient world, to the death of cities who have married civilisation each with a ring of their own, which cannot be made to fit another hand.

It did not seem necessary to compare their thoughts. They sat straight side by side, each in a precinct of pain and delight. Watching a dance of love, love when it is nearest to death. Death of Vienna. Death of Anatol. Death of Saki's Clovis and Comus Bassington. They were dead. They were dead. Had those dead boys found any Paradise in which to go on playing? (Was it a spoiled Anatol she had sitting beside her?) As the curtain came down, "No," said something distinctly.

The next was the "Boutique Fantasque." Alan did not want to stay. "Not after that, Anne, please." Anne wanted to stay, because she loved the "Boutique," because it was something like bad discipline to run away, instead of tuning in to another kind of joy. A better kind perhaps of a very different best. "Stay and laugh," she said. She often gave in, but this time she did not want to give in. Or, when Alan began to sulk, damn well mean to give in. "Alan, stay and play." "Play!"

he cried out, turning his ravaged head: "My play died with that. Why should I stay? Tell me that."

She said coolly: "Because of courage." For a few moments he stared down. "All right," he said at last. The curtain rose again. She leaned forward, ready to lose herself. Not quite. Aware from time to time of a fleeting look he gave her. Of the kind a lover would rather not see.

When they had left the theatre he said: "I wonder how long it will continue to amuse you, going about with a corpse. Can't you see, you blind woman-thing, that I died when that died?"

"The answer is that I should dislike it very much. Only I'm not and you haven't."

"You're like all women—you only see what you want to see. And what you want with me, God knows. I can't even ask you out to tea. I'm sorry to be so poor, but the tickets cleared me out."

She knew these pettish fits. At first she had thought to tease him out of them by a cheerful generosity, and for a time it had seemed that she *had* teased him. This afternoon suddenly palled.

"I am going home to tea. And I'm not going to ask you because it's my housekeeper's day out, and I have to get it myself, and it's such an awful bother putting an extra teaspoon into the pot. Besides, think of the expense." The tube station was mercifully near. She knew him hesitating behind her. Would he dash after her as he had sometimes done and, penitent, eager, exceedingly forgivable, laugh at himself? Explain all over again: "I come all over beastly about money because of *her.*" This time he did not follow. She reached home unhappy, vexed at the stab—worse than pain—of contempt that nagged at the being of love. The love she thought they were making, and of which she could never be utterly sure if it was makeable or not.

The tiny crisis passed. It seemed more and more as though she had accepted to marry him. Not that there was any hurry. Then one day they were together at her house when the news came that Alec was very ill. He was going on tour, a first-class tour, to play lead. He could not go; and when he recovered he would be out of work. It was possible that if an expensive treatment were given instantly, he might recover enough. Anne got out her passbook and looked at it thoughtfully. Did sums. Asked Alan if he could help to make up the right amount.

"We owe him a bit, *mon ami.* No two people had a better friend. Besides he is one of the very few who will pay back and pay back quickly." She had not time to be horribly afraid before she heard Alan saying:

"Twenty pounds? My dear girl, I'm afraid I can't do that."

But Alan, it's only a loan and a short one. You've told me your income. You've no real expenses. You're living at home—"

"I'm out of work if it comes to that."

"My dear, you could have gone touring with Alec. They wanted you; he wanted you—"

"And leave here—you—this?"

"As you like. But don't call yourself out of a job."

The usual fatuity followed: "I thought you wanted me to stay." And she must make the obvious reply:

"For myself, yes, of course. But for you, and also for myself—don't you understand—I want to see you act."

He said with a sneer:

"And play second lead to Alec." There was a nasty silence. Then he began to tell her witty stories of life on tour, and left her, promising to go home and see what he could do. Left her reflecting. He had said no more. He *had* changed his tone. Perhaps he had seen for himself what it would mean if he did not help his friend. Anne wrote a cheque for her part, and went round to the far harder business of persuading Alec to take it.

.   .   .   .   .

The next day she went to Kensington, to Alan's house, to the tea she shared once in a week, alone with his mother; a visit now become a custom between the old woman and the young. The ritual was that Alan should appear later to take her away, dine with her or take her out to dine. Still Anne could not determine what the old woman thought. Was it her french training, ignoring what she could not prevent? How far was she in her son's confidence? Were they together—uncomfortable suspicion—using her—as a medicine, a cure, a prophylactic against something worse? (Stupid. Of course they were. Exactly how much?)

How much *did* he tell her? Anne smiled and blushed. Well, old Madame Courcy was the right kind of mother to appreciate that.

They had tea in the garden. The old lady began cheerfully:

"Alan will tell you when he comes. He won't have had time before. It's sad that your poor friend Alec is so ill, but they've offered Alan his part on tour; and, thanks, my dear, to the way you've encouraged him about his work, he's accepted it. He says, too, that he's sending Alec something to help pay off his illness."

Anne stared at the grass. A caterpillar on a blade stood up on its green tail and waved a black head at her. Two worlds, caterpillar world and man world for an instant in contact. Anne thinking man thoughts, the caterpillar, caterpillar thoughts. So Alan had sneaked off and stolen Alec's job. (Innocently she was responsible. She had told him about Alec's illness and his need and the tour he had accepted.) On such conditions the loan she had asked for had been granted. Alan would have the work and the pay and the fame, if any. And be paid back the money he had invested which had obtained him these things. He, the spoiled gentleman actor, too good for this and too gifted for that. The bitterness that is the reverse and the measure and the proportion of love welled up dreadfully in her. The amateur had robbed Alec, Alec who gloried in his profession. The profession Alan gloried in being too good for—the fine art of the actor—picking and choosing and turning his back on the mill to which Alec offered his body as a grindstone.

(And how had he got the job? Was that the way the money went? Was it possible? Anne only knew that anything is possible.)

Madame Courcy was looking at her:

"Have I distressed you, child? I mean, do you not want him to go? Of course you don't, but you've always been so sensible and intelligent in wanting him to work; in seeing what his work might do for him. Only it has been a shock, the separation—I see. I have been careless. But if you only knew, my dear, how I have come to rely on your courage. It has not always been easy to be Alan's mother—"

('Tell her? Tell his mother? Why not? She would not understand by herself and she'd better. And if she's a cheat also, I shall know. Those last words of hers sounded sweet. If they were, then she's worth truth; and if she'll stand the truth, Alan won't quite get away with it…. Besides, I'm so angry, it's bound to come out…. Lovers can't be cads…. How dare he do that to love?') Hoping piteously that Madame Courcy would understand, grimly prepared for an explosion of mother-love, she said:

"It is not that, *Maman*. It is because Alan had no right to do that." She explained with her head averted, her eyes on the caterpillar, now gathering itself up, head to tail, in a loop, and shooting forward its own length, to wave a moment and repeat. Very neatly done. As if, too, it was showing off. Alan liked to show off. *I am a worm and no man.* She began to look hard across the garden to a tree, the tree the French called Golden Rain, most beautifully in bloom.

"You see, it takes away one's respect that he should do a thing like that. And how can one keep love without the honour that goes with it? I mean I can't. And forgive me the priggishness." To her great comfort, Madame Courcy's voice reassured:

"I see, my child. Of course I see. Yes, I am glad you have told me. It is as well to face these things." Blessed french mind, accepting things as they are; keeping values pure and intact.

"I quite see that he has done wrong. And what it means to you— for you have tried. We have all tried...." (Anne thought: 'Even if she would be glad to be rid of me, this woman is honest. Not a touch, thank God, of "my son, right or wrong."') She heard her add rather grimly:

"I think we will speak to him when he comes in—and yet—" Their eyes met and both women nodded.

"You mean, *Maman*, that it might put him off acting forever if he is told not to be a cad and to leave this?"

"Yes, I fear that. You see, I know—oh how well I know—his perverse mind. Presently he will be saying: 'You made it a point of honour, when I had the best chance in my life, that I should not take it....' You can imagine what he would make of that."

"You are absolutely right. Dear God, how difficult it is." And from the mother's face she understood what a lifetime had been.

"*Réfléchissons-nous*. And what perversity it is again that you should have so stimulated him—for this.

"It has always been like that. From his childhood—how often I have been unhappy. Feared too for the woman who—how do you say it—should tackle him. But except for the *amourettes* with the lower classes and with, shall I say, *grues*, he avoids our sex. Always it must be one who is paid to please."

Anne sat up sharply. Of course he was that sort. All the horrible things, as is their way, were coming out at once. If she had not been drugged by the Vienna story, she would have known that. Now it was intolerable with what distinctness she could see him making love to a girl of easy virtue from the corner tobacconist. And did he get his cigarettes free? Reaction was making her beastly. He had called her Anna Perenna. Moments of exquisiteness flashed back, flashed past. Flying things, coloured and winged, to lie preserved only in the amber of memory. She heard herself saying in a sensible voice:

"While we must always remember the Vienna business. To have lost one's first young love like that. When a thing like that happens there is always something final about it. Something for which one must have extraordinary patience, extraordinary understanding. After which, heaven help us all, perhaps we can never expect too much." Madame Courcy interrupted:

"Vienna, my dear, what was that?"

"Why, about the little Elizabeth, about Babette." ('Perhaps he didn't tell her. That's nonsense. He tells her everything, let alone *that*.')

"Babette Cosmas he was engaged to and who died so awfully." ('She is staring at me. This is like finding a person you supposed a Christian hadn't heard of the Crucifixion.') Clear and distinct she was being answered, plain words within the range of cat and dog and no and yes.

"Babette—bless our hearts, why should he say that she is dead? Or that he was engaged to her? Yes, they were a family we knew very well, in Vienna, just before the War. Charming people—she was a good deal older than he was. He made a few calf's eyes at her as a boy will. Engaged? She was engaged already. Married when we left and managed to spend the War with her baby in Switzerland. They had property there. They all managed to get through all right. I still hear from them occasionally.

"Child, you were angry before. Now you are white. What is it? Speak out. We have not kept secrets from one another."

As Madame Courcy spoke it seemed as though, instead of trees flowering and new grass and borders opening with flowers, they were sitting in a place that was a desert pocket, full of clean dry stones. In the middle one large stone, like an idol, called The Truth. And why all time had she been calling the place a garden, when actually it was made of dry stones? Bones among stones. *Can these stones live?* Instead of the heart's desire, a stone. All this time she had been serving the image of a love which had not been there. The moon had come to Endymion; Endymion had got the moon down under false pretences. After all the moon is a stone. Who was it called the moon a "luminous stone"? In the centre of everything there was this large stone. A stone instead of the heart's desire. It occurred to her that perhaps she now saw the stone because she had wished for truth. Truth in love. No love without truth. There was singularly little consolation in it.

"I will tell you the story Alan told us," she said. "The story that was his passport, through Alec, to our society. To me most of all. The story we believed utterly."

She told it, the passion and death of Elizabeth Cosmas. Which had not taken place, whose shadowy and metaphysical existence had so affected her own. With its details: the money Alan had sent, the things he had gone without, the money he hoped to send. His mother listened silent. At the end she said:

"There was no one like that: no one of whom that story could be true. Nor was he in the Army for more than a few months at the end. Clerk's work at some base: his health alone made a commission out of the question. On that account I never suffered the least anxiety." Then, "I remember, Alan said to me once, quoting one of your modern poets: *I must find a gesture of my own.*"

"He seems to have done so." The old woman waited a few moments. Then she said:

"My dear,, I have one question to ask you. From you I know I shall hear nothing but the truth. Can you forgive him? If you do not yet know, say so; but I believe it to be one of the occasions when if you look in your heart, you will know the answer." Anne did not hesitate at all: all anger apart, the mother was quite right. She knew the answer, as if it were prepared for her.

"No," she said.

"I understand. With you it is inevitable." Anne nodded. The old woman stared down the garden, in which she saw no more flowers.

"It is not necessary for me to say that I am sorry that my son has done this to you."

"Done it to love. If I stayed till he came and we taxed him." She went on staring; both women thinking the words he would say: "I'm glad you've found me out. I'm glad I've been exposed to you. Now you know exactly and for keeps how vile I am." Roll himself in his poisoned shirt, till she, too, was fiery with the prick of his disease. Now there was just time to escape. No gifts at home to remind her. Half an hour would purify her house of the memory of him.

She picked up her long gloves. No need to hurry. The gods had this in hand, and she had already escaped him.

"Good-bye, Madame Courcy. Thank you for all your *gentillesse* to me." She walked across the green grass which had turned to stones.

'What am I leaving her alone with in this garden? Something she did not know before. Thrown him back on her? I had to. Leave him to her. What have I to face—some pain and more shame? But if she were not his mother, she would no more forgive him than I would.'

❖ ❖

From Altar to Chimney-piece

H E WAS EXQUISITELY in love with Paris, his *sweet profound Paris.* Great Paris—

where the sights are—
where the nights are
and the lights are.

In love as young Englishmen used to fall in love with her, who had come to her just after the War, after doctors and hospitals and sanatoria had done their best and worst for them. After the country-life prescribed had done its best; and after a year or more had sent them out with the minute drop of sap, without which health of body is no more than the carrying-round of an active corpse and health of spirit does not exist, running once more in their blood. A supreme tonic was all that was needed, and here Paris played its lovely part; and, though it seems incredible now, just that part of Paris the newspapers have learned to leer at, which has now become an american side-show and an alcoholics' parade, Montparnasse. Montparnasse—at that time still old and shabby and merry and wearing a crown of little stars at night. Twelve years ago, when Vincent first went there, it was still like that, still French, still serenely uncomfortable, still adorable and full of great and famous people and those who would become great. Famous Americans too, but come to enjoy France, not a bad copy of New York. Their imitators, their failures, their complex-ridden repression-loosers had not yet arrived to violate and corrupt it. It was not until five years ago or six, that a demon of vile intelligence stepped off the boat-train, crossed the Seine at the Pont Royal, followed up the Boulevard Raspail to where it meets the Boulevard Montparnasse, and at that wide, untidy, sun-struck, tram-clanging crossroads halted to see what he could do to change all that. He found a quarter in a princess of cities where people were being good because they were being happy, because, after the lost years, a small tide of earthly joy was rising gently in that place. Or winding in and out of it like a little stream no evil thing could cross. A place where, even if people suffered, the sorrow had in it something that was exquisite, a touch of rapture, as though the pain was about something real, a necessary part of something like immortal life. A place where men and women were beginning to live again, beginning to make up for the years that the War had taken. A place where work was being done, by people of all kinds and races; and France at her work again, modulating, civilising, evoking, praising, setting free.

In those days you could see, springing, timid but sturdy, like plants an east wind has shriveled to the earth but whose roots have lived, men and women in bud again, hardly able to believe the blue air's caress, on the warm soil firm and nourishing, but lulled by them and fed—looking out at life again from the shoulders of Paris, from the arms of France.

This story, suppose one could bear to write it, is not about how the demon changed all this, how those who should have guarded the stream let him across. Or how, like a good strategist, he attacked the French where they are weakest, telling the proprietors of hotel or restaurant or café how much money they could make by giving the nastier or more ignorant kind of American the drains and baths and bars he thinks are civilisation, because they are all he has to distinguish him from the least finished kind of man. Hell found no difficulty in transporting them, the men and women who think art synonymous with vice, and delirium tremens an ornament if acquired in an artists' quarter. These and the hangers-on of all the arts, their failures, the silly-rich, the neurotic, the intolerably-repressed. They came—and the place is hardly recognizable now. They came—demoralising their hosts, who grew fat and brutal and time-serving under the rush of dollar bills. They came—and the old delights went, the love of work and the love of play. The love of a party, work, solitude, study, indolence or an exhilarating row. Love of loving Paris, of good wine, good food; love of one's friends, one's enemies, one's beloved. The lovers went, as the old cafés were pulled down or came back after an interval of hammers and scaffolding in new and horrible clothes, with doubled prices and waiters ravenous for tips, and with no eye for the old clients who made or would make their Quarter and their service illustrious. The great arts withdrew with the men and women who practised them, and with them went the lovers and the men and women who were beginning to live again. They went—to be replaced by the parasites on all the arts and all the passions, the men and women harlots and the fashionable purveyors of sexual excitements disguised as art. And with these, *their* panders, not of social or sexual tastes, but the neurotic vices which follow fashion and have nothing to do with desire. Also the men and women whose hell had not been occasioned by any dislocation of our society, but by the putrid state of their subconscious selves, occasioned by fear, by over-indulgence and sometimes by the intolerable repression of american life.

Anyhow, their arrival closed Montparnasse as a temple of Æsculapius; and Vincent, the young man who began this story, went to live in another quarter; and for a time, again, it was well with him.

. . . . . .

Years passed, and Paris remained in part his home; and as happens to people who become imaginatively conscious of a great city, he came to have a private map of it in his head. A map in which streets and groups of buildings and even the houses of friends were not finally relevant, or only for pointers towards another thing, the atmosphere or *quality* of certain spots or spaces or groups. These maps are individual to each lover of a city, charts of his translation of its final significance, of the secret workings of men's spirits, which, through the centuries, have saturated certain quarters, giving them not only character and physical exterior, but quality, like a thing breathed. Paris is propitious for this making of magic maps. While one thing that Vincent, the cornish gentleman, found out was that the hillside, across the river from the Tour St. Jacques to the top of the Rue du Cardinal Lemoine is still given over to witchcraft, a winding stream of passionate and infernal air, in and out of the old Latin Quarter. Also that, in Passy, there is a river-strip and a small low terrace (now in the hands of housebreakers), looking across to the river over green tree-tops where the tears cried in the Revolution are still audible. A blind rain among the almost visible gleam of ancient silks, the tapping of heels, the stir of powder, a terrace where the soul of elegance still breathes, and, like the heart beating, one hears the passionate continuity of french life.

In the Rue St. Dominique it is difficult to tell the living from the dead, and he could never be sure if he were not buying cherries off a talking ghost. The west wind sweeps them out like leaves, in handfuls, especially at dusk, when the Eiffel Tower is putting on its crown and the necklace which hangs to its feet; while the wind roars in the mouths of old courtyards, springs like a cat in and out of their corners, and with its broom sends out spinning leaves, torn papers, ghosts and the street-swarm, to scatter them on the starry, roaring space before the Invalides; where, looking down towards the river, you can see Imperial Paris with its crowns and tower. For Paris is a city divided—not like London, with all that she has of splendour and government, of learning or pleasure or art on one bank of its stream; and the other a place not one half of the city has ever set foot in, being given over to workmen at their meanest. But of Paris it can be said that the right bank of the Seine belongs to the world, and the left bank to France. This could have been said once, and is still partly true—but this story is not about a city, a few bars only out of the Song of Paris, and perhaps, of something more than Paris. So that for its introduction, a few notes on the present state of that capital will serve.

Two years after the War imagine Vincent at least half-healed, and as the years pass, see him half-established there, but going less and less often to his first love, the quarter of Montparnasse. He has struck roots here and there, in a small Passy flat and in several french homes, in a few cafés and restaurants and among certain groups, english and american. He would arrive now at any time or leave—for his small, ancient home and estate, which was in Cornwall, and of which he was a careful steward. Less consciously now and by habit he would leave England— for that exhilaration which is also rest, for that delight which is peace and Paris' loveliest secret. For, like many men of profound patriotism, he liked less and less the way England was going, what she was doing, and still less what was being done to her.

While this also was true and he knew it, that, since the War, he had never achieved full life again, not quite. He did his duty as a small country gentleman, kept up his classics, his science, his contemporary letters, his friends. Had neither—and he noticed the omission—either love-affairs or any work that implied creation. Not up to the limit of his powers. For he was a man to whom quiet power would have come in life, in his case perhaps in moderate public life, with a fair chance, too, of private and enduring passion. "They castrated me, after all," he used to tell himself. "I'm just wholly alive, but only just. I can't use all of myself. Like a man who plays clock-golf perfectly, but not on the links. There must be a million or so like me." Not quite forty, he had not given up the hope that the check was inside himself, that the minute barring of his energies and impulses would disappear of itself, if the right, exactly the right, stimulus came. Scrupulously honest, he was hard with himself: gave life every chance to have its way with him. And it seemed that life delicately evaded him. "It is like being thirsty, a thirst only one drink would satisfy, and I don't know its name. Still less if it'll ever be offered. Neither I nor anyone who is in the same boat." This is not a state which can be talked about, but Vincent was a much-liked man. A man, lacking at any time the power to seize life by the throat and strangle it into submission, he was one of those who work joyfully for whatever in their age is best. The stuff out of which the "perfect, gentle knight" was made; and at any time, in war or medicine, in government or agriculture, in works of organisation or mercy—a man who needed, for his full development, a law, a worship, if possible a congregation and a church. At best, a hero. These he was equally without, in the west of England from where he came by long descent, or in France. Or among his friends, who were all in the same state; who also, that being one of the reasons why they were his friends, knew it. The adventures of such men are important because, whether they are fatal or not, they are honourable adventures, and because they are significant of our time. For it seems that none of their traditional occupations are able to take them over and use them as they once did, neither religion nor politics nor any traditional occupation, no cause or leader or conception of human relations with the divine. However they survived as individual souls, the same minute sap-gland, in them just saved, seems to have dried up in the clan and the group—almost in the nation; and its loss has left the most vital of human affairs some-how inadequate. Insufficient to take a man by the shoulders and swing him off into full allegiance, able at once to take the rough with the smooth, to judge as well as to save; to pour a life into a chosen mould, and feel it in the end sufficient, a mirror for all that there is. What is wrong? Was it his own fault? It was too easy to say "yes" to that. While he knew that he was not without ambition, and that it has never been easier than it is today for a man to boil his own egg. And not only the worst men. There is still a modest place for the Vincents. Only Vincent who had never wanted more than a modest place, whose instinct was to give his life up to something greater than himself, found that he did not want *that* modest place…. He had a dream of himself as a little fish, standing on its tail and bowing to one of the present Great—say a newspaper lord—on an Albert Memorial throne and being asked why he did not do anything. His answer was like the Bible: "because no man has hired me." On which the man on the throne would begin to tell him all the things which a "straight, intelligent Englishman of goodwill" ought to be doing. He heard himself say, "I'd sooner be a dago-moron than serve you: but I'm a fish: that lets me out." And then he tried to run away on the point of his tail, until he noticed he had changed into the little Sea Maid who walked on knives. But that was for love's sake. For what love was he bearing a lifetime's loss of honourable employment? For a love which had left the earth? Gone off somewhere behind a space-time curtain into the inconceivable?

It was this that drew him and his friends to artists. They had something. Mysteriously, tiresomely, or noisily or crossly, or savagely or piteously, the arts went on, weathering the chill dark storm, blowing across the earth as if from outer space. Yes, art was still going on, most certainly in literature and particularly in Paris. The men and women who did it had something they held to and which held them. Theirs was essential health, and it was among their hangers-on, or— and here he smiled—among their admirers, that the death-rate was so high. But all men cannot be working artists, not in the strict sense. If the artists' secret was one form of a universal secret, there must be a re-statement of it, in terms equally life-giving, for his sort of man, for every sort of man. Nor was it, he suspected, quite enough even to meet the artists' full needs. For two things are needed today, an art in the terms of Dante or Æschylus, which is also first-class in terms of our age and of itself.

When he came to think of it, he did not know any writer or any painter whose work fulfilled such terms; but only for such would their art be enough. While they were all suffering from a singular new set of prohibitions: forbidden in the past to refer to the Deity as a wish-fulfilment, they now seemed unable to refer to It as anything else: unable to mention the lavatory, they forced the reader to spend more time there than he would in fact. While the bed, once tabu because too stimulating, now appeared discouragingly as a trap, baited with all the ills that flesh is heir to, source of disease and abortion; or, if not in the body, of the cruelest terrors of the mind. As for painting! Why was Titian able to paint a picture of Sacred and Profane Love, while, today, no one but a bad painter would try? Vincent noticed all this, noticed also that, traps or not, beds did not come into his life, who filled them with no more than his own lean body that he kept in scrupulous condition—for what?

Time after time, a moment would come and a desire—to fling himself out, abandon himself to the flashing hurry of contemporary affairs as they tore past him, a ravelled web of cross-colours, a stream whose rapids so many bodies he knew were shooting, their heads bobbing under and out, their hair splashed with spray. Or piled like mounting salmon before some obstacle. Which usually turned out not to be there. Or, more frequently, turned out not to be the barrier they thought, but something different, neither to be changed nor circumvented. Part of the structure of reality, in fact.

Still, he envied these swimmers, those delicate or vigorous, fastidious or powerful specialists in pleasure or dissipation, in the pursuit of power or wealth or notoriety, or of social or sexual success—rioting in their Paris-playground, incomparable *terrain* where, for once "work was play and play was life." But what play? And what life? He sneered, as near as ever he came to a sneer, at it and at his inability to yield to it. While the image of the Poor Fish pursued him and distressed him.

> *"Par délicatesse*
> *j'ai perdu ma vie."*

Here his humility protested. Who was he to compare himself with Rimbaud? If he had chosen to forget "the ardours of an incomparable adolescence," it was because he had preferred to go about his own mysterious and delectable business. Vincent's youth had passed on Vimy Ridge, in hospital, and on the Somme.

Meanwhile, there were the artists of contemporary Paris, and the modest collection, part prudent investment, he was making to set on the shelves and along the panels of a cornish manor-house. There an Atlantic sun and airs from half-way across a planet would look in on the café scenes, the abstract plates, plants, pots and musical instruments, the austere landscape, the magic horses of contemporary painting.

"I have brought back tangible treasure," he would console himself—"for the more I look at some of these, the more I like them. I have brought back, too, a piece of France." Noticing that whoever brings home french work does that; and finally, that what he had acquired owed as much to the spirit of the land as to any particular painter. Or, in another way, that in France, the most individual artists are more the transmitters of a supreme tradition than of themselves.

Matchless discipline! Was he dying slowly for want of the version of it proper to himself?

If he had been driven away from the famous crossroads where his life in Paris had begun, there was still a half-way house; still in the Latin Quarter, still itself, still brimming with young life; a place where there remained a taste of the old delights—the Café des Deux Magots on the Boulevard St. Germain. At the end of the still noble part of a noble street, on the edge of the space in his map coloured "witchcraft," it stands close to the river at its most adorable strip—the Quai Voltaire. He would sit there, with the pleasure at the back of his mind that comes from the right geographic situation, from being perfectly placed with regard to the whole environment. At any moment he could get up and go for an enchanting walk, with, a few yards off as he crossed his sorcerer's line, a hint of danger about it. A delicious sense of walking into the part of a town which was literally supernatural, charged with it, a charge put in during a part of the Middle Ages, too strong to wear off. Also that he, and a good proportion of its inhabitants, were in tacit agreement about it—and the less said the better. Meanwhile, one could always retreat, back to "the Maggots," as a swimmer out of the haunted caves of the ocean to the warm beaches of a pleasant shore.

It was there that he met his american girl.

She was the freest of free things—a young woman sent with her people's blessing and a sufficient allowance to stay in Europe as long as she liked. (He could never quite make out what her people were, her credentials were not those of some of the New Englanders he knew; but he judged the situation to be that.) Of course she was to return— to an address which geographically baffled him—filled with the last culture; her pretty gift for painting improved, with ravishing clothes and interesting friends. Something like that seemed to be the old people's kindly wish, not nervous about her—that, heaven bless it! not in their tradition—for she had friends who would keep an eye on her, and her own good sense would keep off undesirable foreigners. There would be plenty of the right american boys there, for sure.

This, at any rate, was Vincent's kindly translation. He saw her saffron scarf fluttering along the Boulevard one spring morning, heard her little heels tapping on the pavement and "registered"—the word had just come in—nothing but delight. She *was* enjoying herself, bless her! He saw her eating cream-topped ices and wave her spoon; and when some friends of his spoke to her, he spoke to them; and finally took her to a place where the ices were larger and better, and fed her several more. So they became friends.

After that he saw her every day, with that utter Paris-freedom which allows people to do exactly what they want to do. Not all people. In practise, the people who achieve it are the people who are "most right." Others, unless they are strong in character or long-practised in evil-doing, find that liberty a snare at least; at most, a terrible thing. These fall continually into traps they have set for themselves, create imaginary barriers and fall down before them, feel emptiness where others find open air, and conjure up demons to people it. She was not like that, he said, his lass with the delicate bones, her coaxing, slightly hoarse voice, her sharp young appetite for everything. Vincent immediately forgot to think of himself as a piece of middle-aged war breakage, and tore round with her all night and half the day.

If he had thought of himself as a little older or a little younger, it would have been better. Older, he would have assumed authority; younger, he would not have thought to let her be. As it was, he used often to withdraw himself respectfully, in a sort of homage to her youth. While all the time he noticed that he was asking himself questions about her. For one thing, he could not find out how much she really knew. Was she really so keen on everything, and so intelligently? Or was she—it was an uncomfortable suspicion—a kind of wonderfully trained automaton, for response to whatever was presented to her, but without criticism and without real choice? Without effective memory, and the working-over the creation it implies? *Was* it sheer youth, trying everything at once? (Or was it looking for and would it find something that was outside the range of his understanding at all?) Was she a puppet, who might even now be dancing to lures he had never heard? Or a bit of both? The last presented appalling difficulties. Suppose the part of her that was not an exquisite doll had no connection or the slightest real interest in what was important to Vincent, to Vincent's race, to high european life? Suppose she represented another, an in-the-bone-and-nerve raw thing, a tricky race-mixing? A wild animal with an instinct for adaptability, inquiringness and protective mimicry that masked—well, something that since the Stone Ages man has been muzzling, keeping on a lead, destroying, lest it should destroy him—even though it were one of his eyes, a part of his right hand? He could not place her in any of the Americans he knew something of, in New England or the South or the East or well-accounted for New York. While "from somewhere near Kansas City"—and where *is* Kansas City?—was the nearest he ever understood of her address.

These tiresome questions represent the further side of the moon of his love for her, the questions, as he afterwards remembered, he had put about her from the first; that had grown until they made shrill noises at him, in proportion to his love, the other, the visible side of the moon. Was she real, or was she not? For if she were real, his real, she was too good to be true. If the child were true, there was no imagining how far she would go nor the miracle it would be to have the care of her, "to watch, to encourage, to restrain, the royal young creature by his side." Was she infinitely sophisticated? Or nobly innocent? Or of such intelligence and native virtue that she *did* know, dealing with good and evil like a young warrior from heaven? Her "Come on, Vincent," "Look, Vincent"—her eyes, the curve of her parted lips—was their strength that of a spirit or a wild beast?

It was one of Vincent's simplicities that he did not see what value he might have had for her; or that, whatever she was, she was a young girl, and so, to some extent, what the man who took her in hand expected her to be. That what he had to do was to assert himself, muffle any protests with "that's what matters over here, sweetheart" and a kiss. He had not learned from life how much time and trouble kisses save, still less the romantic figure he might have seemed to her, had he been a little more explicit, had not assumed that she could place him as an english girl would have placed him; not realising that where the tradition is different, a common language may be a trap. In fact he made most of the mistakes we make in dealing with young America.

What happened, when it happened, happened quickly. The quickening appalled him, who forgot that however long it may take to prepare, a fall is a matter of seconds. Later he reminded himself, that if it had not happened, he would have given himself up to his love. Taken back with him to the West Country a strange woman; and that it was not without some mercy—even her mercy—that he had been prevented. That if he had seen an infernal curtain lifted, he had been left with a closer apprehension of the world. For a curtain was lifted for him, but not before the last minute of the last act. The rest of the story had been played on the stage of Paris, as if before one of those drop-scenes which came down close to the footlights, leaving the stage a strip, for the actors to enter in twos and threes and the chorus to dance across. A drop only lowered for scenes whose significance is momentary, while the full stage is being set behind.

They went about with artists as before, but Vincent's friends were usually English or some French; it was Cherry, the girl, who had discovered and furiously cultivated some of the Americans; who, so far as he could see, had taken over all that was left of Montparnasse. He found himself telling her: "Of course you have to make an art of your own now. Your great men of letters were so much pure Europe gone across the Atlantic. Now you've half a continent wanting to express itself, instead of just New England. Though how the place managed to breed Melville and Poe..." But these, as he expected, she had hardly read, while the others were no more than school-books to her. What excited her was a number of quite young men and women, whose master was James Joyce; and what *they* were about, he could never quite determine. Unless it was to turn themselves inside out. Very natural to youth, but he did not much like their interiors, not quite wholesomely raw they seemed, and furtive and afraid, wanting in candour and simplicity of perception, in faith and essential courage or the rudiments of fine taste. He even called them to himself a set of unprincipled little bastards, blackguards or milksops in the making. Which was not at all fair; but, in his heart, he was blaming them for having hurt his Paris, who of all their countrymen were least responsible; whom poverty kept reasonably sober, who were not to be blamed for not knowing what they really wanted, or for the growing-pains of a nation, or for homes where the wrong things were held in esteem. For in America it would seem that a cheap and strident idealism often takes the place of true discipline, the love of country or of mankind. All this he made himself allow for, reduced himself to wishing and wondering why, with all their chances, these boys made no effort to make over their lives with some sobriety, pray for peace and quiet and practise them. They spoke as though nothing had ever happened before they happened. What was worse, they wrote—some of them—as though man had never put pen to paper before. Incidentally he noticed that they were not without friends among certain young Frenchmen, busy on the same experiments. But, then, on this last point, the Frenchmen would not be able to judge.

Perhaps the abyss that Vincent saw opened, that for an instant he leaned over, gave him a glimpse of something final, as the colour of the infernal spectrum might be held, for a split second, in a drop of dew.

While if, at the same time, his glimpse was his salvation, the danger and the escape came together oddly mixed, treading on each other's heels. And it was with difficulty that his mind held, clearly and continuously, what he had seen. As he told it to himself and as I learned it from him, he called it "the translation of a translation of a translation."

"We're at least two languages out," he said. "But at least we both make the same thing of it."

What happened was this.

Between Montparnasse and the Boulevard St. Germain, the tide-line between the rest of the city and his magical strip, there lived an old woman of some consequence, in herself like a received and accepted and perfectly reputable witch. A local sorceress, and therefore, to some extent, international, long become part of the landscape—who *might* accept an invitation to a fashionable christening, but had never been known to resent it if she were not asked. Her spells were composed with the help of the english language used as if it had never been used before; and were not calculated to inspire fear. She had a house in impeccable taste. Her entertainments were formal and much sought after. But the people who were always to be found there were Cherry's young Americans. And their french friends. The art of the latter was based, partly on mystical reliance on the subconscious, partly on extreme Communist theory. In essence a belief in magic—"*Le Moi est le Verbe, et le Verbe c'est Dieu.*" In practise, a measured brutality, a logic of destruction, all somehow made elegant, flashed with "chic" by the qualities of the french mind, its instinct for proportion—even in the realm of chaos and old night. While for reasons Vincent could not make out, the French who knew everything and the Americans who knew nothing, met, at the house of the old woman in a kind of uneasy dance.

One day it was Cherry who insisted that he should visit her. He asked: "Why do you young things go there? Why do you want to go? You can't have much fun. Your best behaviour and no drinks. Yet I believe you spend half your time there, when you aren't with me. While what I'd like to know is—which is the agreeable change from which?"

She gave him a little smile with closed lips, what he thought of after as a far-too-wise smile.

"She's an old dame of course. I reckon she likes it that way."

"Why should a flipperty-gibbet like you mind what she likes?" The girl hadn't an answer—she evaded all such answers. Yet go she would, and now she would have him go with her; and amused Vincent by telling him how very carefully he must behave. Though he did not believe it was snobbery; always he had felt her to be far more interested in her boyfriends than in any of his celebrities. He did not know what to make of it. He flung it away from him, determined to make nothing of it at all.

From the beginning he had loved her. For the last few days he had fallen in love with her. No one knows what that is—only the infinite variations of what it looks like. But this one property it always has, that the beloved becomes harmonised in the lover's sight. As though seen in some magical glass, which mankind has always insisted, and probably rightly, that the image it gives is nearer to reality than any other. Closer for the instant, but liable to vanish, liable also to burden the original with its loveliness—(for it is rare, for women, at least, to wish to live up to the image the lover has seen). So Vincent saw Cherry now, marvellously the same, but now all true, all one. Girl of the Golden West, young maid "*prochaine Aphrodite*," ready for adventure, yet a wife in the making. He would take her back to the West Country for her journey's end—the end that is a beginning; incorporate her into the saga of England by way of the saga of his house. He had put it to her lightly, a few nights before, during a wild evening in Montmartre. She had danced away, said "no," implied "yes." It was the look in her darkening eyes he had not understood.

He was now asking her again:

"Cherry, my heart, will you make up your mind to it and marry me?" She became very serious:

"Sure, I ought to tell you. You come up to tea with me at Miss Van Norden's, and after that you'll know—I mean, I'll know—I mean—." So he had seen many small beasts pursued and casting around, but he was not thinking of things like that. He drew her hands to him and kissed her small brown wrist bones. For the last week a clean and quiet content had been entering his life, as a man sees—not the other side of a wood, but a path that will lead him there; and already, ahead, a thinning of dark branches, a promise of open country not too far off, at last. As, with a turn of passion, he drew her to him, she did not draw her wrists away; it felt almost as though she were pressing them against his mouth. He expected her to dance off, but instead he saw her, now standing upright, straight before him, a young gold tree between him and the Paris-winter fire. A moment later, she was fallen between his knees and her shell-curled head was burrowing blind towards him. She was saying: "You're strange too. It's another kind of strange, but I tell myself it's the kind of sort that's quiet because it's strong, and so strong it can afford to be kind. Like one kind of strength, whatever people say. Sort of thing I thought I wanted—till I found something else. Or what I'm like myself. I thought *that'd* cure me of being afraid, but maybe it hasn't. I'm not sure I'm not afraid still of what they call life—." He supposed that she meant that life hadn't turned out what she had expected, not like *him*. That she expected him to give her courage again; and he was filled with the infinite—there is no other word—delight of the lover on whom the beloved calls for help.

"Life," he said, cheerfully, "it's our friend from now on." He gathered her up. It was all right. The beginning of the way: first with this precious thing—

"I didn't know that you'd found life too much already."

"Like hell I have!" She answered harshly, with a wriggle out of his arms, where for a minute or more she had lain exquisitely, and a spring onto the arm of his chair. He saw her face in the mirror. It had not the Artemis-look of the girl he had met a year ago—but the look of another hunter, who had become the hunted. A song tolled in his head:—

> *Thy lovers were all untrue,*
> *Thy chase had a beat in view,*
> *Thy lovers were all untrue.*

Then:

> *Time the old year was out—*

What sort of passing-bell was it? A rare accompaniment for a man about to take his young love out to tea.

They left his warm flat and went down the wide, shallow french stairs, side by side. In the grey street he thought that the small gilt curls growing under her scarlet hat were like some delicious fruit, gilding winter with promise; and that her face and her slight body and flying legs made her like a boy-angel. He strode beside her, tall with pride and possession, and approval that she should choose to walk, like a country girl and not like a town miss; and that her walk was fit for the wild land, hills and dark valleys and hollows and sea-terraces, where her home would be.

They reached the house of the old woman, across a courtyard in which there were true city trees, whose branches stirred in the small bleak wind as though they wept. The long room was full, and he, except his hostess, the oldest person there. Why was it full of young men? Why should they go there? Cherry seemed to know them all. English or French. While it had about it the indefinable air of a group, meeting in a familiar place. But what a place to choose, an entertainment as conventional, indeed it reminded him of it, as the hospitality of a cathedral close. If indeed the Frenchmen found the formality agreeable, would the american boys, come to Europe, as he knew, to throw off all restraint?

There was tea on an ancient table, before a magnificent fire. Their hostess sat and spoke to them, one by one; giving the newcomer a little more of her attention. Then he noticed that, after a time, people found themselves in circulation. One after another, in twos and threes, and one or two accompanied by her, they would make the circle of the long room, down whose centre ran more heavy tables. Exceedingly slowly they went, a flowing stream, turning their heads up from left to right to look up at the celebrated collection of pictures, or down onto the tables, at books and manuscripts and *objets d'art*. With pauses and repetitions, jerks and restarts, but always round and round the same way, counter-clockwise; so that, unless you caught someone up—and that you somehow felt was a thing you should not do—you hardly met anyone who was there.

The first time round, the old woman herself had taken him. He saw Cherry with a pale Frenchman, what he thought of as five bars ahead. The pictures were superb and he enjoyed them. But when he spoke to her across the tables, he felt that he had not been discreet. Much later, when he had been round again, once with a stranger, once by himself, he anchored himself with a bun and more tea in a dim corner, and it came to him how strange it was; and that this was a place where this party was going on all the time, a ritual of some particular significance, a kind of enchantment. (In situation the house was off his magic map, too far west, between Raspail and the Boul' Miche. He remembered this almost with relief.)

It grew dark. Candles, many of them and nothing else, were lit. He still sat in his corner, his teacup balanced on his knee, opposite a famous picture which was his excuse.

For many years after that winter evening's entertainment, he ground and burrowed into his memory to recover how Cherry had appeared. They had hardly spoken to one another, he purposely insisting on nothing, believing that she was trying to see what he looked like among her friends. All that he could, with infinite effort, recall, was that she had been very quiet, possibly uneasy, respectful even to the old woman, who, and he disliked her for it, patronised the girl as though she had been some little silky dog. Again, that on their round-the-table dance, she had been partnered by a pale young Frenchman, in a light suit. The dying light had shown up his bright hair, the dull white skin of his nose and forehead. This was the sharpest image Vincent's memory threw upon the screen; and that he had called the Frenchman's hair "green-gold" and smiled at it and had not liked him. His eyes were probably grey to match, and Vincent's mind insisted that they were red-flecked on the whites and red-rimmed. He had seen that, inside his slack clothes, his body was slack and would be slacker. Cherry and he had talked, when they had spoken at all, without looking at one another. Her French had remarkably improved, low and vibrating. That was all. All. All. All. Night-out, day-in, he could recall no more. The talk of the room—in rapid French or most pronounced American, ran past him. All gossip or the latest experiments in the Arts. That was the old woman's *forte*, as all Paris knew. The stratum of public-school boy which underlay so many of Vincent's judgments, kept insisting that if they were really doing so much to the Arts, they would talk about it less: until his sense of justice corrected him, reminding him that they were in France, where it is not incorrect to speak of the things of the mind.

Yet everything in the room that had to do with the Arts was ancient, and the picture that had anchored him, a Fragonard. While, among so much lively and controversial youth, the decorum was peculiar. There was animation, no doubt, but spiritually, if not actually, in whispers. His own lass had appeared actually prim. It had been, too, something more than repression; there was something automatic about it, as of a coterie, a set, repeating what they had often done before; and, behind the hypnotic winding round and round the room, as though there was something known—to everyone in the room but him; something— these were the words that rose—large and raw, yet exceedingly subjective; a common knowledge, a secret, even a mysticism, funny, beastly, witty, mad, untrue—but neither mad enough nor false enough to be inoperative and inactive. Yes, there was a secret in that room. He had quickly become aware of it, but not at the time with any reference to Cherry; Cherry who was walking in his mind in a cup of wind and a lance of sunlight off the Atlantic, where England begins to thrust its bones up out of the sea.

Nor did he wonder, at the time, why she had so completely deserted him, his sensibility suggesting to him that girls at such moments are apt to hide. Nor did he give a thought to the young Frenchman, except to wonder if he had seen him, as he had certainly seen some of the american boys, enjoying themselves in a very different manner elsewhere. Certain of them, highly intoxicated: up to larks, in fact.

It was time to go. He looked round the room at the figures passing. The girl did not look up at him, he had to fetch her. They went out together silent; and when they got into the taxi they were silent. They parted to change and he took her out to dinner; and after dinner she told him that she would not marry him. As she said it, he knew she would not: he would never take her home to the West, nor would they, two lovers, play hide-and-seek there, in and out the curtains of the wind. A sea-noise rose in his head.

"You made up your mind then this afternoon, my dear?"

"Yes, I suppose so. I told you I'd tell you."

"But you haven't told me enough: I mean what it would be fair for me to know. What was it that decided you?" (It means so much to know that: then you know who your enemy is, and believe, at the instant, that you have only to know who he is to destroy him.) Cherry was looking at him wretchedly.

"I'm not going to explain. I know all right. You take it from me— you'll be glad enough."

"You mean, don't you, that I shall find something out? I don't care if I do. You mean that you've been having an affair with someone else, and perhaps can't make up your mind? I'd understand that. While you're only a child, and I can be of use to you." She began to laugh, a miserable laugh, but with a note in it that made him recoil—a movement in the mind which often alters, and for good, the previous angle of vision. It was bad, that laugh, a note in it at once curt and unpleasant, as though there was a dirty impulse behind it. Not the laughter of a slip of the moon. She was saying:

"Had an affair! Can't make up my mind! Be of use to me! Who in hell cares for you and your uses? Child am I! Bet your grandmother— Who cares about being fair to you, you poor fish?"

"I for one," said Vincent, a touch of anger helping him. (All the time she was on the edge of crying, which made her actual words less significant.) He went on: "You had not made up your mind until this afternoon. I think you had better tell me, for, one way or another, I mean to find out." It hurt him to see her slightness, trying to bury itself in the folds and the fur of her clock.

"Go on and find out then."

"So I shall. As a matter of fact, you're going to tell me now."

"Why in hell should I?"

"Because I'm going to leave you with the memory that you'd that much courage." She said hurriedly in a low voice:

"It sounds somehow different in English, but you can take it I was in with that set before ever I knew you: belonged there: wouldn't leave them if I could. You were Blaise's joke. That's why I told you you'd be glad to be out of it."

"In with what bunch?"

"The lot there—there this afternoon. You can make what you like of it." Then he remembered the young Frenchman. She sprang up. He saw her out of the restaurant, into a taxi; and came back to his table, the room swimming across his eyes.

. . . . . .

Several days passed before he pulled himself together enough to do a little serious thinking. *What* was behind it all? He was not so stupid as not to know once he came to think of it that he had a great deal to offer the girl. Why had he been only a joke? Had he been *only* a joke? He asked himself the rejected lover's questions: "Where did I go wrong? Who did she prefer to me? What should I have done '*to lure this tassel-gentle to my wrist*'?" That she had perched there an instant, several instants, he knew. What had scared her off? He suffered, not, as he knew after a short time, so much for her, as for what she had meant to him. By means of her he had sensed a way by which his full life would have been restored to him. She was not that life, or only a part of it, but married to her, he would have been able, at last, to use all of himself. Nor had his love been selfish, he would have done his best to insure the same fullness, of thought and experience, for her also.

How had they missed it? What was the meaning of that laugh? He remembered her warm confidence at first, in the summer and in the spring. That had not been *all* acting. In the early autumn he had lost sight of her, but not for long. What had happened during that time? And, above all, what part had the shadowy room in the house whose doors gave on to the courtyard full of weeping trees—what part had it played, and its mistress? Conscious inquiry came hardly to him, outside his code and training, near spying; until he remembered a Frenchwoman of distinction who knew everything that happened in Paris, and went to call on her.

Alone, in her salon, she spoke very readily indeed. As a matter of fact, his simplicity took her in, and she imagined nothing personal in his curiosity; while it amused her to display the strangenesses of her city to a well-bred man from another land.

From her he learned what he instantly felt that he had known all the time—that the young Frenchmen—she could not answer for *ces Américains*—who went to the old woman's house were a very bad lot indeed. Of course their idea, as they explained it to the Paris public, was to make as close a copy as they could of the principles and practises of Revolutionary Russia. "*Ces sales Bolsheviks*" were their masters, which meant in practise chiefly in their sexual conduct. It was the same in their art; but there, as many of them had talent, the results were sometimes stimulating, exciting, and anyhow very much *à la mode*. But in themselves they were horrible young people. They played obscene practical jokes; they had a cult of cruelty—psychological cruelty; and those whose nerves would stand it made a study and a practise of physical torture. They stole things, very cleverly too, for an excellent joke and a high feather in their caps; there were people in prison on their account. They had a system of blackmail which helped them to live—they were quite open about it—called it a protest against bourgeois morality. But what made it quite intolerable, what, as Vincent agreed, implied a particularly nasty mixture of ignorance and hypocrisy, was their spirit of which they boasted of cold scientific inquiry. Dragging science into that *galère*. Of course, she added—she was a really intelligent woman—Russia was just an excuse, or possibly, and in parts, a useful model. It had happened before, was happening perhaps in a lesser degree everywhere, the cult of *le Moi* in excelsis, and of the private dream. In Art, a cult of the arbitrary use of words to express the private dream. Of course, if your dreamer were a Rimbaud or a Mallarmé, you got an art to match. "Art," said Vincent, "is not life. At least…" "*Exactement*," said the Frenchwoman, and that whatever the art of the private dream might be, the life of it was another thing: usually a much nastier thing. "Subjectively run mad," said Vincent, "but it would all depend upon the dream." "And what sort of stuff are the run of our dreams made of?" said the Frenchwoman. "Who out of a million has an inspired dream? While for the rest…" "Where will it take them?" said Vincent. "To suicide, often," was the answer, "or back into the Church." She then asked if we had such phenomena in England. He considered. He supposed that we had, though he had never met it; that it must happen, but less publicly, less in groups, perhaps less staged. Tentatively, that would do. "I believe," he said, "that we're a less intelligent, certainly about aesthetics, but a more sensible, people. We do not laugh at life or at each other so brilliantly as you do, but we do laugh at ourselves. I can't see one of us setting out to be a conscientious blackmailer or a thief on principle. Though I've known seduction carried out that way. An english boy of gifts, however bad his character, would find it too much to believe that there was nothing in the Universe except what he and a few of his friends felt. Even if he knew the arguments. For there is a logic of it.

"But tell me some more about it. Have they any women among them?"

"What young men will always have. A number of young women who like them, and so pretend to understand and adore what they are about. It would be the kind of young woman," she added, "who likes to be hurt."

"Do they?" said Vincent, simply.

"Of course. I have remarked it too among american girls, even—I suppose by reaction—those who have been spoilt by their men into petty tyrants. If they do, they will get what they want: they will be horribly treated there. The stories that one hears! Last year it was the great joke to make the tour of all the houses of their families' friends—good people, you know, of the higher bourgeoisie. Then, when they had established themselves, to see how many of the young daughters of the house they could seduce; the one who had accomplished the most being elected a kind of Commissar of the Alcove. But seduction was not considered enough: the girl must become *enceinte*, and then there must be an abortion—and—if possible, her suicide or death. Oh, there was more than one, I assure you; and a charming child I knew is in a madhouse, and another is a cripple for life. Another—again I knew her slightly—was like one hypnotized. She ran away with him, with one of the worst of them, I mean, Blaise Boissevain. He's the cleverest, too. It is said that he sent her out onto the streets to solicit for him. She went, and afterwards killed herself, but very carefully, so as not to compromise him. She left a letter, too, in which she called him the Liberator, and said they were all pioneers of a new civilisation. They all, and he especially, have some power over women's minds. They are virile, too, you know. It is not a question of that '*Apostolat pédérastique*' so fashionable a few seasons ago. They leave that to the older men, whom they persecute in a quite particularly detestable way. You know how Frenchmen adore their mothers…" But Vincent was not at the moment interested in the sufferings of homosexual Frenchmen of his own age. "Blaise" was the sound in his head. "Blaise. Blaise." That whisper of a name had passed Cherry's lips. "*You were Blaise's joke.*" That pale slug of a lad had been with her at Miss Van Norden's tea-party, turning, turning round the tables.

"Blaise, Blaise Boissevain. I think I've heard the name. Did you say he was the worst?" "I think so," she answered cheerfully. "His young women usually die one way or another. And, as happens, his gifts are remarkable. He quite openly practises spells, some based on a desecration of the Host. And they work. But I have horrified you, Mr. Penrose. You know Paris too well to think that one set of corrupt children can affect, let alone typify our civilisation. Only, as you say, wickedness is staged here. It is perhaps safer so." His answer made her, for the first time, glance at him sharply:

"A girl would stand no chance with them whatever?"

"I'm afraid not. Not if she ever got among them at all. You see, if she did, she would not stay unless she liked that sort of thing; unless it corresponded with some hidden need in her or some taste. You see, they are not particularly attractive physically or well-off. And, *mon Dieu!* they are not kind."

"Tell me one more thing," he said slowly. "Why do they meet at the house of that old Miss Van Norden? I went there and I could not make it out at all." All the contempt which it is possible for woman to feel for woman was in her answer. She raised her silver shingled head, twisted her pearls, flung out one full, still lovely arm, its nacre skin shining under black lace. He thought of old Miss Van Norden's boots, square like a footballer's, her lank, cropped, iron hair, her shriveled body in an overall tied round the middle with a twist of cord, her nutmeg-engraved skin.

"The poor old creature! But is not France large enough for all? It is the hunger they have for it, the Americans. She knows nothing of her circle, nothing. She sees herself—into whose eyes no man has ever looked—as the *salonnière*—her house full of young men of genius. And how it amuses them! To be so decorous: to mingle there, as happens, with the innocent, the respectable, the lovers of ancient painting, the eccentric-art snobs! To go there before some secret party, some dreadful escapade. To leave it—to vanish on strange errands into those ancient palpitating dark streets. They are connoisseurs in their way: to them a bad nut is *délicieux à croquer*. If she knew! But she knows nothing. But if I know anything of them, they are preparing for her a charming entertainment. She is a woman of letters, she takes herself seriously. One day she will find herself embroiled in one of their scandals…." Vincent gathered that, when that happened, at least one woman of Paris would laugh. Soon after, he took his leave, with the sincerest thanks, and went for a long walk.

So that was where the girl had been, secretly, all the time. There had been the centre of her life and he had thought her without one; would have given her one. In such a set as that she had found her feet, his young Artemis. There had been her hunting-ground, with such huntsmen—and such a prey. *"Thy chase had a beast in view."* For an instant he saw himself, as a quarry that had been spared. The thought humiliated, but why had it happened? Some wisp of compassion—of love? Or had Blaise got bored and early called it off? He was not yet in his sense about Cherry, but a reserve of clarity in his nature told him that he would be. Again, he had not wanted a captive, but she a master. And had found it in Blaise. He imagined her intonations when she said "Blaise." Imagined other things. It hurt.

A moment later he reproached himself, thinking: "I did not love her enough, or I would have saved her. I would have found a way." Until he could not help hearing the angel of his *clarté* saying: "You are old enough to know that you cannot: that it is impossible. She cannot now eat natural food. She never relished it: she is feeding now on what she likes. No, she was not wholly an evil child, or she would not have spared you at all; would have married you to make sport for Blaise and his crew." He had the dislike of his kind for the abnormal, though he criticised his distaste, and began to realise again how she had been carried into a world where he could never penetrate. Only the utmost height of passion would have given him the power and the insight, and that he had not felt. "Love one of your own kind," was the answer of his angel, "if ever this comes your way again." He walked fast, striding over a delicate Paris bridge into the darkening afternoon, into the tall shadows of the Left Bank.

Then his mood changed for a moment into a great pity. Pity for the girl, pity also for the boys, caught with their victims in the traps they had set, whose artificial hell was only too likely to turn into a real one. Passionately he wished, as he had often wished, that his own wounds had won a better world for them, a world wherein they would not have found it possible to invent the form of life they had. Then cursed himself for a sentimentalist. Part of this Actæon they had spared would have liked to turn their own dogs on them. Then thought that France might have done better by her most brilliant children. Then that their sickness was part of the world's sickness.

He was not unhappy now, walking in the understanding of the meaning of events, which of all experiences puts suffering and disappointment most in their right places; conquers them, if it can keep them there. "Rapture of the intellect at the approach of the fact" this state was called once; and he went on moving in it, until the beginning of fatigue from city-pavement walking pulled him up.

He found that he was not far off from the old woman's house, and an impulse seized him to return there. Cherry might be inside. The thought of a sight of her was still exquisite pain. He would take one last look at her with the knowledge he had gained: one more look at that infernal dance, going on, counter-clockwise round the tables. A first real look and a last, at the people who had taken Cherry away— (was it possible that it might not be the last, that he still had something for Cherry? Could do something for Cherry? Would find a way to take her from Blaise and what Blaise meant?). One more look at the Fragonard, laughing on the wall, work of a saner age. One more look at old Miss Van Norden, who did not know what happened in her house.

He went into the courtyard. The trees were still crying in low voices. He rang the bell. She was at home. Cherry was not there. But it was all going on as it had gone on before, a replica of that day he had brought the girl and of all other days. "Weave, weave your infernal dance," his mind murmured. But today they did not seem to be, any of them, the same people; nor could he hear any French spoken, only American. "They" were not there. Anyhow, it mattered nothing, since Cherry and Blaise were not there.

As before, the room was not lit until it was almost too dark to see; and for some time the noble fire burned by itself, like a giant rose. He had finished his second cup of tea, sitting where he had sat before, with the Fragonard for company. The ancient furniture gleamed, the huge cabinets along the wall repeating the fire in their panels. An ancient servant came in and put a taper to the candles, and the whole room was picked out with gleam and reflection, the repetition of their pointed flames.

As it had been before. One part of his brain had observed for the first time a particular series of brightnesses, which in daylight had been invisible, as if candle, not daylight, was needed to pick them out. Again they sprang into being, all round the room, on top or along the higher shelves of the wall-furniture; something in metal, a series, a sequence. He could not determine what they were. His hostess, who had been circling with her guests, came and sat beside him. She poked forward her cropped stringy head at him: "Seen everything you want to, Mr...?" She spoke shortly. She would not, he saw, welcome stray Englishmen of no particular "chic," who might be using her house as hunting-ground for a pretty girl. He remembered what the French-woman had said, shared her opinion of the woman. He gave a conventional answer, while she must have seen his eyes straying along the high shelves and the cabinet tops.

"Have you seen those?" she asked. He rose with her and they crossed the room to one of the shining objects, now level with his head. On the next cabinet stood another: and another. They were all the same. About a foot high, of some common metal, gilt, rough, traditional. But the design was pure, the whole representing a flame or a star on fire, inset with a circular disk, rubbed silver-bright and painted on it in blue, the letter Chi. It was clear now what they were: they were frames, supports, stands for the ciborium, the box—in this case a round of hollow glass, fixed onto the disk—to hold the wafers of the Host. The box taken away, they now made delightful chimney piece ornaments. He saw it for himself and Miss Van Norden explained, and told how they had been sent to her from Spain, and had once been part of the traditional altar-furniture in country churches.

"Those Greek letters are the only relic of piety about them," she added, "and cleaning will soon wear them off. Interesting parochial baroque—and from the country of its origin too. For they are not old." She picked up one and began to rub it on a filthy handkerchief of khaki cotton, on which she spat. The old paint was dry and cracked and the signature of Christ rubbed off at a touch.

"I must be going," he said. "I only wanted to thank you for showing me your collection. It is superb. I shall never forget it."

She was looking hard at him. Her head was like one of those carved out of a dark nut. She grinned. In matter of practise it was not the face of one who does not know what is happening in her house. Her contempt for her body, but not for her surroundings, and for all that otherwise makes life worth living, had something enormous about it, as if a rock could fling its shadow evenly around itself in an ever-widening circle. They were standing near the fire. He looked down the whole length of the room. Point after point, the empty flames burned up the boxes which had held the bread of life broken off them. He looked at her again. The old eyes twinkled up at him:

"Two of my little friends, Cherry and her Blaise, aren't here today. They've gone off somewhere. No hope, I fear, of wedding bells. I'm afraid that some of my countrywomen have less morals than your english girls. While Blaise's affairs never last long. Just the conventional change of sweethearts, with a new excuse. It's only his endings that can be called original…"

She had hardly done speaking when his courtesies followed. Walking slowly down the room, touching with his left shoulder or his right the dancers as he passed, his eyes stayed fixed on the stripped stars of the Host. The Frenchwoman had been wrong, but now he understood.

With and Without Buttons

I T IS NOT ONLY TRUE, it is comforting, to say that incredulity is often no more than superstition turned inside out. But there can be a faith of disbelief as inaccurate as its excess, and in some ways more trying, for the right answers to it have not yet been thought up. It was only because Trenchard said at lunch that the mass was a dramatised wish-fulfillment that what came after ever happened. At least I wish we did not think so. It was trying to get out anyhow, but if he had not irritated us and made us want to show off, we would not have made ourselves serviceable to it. And it was we who came off lightly. To him it has been something that he has not been able to shake off. When it happened he behaved so well about it, but that didn't save him. Now he cannot think what he used to think, and he does not know what else there is that he might think.

I am seeing him now, more vividly than I like. He was our next-door neighbour in a remote village in Kent. A nest of wasps had divided their attention between us, and we had met after sunset to return their calls with cyanide and squibs.

He was a sanguine man, positive, hearty, actually emotional. He had known and done a great many things, but when he came to give his account of them, all he had to say was a set of pseudo-rationalisations, calling the bluff, in inaccurate language, of God, the arts, the imagination, the emotions. That is not even chic science for laymen today. He might have thought that way as much as he liked, but there was no reason, we said, to try and prove it to us all one hot, sweet, blue-drawn summer, in a Kentish orchard; to sweat for our conversion; to shame us into agreement. Until the evening I told him to stop boring us with his wish-fulfillments, for they weren't ours, and saw his healthy skin start to sweat and a stare come into his eyes. That ought to have warned me, as it did my sister, of whom I am sometimes afraid. It did warn us, but it wound us up also. We went home through the orchard in the starlight and sat downstairs in the midsummer night between lit candles, inviting in all that composed it, night hunting cries and scents of things that grow and ripen, cooled in the star-flow. A world visible, but not in terms of colour. With every door and every window open, the old house was no more than a frame, a set of screens to display night, midsummer, perfume, the threaded stillness, the stars strung together, their spears glancing, penetrating an earth breathing silently, a female power asleep.

"All he hears is nature snoring," said my sister. "Let's give him a nightmare." It was a good idea.

"How?" I said.

"We'll find out tomorrow. I can feel one about." I got up to close the doors before we mounted with our candles. Through walls and glass, through open doors or shut, a tide poured in, not of air or any light or dark or scent or sound or heat or coolness. Tide. Without distinction from north or south or without or within; without flow or ebb, a Becoming; without stir or departure or stay: without radiance or pace. Star-tide. Has not Science had wind of rays poured in from interstellar space?

There is no kind of ill-doing more fascinating than one which has a moral object, a result in view which will justify the means without taking the fun out of them. All that is implied when one says that one will give someone something to cry about. It was that line which we took at breakfast.

"We'll try his simple faith," we said. "We'll scare him stiff and see how he stands the strain. We'll haunt him." And asked each other if either of us knew of a practising vampire in the neighbourhood or a were-cow.

It was several days before we hit on a suitable technique, examining and rejecting every known variety of apparition, realising that apparatus must be reduced to a minimum, and that when nothing will bear scrutiny, there must be very little given to scrutinise. In fact, what we meant to do was to suggest him into an experience—the worse the better—wholly incompatible with the incredulities of his faith. That it would be easy to do, we guessed; that it would be dangerous to him—that appeared at the moment as part of the fun. Not because we did not like him, but because we wanted to have power over him, the power women sometimes want to have over men, the pure, not erotic power, whose point is that it shall have nothing to do with sex. We could have made him make love, to either or to both of us, any day of the week.

This is what we planned, understanding that, like a work of art, once it had started, its development could be left to look after itself.

"Suppose," said my sister, "that we have heard a ridiculous superstition in the village that there is Something Wrong with the house. We will tell him that, and when he has gone through his reaction exercises—it may take a day or so and will depend on our hints, and if we make the right ones, the battle's won—he will ask us what the story is."

"What is it to be?" I said, who can rarely attain to my sister's breadth of mind.

"That does not matter. Because before we begin we'll *do* something. Anything. A last year's leaf for a start, so long as it can go into a series—on his blotter or his pillow. We're always in and out. We'll put them there and get asked round for the evening and start when we see one, and that's where our village story begins. All that he has to get out of us is that there *is* a story, and that wet leaves or whatever it is we choose are found about. Signatures, you know. If he doesn't rise the first night, he'll find that leaf when he goes to bed. It depends on how well we do it—"

I recognised a master's direction, but it all seemed to depend on our choice of stimulants. Last year's leaves, delicate damp articulations; coloured pebbles, dead flies, scraps of torn paper with half a word decipherable.... A mixture of these or a selection?

"Keep it tangible," my sister said—"that's the way. Our only difficulty is the planting of them."

"Which," I asked, "are suitable to what?" It seemed to be necessary in laying our train to determine the kind of unpleasantness for which they were ominous. But I could not get my sister to attend.

"It's not that way round," she said at length—"dead bees, feathers, drops of candle-grease? Old kid gloves? With and Without Buttons. That will do."

I felt a trifle queer. "Well," I said, "they're the sort of things a man never has in his house, so that's sound so far. But women do. Not the sort of things we wear, but he'd not know that. And how do we get hold of them?"

"There's a shoe box in the loft full of them, by the door into his place when these houses were one." (Our cottages were very old, side by side, with a common wall, our orchards divided by a hedge. We had rented ours from a friend who had recently bought it as it stood from a local family which had died out, and of which very little seemed known.) My sister said:

"Shiny black kid and brown, with little white glass buttons and cross stitching and braid. All one size, and I suppose for one pair of hands. Some have all the buttons and some have none and some have some—" I listened to this rune until I was not sure how many times my sister had said it.

"With and without buttons," I repeated, and could not remember how often I had said that.

After that we said nothing more about it, and it was three days later that he asked us to supper, and we walked round through the gap in the hedge in the pure daylight, and sat in his little verandah, whose wooden pillars spread as they met the roof in fans of plaited green laths. Prim fantasy, with its french windows behind it, knocked out of walls of flint rubble three feet thick. Roses trailed up it. A tidy little home, with something behind it of monstrous old age one did as well to forget.

"By the way," he said. (As I have said before, his name was Trenchard, and he had come back to his own part of England to rest, after a long time spent in looking after something in East Africa.) "By the way, have either of you two lost a glove?"

'So she's got busy already and didn't tell me, the spoil sport,' I thought.

"No," we said, "but one always does. What sort of a glove?"

"A funny little thing of brown kid with no buttons. I didn't think it could be yours. I found it on the top of the loft stairs. Outside the door. Here it is." He went inside and came out onto the verandah where we were having supper, a moment later, puzzled.

"Here it is," he said. "I put it in the bureau, and the odd thing is that when I went to look for it I found another. Not its pair either. This one's black."

Two little ladylike shiny kid gloves, the kind worn by one's aunts when one was a child. I had not yet seen our collection. The black had three of its buttons missing. We told him that they were not the kind that women wore now.

"My landlady bought the place furnished," he said. "Must have come out of the things the old owners left behind when they died." My sister gave a slight start, a slight frown and bit her lip. I shook my head at her.

"What's up?" he asked, simply.

"Nothing," we said.

"I'm not going to be laughed at by you," said my sister.

"I'm not laughing," he said, his goodwill beaming at us, prepared even to be tolerant.

"Oh, but you'd have the right to—"

After that, he wanted to know at once.

"It's playing into your hands," she said, "but don't you know that your half of the house is the Village Haunt? And that it's all about gloves? With and without buttons?"

It was ridiculously easy. He was amiable rather than irritated at her story, while I was still hurt that she had not first rehearsed it with me. She began to tell him a story about old Miss Blacken, who had lived here with her brother, a musty old maid in horrible clothes, but nice about her hands; and how there was something—no, not a ghost— but something which happened that was always preceded by gloves be- ing found about. This we told him and he behaved very prettily about it, sparing us a lecture.

"But it's not quite fair," he said. "I mustn't be selfish. She must leave some at your place. Remember, in her day, it was all one house."

Then we talked about other things, but when we had gone home I found my sister a little pensive. I began on my grievance.

"Why didn't you tell me you had begun? Why didn't you coach me?" Then she said:

"To tell you the truth, I hadn't meant to begin. What I said I made up on the spot. All I'd done was that just before we left I ran up to the loft and snatched a glove from the box and left it on his bureau. That's the second one he found."

"Then what about the one he found outside the loft door?"

"It's that that's odd. That's why he never thought it was us. I haven't had a chance to get to that part of his house. I didn't put it there."

.   .   .   .   .

Well, now that the affair was launched, we felt it had better go on. Though I am not sure if we were quite so keen about it. It was as though—and we had known this to be possible before—it had already started itself. One sometimes feels this has happened. Anyhow, it was two days later before I thought it was my turn to lay a glove on his premises, and went up to our loft and took one out of the box. There was nothing in it but gloves. I took a white one, a little cracked, with only two buttons, and having made sure he was out, slipped through the hedge and dropped it at the foot of the stair. He startled me considerably by returning that instant. I said I had come for a book. He saw the thing.

"Hullo," he said, "there's another. It's beginning. That makes four."

"Four?" I said. "There were only two the other night."

"I found one in my bedroom. A grey. Are we never going to get a pair?"

Then it occurred to me that he'd seen through us all along, and was getting in ahead with gloves. I took my book and returned to my sister.

"That won't do," she said, "he's sharp, but we didn't begin it. He found his first."

I said: "I'm beginning to wonder if it mightn't be a good thing to find out in the village if anything is known about Miss Blacken and her brother."

"You go," said my sister, still pensive.

I went to the pub when it opened and drew blank. I heard about diseases of bees and chickens and the neighbours. The Post Office was no good. I was returning by a detour, along a remote lane, when a voice said:

"You *were* asking about Miss Blacken along at Stone Cottages?"

It was only a keeper who had been in the pub, come up suddenly through a gate, out of a dark fir planting. "—Seeing as you have the uses of her furniture," said he. We passed into step. I learned that after fifty years' odd residence in the place there was nothing that you might have to tell about her and waited.

"—Now her brother, he was not what you might call ordinary." Again that stopped at that.

"—Regular old maid she was. If maid she'd ever been. Not that you could be saying regular old man for him, he wasn't either, if you take my meaning, Miss."

I did. Finally I learned—and I am not quite sure how I learned—it was certainly not all by direct statement—that Miss Blacken had been a little grey creature, who had never seemed naturally to be living or dying; whose clothes were little bits and pieces, as you might say.

Anyhow, she'd dropped something—an excuse me, Miss, petticoat, his wife had said—on the green, and run away without stopping to pick it up, opening and shutting her mouth. It was then it had begun. If you could call *that* beginning. I was asking to know what that was? In a manner of speaking he couldn't rightly say. It was the women took it to heart. What became of the petticoat? That was the meaning of it. 'Twasn't rightly speaking a petticoat at all. There weren't no wind, and when they came to pick it up, it upped and sailed as if there were a gale of wind behind it, right out of sight along the sky. And one day it had come back; hung down from the top of an elm and waved at them, and the women had it there were holes in it, like a face. And no wonder, seeing it had passed half a winter blowing about in the tops of trees. Did it never come down to earth? Not it they said. Nor old Miss Blacken start to look for it, except that it was then that people remembered her about at nights.

A little pensive now myself, I asked about gloves and was told and no more than that "they say that she's left her gloves about."

I returned to my sister and we spent the evening doing a reconstruction of Miss Blacken out of victorian oddments. It was most amusing and not in the least convincing.

"Tomorrow, shall we feed him a glove?" I said. It was then that it came across our minds, like a full statement to that effect, that it was no longer necessary. The gloves would feed themselves.

"I know what it is we've done," said my sister, "we've wound it up."

"Wound up what?" I answered. "Ghost of a village eccentric, who was careful about her hands?"

"Oh no," said my sister. "I don't know. Oh no."

.   .   .   .   .

After another three days, I said:

"Nothing more has happened over there. I mean he's found no more gloves. Hadn't we better help things along a bit?"

"There was one yesterday in my room, unbuttoned," she said. "I didn't drop it."

I was seriously annoyed. This seemed to be going too far. And in what direction? What does one do when this sort of thing happens? I was looking as one does when one has heard one's best friend talking about oneself, when the shadow of a heavy man fell across our floor. It was Trenchard. My sister looked up and said quickly:

"We've found one now."

"Have you?" he said. "So have I." He hesitated. There was something very direct and somehow comforting in the way he was taking it, piece by piece as it happened, not as what he would think it ought to mean. It was then that we began to be ashamed of ourselves. He went on:

"You know my cat. She's her kittens hidden somewhere in the loft and I wanted to have a look at them. I went up softly not to scare her. You know it's dark on that top stair. I got there, and then I heard—well—a little thing falling off a step. Thought it was a kitten trying to explore. Peered and felt and picked up a glove."

He pulled it out of his pocket and held it up by a finger with slight distaste. A brown one this time.

"One button," he said. "The kittens aren't big enough to have been playing with it and the cat wasn't about. There's no draught. Funny, isn't it? Reminded me of one of those humpty-dumpty toys we had, a little silk man with arms and legs and a painted face, and a loose marble inside him to make him turn over and fall about."

My sister said:

"We've found a box of loose gloves in our attic close to your bricked-up door."

His answer was that it was bricked up all right, and had we thought to count them in case either of our maids was up to some village trick. We hadn't, but I noticed that he mistrusted our maids as little as we did. Also that his behaviour was so reasonable because he had not yet thought there was any cause for suspicion.

"Let's do it now," he said. "Put them all back, yours and mine. Count them and lock your door."

He went back and fetched his five, and together we went upstairs. They sat on a basket trunk while I emptied the box.

"Twenty-seven. Eleven pairs in all and one missing." I shovelled them back into the cardboard box, yellow with time and dust. I looked up at his broad straight nose and my sister's little one that turns up. Both were sniffing.

"There's a smell here," they said. There was. Not the dust-camphor-mouse-and-apple smell proper to lofts.

"I know what it is," Trenchard said, "smelt it in Africa in a damp place. Bad skins."

The loft went suddenly darker. We looked up. There was no window, but someone had cut the thatch and let in a sky-light. Something was covering it, had suddenly blown across it, though outside there was no wind. I took the iron handle with holes in it to stick through the pin in the frame, and threw it up. The piece of stuff slid backwards into the thatch. I put my arm out, caught hold of it and pulled it in. A piece of calico with a stiff waxy surface, once used for linings, again some time ago. It seemed to have no shape, but there were holes in it. Holes not tears.

"Nasty slummy rag," I said. "I suppose it was lying about in the thatch."

Our thatch was old and full of flowers. This thing went with dust-bins and tin cans. One piece was clotted together. A large spider ran out of it. I dropped it on the floor beside the box and the gloves. I was surprised to see Trenchard look at it with disgust.

"Never could stand seeing things go bad," he said. We left the attic, locking the door, and went downstairs. We gave him the key. It seemed the decent thing to do.

Over a late and thoughtful tea, we talked of other things. We did not think it necessary to tell him what the keeper had said.

.   .   .   .   .

The evening was exquisite and the next day and the next night. Days refreshed with night-showers to draw out scent, and steady sun to ripen; a pattern on the world like the dry dew on a moth's wing, or the skin on a grape or a rose. And nothing more happened. The next evening Trenchard was to give a little party for his birthday, for some friends who would motor over; and my sister and I were to see that all was in order for it, flowers and fruit and wine and all the good cold things to eat. We had the delicate pleasant things to do; to slice the cucumbers and drench sprays of borage and balm-in-Gilead for the iced drinks. The almonds did not come, so we salted some ourselves, blanching them in the garden, getting hot in the kitchen over pans of burnt salt.

At about six o'clock we went back to dress. Trying, as was appropriate, to look like Paris, in compliment to Trenchard, but principally to the garden and to the weather and to the earth. There was a bump overhead from the attic.

"What's that?" said my sister, painting her face.

"I left the skylight open," I said. "It must have slipped. Let's leave it. Am I in a state of dress or undress to go up there?"

She was ready before I was, and said that she was going across to

Trenchard's to have one more look to see if all was in order there. Half of our day's work had been to keep him out of the way. We had just sent him up to the village after more strawberries and hoped that he would be back in time—and there was still plenty of time—for him to dress. As she went, I heard his step at his front door, and a few moments later, my dressing finished, I went downstairs and out across the orchard to join them. He had gone upstairs to change, but just as I reached the verandah, I heard a short cry which must have come from him. I ran in with my sister, who was also outside, building a last pyramid of strawberries on a dish shaped like a green leaf. He came out of the dining room.

"Who's done this?" he said.

The supper table was set with food to be fetched and eaten when people pleased. There were little bowls of cut-glass set with sweets and almonds. One of these had been sprinkled with buttons, little white buttons that had been torn off, still ragged with red-brown threads.

"I filled it," said my sister in a small weak voice, "with those sugar rose leaves, and a real one on top."

"Your servant—" I began, when he cried out again:

"What's that glove doing up the back of your dress?"

It was a little silver coat I had on to begin with. I pulled it off, and there fell off the collar, but with a tiny thud, another glove, a black one. It had no buttons on it and was open like a hand. Trenchard picked it up, and I thought I saw it collapse a little.

"No time to count them tonight," he said, and looked round. It was too hot for a fire, but they were laid in all the rooms. He put the glove down and struck a match. The huge chimney used to roar with its draught, but the fire would not catch. He went out to the lavatory with the glove and the dish.

"Go up and dress," we said when he came back; but instead he sniffed.

"It's what we smelt the other day," he said. "Up in the loft. Dead skin."

Outside, the air was hot and sweet and laced with coolness, but we noticed that here indoors it was cold, stale cold.

"Go and dress," we said again, with the female instinct to keep the minutiae of things steady and in sequence.

"They won't be here till eight: there's plenty of time," he said, feeling not fear or even much curiosity, but that it was not the proper thing to leave us alone with the inexplicable unpleasant.

"Your servant," I began again.

"My servant's all right," he said. "Go out and wait in the verandah. I'll be down quickly."

So he went up. We took a chair and sat each side of the open glass doors where we could see into the house. We remembered that his maid as well as ours had gone back to her cottage to get ready for company. So there was no one in either house.

"He's taking it well," we said, and, "What is it?" And what we meant was: "What have we stirred up?" And (for my sister and I cannot lie to one another), "You did not do that with the buttons in the dish?" "Dear God, I did not."

"A dirty old woman," said my sister, "nice about her hands."

I said: "Dirty things done in a delicate way. There was that piece of stuff."

The house and the little orchard were backed with tall trees. There was a hint of evening, and high branches black against strong gold. Was there something hanging high up, very high, that looked like a square of stuff that had holes in it?

Upstairs, Trenchard must have gone to the bathroom first. Then we heard him, moving about in his bedroom, just above the verandah roof. Then we heard him shout again, a cry he tried to stop. We ran out across the grass and called up at his window. He answered: "No, don't come up." Of course we ran up, in and through the sitting-room and up the stairs. The dining-room door was still open, and with a corner of my eye I saw a candle, guttering hideously in the windless room.

"Let us in," we said at the door.

"Of all the filthy nonsense—" he was repeating: "—Look at my shirt."

On the top of the chest of drawers out of which he had taken it, his shirt was lying; and on its stiff white linen was what looked like a patch of grey jelly. Only it had spread out from a clot into five ribbons, like a hand or the fingers of a glove.

"Fine sort of beastliness," he said, "that won't let you dress for dinner." I heard myself saying:

"Are all your shirts like that?"

"No," he said grimly, "and if you don't mind waiting here till I've finished, we'll go downstairs and see what this is about."

He took another shirt and finished his dressing, wincing as he touched things; while we felt as if there were slugs about, the things of which we are most afraid; and that we must keep our long dresses tight about us.

We went down together into the dining-room, and there my sister screamed. On top of the centre strawberry pyramid, hanging over the berries like a cluster of slugs, was a glove, yellow-orange kid skin, still and fat. A colour we had not seen in the box. The wrist and the fingers open and swollen. No buttons.

"What witches' trick is this?" he cried, and stared at us, for we were women. And like a wave moving towards us, rearing its head, came the knowledge that we were responsible for this; that our greed and vanity in devising this had evoked this: that we would now have to show courage, courage and intelligence to put an end to this, to lay this. And we had no idea how.

"The fire must burn," I said. "A great fire." He turned towards the outhouse.

"What's that lovely scent you wear?" he said to my sister.—"I want to smell it. Get that."

She ran away, and I stood still, aware of my shoulder-blades and the back of my neck, and all of my body that I couldn't *see*. Doors would not open easily. I heard him swearing and stumbling, the clang of a bucket tripped over and kicked away in the yard. My sister ran in, a scent-spray in her hand, crying:

"It's not scent any more. I tried it. It smells like the attic—"

She was squeezing the bulb and spraying us all violently; and I could not smell the dead smell of the loft, but the sweetness, like a lady-like animal, of old kid gloves.

Outside, the delicious evening was pouring in, to meet the original smell of the house; smell of flowers and tobacco, of polished furniture and wood-smoke and good things to eat. Trenchard had brought in a gallon jar of paraffin. He tipped and splashed it over the sitting-room fire.

"Get all the gloves," he said, looking at our helpless skirts: "I'll go across. I've got the loft key."

We peered again into the dining-room, that the kitchen opened out of. The candle guttered in fat dripping folds; a spider ran across a plate. My sister said:

It's got only five fingers. Like a glove."

We waited. "Let's have the fire ready," we said, and I staggered with the can at arm's length to the sitting-room fire and drenched the piled wood. The ugly vulgar smell was sweet with reassurance. My sister threw in a match. A roar drowned the crackle of catching sticks.

"Now for it," we said, and tore open the bureau drawer for the gloves. I ran up for Trenchard's shirt, and when I came back, my sister, her hands full of strawberries, threw them, yellow glove and all, on the leaping pillars of fire. I shook the guttering candle out of its stick; my sister unscrewed her spray and emptied the precious stuff, that waved blue and white fingers at us out of the fierce, shrill yellow flames.

"So much for that," I said. "Where is he?" said my sister. We looked at each other.

"This is our fault," we said. —"We must go over. If it starts here again when we're gone, God knows what we're to do." Then she said:

"The loft's the place. It started there."

Outside, the orchard was full of bird-conversation. Inside, in half an hour we were to give a birthday party. We ran through the gap in the hedge and into our side of the house, which had become again part of one house.

Inside it we expected to find one large, troubled man, upstairs collecting things. Instead there was quiet, a kind of dead quiet that came to meet us down the steep stair. The loft door was open. On the flight that led up to it he was lying, feet down, his head upon the sill; his head invisible, wrapped up in what looked like a piece of dark green cotton, dirty and torn. We dragged it off.

"Burn. Burn," my sister said.

Some of it was in his mouth. We pulled it out. His tongue and mouth were stained. We slid him down to the foot of the flight and got water.

"Draw it fresh," she said. And, "Keep it tight in your hand," for I wanted to drop the cloth, to pull it away, as if it were trying to wrap itself round me, to stick to me.

We threw water on him. (Two shirts already; what an evening! thought a bit of me.) By this time I had hold of the cloth like grim death, for it felt as though it was straining away in a wind that wasn't there. "Gloves," she said. We went into the loft. The skylight was open, and the cardboard box lay open and full. She put on the lid and put it under her arm, and we left him on the stairs and made off again, across the orchard to the fire. It was dying down. The room stifling, the wood sulky with oil-black. My sister flung in the box, drenched it with the oil, and stiff grey smoke poured out on us. She tossed a match on it, and there was the grunt of an explosion, and, as we jumped back, the fire poured up again. I felt a smart in my hand, as if the cloth was raw between my fingers.

"It mustn't fly up the chimney," she said. "If it does, it will come back all over again."

There was a box of cigars on the table. We turned them out, and thrust it in between the thin cedar boards and shut it up. Flung it into the fire wall and held it down. The box rose once or twice, bucked under the poker and the shovel.

Then we went back to Trenchard. He had come round, and was sitting at the foot of the loft stair.

"Everything's burned," we said. "Tell us what happened to you."

"God knows," he said. And then: "I was stooping to get the box, and something flapped against the skylight. Blew in, I suppose, and the next thing I knew it had wrapped itself round my head and I couldn't get it off. I tore at it and I tried to get out. Then I couldn't bear it any more. It was winding itself tight. Then I must have passed out. But, oh God, it was the smell of it…"

❖ ❖

After the Funeral

WE WAITED IN THE ice-dark, star-pierced church, under the sea of dead incense and winter-chilled stone. Under the sea of our sorrow and our memories. More memories than sorrow? More sorrow than memories? Memories won in my case, pushed in and thrust out sorrow. Sorrow which came back; hid behind a pillar on which mildew had drawn green scrolls, lounged against it and watched us where we sat, slender and very tall, as the body we were waiting for had been. Dead cold in the church and very still, outside a storm yelled, black and visible over London; and the coffin which had to cross the sea to reach us was late. Late like she had been, who had *always* been late, who had said with her lovely laugh that some day she would be late for her own funeral.

We were all there who had known her, like a party gone to church. Who did not usually go to church. Each alone, for once, sitting side by side, but alone in a little precinct of grief. And physical wretchedness and shyness and impatience. And the question: "When will this be over?" and "When will the coffin turn up?" and even "Why did we come?" But alone. Here everyone knew everyone else so well, there was little recognition. The men with their uncovered heads were the most visible. I sat back. Somehow a whisper passed along. The boat-train was late because of the storm, in another half-hour…

In another half-hour the box would be here, and in the box would be that, that, that which had been her.

> Because she was very tall and quaint
> And gold like a quattrocento saint.

That would do. I must shape my memories of her. Hold on hard to something that would focus feeling; drill the memory-swarm.

> Here we solemn vigil keep
> Where all beauty lies asleep.

On this awful London winter afternoon. Not where it should have been, in the south, under a light sun, under flowers.

"I am a woman," she said. *"I was happy when you loved me."*

About all there was to it, if you left out the wit and the divine inconsequence and the sorrow.

"Who has remembered me? Who has forgotten?" I thought a little grimly:

"You won't be forgotten, my lass. A fair amount of trouble you gave, and as much joy. People can take their choice, and the joy and the trouble cancel down to a number in magic. By your magic we have known you. Which is the last thing you can say of anyone. And the best."

I sat back. There were two empty chairs beside me and then a man we had both known, and then a painter all our lives our friend. Glancing at her, I saw her eyes watchful, turn abstract; out of the inside of her fur coat saw her pull out a sketch book, and with loose matchless precision begin to draw. Stare and scribble, stare and scribble. I shouldn't be able to do my equivalent yet, which was damnable. I should have to wait. Wait and register. Wait and register. The emotions one is expected to feel; the emotions one wanted to feel; the emotions one felt.

Behind me someone was crying. A man's crying, torn, ludicrous, ashamed sobs. I wanted to turn round and stare; wanted to leave him alone in a church's assumption of privacy. There were very few women. It was a man's party. Three rows ahead of me, one of them pitched forward suddenly onto his knees.

. . . . . .

Was she really inside that box, between a parterre of candle-flowers? Their white stalks would be shortening, each fire petal would be dead, even before the flowers that heaped the thin boards that separated her from us.

What was she looking like now? Had they painted her face? What had they done to her hair? What had she on? Very fine white linen, I hoped, embroidered with white flowers. (Families see to that, and families don't care.) She would have chosen a frock in which she had every confidence. I remembered a blue one, with a skirt made of short curled feathers, the colour of an April sky.

On a cushion of jonquils, her name was written in violets: Clair. Clair. Clair. Clair… How badly the *Dies Irae* goes with spring. "Light things and winged and holy" were fluttering, flower and fire and tear and willful memory-drifts against words of majesty and passion.

> *Dies irae, dies illa,*
> *Solvet saeclum in favilla,*
> *Teste David cum Sybilla.*

What had that to do with her? What sentence of it was in relation to her? What memory had we of her in terms of salvation or of death?

> *Quaerens me, sedisti, lassus*
> *Redemisti Crucem passus;*
> *Tantus labor non sit cassus.*

Not in your line, Clair. With what divine inconsequence would you have evaded equally salvation or damnation, or even devotion such as that. To each his own *labor*. Yes, your *labor* was not unlike love. Yes, it was love, who set everybody loving, loving you, at least. *Tantus labor*—let's leave it at that, and by that work be remembered among us, my dear.

II

It was next spring that I met George in Conduit Street. He stopped me, his handsome head looking down on me, standing on the curb, a hand on his hip, swinging from one foot to the other. His great good looks somehow emphasized what was common in his bearing.

I was wanted that night for a party. There was an american husband and wife in London who were a support to Lionel's muse. They had already bought two pictures, and their reward was to be an evening they were to think had been spent between Bohemia, Fashion, and the Underworld. I listened to George's arrangements: we would dine here and dance there and take them on somewhere else. After that George would improvise. He has a genius for parties.

"What sort are they?" I asked.

"Quite overpoweringly serious. Both of them. From Boston."

"Erudition?"

George raised his eyebrows.

"Erudition *and* uplift. And she wouldn't be bad-looking if she wore less hair and more leg.—Eight o'clock then, my pretty. Put on that jade dress."

George is a man who must be loved wherever he goes. So he left me feeling that he must love me. Which he does not. I saw him flaunt off, watchful for admiration and nervous of criticism, and hoped that Lionel's patrons had not found him an embarrassment.

I need not have wasted a moment's consideration on that. Lionel's buyers were perfectly able to keep people in their places. The husband was delightful, a lean slip of intelligence, detached even when he followed his wife like a racing schooner in a liner's wake. George had been right about her looks, though I judged that the legs under her long skirt were not good enough to show. She was one of those unfortunate women today who are really nobly-proportioned, and had the singular courage to feature it. Her fair hair, which must have hung to her knees, was pinned onto the back of her head in a boss, a corbel, an escutcheon. It only needed a device in high relief to complete it.

"A fish," said Lionel, and that she was more like a building than a boat. At that second I remembered another very tall woman, whose thin arched feet would not step our way again, a woman who had been like a tree moving in the wind.

> In the deep-feathered firs
> That gift of joy is hers
> In the least breath that stirs—

But that night we were not thinking of Clair, as we fed our Bostonians and danced with them and took their intelligence as seriously as we knew how. She was very much married to him. It was always "we" and "my husband" and the works of culture and virtue on which they were occupied, and what similar interests and institutions we had in England. She seemed to us a marvel of over-education, which he did not, as she passed from Mantegna to Mendelism, deferring at the right moment to his opinion, and when he hadn't one, inventing the right one for him. Nobly, only too nobly planned. Indeed, after a time, I married her to George. George would not be able to elude her like the lean brave at her side. She would take over George and run him, gag his loose tongue, fix his wanton eye. George had earned that something like that should happen to him. George, whose sex-appeal was his life's work. He had tried it on her, but automatically; if he was not trying it now, it was because she had gone through his attacks as a tank might pass through a wall of butter. He was now as douce and sensible as I had ever seen him; so that forever after I thought of her as the woman who had put the fear of God into George. And as I watched I saw that everything that she did with purpose, her husband did without effort, outstripping her, but in absence of mind, and on instinct adjusting his pace.

Her earrings, each tassel of antique pearls, swept her shoulders; on her long hands, with unlacquered nails, were three choice rings beside a wedding-ring of stout gold, unashamed. With her husband I rejoiced to dance, and rejoiced to see her guide George while she followed him. Lionel's sister said that there was a key-pin to her hair-knot which kept the escutcheon up, and was young enough to want to pull it out and see what she would do with her hair hanging down her back.

"Replace it with a gracious gesture," I said, "and look rather superb with her arms raised and gold ropes running through her hands."

"Queenly," said Lionel, and something about "what a constitution," and giggled as he saw George try and rush her into a fancy step and be frustrated and get out of time and be ushered back into it.

In such decorum the evening passed, and George's finale was a party improvised at their studio, and more to eat and more to dance and drink. There I went off duty, and the Americans showed how well they could mix, and as at all George's parties, the room flashed into movement; movement of bodies and glasses, movement in mirrors and air filling the long curtains, movement of candles streaming and fire on the hearth rising, movement of voices and music the bodies repeated, the movement of each person a variation on the whole theme.

It was late when I found myself next to the American again, on a divan, and he fetched me a drink. He had a portfolio of Lionel's drawings and we looked at them together, drawings of plants and birds and eggs and fish.

"I want a figure-study," he said. Then sat still with—"Does he never draw anything human?"

"Not well and not often," I said, as he pulled out at hazard a drawing of Clair, her hand on a wine jar, upright against a Provençal house, in the Provençal light.

"Clair Lorrimer," I said. "Did you ever meet her? She is dead."

"Yes," he said, "I knew her well." And then sat still with the drawing in his hands, and looked at it so long and in such abstraction that he became almost invisible. Someone fetched me away.

III

It was many dances later, the party going with a roar like song. The American's wife was queening it by the hearth, but a queen unbent, her hair's architecture in ever so small a landslide down the nape of her neck. I thought of the garden behind the studio and that there would be pouring down into it an April moon; and went down to the passage and opened its door. Outside I found that I was not alone, for there was Alan Crane, standing in the centre of the colourless grass holding up a drawing of Clair, looking at it by the light of the moon. Like a man before an invisible altar he held her picture.

"Clair. Clair. Clair,? he was saying: "Azay-les-Rideaux. Oh my God, my God."

I thought: 'Clair and Clair again. You've done it again, my girl, even now you're dead. Out in the moonlight a pencil ghost of you. This man. Where did you know him? How did you impose yourself on his virtue?' He must have heard my shoe on the path, for he turned. Came over to me, and I saw his face glittering with tears in that light.

"Tell me all you know about her," he said, with a directness of passion which was in keeping with his quietness, his decorum's complement. "Azay-les-Rideaux. We were there three days. I have not slept one night since she died."

It seemed to me that the time had come to speak the praise of Clair. I made it and he listened, in a rapture, as though I spoke for him, as though he was telling her himself.

"Azay-les Rideaux," he said again, turning his face to the lightly-starred heavens.— "Azay-les-Rideaux. Three days she gave me. Three days in the boat called millions-of-years…"

Again I heard the garden door opened. It was Mrs. Crane come to look for him, and George with her; George called to seemly order, George frisking in attendance, George repressing tiresome comment at finding us alone there. So did she. The perfect wife, indulgent even of flirtation, rebuking it only by absence of comment, her "Alan, don't you think we ought to go now" shepherded us inside. George and she went in first, then I, he last. So I could not see what change took place in him in the ten-second corridor-transit. Only, a minute later, the man who had wept in the moonlight was the pleased and pleasant host, who had drawn Lionel aside and was writing him a cheque; to whom his wife was saying:

"Another enrichment for our lives. What an interesting drawing. Did you invent her or did you draw her from life? Who was she?"

❖ ❖

The House

ONCE THERE WERE four friends who shared a house between them: a husband, a wife, and two sisters. The sisters' old nurse looked after them. They were poor, and the house was principally furnished with mirrors and pictures and books. When the things they had were dirty they washed them; when they were shabby they painted them. The house became a place where all their friends were equally glad to come, and where they could do anything or nothing, as they liked. There the four lived without a quarrel for three years.

At the end of that time they decided to go abroad for a spring and a summer, and inquired among their friends who would care to take the house and pay the rent and a little over while they were away. They could not find another family like themselves, but the husband and wife found a girl called Pippa to live in their part, and a young man called Arnold. They had known them a long time, and the arrangement seemed good.

One day the eldest sister said to the husband and wife who were called Julian and Anne:

"Our married sister—whom you don't know—and her husband and her babies and their nurse and their cook want to come to our part of the house for the summer. We could just get them in, and they always pay their rent." Julian, who was not listening, said, "All right," and Anne said, "That sounds all right." The old nurse said nothing at the time, but when Anne came down to the kitchen late in the evening for a cup of tea, she said to her:

"So Christina's coming when you're away, duckies?"

"So I've heard," said Anne. "Well, if she's anything like Charmian and Chloe, it will be all right." The old nurse tried out a fresh iron and said: "I shan't be here, I'm going to my brother's while you're away. I don't want to see her nosing about my kitchen."

"Does she nose, Nurse?"

"Always did, as a child, and always will. I don't care to see any of her servants washing up at my taps."

"Isn't she nice, Nurse?"

"I wouldn't care to say that, dearie. She's a lovely little housekeeper. But you'll see for yourselves. She'll be here for lunch tomorrow."

Anne went to look for Julian.

"There is a horrid woman coming," she said.

"How do you know? She is Charmian's sister."

"Nurse says she doesn't want her down in the basement with her cat. And Nurse was her nurse."

"Well, we shan't see her."

"Yes, we shall. She is coming to lunch tomorrow."

"Well, we can be out."

"No, I want to know the worst."

"Why hurry so? Anyhow, Pippa and Arnold will be in our rooms."

"I don't want the wrong sort of people in our house."

"What we want is the rent."

Next day Anne was late for lunch. The nurse was too busy carving to scold her, and there was a feeling of unfriendliness. She sat quiet, observing the woman who was Charmian's sister. She was not like either Charmian or Chloe. She was rounder and redder and not so quiet and not so gay; and she talked positively about babies and about books. She was very pleased that she was married, and wished to appear seriously intelligent and a woman of the world. Anne was thankful Julian was out.

The husband amused Anne. He was little, and reddish-dark, and there was no fat on him. He was restless and genial, but every time he began to make her laugh there was something in his voice that only allowed her half a laugh. Each time she was ready, each time he checked her. She thought he was like a hill pony, and understood that she did not know the hills he came from. She sat back in her chair and attended to Christina, his wife.

"I am convinced we shall go back to the matriarchate again," she said. "I don't agree with Frazer there. He is right about many things, but I feel that a partial return to that phase of primitive life—"

'Prunes and prisms,' said Anne to herself—'and it's not her style, anyhow'—and forgot her manners and answered back: "I don't think he ever said what ought to happen. Anyhow, a matriarchate, if there ever was one, sounds unpleasant. Think of all the old women bullying the young." Christina went on: "I'm sure that when descent is traced through the mother, it has immense influence on society. Think of the position of women in Homer."

"But," said Anne, "d'you think the people in Homer wanted to be traced through their mothers? Think of all the stories they invented to call themselves Zeus-born—" and was out to argue to win. But Charmian got up from the table, and took her sisters with her, and the old nurse.

Anne had tea alone with Julian, and told him: "She's a woman who has all the wrong points. She reads *The Golden Bough* to keep her husband in order. She has married a little black man from somewhere queer—"

"Horrid little man," said Julian. "Yes, I've seen him. We passed the time of day on the stairs."

If Julian and Anne had had any sense, they would have gone to Charmian and Chloe and told them that their sister and her husband would not do. That, though they would pay the rent and preserve the linen, they would alter the house. Instead, Julian bought drinks and Anne bought flowers, and they gave a party for their friends. As they were arriving, Anne went upstairs and asked Charmian and her sisters to come down. Taff and Christina were not there. Charmian was making a cluster of grapes for Chloe's hair. She put them away, and said, "Yes, we're coming." Chloe threw her book away. She was so young that she still pretended not to care for parties, though she was the last to go to bed. Charmian, who was a Tuesday's child, stood up, folding her sewing away in a linen cloth, lit a cigarette and followed Anne lightly down the stairs.

It was a good party. They lit a bonfire in the garden, and threw the cat over it because it was the spring equinox. The cat did not care. Pippa and Arnold came, who were to live in Anne's part of the house. Pippa was more beautiful than Charmian or Chloe, or Anne, or any of their friends, but nobody minded. Arnold fell in love with Charmian.

When the bonfire was over, and they were sitting out on the round balcony, and some were drinking, and some were singing, and some were looking at the sky, Taff and Christina came in and joined them. Pippa was running about, and Taff said to Charmian: "Who is that very pretty girl?" When Charmian introduced them, he said: "Delighted to meet you, Miss Arundel, delighted to meet you," and shook hands up and down. Christina looked at Arnold and said: "Who is that young man?" and Anne, who was watching, got up and said: "You will all know each other before long. You will be sharing the house while we are away." Christina said: "How I envy you all. But, you see, mine are only babies."

Anne knew that Julian was missing this, and saw Pippa attending with round eyes. They went down to the basement room to dance.

"Are they your friends, Mrs. Ker?" said Christina to Anne.

"Yes."

"Do they give many parties?"

"A great many parties."

"I only ask because of my babies, you know."

Anne thought: that is reasonable. "I will explain to them," she said, "that the parties must happen down here, where you won't hear them. It will be quite all right." But as they went downstairs together, she thought: 'It won't be. And I don't care what happens to these people at all.'

The long room in the basement was full of young men and women. There was a brilliant fire, and the doors into the garden were open. There were glass panels on the walls, and the green floor was waxed like a sheet of dark water.

Anne was not at ease. She went to find Julian, but as she sat down beside him, he said: "I am going to bed," and Anne knew why.

He did not go, and Anne could not blame him, because his room was exactly over the party, and he would not have been able to sleep. He tried to talk to Taff and make him say what he thought about something, but Taff would not play. He enjoyed himself by pretending to be one of the party, but the fun lay, as someone said, "in only pretending to be a bee." All the time he talked a great deal, and now and again he looked at Pippa. Anne went and sat by Arnold, and they watched what was happening, very comfortably, with a box of chocolates between them.

First of all Pippa danced, and her round bright eyes looked at nothing. Taff's little eyes looked at her, and Christina looked too, not with attention but between her stitches, as if she were keeping a child in its place. Then she cried: "Really, how delightful. Will you show my babies how it's done? It must be so good for you. I believe in eurhythmics. Do you think of these dances all yourself?"

Pippa stood with her bare legs apart.

Arnold and I make them up together, and when I do them on the stage, he produces me. Yes, I'll show your children, if they like. How old are they?"

"Only babies. Three and four. But Joan has some idea of dancing already, and I want her to express herself." Then she went on: "Now the fault I find in the Russian ballet is that they insist on technique for its own sake.—You see what I mean?—One is interested only in the wonderful way it is done."—Everybody listened, excepting Julian, on the floor between two mirrors, playing a very small game of bowls with some walnuts. He bowled once, much too far, and the kitten chased it. Christina went on: "You are not shown the emotions of the characters taking part, only their gestures."

"But don't you think that you get it all in with the gestures?" said Pippa. "I don't know; it seems to me all right. I wish I could dance like that. Anyhow, I can turn cart-wheels. I'm sure your kids would like that."

She turned cart-wheels across the floor to Arnold and Anne's corner, and laid herself down between them, very warm, her child's face turned to the ceiling.

Anne thought she heard Julian gnashing his teeth, but when she looked he was cracking nuts.

Later on, when Pippa was running about again, Taff came over to Anne and sat down by her and said: "Tell me, Mrs. Ker, who these people are."

She wanted to say: "They won't interest you. It would be much better to leave your acquaintance with them as it is, and then, please God, we may get through this summer in peace."

She was not brave enough. She tried to amuse him, and felt that if she amused him she would have to be disloyal. Then she said: "Charmian is the best story-teller I know. She knows everybody. Ask her."

She saw Charmian, looking like a woman in an old song, with her hair over her eyes in gold shells and a scarlet dress to her feet. She thought that Charmian would not be hurt, anyhow, and contrasted her choice words and conversation with her sister's streams of opinions it was impossible to cut short, examine, or in anyway chasten. In fact, do anything but enjoy. Only she could treat it as a play. She got up and caught Pippa, passing, by the hair.

"We'd better dance. Make us."

Arnold went to the piano. Taff and Christina danced once together and went to bed. Charmian followed them.

Some time later they were singing songs. There was a pause. Julian got up and said: "Sing this," and whistled. They heard it, and the room roared.

> "Taffy was a Welshman.
> Taffy was a thief,
> Taffy came to my house and stole a piece of beef.
> There I met a little man who wouldn't say his prayers.
> I took him by the left leg and flung him down the stairs."

Anne thought: "Where's Chloe?" She was there, but she did not seem to mind.

Much later one of the men, who was a painter, said that he must see a picture that was in Charmian's sitting room at the top of the house. Chloe told him the door, but in a few minutes he came back, embarrassed: "I say," he said, "I must have gone in at the wrong door, because before I turned the light on, a man's voice said, 'Goodnight, sir'."

"I suppose," said Chloe, "that they missed their train, and you went into the room where they were asleep."

"But," said the painter, "why did he say goodnight to me like that? It was a mistake. I wasn't even drunk."

"That's how they do be talking," said Julian, surprising Anne by using one of the turns of Charmian's speech. Agreeable from her mouth, it sounded ridiculous in his. Or spiteful. The painter protested: "It sounds silly—I don't know why, but I feel embarrassed. Not as though I had blundered into your room, Anne's, in the middle of the night."

"He only wanted to go to sleep," said Chloe.

"How did he manage to make you feel a Don Juan *manqué*?" said Arnold anxiously, who was in love with Charmian.

Next day Anne got up early, made some tea and woke Julian, and said: "What about that woman?"

"What about her?" said Julian.

"She won't play up, and our tenants are half across each other already."

"She plays her play. The common and ancient game, if you like it, of putting one's neighbours in the wrong."

"Envy," said Anne.

"Perhaps," said Julian.

"Patronage," said Anne.

"Principles," said Julian.

"What about the rights of man?"

"She has them too."

"She'll bitch up our good house."

"Probably," said Julian.

"Malice," said Anne.

"Position," said Julian. "I can't stand her husband at any price."

"Snobbery," said Anne.

"Certainly," said Julian.

"What has a woman like that got to be a snob about?"

"What are english people snobs about, anyhow?" said Julian, who was a Scot.

"What are we going to do about it?" said Anne, who was not.

"Nothing," said Julian, and went to sleep again. Anne sucked her thumb, but after tea she called on Christina again.

"I'm sorry if you were disturbed last night, it was a stupid mistake," she said.

"Of course," said Christina, "I understand. It was only an accident. I am sure we shall get on very well." Anne thought: 'Now that sounds kind.' Charmian smiled. Her smile usually quieted Anne. Now, for the first time, she noticed that she was critical of Charmian's smile.

The three young ladies went downstairs.

II

Julian and Anne sat out in Paris in the sun and read a letter from Pippa which said:

> We have not got on badly, so far. One thing went wrong, but I think I put it right. It is light very early now and I came back from a dance with three boys. I went down to the kitchen to cook breakfast, or it wouldn't have happened. Cherry began to play Purcell in the room under their bedroom and they thumped on the floor. Cherry didn't mind, I mean he didn't stop, and the sausages took a long time.
>
> Next day I stopped Mr. Guest, you called Taffy, on the stairs and shook hands with him and told him I was very, very sorry.

> He said it was all right, and next day there was a box of cigarettes, with a message, "from a disagreeable neighbour" on it, and next day there were fireworks in the park, and he and I were alone in the house except for the children, and we watched them a little. They shot up over the trees. It sounded like air-raids and I was rather frightened. He told me at first it was guns.
>
> A vest of mine got mixed up in their wash. I don't know how. Or why. Do you? I think it is all right...

"It might be much worse," said Anne.

"Or, you might say it has begun," said Julian.

It was a long way off, and they were happy. It was interesting to think of two kinds of life going on in the house, and wonder which would come off best. Anne said it would be all right, because if Pippa was naughty Taff and Christina knew the rules of behaviour for people who were not living under their own roof. There were going to be amusing stories. That was all.

After this Julian and Anne left Paris. A huge train took them out into the middle of Europe, and they went on, always through new countries, till they forgot that there was a house in England from which they came, to which they would go back. Julian would never have remembered. Anne only partly forgot; both would have been content to go on, she for a long time, he forever.

In the middle of a black Silesian wood a letter found them. Anne read it aloud. It made a small tinkling noise that did not sound real:

> You know Charmian and Arnold like each other. They arranged that he should meet them for a time when he went away. A postcard came from her to him, and Taff and that woman Christina saw it. I know he took it upstairs to read and put it back. Arnold asked him for it. That didn't matter because Taff was in the wrong; but a little later there was more trouble about bedroom doors. Another friend went up to look at that picture and walked into the room where Christina's servants slept. They shrieked; I suppose they thought they were being ladies; but Taff wrote us a letter. He said it was the second occurrence, and he must mention it because a servant's feelings had been hurt. There were two and and he didn't say which. Arnold apologised at once. They were all right about it. "We know the young gentleman" sort of touch. It wasn't that anyone was drunk but there were lots of doors. Dear Anne, I am very sorry about it.

"That's that," they said, and forgot about it.

They went out into the black woods that go on forever and ever. Anne made up a song called "Quiet in the Woods," about a tall, magic animal with cold, innocent eyes, walking between the trees when no one was there.

Anne wanted to turn east and follow the Danube, but Julian's mind went north always to the edge of the snow. They went to the Baltic and ran in and out of the water all day, and lay stretched on the beaches. The memory of England was like an old top humming, turning slower and slower until it fell off sideways into the sea.

In September, when it began to get cold too soon, they turned south to meet Charmian and Chloe in Berlin. (Anne said: "In autumn it should rain, and there should be a warm wind. This wind comes from another place and I want more clothes.") They walked in the Tiergarten through a storm of leaves. Only Julian liked it. In a week they were going home. It was then that Anne remembered the two letters, and one day when they were at dinner she said: "Charmian, you have not been so far away. What has happened to the house?"

Charmian said, without moving an eyelash: "I think it has gone off as well as could be expected."

Anne wanted to go home. "Then there has been trouble?" she said.

"Tell us about it, Charmian," said Julian.

Chloe began:

"There was the fuss about a postcard Taff read. Do you know about that?"

"Yes, and about the maids' room."

"Well, when Arnold was away, I expect Pippa did what she liked. She is quite young enough to show Taff and Christina she didn't like them."

"All right, young Chloe," said Julian.

"There must have been a great deal too much noise," said Charmian. "I think you will find Taff and Christina were so far in the right."

"But what has actually happened?" said Julian.

"Nothing," said the sisters.

Anne thought: 'I don't believe you. I have never not believed anything you have said before, but I don't believe you now.'

"I can tell you one thing," said Chloe, "the house has been sold. To an old man who lives up the road. Anne, we really don't know anything more. That news came in a letter from Nurse. Christina's cook told her."

But Anne was irritated and said: "Nurse said that your sister turns the gas off and keeps the fire down as though to have two saucepans boiling at once was the shortest cut to ruin."

"It sometimes is," said Charmian, in her light voice. "But those two never got on. Christina is used to authority, and so is Nurse. It is better to keep them away from each other."

"Anne," said Julian later, "Chloe and Charmian have nothing to do with whatever has happened. If you let houses to people like that, you take the consequences."

"Little squireens," said Anne.

"A managing woman, two ordinary servants, Pippa and Arnold—casual people—"

"—People like Taff and Christina dislike charm—"

"—Certainly they do."

"Never mind," said Anne. "I'll have them all out in a week."

A small grey letter came for Julian. He turned away, read it, put it in his pocket and looked at Anne. He went out, walked half the way down the Unter den Linden, and turned back. He met Chloe and they went to drink beer and read it together:

> How awful for you and Anne about the house. I take it that
> you will have to go, but that it will be all right for Charmian
> and Chloe.

Chloe shrugged her shoulders. "Julian, you know this may be nothing but gossip from the club."

"So I suppose, but I must tell Anne; and Anne loves the house…."

Anne snatched the letter, read it, and backed away from them, staring.

"This is how it stands. The house is on a lease in my name. I have broken the lease. Apart from any lies the new landlord may have heard, I have sub-let. I have left the garden to be a paradise of dandelions, and people have hung out their washing on the balcony rails. God only knows what Pippa may have done. But the point is that Pippa does not know. I have a letter from her today about fun, and nothing else.

"I want to go home at once."

III

It surprised Anne that the house was still there. She stared over her shoulder as she kissed the old nurse, trying to see into her rooms that seemed hollow with dark, and colder than the October night. She worked till past midnight, setting her own room exactly, dragging out of her boxes colour that would cover the disorder, sleeping under a leopard-skin and a polish shawl.

Next day they all worked at the house while the telephone bell rang, and their friends found out they were back, until they realised it themselves. Anne found two letters from a lawyer on her writing-table. They frightened her. They said the garden was full of weeds. Which it was. They said that there had been noises at night. Which no one tried to deny. They said that to sub-let to an unknown number of people made a break in the lease. Which it did.

But Julian said: "This is a new landlord asserting himself. What he minds is that the house is let so cheap. Order a gardener at once. Tell him to take out the dandelions and put in geraniums. I don't care if geraniums will grow now or not. You must do that, Anne. Send these letters to your lawyers. Tell them you are allowed to sub-let, which you are, though you interpreted it freely. Say that your tenants were the children of bishops, and that there will be no more noise. Don't pay the rent. I tell you, it will be quite all right."

Anne left off polishing the surfaces of the house, the glass, the brass, the wood, and did what he told her. But she was full of fear and pain, and the realisation that something had been spoiled. Never before had she loved the house so much as now that its unity had gone, destroyed by Taff and Christina, not deliberately, but naturally. Her innocence was to suffer, and Charmian's and Julian's. But Charmian must have known.

She went to see her lawyer.

"He told me that I had done everything wrong, and that the landlord has a case. But I think he means that there is something which hasn't been said yet. I am going to see the landlord."

"Would you like me to see him?" said Julian.

"No. I have told him to come here. A woman had better see a man."

Pippa came at once. She said:

"Since the last row, when Arnold's friend got into the servant's room, I thought it was all right. There were a few parties, but they were downstairs and indoors. I don't think we ever saw each other. Not once in three days. I used to play with the children now and then, but even that stopped. Yes, I hung out chemises on the balcony railings to dry. I'm sorry about that. I saw an old man walking about the garden. I ran down the steps to him, and he said: 'I have bought the house,' and he looked at me and went away."

"Had you much on?"

"Everything, Anne, except my shoes and stockings."

"No one," said Julian, "is going to law about Pippa's bare feet."

"Who cares about the law?" said Anne, "when the house itself is broken up."

Anne went upstairs to see Charmian and Chloe, and found Taff there. He sprang up. She did not like to look at him, because she thought that it would be difficult for him to look at her. She gave Charmian back two books, borrowed another, and said:

"What did you tell the landlord, Mr. Guest?"

He began to talk at a pace, to a tune that made her feel that it did not matter, and she was not there. It did not matter because he would never, unless it went with his plan, tell the truth. He always had a plan, and the plan did not matter because it had nothing to do with the truth. He said that he had never seen the landlord, it was his wife who had seen the landlord, and that she was in the country, and that Charmian must write to her, and she would tell them about it. This was the truth, and the truth did not matter. Anne left them.

An hour later, the new landlord called on her.

"Mr. and Mrs. Guest—" he said.

"Of whom are you speaking?—Of Miss Trelawney's married sister and her husband?—yes."

"People in their position—"

"In their position—?"

"Have been very seriously offended—"

"And by what?"

"By the conduct of other tenants who have lived here."

"What did the other tenants do?"

He looked out into the garden, where an old man was setting geraniums in a plump bed of dark soil.

"I had several conversations with Mrs. Guest—She has returned, I understand, to her country estate."

"She is out of town."

"She was naturally very much surprised—and that the neighbour-hood should complain—"

"Of what did the neighbourhood complain?"

"Of noise, and of articles of dress hung out on the balcony to dry—"

"The clothes of Mrs. Guest's children—"

"Colonel Hicks, who lives next door, did not mention any children's clothes. There was a young woman, commonly referred to as Pippa—"

"Miss Arundel. Go on."

"And a young man, Mr. Copley—"

"Arnold," she said, to be sure that he was meant.

"—entertained their friends in a suspicious manner."

"Tell me what they did."

"Mrs. Guest had doubts of their relations."

'Ho!' thought Anne. 'More fool she.'

"Their friends came here at night to sing and drink. The piano was played at all hours. They even found their way into the upstairs bedrooms. It was impossible to foresee what strange young man or woman would be found in the bathroom, in the morning—"

"It was agreed upon that the bathroom should be shared."

"This Miss Arundel was seen in the bathroom with a man. She was seen by Mrs. Guest's nurse—"

"I do not think that the relations of landlord and tenant are affected by Mrs. Guest's nurse."

"Mrs. Ker, you must know what it is I wish to say."

"Say it, then."

"I can only remind you of the number of persons who were known to have slept in the long room downstairs. From that it seems plain to me that, for some months, this has been little better than a disorderly house."

"You mean a brothel?" An image of Christina as Bawd created itself in Anne's mind. Brothel. Arnold. That splendid child. "I think Mr. Guest is upstairs. He had better come down."

"I have not, up to now, become acquainted with Mr. Guest. You must understand that I am reluctant to offend them—"

(Can I say that Christina is a *divorcée*, trying to get up in the world again? Oh, my soul, how mean you are. Besides, that is the kind of lie that is found out. I must try dignity, whitewash, and truth. But what am I to say?) She heard herself saying: "Miss Arundel is young. Mr.

Copley is an actor. Mrs. Guest is quite unknown to us. Young girls who are dancers do not understand that women like Mrs. Guest are specialists in impropriety." Julian came in. She heard him say to the landlord: "I'm sorry there have been difficulties, and that a lot of nonsense has been talked; but you realise that we have our lease and are now in possession. There is no need to discuss Mrs. Guest's misapprehensions."

"But," said the landlord, "I saw Miss Arundel run up the road in her nightdress to see a fire myself."

"I expect it was her practise dress. Anyhow, Mrs. Guest should have complained to us. From her point of view, it was our house—" She was surprised that the landlord had no more to say to Julian, and that when Julian saw him to the door, they left the house together. She went down into the kitchen, where the old nurse was ironing, and sat on the corner of the table and watched her. The nurse's cat rubbed her ankles.

"Glad to see us, Nurse?"

"Yes, dearie. Now you're back I don't want for anything." Anne kissed her. The warm smell of ironing was like peace, it was peace to be scolded a little for cigarette-ends left on the dresser, to bring frocks to be pressed before parties, to have rings found left about the house; all the things old nurses do.

"Tell me, did the cook next door tell you anything about what happened last summer?"

"Well, dearie, she said that there were rare larks going on, high old times, as you might say; and that Miss Pippa was a little love with her boys and her bare legs, and Mr. Arnold behaved quite like a gentleman when her cat had kittens in his portmanteau."

"You know that Taff and Christina tried to get us turned out?" The old nurse said nothing. Anne said: "I hate them."

"Well, precious, I know whom I like."

"Why did they try and hurt us? Hullo! there's Julian."

The night was wet. Julian shook the drops off his hair like a dog.

"Why did you take the landlord out?"

"To give him a drink and find out what it's all about; and I have. Taff and Christina were trying to buy the house off him. Between them they might have turned us out, and kept Charmian and Chloe. That, I suppose, was why it was worth while to suggest that Pippa was a harlot." Anne stared. The old nurse went on ironing....

The next night Arnold came to dine with Charmian, but after

dinner he came down to Anne's room, and Julian gave him a drink.

"This room is the same," he said. "It was my room when I was here. I had Taff Guest above me. I used to fancy he sat with his ear to the window to hear if I was talking to Pippa or not. He is still here; that was why I came down."

"Why should he?" said Julian.

"To tell Charmian who his friends were," said Anne.

"Have another drink," said Julian.

"I was asked here tonight to hear a letter," Arnold said. "After I'd heard it, I should have come away anyhow."

"Do you remember it?"

"It was written to be remembered. It was from Charmian's sister."

"Say it."

Arnold repeated: "'Of course one is not intolerant. But the children's maid made me understand what common women think of a type like Pippa. Especially one like ours who has worked in a rescue-home. She asked me if I thought it was safe to use the bath after her. Of course, I explained that it was not quite like that, but she recognised the type.'"

"Stop!" shouted Anne.

"Go on," said Julian. Arnold went on:

"'As for that unfortunate child, Pippa, when I think of what her life must be in ten years, I can only hope that she will suddenly fall down dead.' And Charmian said to me: 'It's a point of view, Arnold. So many people think like that.' So I came down here."

. . . . .

Julian shaved in the bathroom and talked to the old nurse. Anne came restlessly upstairs to join them.

"See what I've found," said the old nurse. "It isn't often they leave anything behind them. It's a bottle of something that'll come in handy for the dustbin. Mr. Taff's written something on it, too." Julian took it from her and read: "*You may find this useful.*"

"Why?" said Anne.

"I think," said Julian, "it's the disinfectant for Pippa's bath. Yes, it must be that. The last word's with them. Don't tremble so, Anne. Remember, if you play any game, you must play it thoroughly and well. Even games likes that—and not shy at details. Try and think of it like that, my dear; try and think of it like that."

"She said," said Anne, "she said: *'Mine are only babies.'*"

Honey, Get Your Gun

PERFECTLY SOBER, exquisitely clean, very young, and somehow not quite respectable, the young man looked round the place where he spent most of his evenings. Not a bad place, small enough, smart enough, rowdy enough; and if there wasn't much room to dance, there were people to watch. He liked watching, to observe all that was going on but without analysis. Reflection exasperated him, even words; because they would be a delight if you could be sure exactly what they meant. And people used them to dope you, and then made them bleed you to death.

He stuck out his little chin, very much *le beau gosse*, caught the eye of two girls, and sucked his drink softly up a straw. He knew all about them and about everyone in the place. Some day he thought he would tell them exactly what he thought of them. As a matter of fact, he had already given them extracts. Perhaps that was why he wasn't so popular now, now that his money was gone, and he too sick to earn more, and his temper like a devil who is sorry for itself. But *they* hadn't got tireder and tireder, till, one day when he had cut himself shaving, the blood hadn't come, only stuff like water. Very useful that had been, with a shaking hand, and a result of the war, and the cure had been worse than the disease, and he was getting all right now, but somehow different.

He got up and asked the girl, in the most charming way imaginable, if she would dance with him. Thinking about her all the time disagreeably, coldly undressing her. His thoughts were his own, but his small, disciplined movements were his protest—against every American he had ever known, against being an American himself, against all their standards, and the existence of the place. He had made other protests, so many that, in detail, they had ceased to be protests and become natural. Not a bad bit of work, he flattered himself, and it went down. The girl, and not because she thought he had money, had her eye on him all right. She did not dance well, but he made her, the sharp foot turns marking the professional. When it was over he ignored a certain appeal in her eye, put her away and went back to his table.

The worst perhaps of the heroic exercise of dragging yourself up by your roots is that, once it is done, you have nothing else to do. It was really the young man's luck that, so far from becoming a pale European from nowhere, he had done nothing that was not physical but accentuate his temperament. And there is another thing about being born "over there," that you know good jazz from bad. The place had only a piano, and a handsome half negro for the cymbals and drums; but the music was good, good like the plain gold walls and glass panels, the lines of scarlet, the notable clients, the clothes of half the women, and the food.

The tunes affected him, who disliked all the arts; because art was "camp," and the people who did them couldn't do them, and when they were done they told lies. You can get in a great deal of dislike that way; but he was inclined to make a slight allowance for tunes. Jazz was not art, whatever his french friends liked to say. (He took no notice of Americans, they would not know.) And some tunes were exciting, like going to bed with a pleasing girl, and he judged them as he did his women, for the most unsentimentally, or else with a fury of sentiment. He did not excuse himself where that happened, he raved and wept. People could take his tears or leave them. Now they generally left them. Once they had not left them, and he had absorbed the sympathy and forgotten it. Now people did not care. A lot he cared for that. He knew the world now. It was a filthy place, and it is good business to have learned that, and telling off the filth an occupation. He had his own vices and virtues also pat. He was sentimental and jealous and mad about women; and if he heard any more about their damned american morality, or their vices, well, he knew what vice was. Something to make them sit up. He smiled, a little tight smile, remembering what he had done, and turned his flushed cheek as if away from himself. How many girls he had had, and which and how. And he knew this too about himself, that he worked in two streaks, the young man about Paris, the young man from Massachusetts, and that the two fighting it out found him a bewildered battle-ground. All the same, vice was his *métier*. Vicious to have such a *métier*?—(vicious to have it *as* a *métier*, a woman had told him, who had wanted him and he had not wanted her). That might be that, but it suited him.

He was quite alone. Except for one or two women who had not been his mistresses, lonely as anyone young and delicately attractive could be. He did not mind it much, because he understood perfectly the sensual production of himself. Perfectly up to a point. He screwed his little mouth up even tighter at a memory. Not perfectly enough to have kept Renée. Well, he had made a fool of himself and lost her, not by his infidelities, but by an indiscreet loyalty. Life had shown him that also the knowledge "shaken from the wrath-bearing tree," that virtue, may be the producer of disaster. Only very large natures can understand this and use it; but the boy was one of those who grow a flint armour and sometimes cry through the stone.

Then he began to recollect with pleasure one or two things he had said at dinner, when he had pointed out to Clara that she had got her movie job by sleeping with her director, and offered her a few hints how to keep him. He looked round. There she was, over in the corner, getting drunk as usual and glaring at him. Common slut, but he hated to see women drink like that. It ruined them slower than it did the men, but it did it. The little grey heart under the gilt head hurt him a moment then. Ruin, he was ruined himself. If you like to call it ruin. He didn't, because he could steer his boat in sewage and fancied that sort of sailing, and had no illusions. And hard drinking disgusted him, and getting into debt. Only he was alone, partly because of four walls which came in and stood round him. When he told them to go away, they joined corners and held him inside them. They made a dirty grey small room, lit from the top with a grey light very high up. Filthy because he had been left alone inside them for over a month. He was thinking of that bit of his actual imprisonment again. Then he half got up to look at himself in a mirror, to be sure now that he was now not only perfectly clean, but exquisite in every detail. Reassured, he stared round the room, indefinitely expanded with mirrors; but he knew that the other walls came back in sleep, the place where he had been put for innocence and childishness and hero-worship of a young swine who had betrayed him.

> Honey, get your gun,
>   get your gun,
>   get your gun.

It was late. The little Paris cabaret had settled itself into a large family party. The band was amusing itself. Any old tune would do. He thought that getting his gun had had a peculiar end for him. "Over there" was over here now, and for good, away from the country of his birth, where he had been insulted and tortured and left for dead. Like a cinema flashback, he began to live again his imprisonment.

He had been chained between a tough and a negro. The negro had murdered a child whom he had violated. When they had got back to New York Harbour, both the men had jumped into the water and had swum away; but he remembered them, chained to each side of him, as the ship rolled. At his court martial he had refused to speak. There is a great pride in saying nothing when you have a great deal to say. He was not quite grown-up, and the sentence they gave him would have lasted until he was old. When he had given himself up in Paris they had sent him to a guard room, where the men had beaten him up. When he had got back to America they had locked him up, and made that part of the memory which was four walls coming in and out of his sleep and his bad living moments. Then they had sent him out to work in the yards, work shifting coal that skinned his hands; and for all that he had been an athlete, tired him with extraordinary fatigue. It had been shame; first fear and hope, then shame that parched him. That had dried him up, once and for good. And it had happened because his friend Peter had said that now that the war was over, they could overstay their leave. He had been over a long time and had had no leave. They had gone off together, and there had been Paris, crazy with joy, to play with. His friend, who knew the high command, had said it would be all right. Then one day Peter had gone, and he had not known what to do. They had had some sort of a quarrel, and pride is a good gesture after that. He had reported himself to the military police, and had been tried and condemned to begin life again for ten years as a navvy in the yards.

He had written to Peter—that had been the hope several times. He knew where Peter was, and that he was quite all right. His mother did not know where he was, only that he had been posted as a deserter, and he had not expected that Peter would have left it at that. Then one night he had gone to bed particularly tired, and in the morning he found that he was paralysed, he and six others. They all died in hospital, or went blind ; but he got well, because when your body winds itself up again, it winds itself up. They sent him back to prison

373 * The Complete Stories of Mary Butts

and it began again. By this time his people knew where he was, and they put him in a cell with naked madmen for his sister to see. His father was dying and his mother left him to go to Washington and get her son back. It had been all right there. The President had listened to her, honourably discharged him from the service, and afterwards there had been medals. But he had not known how to cross the street when, sometime after and reluctantly, the prison governor had let him go. And when he had got home, his mother had held him and cried over him, but had not been able to help him much because she had suffered so much herself. Also, there is nothing but qualities in you for which you are not responsible to fit you for an occasion like that.

So he had become what he was, sensual and bitter, old and still a child.

Honey, get your gun. Honey is sweetness like gold. For him there was no sweetness. Like poetry it was invention, and like love as he had looked for it and found it; screaming for it like a child, getting it with his charm, spoiling it as a child does its toy, breaking it, burning it, burying it, leaving it in the rain. He did all that, and regretted it; but cynically, not like a child. And like a child comforted because there would always be something fresh to play with. And if the playthings were not amenable, he'd scream. He used to do that, up to suicide point, with the sense left not quite to bring it off, and not sense enough not to pity himself.

Still, he half admitted that somewhere there was pure sweetness, like the *Chant Hindou* out of Russia they were playing now as a waltz. Running sweetness poured like scent out of a jar. (The critical mind thinks of bad illustrations of the *Arabian Nights*, but he did not.) He felt before he thought, and his feeling was a kind of thinking, that ached always before memory and even before desire.

Only the body and the imagination can be exactly aware of each other. The rest is the critical business. If the boy was curled up at one end of Jacob's ladder, usually sound asleep, he had no place anywhere else; and perhaps all that was wrong with him was that he thought his occasional waking was the dream. As all that was right was the art and the laugh and bright, sensual, stare he used to get from out of his world.

He thought that it was time he had another affair, but never again except with a woman who wasn't more or less of the streets. So that the imagination of love could be kept to himself. Anyhow the Sadko waltz held all his imagination, and there were women outside to realise it physically, and take the chance.

He had another look at Clara, the girl he had told off for sleeping with her director. She was getting pretty drunk. She would come to a bad end. He knew that, principally because she would not take the advice he had given her how to keep the man and improve the job. Oh no. The common, silly bit she was. A Frenchwoman would have made a better job of it. She was telling her two boys exactly how fine she was and how awful he was. They were enjoying it; but they had had some drink, and presently there would be a row. A row over the sweet tune like water running, loud but not deep, through a place where he would like to be. The late night was drawing his mind back again into what had happened to him; quietly this time, not with the thunder-bang of "Over There." He remembered the summer before, down in the Pyrenees. There had been a dancing place built out over the sea, and the Atlantic had run up under its piers and run back, hushing the bright crowd the stars shook over. Over the sea-wash the Sadko tune had poured, a kind of middle-note between the sea and the sky. He had sat at the bar, watching three tall persons enjoying themselves. Part of a part of the english crowd that follows the sun. He had seen them about in Paris, and heard of them all over the place. Over life-size all three; and he envied their light ease, so different from his bitter ease. They were drinking with the commonest of his people, anyhow. That had made him angry. But how they got away with it…indifferently playing because they thought the earth belonged to them. How much of the earth did? Precious little now he guessed, and precious little they seemed to care. Uncritical as lambs or lions, they were an accusing pleasure to him. Also a kind of pride, because he had always known that, if what had happened to him had not happened, he would have been with them. He remembered how he had watched them, observing their difference from the other people, and that their assurance implied a kind of magnanimity. Then he had felt pain because he knew that magnanimity was denied him because of what had happened to him.

But this was too much like thinking. He let the memory of them make pictures for him again. Tall as trees or the figures one sees in sleep, two men and a woman. They were all three filed down to points, like delicate, exact instruments. Or even sharp pencils. No bluntness anywhere of body, or extra fold of flesh. One man was like a black and white eel, the other dark gold, grinning all the time, saying what he thought of the people as though he was invisible and the earth belonged to him, but he not one of the creatures of earth. If he had been bright green all over and worn a fairy cap, he would have looked exactly right. They were talking in the Casino about baccarat and bullfights and bridge, growing taller all the time, and the tide was turning, the noise of the sea growing louder, and the band playing against it, the waltz and the tide pouring across one another, over and under the other. And it seemed to him that only they would be aware of it, and, being aware, not afraid of it; that they belonged to music and the sea. At any rate, they had moved him in a way that was too like torture. He had pulled himself together, placed his hat low over his eyes, and left the place.

On the promenade he had found a girl and left her. Returning, he had met them again, going home, he supposed, and, curious to see where they were staying, had kept near to them. The night had not diminished their height, as they walked along the wall, below which a white line of torn water rolled about, whose noise now was all the noise there was.

The sea was changing its place, a longer pause between the beats and a louder crash. He was alone with them in the world, in a group of three and one. He remembered beginning to be sorry for himself and wondering if he went up to them they would take him for a child and talk to him. He had decided that they would think he was drunk, when it was much more likely that they were; and had trusted to the night to hide him as he sat quite close to them on the wall. They were looking out to sea. He heard one of the men say: "Sing us something, Cynthia, before we get back."

"What sort of a song?" she'd said: "'She was poor, but she was honest'. Will that do?" The gold man had kicked the wall and yawned. She had said: "I'll sing about God if you like."

He remembered his surprise, and his question whether the maddest English ever broke into hymns, when suddenly she was singing an air he could never remember, never forget.

"*Voi che sapete*," she began, "*che cosa è amor.*" His really good Italian had not followed hers, the cold, northern voice formalising the air. She stopped and the black and white man he had placed as her lover or even her husband, said : "Shocking accent she's got; but I like to hear her sing 'You who know what love is'. Because I suppose we do know what it is." Then they had begun to discuss their losses that night, which seemed to have been disproportionate to their fortunes.

They had gone home, and left him wondering what on earth that tune had to do with love, let alone God; and were they all three poor fish; and which would be the most surprising, that that song should have been a love song, or that those three were poor fish. He had never made up his mind, but after that he had cultivated the English with varying results. Always puzzled, sometimes irritated, sometimes pleased, because he was looking—not for the people of that night—but for something which would recreate that night with explanations. Explanations which would make his heart well again—(not that he was at all certain that he wanted any change of heart).

Then, by some trick of memory, some chord played by the pianist who was now fooling about, the air came back to him he had heard that night in the Pyrenees. Made a little deliberate by the drink he had taken, he went through it from beginning to end.

It had been sung as an alternative to "She was poor, but she was honest." "You who know what love is." A song about God and about love. Sung in the Basses Pyrénées, after the Sadko waltz, over the sea with the tide turning, the black water travelling in from "Over there." Sung by one to two, carelessly, their minds full of losses at cards. But what had their hearts been full of that accepted music and the night and everything? He didn't know, and could not find out. Meanwhile, there was Clara, preparing what he understood perfectly, a "send-up" for him. She was getting up to go with her boys. Very drunk, and they'd have to pass his table. That was all right. He was ready. He heard her cockney voice, pitched to be heard, whining across the tables:

"There's the snobby american boy who was rude to me, Steve." He waited for them, pinching in his smile. A moment later, she was saying to him: "Going about with the gentlemen these days aren't you, Innis? Preaching to poor girls. But I haven't slept with you, and I wouldn't." This was too easy.

"Haven't been asked, have you?" and see her flounce. She went on:

"Thinks I'm common English and I am proud of it. You'd like to know the grand kind, the sort that throw you a word as though you were throwing a bone to a dog?"

Answer: "Why be a bitch?" and watch her go, unsteady, complaining, making vague rude noises. Both her boys winked at him.

But he wondered how she had known even as much as that about him. He did not mind her knowing in the least. He ordered a coffee to temper the slight effect of the drink. It did not soothe him; he was thinking again. So that was a song about God and about love; and what was the use of thinking about a thing like that. It was silly, an idiot's lie. God was a person who objected to him, and all he was and did. And God does not exist. And that night's memories were too ambiguous. Those people—*You who know what love is.* Had they known? To answer "yes" would have been a surrender to faith. And it was his faith to have no faith. And because he had never lost his courage he told himself that he would keep faith with his faith.

He collected his hat and cane, and went out into the brilliant street, thought of a taxi, remembered his poverty, and started to walk home.

❖ ❖

In the House

So IT IS TO BE like that again: hunger, no, not exactly hunger, because when the brother one loves has gone away in cold anger, one
is not hungry. Rather sick at meal times, and thank God there is "tick"
at the *crèmerie*, and a drink of milk stops the pinched feeling inside and
can't cost much. Only, as my friend went on explaining, his coming
had made it easier, easier after those years of it. There had been enough
money in the house to buy a delicate fish, and a good bottle of wine,
and a new picture of birds. Feathers enough to stuff a cushion. Rings
of prawns in a glass dish, round a parsley-spray, a bunch of marigolds
on the bed-table; and one to sit, picked off to a head, on damp cotton-
wool on the Buddha's hand.

And not a cent owing anywhere; not a shop she hadn't liked to pass;
nor one where an earring was waiting, mended, that one could not
pay to get out.

He had given her the money for that; and only got paid in love.
God knew quite why he had gone away, and with the pain of his going left a thousand little pains, fluttering like Pandora's *kêrês* through
the rooms which had done their best to be made lovely for him. One
was called "ten francs," borrowed, from the very poor woman who sells
newspapers, to buy horrible yellow cigarettes, and a taxi on the day it
rained, when she had gone to see if the people who had taken a great
sum from her would pay back a little. They were out, and when they
came back they wouldn't; but the rain shuddered along the wet streets
and wind-arrows drove through them and there were no friends. There
was another *kêr* also, which might grow large like a lion and spring;
and a tooth gone from the front of her mouth which spoilt her smile,
only there had been nothing to smile about. But she would have found

it easier if he had knocked it out himself than taken away the promise to have it put back. She had had it put back, so there was a great debt of honour apart… Apart from the café, which still gave a packet or so of her own cigarettes on "tick" because she "had not had time to go to the Bank"; and the coalman for whom she had only been able to rake up a few centimes out of an old box for tip after he had carried that great weight upstairs.

Would they give her credit a little longer? She wanted me to tell her. Long enough for the day when he would come back and say he was awfully sorry, and bring a great curly chrysanthemum head, a goddess among flowers?

By the evening it was quite easy for both of us, sitting together, to raise the ghost of him doing that, when all the food that could be got was ready, not for the real brother but for the *frère, doulx amy*, who was very ill, and who dragged himself out of his cold hotel room to her door. Good thing that one couldn't eat much, so that it could be left for him whose only food it was. I saw her hang up his thin coat, and hide her face on his much thinner shoulder, and knew that while she did that the pains stopped fluttering and whispering. When he was gone she would re-tell what he said: "We fasted before together; sometimes we had feasts. Now we must fast again." But she didn't want to for him. Nor for the old servant who worked so hard because "Madame would pay when she could." A little anxious she was, being a woman; her little wages a thin, thin hair between starvation. And if my friend was starving a little, it was because his promises had made her so hungry. Without hope you are not hungry at all. He had said: "You shall never want for anything again." More precise than that he had made lovely promises of things one does not have to have: made them so near that she felt light, walking the streets among gold-whirling leaves under the heavy autumn sun.

Strange how ghostly her flat grew, as though it had a soul, pinched with her pinched face, wasting with her heart whose blood had been pressed out of it. On the evening of All Souls, we heard one of our dead say: "Is it well with the child?" And sighs and little whispers like clicks repeated; "It is not well." And it was as though he sighed, whom we had known each. He and another, maybe, one for each. And what does one know of the grief or of the anger of ghosts? Only the rain beads passed, stripping a little dirt from the brick wall opposite, and from our long glass panes. "*Low, faint, sweet sounds, like the farewell of ghosts.*" Only it was not a farewell: they did not leave us, but their love distilled through, too pure perhaps to be all absorbed by us; but not as the strengthless dead.

The house did not miss him, the brother who had left his sister; only its life wasted as our lives wasted; as the coal went, the last drop of scent, the bowl of figs, the flowers. Just as there were to be none of the things he had promised, nor the dress to make her splendid at night. For as there was not to be any of him anymore, so there was to be less of herself; less at once, because the spirit, unnourished by love, wastes swifter than the body. And fed, grows faster.

There had been so much for that love of his to do. Principally to make a ring; as near a ring to a magic ring as men wear in this world where…where the quick thrill of death-making is preferred to the slow opening of life. Death of other people, of course, one's own flesh, maybe, preferred; sought as a food for the hungry, separate souls, who have no part in the ballet of the world.

So were left with the *frère, doulx amy*, who turning saint, might easily lose his body. He who had left her might have fortified him also.

And so all the copains might have moved, for once, *en ronde.* We would have been satisfied with that, comforted for all that had happened before. When Achilles' set were no more dog eating dog.

And one would have been comforted for what had been lost; for one's ghosts of land and rent: of books and of the things to ride and wear and eat. Of friends and lovers: for the dead and the living. For all the dead.

Taken away from her too soon, the good company, the plans. What would have made her well. "Not to be alone any more." "Not to be afraid": reversed again too soon into solitude and the fear of diminishing things.

Paris. Autumn 1929

❖ ❖

Lettres Imaginaires

I

MY DEAR,
I have learned that I cannot speak to you any more as to my temporal lover. If I tried you would force me into sentiment, and special pleading. I might appeal to your pity. We have not known each other very long, but I am assured that with you such a demand would be a piece of ill-breeding.... There is an image of you in my breast, and an image of the world. But truth does not lie in these presentments.

Let us suppose then that you have a Pattern-laid-up-in-Heaven waiting to touch my elbow as I write.

"Sir, you and I have loved," but that's not it.

"Sir, you and I must—." I find it difficult to continue.

The business should be commonplace, but a bizarre streak seems to accompany my lapse into passion. It has been a freakish crucifixion— from a delicate approach, conventional as a harlequinade; for ten days we loved one another—as I thought with some quality of passion. You assumed my nature, I took on yours. The change of spiritual hats was no loss. No one knew. We were too sure to need confidants. There was no one to forbid. Our aptitude was perfect and our opportunity. Then one night we had arranged to meet, and you sent me a strange telegram. Two nights later you came in late to our little restaurant and said: "This won't do. I smell burning." Now I like fire. I looked at you and saw you were Wyndham Lewis's drawing of the starry sky, a cold Titan, a violent Intelligence. You were holding away from you a jewelled image which was myself. Then I knew that friend I might be, or mistress, but not lover. That dance was ended. Essentially you were "through" with me and resentful. But I do not love like that. I will not have this sensuality and this friendship. I march to a better tune. I will not listen while you play both air and accompaniment with your heavy alternate hands.

Dear, I was tired that night. Couldn't you have been gentle with me? It was not lust that I wanted then, or philosophy, only peace. I sat opposite to you, "tower of ivory, house of gold." Your eyes narrowed. Then, with some ingratitude, you damned me for the vitality which has sustained you. Gallic realism? perhaps—your Latin analysis stripped the beauty you had enjoyed. I matched my wits with yours, answered your questions, parried your threats, folded myself in my sex, offered you a delicate candour.... You were not pleased. Then I saw that it was not a game. Throughout your analytical protests there was a recurrent note. I understood that I was target for some sacred male encounter with its own might. Scorn for me was to reanimate your virtue—assure you of something you had lost. But then I could not make the analysis. Your sneers were too effective as you held my image from you. Your brilliant eyes swept past mine, you spoke with your hands. Then, with some irrelevance, you said there was nothing to make me unhappy. I was a cocotte who had attempted your seduction.

Sadism? Well, yes. Innate need for violence, vulgarly called love of a row? In part. But there is an x in the equation. Not since Valentine...

It is too soon for this to have happened to me again. It is making me cry and quiver. I remember how by your Sussex fire you laid my head on your hands, and crossed the hands I clasped lest my virtue should escape you. My rings had bitten into my hands. Your eyes were dark and profound, heavy with peace. I would not have had you change yet to this pursuit of a truth whose "chic" lies in its perversion.

All this in three weeks. You say: "She will get over it."

II

It was too soon, my dear, to be hurt again. That's my text for to-night. You should never have comforted me if you were going to submit me again to torture. All my life I have been accompanied by a ghostly pain. Lately it has become substantial, and I have recognised it in some absolute sense as cruelty. First there was Valentine, then you. You know how you found me—grey and sullen—wasted through too much knowledge. You knew what I had come to see.

There were your compassionate words, you've unsaid them. Can't you understand, you fool, that you've unsaid them?

. . . . .

Look here. You must not imagine that this is a complaint, a whining because a man has refused to love me. You are under no obligation to find immortality in my "white and gold and red." But I think that you should have made up your mind. Do you remember what you said—"If there is any goodwill that can help you through this business, remember that you have it." Within a month you faced me across Porfirio's table—my evil personified. What does it mean? You see I have the mind's curiosity to understand and incorporate. It sustains me, nearly all the time. You need not have loved me, though it would have been better that you should. But your voice is flaying me like the noise of a scythe on stone. Why should my vitality have moved this impulse in you? Through you it returned to me augmented. Did you hate it? Did you crave to diminish it yourself?

Love, dear love—how dare you speak to me of love?

III

You have said that you do not trust life, so why should you trust me who am, at best, one of the "naughty stars"? And I imagined that I was to be your reconciliation.

From such divergence where could we have found a meeting-place for love? If I, "the brother whom you have seen," could not enter your house, where will God come in? In my vanity I thought that where one went the other followed. Sir—you have undeceived me.

What did you call me?—"*dangereuse*," "false," "essentially outside truth." Has that last phrase any meaning? To me, it is plain tripe. I can only tell my part of this adventure. Louis—there have been times, often before some humiliation profound as this, when I have known myself for an artificer in a better way of love than men practise in the world. That does not "prove me base," but may prove me dangerous. Did I offer you too much freedom, too much passion? When I stripped myself of jealousy and possession, did I strip you of some armour you would not be without? You allow me words. I might talk with you on those matters till dawn. But love is not a conversation.

An adventure has been lost. We shall not be together again, and in love how can one have the adventure alone? You hardly admit the possibility. I said, "I could make it damned good." You answered: "Damned it might be."

Am I to go through all my life looking for the love whose pace equals mine? Is it always illusion that turns me here and there, saying that I have found him in my perpetual error?

The pilgrim rescued the lady in the dewy wood. There, without explanation, he left her to face the Blatant Beast.

IV

Last night when you had gone with your friends I sat down on the floor among the nutshells and cigarette-ends, and cried at the fire. I was alone in my house, and you had all gone home, "lover by lover." I was left, out of your thought, out of your dance. Not one of you but Leila had thought to say that it had been a good party. An empty wine bottle rolled across the floor and chinked against a siphon. It frightens me when inanimate things move about. It can be lonely here, past midnight, under the great shadows of this roof, not easy to leave the fire and mount the gallery stairs and slip into the icy bed. Before I decided to attempt it and take aspirin, I wondered if this fire which you have lit—and will not share—has an "absolute" value, a good-in-itself apart from you—and from me. Eventually one takes the way from one's kind.

This afternoon I went out in the rain and through the streets, not faint with desolation but in tranquility, with my love.

Pathological?

Later

I am waiting for you now. Will it be the same if you do not come? How can it be, when my eyes are starved, my quivering touch cannot fasten. I want our old ritual. I want to play it—to satiety. Don't you remember you would sit by the fire? We'd be alone. I would sit on the chair-arm behind you. You lay there, silent, relaxed, as life flowed from me to you. Did you know what I said as I kissed your neck—that I laid my peace on you—the peace you've not had? "My peace, not as the world giveth...." Your astonishment made me laugh. I slipped from the arm onto your knee, and crossed my feet, and swung there. I can see you laugh. I can see your quarrel with life remembered to be forgotten.

"Oh, my dear, you happened, but just in time, only just in time."

And I believed it. My eyes went hot because of the miracle. I used to watch the flush on your thin face, the sudden fusion....

You used to laugh. "Was there ever woman said such things before? Witty fool!" I would slip from your knees onto the floor and crouch there, looking up at you, silent.

Then it was your turn.

You are not coming tonight. I was mistaken. There is no adventure alone.

V

Half an hour later—a knock. External shapes, the walls, the coloured glass on the dark shelf, became like scenery, flat, two-dimensioned. Crossing from the fireplace to the door, I knew how my body bent as though the great chair had risen and clung to my back. You were not there, but a boy with onions. It happened again. I said: "It is not Louis—it is not."

It wasn't. I saw a girl with a suitcase and umbrella and several kinds of fur—a girl you have not met. She wanted a bed for the night. The sequence was amusing.

That evening we compared our beauties on the floor, by the fire on the white rug, burnished our nails and our hair. Our scents and orange-sticks lay between our feet—my long pink toes and her short ones.

She threw down her mirror. She must speak.

She had gathered—indeed she knew. I had given myself—and to more than one man. I was not married at all. I did not seem to mind. Did I know what I was doing? I was giving men what they wanted... I exacted nothing in return. Did I know the "awful degradation" that was overtaking me? No one could be more passionate than she—but never. Her fiancé would come back from the front and kill her. (There's a chance for Ivan.) She was proud to think that she would come to him. Just all of her— (Price sixpence. Please see that this seal is unbroken.) Incidentally, she considered me a blackleg in a pair of silk stockings....

She has left me to wonder, though—without passion—whether you, Louis, are despising me. (She does not know about you.)

You have called me pure. Do you still think that? Did you ever think it—with your mind? I don't care. If love of truth can make me pure, I'll pass. And so, what woman cares a pin about chastity? She tried to frighten me, damn her.

Then later I saw her puny man, and lunched afterwards with Bill, and drank with him, and comforted him in sexless amity; and then came to me, as there has always come, the answer to her fear.

VI

Well, my dear. We've had it out? I repeat if it had been another woman, lovelier, wittier than I—Dolores, Bill's wife, or some other *amoureuse*—you would be dead now, spitted on a dagger. Or the lady would have hung herself on your door-knocker, leaving you to explain. You are not grateful for my moderation. Yet you behaved rather well. You were skilful. I watched you manoeuvring to reduce our affair to the terms of the harlequinade. When you explained that you were not worthy of my least regard I grasped the setting and gave you your Columbine. What did it amount to? That I, who had brought you peace, had become the devourer of peace. There was no greed of which you might accuse me, but you made your case against a vitality which might destroy.

"It is my deepest opinion that a philosopher must avoid love. I cannot—though I have wished to—recognise your life of intuitions corrected by intelligence. It interferes with pure mentality." And then: "Dear, I have wanted to—I wish I were different. But I mean to draw back before I hurt you any more. It is intolerably disagreeable to see you suffer." Your eyes pleaded for my departure. I stood before your mirror, colouring my mouth. In that glass I saw your magical presentment. In it was mirrored the boy scientist, the 'Varsity philosopher, the emotional adolescent. Heaven's hound called herself off. I left Soho, and you, and the tragic-eyed woman I passed on the stairs. I was almost at peace, on the edge of contemplation. I did not cry when I reached home.

I am become a dawn-cat, pattering back with torn ears and fur. A month ago there seemed no beauty my body could not accomplish. Loved One, there is a great gulf outside formal time between our Sussex days and these.

"When the Lord turned again the Captivity of Sion."

Sion has gone back into her Captivity—"credit me," as Stephen Bird would say.

·   ·   ·   ·   ·

It's all right, Louis—you are not my lover. You are a boy, and have sharpened your senses on the scent of my skin and the colour of my hair.

As a lover you are nothing. But the truth of your presentment does not lie there. I've found it. This also is true. Herein lies your originality. Most minds in the world are cheap, sterile, insincere. They impart their stale flavour to the whole. But I have tasted your mind's fruitfulness and passion like salt and fine bread. There is your way, your truth, and your life. And I have lived with you.

VII

Today we met—almost as strangers. We both wished to resolve our affair into formal acquaintance. We finished a bottle of Burgundy. Old Porfirio, who had watched this and other of our affairs, was pleased to see us. He had noticed that M'sieu came no longer with the tall Mademoiselle. There is a gentleman tucked away behind that round stomach. Do you realise that he is not licensed to sell liqueurs?

We walked down Drury Lane greasy with banana-skins, and you held my arms and spoke of Anne, that "wafer made out of the blood of Christ." I could not point out the ritual error while you were telling me of her trust, explaining that her confidence appalled while it elated you.

O sacred *naïveté*! Has it never occurred to you that I have behaved to you in exactly the same way?

That's as may be. I could have sneered, till I looked up and saw your face. You might have been a flame enclosed in ivory. You were thinking?

To you: Endymion, is it all one moon who in the innumerable phases of women turns to kiss you? Adolescent, sensualist—are all women alike to you in the dark?

We walked under the portico of Drury Lane.

Khovanshchina—I do not understand the full implication of that music, except that it united us for a moment, to separate us, I think, forever.

When we came out the Great Bear trailed over Covent Garden, and the empty pavement rang, and the stars leapt in the bitter sky. The music had ravished and troubled me, but your cold elation gave me the fear of an animal that knows it is to be beaten. "It's all there," you said, "in the last Act. The negation of your passion—your pleasure, and your despair. There is the end of being, voluntarily to become nothing, to evade—courteously—your angel of the adventure. Withdrawal, stillness, immaculate contemplation—there is escape with victory. Isn't that better than your daring and your temperance?"

We came to your door, went upstairs without speaking. You did a strange thing. You came beside me, music in your eyes—and on your lips. Then, your eyes closed, you flung yourself down upon my breast, and clung there.

I held you, sitting upright, dazed. Then I heard Jim on the stairs. He came in and found us very quiet. I went home.

. . . . .

You're a brave man, Louis. I cannot accept final futility, Dostoevsky's bathhouse full of spiders, the ultimate rat in the ultimate trap. You are a great man. I "also have known a lot of men," but have not met one before of such intelligence.

You can put them away—things which feed you: Mozart and Tchekov and Plotinus, ballet and *décor*, your physics which only vaguely impress me, your economics with which I do not agree. You can put them away and bank on the ultimate bankruptcy of all cognition and passion. I love you, I adore your quality. I'm too proud to fight.

Varya.

VIII

How am I fallen from myself
For a long time now
I have not seen the Prince of Chang in my dreams.

Today I went out on the word of a lying map to look for hut circles and kist-vaens in the mist. I believed also that there would be ghosts on the moor. I found those I had brought with me, awaiting me there. The mist filtered down and covered the world. I wandered over those soggy uplands, and listened to the silence made audible by running water and the odd settling noises of the bog.

It was not the stone age that pressed round me, but my metropolitan ghosts. I found them translated in that iron land whose focus is a prison and a house of torture. The images that haunt me—the horror in Valentine, the shadow of the war, the starvation of the human spirit,

the thwarting of creation, the power whose symbol we call cruelty—
rose out of the moor, ghastly familiar. When the sun strikes it after rain
it is the colour of raw flesh. Find me the greatest common measure of
these things.

IX

You asked me once: "What can I give you that other men cannot?
My intelligence—perhaps—but not my person, or my wealth—I am
hardly a sexual athlete." And then the demure smile, and the stroke of
the moustache. Dear fool. Am I to accuse you of idealising me? Don't
you know that there is a sensuality in me no one has ever satisfied? I'm
tired of echoing Aspasia and Egeria, but with you I've been romp and
amoureuse, shared the "ardours demi-virginal" of the Kirchner Girl.

We've had the profundity of infinite lightness. With you I've danced
my solo in that equivocal ballet of the world.

X

Prince of Chang—I think of your pale face and high cheek-bones,
your narrow brilliant eyes, and you seem to me remote as that Prince.
You might be an enamelled lord, and I once an embroidered lady, two
pieces of *décor* in an age and city remote as Atlantis.

I have now been a week on these moors.

> *Great London where the sights are*
> *And the lights are*
> *And the nights are.*

The memory of our affair is not dead, but it has become a magical
objet d'art like some awful tale of India or Japan where the raw blood
beats through porcelain and cloisonné and jade. What has Ivan made
of this? Nothing. I haven't told him. I'm learning to offer myself in
instalments. Besides, it won't make a tale yet, and to cry the raw pain
aloud would not be fair. It is not his dance or his crucifixion. It is
hardly his business. But I cannot give him what I would. I've been too
starved. There are better ways. All the time the moor watches me and
the granite hills. The cold streams hiss between the boulders, the mist
is soft as thistledown and cold as death.

There are better ways than this acceptance of mutilation. We are creatures of time, Ivan and I. Years have knit us, of love and adventure. He is my temporal stability. But we three together? The moor is destroying me. Here nature and the Beast—Sologub's Beast—are one. The moor is a repetition of the war. The town is a microcosm of the moor, stripped of its grotesque beauty. I am a tiny seed in such a mill. There are better ways. When he and I first sat by the fire, I remembered you, Prince of Chang. There is a *pas de trois* in love, two cannot dance…. Another way of saying that I don't see why I should not have you both. The result of the frustration is that I am bored. I sit here, sucking smoke up a tortoiseshell tube. The taste of you burns my memory—like the vile cigarettes of this abominable place.

XI

Dear Brutus,

I am in town again—with more humour than when I left it. At least I watch the completion of our cycle without further illusion. It is like this. Since Sion has gone back into her Captivity, she will drink freely of the waters of Bablyon. My dear—you don't know—women who can stand this can stand anything. I do not know what absolute value it may have, but I remember the night when the thread was cut that tied me to temporal needs. I have lived in a world become translucent. But I cannot gauge the quality of the illumination beyond. My feet have been lighter on the streets than on the day you said that you loved me. Then I strode through them, part of the combers of the wind and the hurrying stars. My bird had left the bush and dropped into my hands. Now there is neither bush nor bird but a stillness like sea-fog. I am relaxed, passive. Then I remember. "For God's sake don't stop loving me. I have everything to learn. Make my world new." And then: "You have come in time, only just in time—" and the tears force themselves out of my eyes, separate as stones, and each a microcosm of my disappointment. But the worst you've done is not these. All that I might have written, all that I might have perceived, the adventure I saw and have not accomplished—these I can present you. You begot them. You aborted them. Now I am barren. That's the worst you've done.

. . . . .

"*Complaints are many and various,*
And my feet are cold," said Aquarius.

There is your side to this tale, and I, perhaps, be none than a green-sick girl.

Last night in your rooms, I could not but laugh. You were so glad to think that you had steered your canoe safe back to interested acquaintance once more. Dear Brutus, there was nothing to forgive.

VARYA.

XII

Faint white world,
I stand at my door.

There is snow on every plane of the street and over them a mist, an ice-gauze. There is nothing more. I can live without you and without any man. Yes—"Be sorry for your childishness," and dance again and run about the world. Nothing more. Not for you. The air is an unshaken silver net. It hangs in suspense outside of time. So with me.

Remember the last act of *Khovanshchina*. I do not know whether I am alive or dead, but that there is another state through the antithesis of life and death. There is a cloister for passion. You by denying, I by acceptance, have come to the same place. But there are no final vows. O Tranquility. There are no more grey-walled houses set to watch us or conceal, or scarlet 'buses grinding up the Tottenham Court Road. There are only masses and spears of light, coloured, interchangeable. All things are dissolved into their elements, all things dance.

Athis....

✧ ✧

Uncollected Stories

A Vision
Magic
Change
A Magical Experiment
The Master's Last Dancing
Fumerie
Untitled

❖ ❖

A Vision

A TORRENT OF SILK poured between overhanging breasts and
spread upon the carpet in a troubled sea.

Vast skirts stood out over the surf, vertical lunar cliffs at the point of
collapse. The core of flesh beneath moved like a troubled worm, and
above the unsubstantial walls eyes watched a gilt hoop hung from a
pole, the late circumference of a dead macaw. The wire was worn pale
where the horny feet had gripped and shaken. To the eyes, meditation
his similitude locked there, till the fantastic banners of crest and tail
contracted into a mouse—like image of enamelled solidity—a chinoiserie of the imagination—suspended by tiny feet under the outer rim.
A tail like a bronze whip followed the line of the circumference.

Dickory, dickory, dock.

The eyes followed the ascent.

It climbed the golden rim, and crept over the farther side at even
pace—a tiny demon on the noble disk of the sun.

"In whom is no variableness, neither shadow, of turning." The weak
eyes gleamed, and at the sigh of pleasure the light cliffs were shattered
and reshapen.

The mouse-image stooped and shook, then whirled about the rim.
From the fury of its revolution there showed only a halo of shaken
light about the hoop.

The eyes blinked and accepted.

The mouse ran out of the dancing air and hung upside down under
the rim.

They stared.

It began another turn, infinitely slow, and another whereon it appeared immovable. Time in the fantastic room moved like the strokes of a gong.

"Get on with it!" The squeal was swallowed in the infinite silence proceeding from the mouse.

It rose, passed, and returned. It leapt and accomplished the circle, a returning ship with cloven time pouring from its bows. It leapt again and paused, checked by an observant star.

The rim glittered and was not shaken.

"It is the soul upon its journey to perfection." With shameless levity the mouse ran down. Again shot up and the hoop trembled. It stopped, suspended by tiny feet. The brown tail followed the circumference. The mouse returned.

The image of that horror recommended its upward crawl *sub specie æternitatis*.

The torrent of coloured silk, the glittering cliffs crashed down. Upon the wriggling body the pendulous breasts touched the knees. The eyes strained up. The mouse climbed the zenith.

> "'In whom is no variableness,'" then wailing—"but it always comes
> back to the same place. What is the good if it always comes back to
> the same place? It can't mean that. Cruel, cruel, cruel."

The mouse that shall run from everlasting to everlasting attenuated in significance.

Projected on the opening panels of a screen an angel in Wattsian deshabille conducted a creeping soul up to the ascent of a mountain. At the telescopic distance on the receding folds a black speck circumscribed a black hoop.

The crashing silks swelled. The angel smiled and pointed up. The little soul pattering along behind sat back on its haunches. A fat white star featured slick on the screen, its spherical nature obscured by long theosophic points.

The eyes tranquilized into rapture. The star's circumference grew till it included its irradiation. It became a threepenny bit melting at the core. A thin bright hoop hung in the heavens. The angel disintegrated till it put forth the plumage of a macaw. The little soul went down on all fours and began to grow a tail and the bright bottom of a mandrill. The star's circumference grew and slid across the diagonal of the screen.

The eyes wept, and through the liquid veil they ceased to distinguish these things. The scarlet lids closed. A telephone bell jarred on the table. The clashing silks built up again the shell of the body's complaisance.

THE EGOIST, *September 1918*

Magic

O N THE WALL behind him and above his right ear a nail-head was
sunk in the plaster. When she had sat down and tranquillized
her perceptions she balanced her eyes on it to keep the tilt of her head.
The north light swam in, upon her cheeks, exposing the shiny down of
the lip, the hollow pores on each side of the nose. In front she saw his
shoulders cutting the light square, and his bent head black against the
light like an auk's egg tilted on the top of a rock.

For ten minutes she listened to his pencil inscribing its version of
her image. Ronsard m'a célébré aux temps que j'etais belle. It had been
a sufficient sentence. She would be what she was for another ten years,
and more than that when she died. In the moment's complacency her
eyelids fell, and the corners of her mouth crept up.

Painters are not concerned with youth or age. They are not finally
interested in your phenomena extended in time and space. They use
it to present appearance in reality. Reality swallows phenomena and
puffs them out in patterns discerned in the arrangement of antitheses.
A good painter is free of the pain of opposites. He leads out the arrangement in reality by hand or claw. He was examining her pattern.

A "rapture of the intellect" stirred her. Her eyes, shifted from the
nail-head, had drawn her chin along under them. She fixed them again.

Time ran on. The plaster round the nail-head blazed and swam.
She clung to the dark point. It put out rays. The shelf above it slid,
and the books became an arbitrary prism. She stepped out of her body.
Immediately in place of his leaning shoulders, a black rock appeared,
a granite bubble, and over it trembled the black star. She crossed the
threshold of the senses, knowing that with the least adjustment the star
and the black mountain would slide again into their terrestrial posi-

tions. In the senses or out they were there together, two creatures, at perception, their relation sustained by her eyes fixed till they swarted on a black star. Why should it be black? Because of a formula the hair rose shivering along her back.

A mountain has roots.

"That will do?"

The phrase followed her about the town. She had said first "Into the darkness at the roots of the mountains," curtseying about the beats. Then she considered its meaning and trimmed it into a respectable statement, training her ear out of its predecessor until each time she said "mountain" and "roots" it was like a harpoon launched from a masthead into a whale at the bottom of the sea.

The next day she walked along the cliffs to his house, shaping her image. She had remembered that when he looked into her it was with no ambiguity of perception. She must hurry where the pace could not be forced. Her eyes picked up the nail-head and held on.... This time she became a bird, wings out, flat against the rock, gauging its surface, its unimaginable volume, gripping a minute ridge with cold, clawed feet. Breast to breast with him. A feather breast was on wrinkled stone, and could not mix. Outside the senses she was repeating the external forms. *Into the darkness at the roots of the mountains.* Abominable sing-song. Jazz to it then. Follow him, cancel it out. A way of speaking that is good enough for the emotions is not good enough for the plainest writing. A great painter was at work on her. A mountain has roots. She became a bird again. The rock was heeling over onto her, it had put out arms. She would lie under it spatchcocked till she turned fossil. *Let him go.* Give it up. She passed out the contact with her wingtips and wheeled off on a fan of whistling air. There was the mountain and under it deep water, stirring, fingering its side, running down, stooping and as silently lifted up. Under that sea the mountain had its roots. When she turned back the sea would be resting on a cushion of conger eels? It seemed that it was ready to be exposed. A diving bird could not part it. The moon must be caught waxing and the extreme spring tides. In the night the water would be drawn back and in the morning she would see the thing it covered and agree for the water to cover it again.

She left him, expectant to the point of tranquility. The days passed.

The house where he worked was down sixteen stone steps, and at the end of a passage all of old stones oozing at the cracks. She walked down them and looked up before leaving the uncovered air and saw a flake of the moon left on the edge of the roof. She looked down and saw the roots of the house were the roots of the mountain uncovered by the moon. With the moon had risen storm, green sheets of water were poured in shaken out and flung back, uncovering what had been laid there from the foundation of the world. In a fury of wind the sea was ripped back and exposed a rock, long dark, of a precise smooth elegance, and a bird was swooping on it. The sun rolled over it. The sea covered it again.

"That's right, old mountain! You would have rolled me out if I had not had wings."

He came out to meet her. She followed him in briskly, and settled herself for a journey with her eyes on the nail. Under the form of a rock she had seen him naked, a pure-shape among the basis of the hills. In bird-shape she had freed herself of his contact. She could now entertain it or as easily leave. She did not know the rock's significance, but at the end of this observation would come knowledge, and out of knowledge power. He had explored her image. He had seen her before she had so much as arrived at their formula. If he reigned. She though late would reign also.

Mais pour regner il faut se taire.

Behind their signatures was the source of signatures, the life which is all life and no death, where he and his drawing moved, were mixed, and poured out.

There appeared the figure of a triangle, the base given in the world. From one known she was to complete this figure of divine geometry. She had seen a black star. Quod superius, sicut inferive est, and this morning it had remained obstinately a nail.

There is an abyss also. She must explore that and as readily as the starry sky. Et pour regner il faut se taire. Accepted also. *Let it go.*

❖ ❖

Change

WHEN I WOKE UP I thought I might do it, cross the belt of villas and the open wood, wade up the sandy lane, climb the hill to the common where we used to pick fir-cone mushrooms, and enter the dark wood that overhangs their house. It hangs on a cliff between the orchard and the home. From it we used to count the planes of the roof with pigeons walking about on them. Over the roofs we watched the harbour running.

I did not tell the old people. My washed-out cotton dress said "disinherited." They gave me a packet of biscuits I did not want, because the child was weight enough to carry.

I thought I might go round by the farm and up the drive, but I was afraid to meet them in the lanes. The drive up from the sea is very long. I should have been crushed under the avenue. The fields would not have hidden me. If one of them had come, I should have crawled into the ditch, or faced them with the embarrassment that would have degraded the three of us.

I walked up the common. There were mushrooms at the top, but few and slug-eaten and kicked. I walked confidently because it would have been easy to hide in the gorse-bushes run through with secret paths.

When I came to the edge where the wood dropped, it was as though I could have leaned over and touched the house. They had so cut the trees that one could look down into the windows. They were black and transparent. I did not see anyone go up or down the stairs. Outside the harbour was empty of ships. I sat with my back against a tree, my feet in an arbutus bush spread out across me. I could see the orchard and the flower garden, the box-edged paths converging on the six wells.

There was a new greenhouse and three men at work. The trees opened in an oval lunette onto the stables at the head of the drive. I heard the side door open. The trees hid a walking body till it came out onto the drive. It was my mother. The flesh on her face was made pink for the morning, her hair was yellow under her hat, her widow's veil hung down straight like a black pillar following her.

She went up to the stables, and stood in front of the white garage door. She did not peer through the grill. She was looking at shut doors. She began to walk up and down the red cobbles where the horses used to be washed, and turned and went to where the men were working, and told one of them what to do. She went from him to a man with red hair, and made him walk up and down the path with her, while she explained. He had a green baize apron and there were times when she took his advice.

She walked away into the rose garden, and stood by the well with the lead lions, picking at a dead tree.

My brother came out of the front door of the house. He looked up to see if the sky was clear. His cigarette was in a very long holder, the smoke was so far from his face. He turned about and about. Once he went back into the porch, once he made off down the drive to the sea. He tried to crack an almond stone from the tree on the terrace, and it shot away under his heel. At last he walked, following my mother very slowly up to the stables. He was not looking for her, but he knew where she was.

She heard him from a long way off. "Boy-oy, Boy-oy." He began to drag. He threw away his cigarette and lit another. I saw the flame a foot away from his face.

"Boy-oy. I'm here. Boy-oy." She came down to meet him, and drew his arm into hers, and led him up the garden. She pointed something out to him asking for his opinion. After a time he began to answer, and changed her arm into his. She put a rose in his coat, he stuck one in her hat.

They stood at the foot of the apple tree where were the graves of my animals. Some had gravestones. The others had been marked out in patterns with pebbles and marble chips. I could not see what had happened to them. They called up a man and gave orders for the tree to be cut down. My brother kicked over my pony's gravestone. They moved away and picked plums off a rich young tree. He asked her for something, and she shook her head. He asked again, and she spread out her hands. She was pouting. He asked a third time, and she shrugged her shoulders. They went down to the house. I heard my brother speaking on the telephone, and the bell ring off.

A servant I did not know crossed the yard, and tore bay leaves from the tree at the back door. There would be a sweet dish flavoured with bay leaves. A gardener came down with vegetables. I remembered our greengrocer, in London, up a side street where the fine fruit was shewn in cotton wool. This man had a huge cabbage for the knife to split like frozen butter.

Behind the stables there would be figs. I could not go down and pick. A workman would ask me who I was, and the child would show. I felt it move. I looked up and saw the harbour streaming out to sea. I crossed the gorse-field where I had lain with my husband and listened to the pods snicking. The gorse-field led into a meadow that belonged to a kind, cultivated woman who did not like my mother, but would have been afraid if she had met me. The grass in her field was heavy, cool and wet. I skirted the hedge that ran alongside our drive. Once I thought she was standing among her fowls looking at me. There was no one there, and I remembered that she was almost blind. When I put my hands down into the pockets of my coat, and let it fall straight and open, down my loose gown no one would have seen the child. My earrings swung. Then I heard footsteps coming down the drive. I thought my mother was walking out to the farm. I fell down under the hedge. The footsteps stopped. I never found out about them. I thought it would be bad for the child not to show courage, and I left the field and walked down the long drive to the sea.

I looked back every few yards, and each time the house sat higher on its hill, its lawns were greener, its trees had more shape. Though they had no car, they had spent a great deal of money on the terrace jars, and inside the house were the cool shining rooms, and dishes piled with fruit, and mirrors to reflect them. And they had got rid of me. It had given them some trouble, but they were rid of me, and I could never go back. There was no getting back. The boy found it dull, but he was ashamed of me. And I would never go back until she would help me, and he thought that if she did there would be less help for him. She had made him see that he could not do without the things with which she had corrupted him. And I wanted money for clothes and books, and not to be hurt when the child was born.

The gate was open. I unhooked it, and it swung across, as we had

been told not to do, my heavy shoes destroying the paint. I made a
face as I went out. The house was too far up for anyone to see it. I went
down to the shore. There were the round stones, the sea-pinks, and
the tough grass that was salt and scratched my nose, but with them I
could make free, and not with the roses in the shut garden. I walked
all round the marsh, and under the trees, and through the damp lane
past the farm. The sea-wind does not blow there. I grew tired. Round
the corner, by the cemetery where they buried my young aunt who
drowned herself because she could not bear her life. I met my brother.
His body was fatter, his face thinner. The pink and white candied face
had green moons under the eyes. His trousers shewed how wide his
hips were. His eyes glittered as he was thinking to himself. He said
"Oh! my sister" and tried not to look at my waist.

I kissed him and said "Darling, I'm not a high explosive." I couldn't
remember properly what had happened about the gravestones, but
that on our left Aunt Vera was dead and buried, and that they had not
been able to kill me.

He took my arm, and we went along together. He said:

"It is such fun to see you. I'm so bored. There is nothing to do here
and we have no money. You don't know how awful it is to have no
money… I suppose you are staying with the old people. I don't know
how you can stand it."

"They are very kind."

"I've known people be kind to you, and you've not been having
any."

"The old people are all right…"

"If it were not for the old hag, I could take you back to lunch. You
ought to try our peaches.…"

I was pleased to hear him call her that. (She would say, "Did you
meet anyone on your walk?" and he would answer "That damned sister
of mine." Did I mind that? No.)

He was like a ball with an open mouth in it. A ball made out of a
turnip head. I looked round at the coral lips, the high cheek bones.
We walked through the dust. He begged me not to go too fast. By the
quarries we sat down on a stone. I thought I was precious to him as he
had once been to me. He was sweating more than I.

"Does she know that I'm down here?"

"Yes, they told her."

Was he kind enough to be asked "Will Mother help us over the child." To know that, only to know that; to sink into the reassurance that opened like a bed bathed in light.

Then I knew with exactly what nervous pleasure he would tell me the truth. I was afraid. I could not speak to him about anything else. I could not speak to him at all.

He began to ask about people we had known in common. I giggled and told him scandal. I should have asked him for an overcoat and a pair of old shoes. I heard myself ask him, and laughing, and laughing and laughing, till the sun threw a hot curtain between me and the huge adolescent.

"Here," he said, "nothing happens, and nothing ever can till my guardians pay what they owe. You don't know what it means...."

"Who should know better than I?"

"O yes. I know that too, but Mother has not had an easy time. We're growing fruit now for the market, and all that I can do is see that the best of it feeds me. In the evening we hunt for slugs. We caught one yesterday six inches long and buried it in salt."

"I hate slugs.

"It kills them at once."

I had pushed up the dust with my toe, and thought of the slug bubbling underneath. He knew.

"Either the slug or the peach had to go under."

We got up and crossed the last field where the country ends. He said:

"You might remember me to the old people."

"I will."

"They're not bad sorts."

"They are very good to me."

"I suppose you know that it was all through Mother she got that appointment."

"Possibly. She is making a great success of it." I thought: You horrible little kept boy, leave Aunt Elizabeth alone.

I wanted to throw him down under the palings where the first villa began, and kneel on him, and dig into his throat, and score his face, and pinch him, and get away from him his watch, and links, and tie pin and shoes. They would do for my man.

My mind recited to me:

The more there is for you the less for him. Can you wonder?...

We were at the field's edge. He said gravely, "I don't know that you have so much the worst of it, Sis. It is awful here. Haven't we always known that there is something wicked about the house? I have to hang about there all day, and listen to the clocks striking."

"Go away and get something to do."

"My guardians won't let me."

"You have friends and books."

"A lot you'll find people want you when you have no money to spend on them."

"A nice set you know."

"They're not used to beggary."

"Thank God, mine are."

That was it. I was looking at the splintered sphere of that world that had given us birth. I saw its ruins turned brothel for him to live and solicit in. An eternal priest. Outside, I was working in the clay. In the woman is the race.

. . . . .

A yellow gravel road ran to the field's edge. There we kissed. I turned the corner of the hedge, so that I should not have to see him go, and craned over to watch the hesitant walk.

There was a packet of sweet, soft biscuits in my pocket. I sat down on the curb and munched and listened to the child twitching. Tomorrow I would go back. There would be stairs to climb. I wanted: Shoes, an ivory-knobbed stick, wine, and a single feather fan. A steak and peaches. A first-class ticket to Town. People to carry my burden and me.

And always there would be more stairs to climb... If it died, would it be their fault? *Oh, the ivory and the gold...*

A bird flew down, and off with one of the crumbs.

THE DIAL, *vol. 72, no. 5, 1922*
corrected from the author's later draft.

A Magical Experiment

SHE LEANED OVER the dark table, and swept the papers onto the floor. She had come in from the street where she had seen the square back of a taxi and its window. Thee was a face in it that screamed at her. As the taxi ran away, the mouth opened and shut till it looked like a black pin-head. This gesture had been made at her, and the circle which had contained her and the origin of the scream had contracted and gone out.

She remained with the painful noise in a huge room where the circle had shot its rubbish.

Already she was imagining a place *east of the sun, west of the moon* where the intolerable loss was made good. She also understood immediately that she could not even begin to think what the face would express when it agreed.

She stuck pennies on the table for the sun and moon, and pushed them about. She spun them between her palms. She shut her eyes and moved them when she was blind.

Sun and moon ran round the table. Other spheres cannoned and shot off. In the wooden mirror they repeated it. She looked for an abstraction of events and for the place where one thing that had happened met its opposite, and touched and spun off in huge ellipses, and cut each other's tracks, and travelled on and met again. She rested there in a sweet futility. There was a place *east of the sun, west of the moon.* If they spent their lives taking knots out of a piece of string, they would meet there.

Through the passages of the house the unstirred air whistled. The circumference lines tore out. The spheres ran into the stream of circumstance. The heavens moved, but she lay across the table, spinning pennies, making circles. Inside the circle were torn papers, and the rubbed out ends of cigarettes.

Three years before she had been out in a quiet street. There were square houses each one full of square windows, and a railing passed them. She dragged herself along the wet pavement observing. Her footmarks were shaped like fish.

A fog slid out of the low sky. It bulged and shook out specks. It lifted and came curling again. It drew up and hung a few feet over her, exhibiting the house and the rails. Round the corner there was a house with a round window, and beside it a conical tree.

The flog dipped up and down. She moved aside into a perception that was cold, interesting and oblique. Look at the most solid and intimate phenomenon, and there remain certain formal shapes. Go on looking, and the shapes will draw into one another, and become a block, exceedingly solid, that moves in. She saw a bundle of iron sticks closing. The most compact form could exhibit another unique form contained by it and exceedingly "ugly." There were people with the same property in the mind. He was one of them. Pleased she stood back on the curb, and drew the house out. It dissolved immediately into its number and its curtains. She looked away and stepped up to it. It went into itself and took a step towards her. She shook it off, and went away, noticing her cold passion with appreciation.

Among the houses there had been one with a round window framed in a scroll, and beside it an elegant tree. In the South there was a house with a round window in its garden wall. Through it the sea glittered. Below it, on one side was a dark wood full of sea-wind. The stones and turf rested night and day, and the sea and the air never. On the hills were circles for war and magic and sheep folds.

These things were not in his mind.

The image-bearing discs that filled her perception went out one by one. Under the edge of the black sky something angry was looking for her. When it came up it would have anger without brightness. It would also be absurd.

She waited, and heard it moving about under the earth-floor. She rose and began to move away backwards so that she could see it.

The sky lit up. A fiery ball slid down. She mounted it and crossed the sky. The sun appeared for a moment, and gave the illusion of morning, and went away into the sea. Another ball of glass with a wounded man in it drew alongside. She stepped in beside him, and they fell away together also into the sea.

A small, square, angry moon came out to look for them.

. . . . .

The wounded man with whom she had crossed the sky was with her.

She said "it is still nosing about under the earth-floor. When it comes up it is square and irritable. We shall have to get rid of it. Go and throw my ring into the sea." When he came back the wind slid in beside him. They listened to the sea thudding on its stones.

Finally a large grey omphalos, neither square, triangular, or round pushed its way up through the floor. It leaned to one side and another, it was like the broken end of a cigarette that swelled till it became like a slug. It was cold. They began immediately to quarrel with one another.

He reasoned with her. "He shewed you the house and railings in the brown fog, and that quintessential shape was not pretty. We have seen what has come out of the floor. And I know what I think."

And she answered:

"He cannot contradict me now. I am free to love him."

"Love him if it amuses you."

"Am I to have had no pleasure at all?"

"What is this pleasure when it is not sentiment?"

"He has a quintessential shape. *Every man and woman is a star.* I am watching the patch of sky where some night he will come out, a little awkward, but it will be quite all right."

"You are pottering about the sky looking for a place where you will have an excuse to go to bed with him again. I hear you whisper it in your sleep. I do not like to see you nurse a dead brat that is not your own."

"I shall nurse it till I find out what it means, if it were a dead brat, or if it were a slug."

"That is not all the truth."

"It is enough for me to go in with."

She went to his room at a time when he would not be there. She was pushing a letter under the door when the key fell out from a shelf under the fan-light. She unlocked the door. The air in the room was clear like a dark glass and quiet. On his bed was a gold rug where he had told her he had had several women. She lay down. The dust on it made her hand grey. He had pinned her photograph upside down on the wall. She sat up at his table and smoked. There was his razor full of scum and short hair. She cleaned it, and cut herself, and licked the blood off her thumb. She howled and laid her head on the square table immovable with books. She munched almonds from a bottle, and looked at an idol full of pits like eyes.

There was a saucer full of broken cigarette stumps. A brown choking smoke burst from one. He had pinned her photograph upside down. She blushed. Another stump she had not rubbed out began to smoke. She left the letter there. She would not see it again. She had completely misunderstood.

.   .   .   .   .

On his table the letter collected a gauze of dust. A long way off she said:

"I make circles.

He is inside a square.

No one has circled a square.

There are the formal shapes that move in, and those, because of him I saw.

There is the irregular and shifting shape from below. He evoked it. I cannot control it. It is like a slug. I think it can control him. Last summer we saw them everywhere; in the grass, in the wheel ruts, and on the tops of the hills.

There is my will.

Wheels full of eyes roll in from the four parts of the air. Daimon, daimon, come from a long way off. I will have my will. I have been a lover, I will be an illumination. That is my will. He shall become my equal. This is my revenge and my love.

Daimon, that is my will. I fix it."

She breathed in and filled herself. She let out the breath and said "The truth will do."

She met a man in a café who said to her:

"He got his fish gilt. The gilt wore off and there was the fish."

And another: "He will remember the time he spent with you, as other men their affair with a celebrated mondaine." And a third: "His people carry their burden. They wish to state a perception that shall clarify and rearrange all values, and from this statement of an essential virtue, they fall aside into morality.

"It is like the fish god with whom they once contended, hatched again, killed again, diverted, refished, lost.

"And they do not break their hearts. They move off.

"You crossed his will.

"That is enough for you to go on with."

In the dead hours of the afternoon she sat in an old man's room while he caressed his mistress. She said to herself—"The little state of fatigue is over. In a quarter of an hour I shall sit out in the café in the sun."

She looked at a nail in the wall. The objects in the room swam and fixed.

Through a square filled with squares she saw souls pour through, rising and sinking like lifts running on noiseless shafts. They were silent and took no notice of the other. There was a square like the back window of a taxi. Out of it the same white pointed face was shaking at her, and opening and shutting its mouth.

·   ·   ·   ·   ·

She had said "The truth will do." A man began to talk about the Italian Renaissance. "The full moon once held an old man gathering sticks. He was being punished.

"That age replaced him by two lovers. Now there is a nostalgia to refurnish that grey moon."

·   ·   ·   ·

You have been a black magician.

Throw your burning triangles round yourself. They are your illumination. They burn him.

You would have shut him up in that moon under your will.

You are in your circle with your treasure.

Rearrange either that, or the universal sphere.

·   ·   ·   ·

You were a lover, and the lover must turn adept. The last move of the lover is the same as the last gesture of the adept.

The adept returns to the café, orders a drink, and lends an acquaintance fifty francs.

She made the gesture, and burned the image, which was reabsorbed slowly into the fire.

From a hand-corrected typescript, n. d.,
likely early 1920s in the south of France.

❖ ❖

The Master's Last Dancing

THE TIME HAS NOW COME when we can look back on parties. There have been so many parties. There will always be parties. Parties are going on now. At this instant there are people just recovered from the party of last night, and there are people looking round their house, kitchen, castle, flat, bed-sitting room, drawing room, studio, and saying, "Is everything ready? They'll be here soon." At the same moment there are people saying, "I must go and change," or dress or tidy myself, put on a clean collar, makeup, or wash, and asking for their sword, dickey, clean white waistcoat, mask or fan, for spurs, furs, cuffs, ruffs, silver shoes or sabots with a daisy painted on each tip. They are all going to a party. How often on leaving their homes have they glanced round and reminded themselves that when they return, drunk or sober, good tired or bad tired, sweetened toward life or embittered, better friends with the people they are going to meet or the reverse, the place will not look the same again. Not quite—however thankful we are to see it, or tired or excited. A change will have come over it because we left it to go to a party. It is the great chance for Something to Happen. We may come back in love, or out of it—in love with one's mistress, with a stranger, with humanity, one's kinsman, or with one's host, or with the salon curtains or the cloakroom cat. Or, best of all, in love with one's society, with the life of the world, with what the party has done to us.

The time has also come when one must say that parties are not what they were, and when, the first glad rush of participation spent, one no longer says, "I must give a party at once," or "I never want to go to a party again." But memories of parties enter the mind, murmur along, and now and then one of them rises like a coloured bubble and makes one smile, winks out on the memory screen as another succeeds it.

Finally, there was the new crowd that began to arrive, and we did not quite know what to do with them. We were forced to explore the tricky half generation younger than ourselves, for if they were raw we were not yet quite ripe. Besides, we were the War lot. We had a secret. Something that they couldn't guess at and didn't want to, didn't believe in, whose mothers had been only wangling enough sugar for them while we— Anyhow, when they were not politely incredulous about our war, they resented our secret, are resenting it at this moment. That has a way of hurting, is likely to make one contemptuous by way of protection, or sometimes really bitter and wholly aloof. It is most unfair. One is thankful that those born after us are having a youth normal and proper to human beings. Nor are we exactly proud of ours, we who know that there is a line to describe us, which says, "*God help us, for we knew the worst too young.*" Nonetheless, I would rather sit next to any elderly soldier and hear him say that the Germans and only the Germans were to blame for what was handed out to us in 1914 than suffer the "don't bore me" attitude of his grandson.

This is the complaint of the neither-old-nor-young until one remembers that there was once little to complain of. Little in comparison with the adorable fun. For there is or was this blessedness about parties: that, like a moon dial, they only count the hours when the night sky is clear and lit. Almost always—for there have been Awful Parties, outstanding for some catastrophe, or that started something that should never have been begun and will never come to an end. The happy party indeed should have no history, no more than makes for agreeable gossip next day, parties that flash by like dancing lightning, leaving only bright heat behind.

Not like the one that this story is about. For some seasons parties had been getting wilder and wilder. I do not suggest that that evening was a culmination, that since that night they have not been getting madder and madder. But this one was as much as most of us could stand. As one of a series, it was never repeated.

It happened in Paris, where everything happens. Its beginning had been a good idea, when, a year before, a celebrated English painter and his wife had hired for their friends to dance in, one night in each week, a tiny café the workmen patronized, in a remote, magical, hardly known quarter, among trees. Here and there in Paris one finds a village, packed tight on a little hill. The luck that follows love had led them to this, with its dancing beside a tiny square, whose *patron* was willing to hire it and let the young ladies and gentlemen do what they pleased. I can see it now. A small place, paneled in varnished wood, with its bar at the entrance, and harsh drinks in coarse glasses, and, inside, the little raised dancing floor with a minute balcony high on one wall, no more than a cage, where the drummer sat. He was a wisp of a man, but his drum was huge, and beside him a gross giant swung a concertina like a giant caterpillar across his chest and tossed it, squealing over the rails, above our heads. There was no room up on the wall for more than those two, but I remember, from time to time, a shriek that cut across their tune, and made us all spin and throw ourselves about, and that it came from a body I could not see and a head I could just see, between the shoulders of the two others, blowing some sort of pipe with stops. They made a glorious noise together, too fast for our blues-trained feet, but nobody minded. We bounded and galloped and twisted about and got hot and happy, and between dances wandered out into the little square, where you could hear the trees talking.

It was a good idea. It was cheap. It was innocent, as only Paris can be innocent. And when it ended something in an epoch came to an end and was written off, but at the same time its successor was announced—a less desirable guest.

.   .   .   .

There was a woman come lately to Paris, from somewhere in Central Europe by way of New York, who made her living by giving us something to talk about. She wrote verse that consisted wholly of noises. We are hardened to that by now, but she was one of the first. Her history was the kind this writer has a personal distaste for, but which many consider romantic, and acclaim, if not in their purses (and it always is), in their indulgence. Hers was the usual kind. She had been a beautiful model; she had made a marriage that gave her a stately title, a name that suited her less than any name you can imagine. He had then killed himself, and his family, ruined by the man, would neither pay her nor acknowledge her. So she had set up in New York, on the strength of her name, to become a family curse, blackmailing them across the water, but innocently, like a child that has been taught bad language. The sort of story one has heard, with its legend of past beauty and boundless wealth and innumerable lovers.

We heard a great deal about her past beauty. She worked a variation on the aged-courtesan theme: now it was gone, so let it go. Indeed, her chief stunt, which made us all laugh and sympathize and even contribute to her support, was a rather witty definition of her lost loveliness. First she dyed her fading hair bright green. Then she shaved it off and lacquered her head scarlet, painting on the skull a phallic sign. She varied this device on other parts, not usually visible. On each knee—and her knees showed—she painted a skull; for an umbrella she carried a hearth brush, and for jewels wore odd bits of tin junk from the dustbin. I remember one of those wire sponges used to scrape plates, hung on a bootlace for a pendant, and a hat topped with a bottle brush for a hat pin. Another hat made entirely from a coal scoop.

I can never make out now whether one is in the wrong when one neither laughs unconcernedly at this nor weeps at its pathos, when on the whole one thinks it rather beastly and shrugs one's shoulders. Most people laughed and were rather kind, some were very kind. One excuse was that it would have been different if the poems had been any good.

In many ways, the Empress, as the Americans called her, was not unamicable. To some of the people who had stood by her in times of stress, she was loyal—picking out, as such persons do, her loyalties at hazard. Nothing was allowed to be said against one woman who had done her such and such a service, while nothing could be too bad for another who had really done as much, if not more. Haphazard caprice, as is the way of such women, and to the Empress it was women now who were kind. Men seemed not to fall for it.

Yet there was a point on which the ageing courtesan (oddly enough, she appeared far older than she was, already something of the crone) would not have a doubt cast, and where the most veiled incredulity provoked fury: the supposition that men no longer wished to take her to bed. It seemed to me that the wretched suicide of her last husband—much as she claimed that he did it on her account and some friends of his that he had only married her when he was drunk and, on sobering, had fled—had affected her in some way she did not explain, driven her actually a little mad. Something had shaken her faith in herself, more than creeping age and fading looks and even poverty shake that faith. So she insisted that, in spite of the lacquer and the hearth brush, she could still snare men. As in youth she must have done, for she had been very beautiful. But it was all too grotesque and rather obscene to be to one's taste. And yet—and yet—one is not proud of oneself for having shrugged so much. For one thing, one did not really *know*. One heard much, and finally saw only one thing.

I had dined across the river with a young man, who was a saga in himself, a whole string of wind songs. I did not know him well, and we sat talking; and when he said "Where shall we go?" I answered, "Let's try the Master's dancing. It's ages since I've been there."

It was a quiet, dark winter night when our taxi drew up. We were high up, with most of Paris beneath us, though we could not see it, because of the tall houses like cliff faces between us and the breakaway down to the river. The little café gave directly onto the pavement. Through its open doors we could see already several of our friends in silhouette. Neither the Old Master nor his wife was there. They had gone away south, and until the spring the parties supposedly would stop; only with the spring—the adorable Paris spring—would they begin again. But here we were, and here was another party, even without the Old Master, for the parties had become a fixture, a habit. The young man, who was called Valentine, went in with me. We were tranquil, not elated. At once, there came over us that sense of dislocation when the people in a normal state enter a ring, a circle of others, threaded by a similar and violent excitement, whirling in it. One had better try at once to get into their state, join them spiritually as well as actually. Or else stay quiet, just outside that ring.

In an instant our friends broke upon us like waves, and the smoke, music, roar of talk, and glitter of lights and glass were like a spray, springing up, drenching us.

Immediately we saw the Empress in the middle of the shiny floor, her hunched body tied up in strips of gold lace, its rags torn in points, with the round bright lids that come off cigarette tins for tassels. Behind her was something that swung and rolled with a hard rumble, audible under the cries and shouts and the swing of the concertina above our heads, as the huge man up there blared out "Valencia." I saw that it was the large coloured-glass knob of a door handle. Valentine handed me a glass of vile and potent brandy, and I stepped over the ring into the run and tap and pounce and shout and stamp and roar of that evening's entertainment.

For we did dance, years of rigidly controlled blues and tangos and neat foxtrots gone west like an inhibition as we bumped and galloped. The men swung the women round, and the women came to pieces and lost their shoes, and their hair hung over their eyes in wet rags and their beads broke. Lionel, an enormous Irishman, picked me up, and I found myself lifted and dropped and banged about and I lost my breath and roared with laughter. I flung myself onto a side table to get my breath and was snatched off again and flung through the air, singing "Valencia" at the top of my lungs with the rest, until we fetched off panting in the outer bar and poured down what did a good deal more than quench our thirst.

When my breath steadied and I looked back, the floor was emptier. Some people began to go away. It was our own set, the group of our friends, who stayed—out to make a night of it, as I was by then. Or almost. Perhaps that long and furious dance had torn a nerve of energy out of me, but I found that I was outside the ring again, not quite comfortable, but more than able to watch.

In the middle of the floor, the Empress was still at her pas seul, something between Salome and a cakewalk. Her head low, she danced with such concentration that it made me think of spells and witchcraft and the winding up of chains. Valentine joined us, along with Alleyne, the lovely, lazy woman all men and most women loved, and who of all people had been the kindest to the Empress.

"She's mad at me tonight," Alleyne said. "She will have it that Lionel's in love with her, because he asked her if he could paint her. Offered to do the lacquer a new way. She thought he meant hand-holding, and nothing I could say, I mean about Lionel not loving *anybody*, made a bit of difference. He would keep dancing with me, and look at him now. I said I wouldn't dance again if he wouldn't dance with the Empress, and all he's doing is lying on the floor under the table making noises and trying to catch her by the leg and trip her up. Won't anybody try and make him give her a dance?"

It was only too true. I could just see Lionel, the Irishman, lying happily on his front, creeping out from under a table and trying to grab the Empress by an ankle. I knew as well as anyone else that the heavens could fall before Lionel exchanged amusement for duty.

As we made again for the dancing floor I saw Lionel take the doorknob and fling it out with a neat spin that wrapped the cord tight round the Empress's ankles and tripped her up, just the way a weighted skipping rope used to do at school. She went down suddenly with a bump that must have split the lacquer, and then she sat on the floor looking up at us. I did not like the look in those sad and starving eyes. A wave of laughter broke out, led by Lionel's high, wild giggle, and then we plunged into it again, stamping our feet in their crushed shoes.

. . . . .

A quarter of an hour later, I limped again to the bar, Valentine with me. We were all there, trying to drink and talk at the top of our voices, through our lost breath. The floor was almost empty, except for the Empress, on her feet again and going on with her solo. She was turning round and round with minute steps in a circle, within her own axis, her head now back like a hen drinking, now bent down, with those starving eyes on the floor.

Then, from under the tables, Lionel came out like a dachshund or a ferret or an exceedingly long young man, and sprang down the steps to the lane between the café tables, his arms wide out, and caught Alleyne.

"One more dance before they close up," he cried. They raced back to the floor together and danced. Before the Empress, alongside the Empress, past the Empress. We joined them, and in minutes we had all joined hands, playing ring-a-ring-of-roses round the Empress, with a song—not the original song—to match.

Somebody slipped and the circle broke and flew out in all directions. Lionel, flung out against a wall, struck his head, staggered, and slipped down full length, unconscious. I remember his long brown hands with the fingers spread as though feeling the plaster as he fell. His friend, another Irishman, rushed to him. I had fallen sideways, and my arm, breaking my fall, had not broken. Valentine had fallen clean down the steps and clear of them and was beginning to sit up. I went to him. A girl had fallen onto a table. A man had rolled under a table. Above our heads, the concertina swayed and blazed and the drum rattled and the pipe shrieked, it seemed now, without a stop.

Again, instantly, I found myself outside it all, as my breath came back and my voice came into control. Time for a bath and bed. I was a little irritated that I had not lost myself and was not now determined to carry on till morning and let the next day's work go hang. Valentine and I helped each other to the bar to get a drink. We were perhaps still a little dazed. Thinking of my cloak, we looked back, and it was then that we began to take in the disaster behind us.

People were picking themselves up and groaning, but Alleyne was lying where she had fallen. The Empress was still dancing where she had been dancing before, but, if you like, a step up. She was dancing on Alleyne, up and down her body. On her belly and on her breast. She gave a little jump, and it was on her face, and already blood was beginning to pour from Alleyne's nose. There was a pool of it on the floor before Valentine went over and knocked the Empress off. As he shoved at her she clung and nearly had him over again, and then we all began to crowd round. I fell on my knees, trying to see how hurt Alleyne was. Her eyes were closed and she was trying to say something. The band, which had paused for a second while it pulled at a beer that someone had handed up, began again with a crash. "Valencia" again. I saw Lionel, recovered, try to beat time feebly. I stayed kneeling by Alleyne, her blood getting over my dress, and now running on my bare arms, and on Valentine's shirtfront, who was kneeling opposite.

Somehow we got her up onto a chair. The band screamed on. There was broken glass on the floor where a table had been knocked over, and at the café door a few workmen of the quarter had come in for a quiet drink and were staring at what was going on.

"We must get her home," said Valentine, and I knew he was still outside the ring, just as I was. I saw the Empress, no longer dancing but sitting malevolently in a corner, counting the tins on the ends of the rags. Two or three of the fallen were making an effort to dance again. Valentine got Alleyne up. I snatched my cloak. Just then the band made a final effort, and someone sprang up onto a table, towering enormously over the tiny room. It was the Irishman, Lionel, who now began to conduct to the wild tune. A rain of something cool and sticky pattered on my face. He was conducting with roses— my roses, the red roses Valentine had given me to carry, which had slipped into the pool of blood from Alleyne on the floor. He whirled them round and the drops flew, a scarlet rain over walls and floor and over our mouths and eyes and hair. It was a benediction calling upon us to thank the absent, infinitely correct givers of our party, and wouldn't they be surprised if they could see us now.

"This will bring down the curtain on the Old Master's parties, I bet," said Valentine. We got Alleyne down the steps, as with one last sweep the Irishman sprayed the room again. The flowers were beginning to come to pieces, the petals flying, and one broken-off head hit the back of my neck. The *patron* had called a taxi, and we took Alleyne home.

For weeks after, before Alleyne was about again, long before she was fit to look at, people spoke of that party as one of the funniest things that ever happened.

Now, was it funny, or wasn't it?

THE NEW YORKER, *March 30, 1998*

Fumerie

THE DUKE SAID: "Next Friday evening, wind and weather permitting, I propose to get drunk." A good statement, but it refers to a liberation of the spirits infinitely rowdy and gross in comparison with the subject of this sketch, which is the inhalation of the poppy-head juice called opium, rightly prepared and worthily received.

"We few, we happy few, we band of brothers." Shakespeare, in a moment of enthusiasm about something else, has described its supreme social aspect as a uniter of friends, a solvent of prejudice, a gentle sapper working beneath the barriers of race.

The people whose existence will be lightly shewn, Helen and Martin, Charles, André and George might have lived in ignorance of each other, in casual contact or, a friendship once made, in squabbles and misunderstandings; might have passed years stealing the affections of one from the others, or in repeating highly coloured versions of what the others had been seen doing out the night before, in their cups. Some diversion is necessary, and life being what it is, few things should be allowed to stand in the way of a good time. But diversions in "boites de nuit" are of the nature of costly public spectacles, necessary, from time to time, in this city, as were the classic games; but no alternative to regular hours of vision or repose.

Helen is american, Charles is english, Martin american and André french. George is almost too english to be true. Out each and every night on a spree, how little they would have known each other, how little race-personality would have filtered through race-personality, the french to clarify, the american to be generous, the english to make subtle. They might have drained their health and their pockets and never discovered each other, or set out on the perspective-opening journey of opium into the secrets of the race and the human heart. What follows is not that story, but some notes it has amused me to make, hints from the Travel Bureau, the opium Baedeker, which, so far as I know, has not been written cheerfully enough in the western world. We have had ecstasy and mystery, descriptions touched with cold fear. De Quincey and Baudelaire. The Halitosis histories America gives us monthly suggest another description of that state which opium can never create but only elicit, the only moments of life whose value remains serene, the hours when man "se trouve, en meme temps, plus artiste et plus juste."

Elsewhere, Shakespeare calls it a "drowsy syrup." Smoked, it is not so particularly, unless you take too much. But what did he mean by syrup? If he meant what we mean, he knew the stuff we use. This touches an enquiry. From the fifteenth century on, the world went mad on pepper and the spices of the far East. They were known in the middle ages, and have passed from an exciting luxury into the commonest of necessities. But did those ships which set out on the dangerous, interminable voyage after nutmeg, cirmamon and cloves return with something extra in the hold? Were the chests of food-and-health-preserving fruits of the earth alternated with such stuff as sacks of poppy-heads packed in clay? Was the spice trade, or what gave it its mysterious energy, a mask for the search after the strongest, least brutalising and most dangerous stimulant known to man?

It seems clear that it was smoked nowhere until the seventeenth century, and then first in China. If Shakespeare knew it as a syrup, he must have drunk it diluted, or, God help him, evaporated and chewed. Did the Doges at Venice throw an opium party? Did a little dinner at the Borgias include it? Subject for a historical enquiry of great human interest. But for such a research the writer must be interested in opium; to be interested, he must have tried it; and having tried it, he must have become a will-less, truth-less victim of morphine. People do not like to be called that. So it is not likely that we shall ever know.

In the sixteenth century, Paracelsus extracted morphia. That most sensible magician also insisted on a supply of pure water for the town whose ruler had made him its medical officer of health. He also restated the practical-mystical theory of "signatures" or correspondences between the visible and invisible regions of nature. Some day Science will have another Clerk Maxwell to spare, and that business will be looked into. Before that day, she might make an effort, and discover an antitoxin to the prison in the unripe seed of a common flower.

FIX YOUR TRAY!

Invitations to "come and smoke" are not always a diplomatic passport to the land of heart's desire. The slips between a jar of B____s and his lip only the apprentice smoker knows. There is the tray. The needles. THE LAMP. The moistened rag or piece of sponge. The pipe, its bowl, the vinegar. Tape. The dross-box and palette.

George has a tray, its original lacquer clotted with oil-soaked dross. His favourite needles are bent. The head has fallen off the mother-of-pearl bee that hangs on the lamp-glass and, choking inside in a pool of mixed opium and olive oil, impedes the flame.

Charles enters, saying "Nien, nien" in what he hopes is Chinese for an urgent need to smoke. Helen, Martin and André are sprawled, impatient; drawing fiercely on cigarettes. The lamp sputters, falls to a bead. Is coaxed: shoots up. The pipe on the bent needle bursts into flame, is blown out, skinned and stabbed again on the bowl rough with burnt dross. Falls off: is caught, licked, thrust on again. Crumbles to dust.

Interval.

George rolls over on his back and gives it up, while Charles cleans the bowl: another needle: licks his fingers. The shrill bubble of a perfectly cooked pipe rises agreeably, while Helen, Martin and André turn over, expectant at last.

Thud. Clatter. The heavy clay "fourneau" drops off the pipe, shatters the lamp-glass (the only one). Charles crushes the opium-ball, which has fallen off the fourneau in its turn and lost itself behind the lamp, in his teeth, and rushes to the bathroom to spit. Like angry dogs, stretched out but not asleep, the party turns on George.

Affairs will probably right themselves in time; but meanwhile temperaments have been exasperated and auras, which had entered George's fumoir all the colours of a healthy rainbow, have now been reduced to a monotony of dingy browns.

Memory-training is the smoker's first obligation.

BE PREPARED.

For insufficient and too sufficient oil.

For waxed or moistened tape, which drying loosens the bowl.

For silver needle-points wrenched off the straight.

For each and every perversity of so-called inanimate matter.

For the live temperament, the diabolic perversity, the ingenious devilry, the highly-strung nature of opium; and each morning in anticipation of your "deux heures de calme" —

FIX YOUR TRAY.

George's pipes are too large; André's are too small. Through undercooking, Charles' bubble on the bowl like porridge. Helen's fall off because the fourneau is cold. Martin is notorious for his burnt pipes. How human nature repeats itself in our simplest acts! But the underlying fault from which these imperfections arrive is Impatience. It takes a year's practise to make a pipe, and each of the band in his impatience to get down quick to a little peace tries to build up the source of pleasure too fast. "Sorry," they say, "it was the bottom of the pot." "My hand shakes." "The stuff is too thin." "The stuff is too thick." Such are the common excuses by which pipe after pipe is ruined; the rhythm of your regime perhaps destroyed. Pipes should be rolled on a palette: any piece of jade will do, and at the same time help preserve that atmosphere of the magic east, about which opium is rapidly correcting a number of our most cherished misconceptions.

DAMN THE LAMP!

Is it a subconscious protest, relic of a misapplied sense of sin which so frequently inhibits the purchase of oil and wick? You are in a hotel, and a descent into the salle à manger at midnight to rob a cruet is hardly the best preparation for your bedtime pipe. Nor is a strip cut out of your finest wool sock a convenient and economical substitute for the "mèche" which should be the smoker's first care.

…Unnecessary, on the other hand, to gild the lily, as Helen did in the days of her debut, when a famous smoker called to teach her the necessary arts, and she, instead of common olive oil had lit her silver lamp with Guérlin's Après l'Ondée which burns a pale blue and scented instead of a yellow, vegetable flame, and added to the smokers' anthology an imperishable joke.

Tape.

By tape I should mean tape, preferably waxed tape, to be cut in nicely calculated lengths. In fact I mean almost any piece of material, including lace shoulder straps, strips of handkerchief, shoelaces and string.

I have seen the bowl bound and jammed on the pipe by the stuffing out of a valuable tie, damp rose leaves, a piece of George's braces.

And I have been present at more shattering moments when the heavy fourneau has crashed off the pipe, broken the lamp-glass and upset the drug; known more ruined pipes, and wasted opium caused by inattention to this preliminary measure than by any other smoker's procrastination.

I do not know the French for tape.

I carmot remember it.

I buy mending for my boy-friends' socks and carry the colours in my head: their different kinds of cigarettes, and all shades of ribbon.

I cannot buy tape.

It is good luck to be a woman: you always wear shoulder straps.

I went out the other day and bought a mile of it.

"What Did They Think They Smelt?"

You are in a hotel. Your friends (non-smokers) gather round your bed.

"Why haven't you opened the window?"

"They can smell it half way down the corridor."

The drug just set on your needle bursts into flame, or crumbles as you press it on the bowl. The window is flimg open, the night wind rushes in: sets our papers flying—rain follows and the uncontrollable outside world. Emotion will spoil your "kief." Spoils it.

And what will the other people in the place, some who are undoubtedly hurrying to their rooms for their daily dose of peace, if they have not smelt what will be most agreeable to them, think they have smelled?

"We are down to twice-cooked dross, and drinking George's bowl washed out with Dubormet—" You sympathise, perhaps press tighter to your breast the little tin you have ordered and paid for a month past, expected for a fortnight, given up hope of a week ago; and, after a rendez-vous fixed for successive days at your flat, received after a two-hours' wait in a workman's café off the Port St Denis.

Perhaps you will share it with them.

Perhaps the last time they left you to derange your interior with three times distilled burnt morphine. BUT —

IT IS USELESS TO ORDER IN TIME. ANTEDATE NECESSITY AS FAR BACK AS IMAGINATION WILL CARRY.

"I DON'T FEEL WELL."

"Yes, make me another— It doesn't seem to be doing me any good."

The novice gasps away at the seventh, seventeenth or twenty-seventh pipe the careless or malicious friend has rolled: while the well-meaning spectator (non-smoker) goes away to prepare black coffee.

Administers it.

DISASTER.

Your pleasure consists not in the number of pipes, but in the attitude, mental and physical, of repose.

OPIUM IS NOT A WHISKEY AND SODA.

KEEP STILL!

How can you expect Nature to do her work if you do not assist her, and frequently outrage her inviolable laws?

Helen is running about making tea for Martin, who has exceeded his ration while he offered battle this time to the french telephone. André has roused himself to argue with a non-invited non-smoker who arrived drunk. George and Charles were late, and could not agree to take turn and turn with the lamp. The interval between tea and dinner was a mere spell of agitation; the meal a discord; the evening devoted to important social obligations, a fiasco.

All this could and should have been avoided.

KEEP STILL.

You are going away for the first time with It. Probably it will not have occurred to you that the problem of packing now presents serious developments.

In default of a travelling set you have followed the usual course in the case of extraneous objects, and your smoker's outfit is secreted in socks, between handkerchiefs, in a shoe.

Lucky for you if you have committed to the sponge bag the bottle, tin, flask or jar on which all depends.

If you have not, on unpacking you may find a morass; chemises, or shirts, toothbrushes, make-up and books gummed together by an inseparable, uncollectable mass of semi-solidified opium.

Useless to repine, you will probably soak each article in your wash-hand basin, bottle the result collected by means of your douche and drink it day by day.

NEXT TIME YOU WILL HAVE LEARNED:

that opium has the qualities of treacle, glue, quicksilver and india rubber.

ALSO:

that liquid, blown to bubbles, cooked to paste, to dust, opium is a living substance, a magic extract. One that knows its own business and who are its own people. If you do not learn its ways, it will leave you, and leave ruin behind it.

The band had brought its dross to be cooked at Helen's flat. Left alone she would be sufficiently competent to deal with it.

In the privacy of her kitchen she assembled a clock, a casserole, fan-folded filter papers. A lawn cloth, a razor blade, a spoon. The stripped wood of more than one matchbox. A slag-heap of volcanic-looking cinders. Tied in a pudding bag, bobbing in a frothy brown sea, the precious extract begins to separate from its ash, when—Martin enters: a minute later Charles and André. Then George, who says, while the others peer:

"I say, are you sure you are doing it right?"

Instead of giving him a piece to suck which would act as a gag, with lovely courtesy Helen stops to explain: to justify. And half an hour later, the clock is ticking frantically, and ascending the corridors above, draft-blown down the stairs to the Concierge's lodge wafts an opium breeze. Over a low flame, in a kitchen littered with debris, a dark surge in the casserole is at the point of thickening. In one minute, five, ten, there will be more opium in the world. But the five midwives are engaged in frantic dispute. Unvarying routine essential to successful delivery sacrificed to conflicting theory.

While Helen, half-stupefied, harassed, aching, stirs and stirs.

God help her if George in a moment of compassion takes her place and, transferring the compassion to himself, raises the flame and finally, in a moment of conviction that André knows nothing whatever about opium-cooking, leaves it to look after itself, in order to persuade him.

Another smell will insinuate itself through the stupefying, vegetable sweetness, a smell of the Pit. Cries, sniffs, a rush to the kitchen to find a split casserole and harsh stinking cinders in place of the honey-smooth black liquid.

But if the final tragedy be averted, there remains still the agitating scene: arguments which continue while the new brew is being tried out, until, overcome by its sheer strength, everyone agrees that everyone else is in the wrong.

There is only one way to prepare opium from dross: convince yourself that it is a bechamel sauce you are making to pour on a fish; and after straining the boiled ash, stir until it thickens over a low flame.

You will stir and stir. Stir and stir and stir and stir: till hope dies and your right arm and your left are attacked by paralysis. One quarter of an hour will succeed another, while black drops, airier than soda water, drip off the spoon. Then, hardly perceptibly, drops which are not so light.

The quality of the brew will alter: fat, gold-skinned bubbles will rise and pop deliberately, like a wink. A wave off the spoon will rise (and try to stick) to the casserole side.

It is over. First lowering the vessel into a bowl of cold water, you can pour, scrape, share, lick it off.

DO IT ALONE.

The room is lit from the low bookshelves by a huge glass wine bottle, filled with water, a piece of the sea at home, topped with an electric bulb, and shaded by a round of lacquered parchment painted with ships. In the open fireplace, a log whistles, another blazes in a level fence of flames while underneath the red-hot wood crumbles ashes charred to a white bloom.

On the black floor-divans are lying Helen and Martin, Charles, André and George. Between them, on the low table topped with a mirror and with dragons for legs, their tools are scattered, the needles and palette, the dross-box and opium-cup. A bamboo pipe bound in ivory smoked to the colour of amber, another of ivory finished with jade. Glass and bronze, silver and enamel, mother-of-pearl and green stone. Objects of virtù and delicate use in their proper employment, lit by the olive oil lamp, the oldest in european use, over whose flame a needle is twirled, redipped and spun again. Bubble clusters blow out, dark, gold skins of opium. They click and whisper, the needle-rod thrills in the hand, the beads enlarge, crisp and trembling. Crushed on the palette, the needle is clipped and blown again. And again. Until—when not too crisp and dry, and not too wet; when no more black drops can be pressed out on the palette, and when no dust powders the jade; when the pipe has been rolled to a perfect cone...

André raises the pipe. In the small light he is a shadow to which, in the light-circle, are attached two fine hands. He heats the bowl, the grey clay incised with small gold flowers, gives a last twist and presses the pipe on. It rests over the needle-hole, pierced, shapely. Helen takes the pipe. For thirty seconds a low whistle rises as she smokes, André guiding the drug with his needle-point. She puts the pipe down and lies back. An instant later André's fingers, delicate as the needle, are dipping and turning again.

"Your turn, mon ami." Helen steps aside into the shadow on outer cushions. Charles draws up.

"Shall I make for you now, André? It's going well today."

Helen says: "I remember now how that song goes."

"Sing it to us later," says Martin, "I'm altering that poem."

Charles decides in a flash how an old quarrel which he had not begun should be ended.

André, following Polycrates, and to protect perfection, cuts out a pipe.

George beams and has another.

"My favourite breakfast, opium and strawberries."

Wake up on a strict and diminishing regime, with a slight chill and a slight ache. Part your hair and wash your face; set your tray and drink your tea; if it is summer, eat your strawberries. Read the paper; smoke a cigarette; listen outside to the morning air, the mysterious plain-chants sung up and down a Paris backstreet.

Imagine a crisis which would turn you out of bed, before you have smoked, to run all day about the city. If you know you can, you are safe.

Smoke three pipes. Lie still and low on your back and let the day fall into its perspective.

Come back at evening to dress. Drink tea with a lemon wheel in it. Smoke what is left of your regime, down to the final sporting event, the scrapings off your palette.

Half an hour for sleep, half an hour for meditation and praise of Paris, preparing for its night's play. Half an hour for bath and makeup; then skip out of the house and into a taxi and over the Place de la Concorde to whatever the night has in its cup, a cup which is usually filled.

"THEY SMOKE OPIUM."

I think I understand the reaction of the non-smokers when they say that. It is what they would feel if we were known to have killed to obtain the philosopher's stone. And got it.

For well or ill, that is to say for fifty per cent of each, smokers are inside a ring. As near a ring to a magic ring as a man can win by his senses. Equally, non-smokers, the people who have heard about it and are afraid to try it—for the question cancels down to fear and to nothing else—are subtly linked. They are not the people with whom opium disagrees; who have been caught by its derivations and sworn off. Nor are they necessarily, though generally, "enemies of the rose." They are, I suspect, people with whom it will have nothing to do. Opium knows its own business. Those it wants, it finds—even out of their ranks.

But I am glad that burning, hanging, drawing and quartering have gone out of the possibilities of fashion.

While, on our side, we have always a card to play. We have excommunication.

Treboul–Paris 1927

CONJUNCTIONS 31, 1998
Edited from manuscript by Nathalie Blondel and Camilla Bagg

✥ ✥

[*Untitled*]

THIS PERFECTLY TRUE story began when Homer Vandermeyer came over from the United States to France. He came to do
the place good, spend his millions and millions on enlightening and
brightening its imperfect civilisation. Over there he had helped to get
Prohibition passed; but over here the only time that he was not helping us was when he was finding out whether drink was so harmful to
him personally as he had decided it was for his fellow-countrymen. He
went on trying to find out, because next day he was never sure whether
the feeling in his inside were that or something else. And those next
days were the ones when he gave France more advice than cheques. But
the cheques, when he had decided that alcohol was just the one thing
he had always needed, were splendid. They were for consumption and
street accidents and babies and golf-links and a good time. The "fors"
and "againsts" may be mixed, but the french authorities hardly knew
how to believe it, and his french boy-friends even learned how to cash
them. All the same, I did not think it quite patriotic of Armande, simply, so it seemed to me, because he liked a good time and wanted to
see how foreigners amuse themselves in his home town, to domesticate
Homer in a bar where he would not hear a word spoken that was not
in good American, and invent a drink for him called a prussian's hoof,
and see that he took it regularly from midnight to dawn.

I thought Armande was going too far. A few nights later, I was sure
he was mad, for I was asked out after dinner to keep Homer company;
and Armande, who is so French that he makes M. Clemenceau seem
like a fine old english gentleman, paid for the taxis. Wouldn't let Homer put his hand in his pocket. Just borrowed a bit off me.

Mr. Vandermeyer, by this time, was a prussian-hoof fiend. I had hoped for champagne and dancing, and found myself perched up at the bar, while Armande, who had forgotten that I could understand him, was tampering further with its original composition of gin, calvados, cointreau and a dash of bitters. So I asked the bar-man, a friend of mine, an Englishman and designed by Heaven for a confidential valet, what it was all about.

"The young gentleman's got something he wants to sell," he said; and a little later Armande, between sips at his Evian water, told me that "M. Homère" was just beginning to think of buying his family castle in the Dordogne, and leave Armande free to slip out through a hole in life's mesh.

The deal, even with my paying most of Armande's bill, was not yet complete. That it was eventually pulled-off is also entirely due to me. They went down to see the place, and the day after I found Armande, his nerve and his patience very badly gone, in the Vandermeyer suite at the Meurice. He was talking to Homer, much too fast and quite often in French; his mouth working like a fish with a complex.

Homer was saying: "I like the place well enough, but I don't see where you're going to put in a lift. Your french châtô are so damned flat." I saw what he wanted, something in the leisurely house which would shoot up and down; and how little scope there was for that in the shallow towers which just diversified the delicate XVII century roof. And Armande was ready to shriek after a vanishing life's dream: a racing torpedo with the speed of lightning and the voice of an ill-bred fury; and a whole series of complicated French 'combinaisons', which included buying the place back cheap when Homer had restored it, and it had gotten sufficiently on his nerves. I was sorry for him, so sorry that I could only laugh. I said:

"If the place doesn't go up, it goes along by the mile. There's a day's walk in those passages. Put in a moving staircase. Up and down the double flight in the courtyard, and one to slide upstairs along the main street."

Armande nearly lost his temper, until we both saw Homer looking very attentively at me.

"If my architect reports favourably on that, it's done', he said. 'I'm meaning to receive there a lot. Nothing like it to bring your guest steadily along. Makes reception the work of a minute."

I faded out. But looking out my window to see what the explosion was in the street below, I have seen pass a scarlet cigar, a plume of blue smoke, a squeal. And Armande in charge of it. And there is a vision with me always: a stream of people rising; pausing a second beside a man, who is not ticket-collecting but hand-shaking: ascending and descending, eternally up and down and round again a sunny courtyard, where statues loll in full classical armour, Armande's ancestors in their miniature Versailles, somewhere in the middle of France.

Hand-corrected typescript, n.d.